Catherine's Cadeau

Catherine's Cadeau

Ann Davidson

Terry Thibodeaux

Texas Review Press
Huntsville, Texas

FIRST EDITION, 2008
Requests for permission to reproduce material from this work should be sent to:

> Permissions
> Texas Review Press
> English Department
> Sam Houston State University
> Huntsville, TX 77341-2146

Acknowledgments:

We wish to acknowledge Bruce Caissie and the Acadian Cultural Society for their support and research assistance, and the Societé Promotion Grand Pré for reviewing a draft of the manuscript.

Thanks also goes to those who read the manuscript and gave their feedback and encouragement: Judy Sarkisian, Cynthia Robertson, Terri Warich, Mary Gutermuth, Brenda Lowery, Evelyn Hasouris-Turner, Cathi Gillette, Jaimie Hebert, Guy Benoit, Becky Guidry Ruddell, Dick Thibodeau, and Charlene Guidry Lacombe.

Special thanks to Marilyn Holman for assisting with the final proofreading and supporting Ann on a personal level from start to finish, to Bill Bridges for his tireless support, patient advice, and great suggestions. Also to Paul Ruffin for his patience and wise counsel.

From Ann: Thanks, of course, to Terry, his wife Paula, and their son Mark.

From Terry: Thanks to Ann, for finding me and including me in this journey.

Cover graphics and design by Mark Thibodeaux

A portion of the proceeds from Catherine's Cadeau will be donated to America's Wetlands Foundation to support the preservation and reclamation of Louisiana's disappearing coastal wildlife habitat.

Library of Congress Cataloging-in-Publication Data

Davidson, Ann, 1954-
  Catherine's cadeau / Ann Davidson, Terry M. Thibodeaux. -- 1st ed.
    p. cm.
  ISBN-13: 978-1-933896-22-9 (pbk. : alk. paper)
  ISBN-10: 1-933896-22-1 (pbk. : alk. paper)
  1. Acadians--Nova Scotia--Fiction. 2. Time travel--Fiction. 3. Acadians--Relocation--History--18th century--Fiction. 4. Nova Scotia--History--To 1763--Fiction. 5. Cajuns--Fiction. I. Thibodeaux, Terry Mark. II. Title.
  PR9199.4.D382C37 2008
  813'.6--dc22

                                        2008004240

Ann's Dedication:
To my children, Joshua and Jessica Davidson,
and in memory of my mother, Leota McKinnon.

Terry's Dedication:
To Mark, for everything he brought to this project, and to Paula,
for her 30+ years of love, support, and proofreading.

Table of Contents

Illustrations

.

Catherine's Cadeau

Chapter 1

Glooscap's Legacy

Friday, August 26

On this summer morning, Michelle Boudreaux sat alone at Evangeline Beach. The sea breeze blew wisps of her short auburn hair across her eyes. As she brushed them back, Michelle watched the waves trickling to shore in perfect rhythm to a seagull gliding in on air currents right above them. The seagull landed on the sand just up from the water's edge.

She suddenly discovered her solitude of the past hour had been disturbed. Someone far down the beach was moving slowly toward her, and she hoped it was Monique, but by the labored gait she soon realized to her disappointment that it was an elderly person. She had needed to have this beach all to herself for the rest of the morning while she waited for her husband Jacques to return, and was now considering where else to go. She looked down at her hand as red sand sifted between her fingers, and closed her eyes to take in the sensation of millions of granules falling away. She focused on this activity for a few moments, trying to clear her mind and calm the anxiety she was feeling.

Michelle's were fingers that played an accordion, and earlier this morning they had been too shaky to hit the keys. She held out her hand and breathed a sigh of relief to see that it was steady once again. How would she ever be able to perform tomorrow without Monique there? She could hear her cousin saying, "*Mais cher*, it's almost as big as you," marveling at the way Michelle was able to maneuver the instrument on stage. She loved to look right down in front of the stage and see her cousin smiling at her.

A knot formed in her stomach. She looked up at the blue skies and blinked back tears. Why couldn't she fly through the air like the seagulls above her? Where is she? Michelle silently asked the clouds that drifted along over the water.

Michelle and Jacques had come to Nova Scotia two days ago

from Louisiana. As the Lafayette Duo, they were slated to perform in *Le Festival Acadien* this weekend and were thrilled to be chosen as the featured performers. Michelle had offered her cousin Monique a free trip to accompany them here, and Jacques had even arranged for his cousin André to meet Monique in the Valley and take her to see Grand-Pré, the home of their Acadian ancestors.

But Monique had disappeared last night, and Michelle and Jacques had canceled rehearsal earlier this morning. She had whispered to her husband that he just had to get them out of their performance tomorrow. Jacques' reaction told her that he wasn't ready to make that decision yet. *Le Festival Acadien* was a two-day event on the scenic Halifax waterfront, and their first gig in the Canadian Maritimes. As headliners, there were high expectations that they could kick it off with the Cajun music that had the whole East Coast talking. With Monique coming with them, it had seemed to Michelle that everything was coming together perfectly. Instead, after last night it was all coming apart.

At rehearsal this morning, Jacques had taken control, announcing, "Michelle needs a break right now." In front of a group of sound engineers and stage technicians, he put his arm around her shoulders and walked her out the front of the auditorium where they were rehearsing. As he ushered her into the passenger seat of their rented car, he said, "Please try to take it easy. It'll all work out. Just give me a few minutes inside." To Michelle, crying inconsolably, it had seemed like an hour later when he returned.

Jacques had said nothing as he checked the map, then drove out of the city of Halifax and onto Highway 101 toward the historic Valley. Now, she sat waiting for Jacques and his cousin André to return from talking to the local police.

A rustling sound in the sand told her that the person she had seen earlier was getting closer. He was an elderly man, limping along. She wondered if his feet were hurting. He stopped, looked out at the waters, and crossed himself, indicating to Michelle that they had their faith in common.

Standing up, she dusted the sand off herself and walked toward him. He turned to her and gave a nod, then lifted a hand over his dark eyes. Michelle followed his shaded gaze toward the ridges of Cape Blomidon, where sandstone cliffs topped with evergreens were reflected in the ocean below. The colors shimmered in the midday sun off the ocean water at high tide.

"This was mostly all mud an hour ago," she commented, waving her hands over the expanse in front of her. A gust of wind caused him to grip the collar of his tattered gray sweater tighter to his neck. "Are you cold?" she asked. She reached up to her own sweater in an unspoken offer.

He motioned to her that he was fine and continued to look out toward the Basin. A hum focused their attention on a small boat going by. The old man crossed himself again. The two of them watched the motorboat move slowly along in the Basin, rocking up and down on the waves. The old man spoke for the first time, his English and French mixed together in a way that rang familiar to Michelle's ears.

"Those fishermen are *mes amis*, the Mi'Kmaq," he said. "*Chaque matin* they come out here to fish. Whatever their catch is for the day they eat, and if they catch nothing they eat fruits and *legumes* until the next morning. Then they try again the following day. *Le Basin*, she does not offer up as much fish as she once did, and sometimes the authorities and local people protest their presence here."

The old man paused for a few breaths, then added, "The simple truth is, their people have been here longer than any of us." He looked over at Michelle, his brown eyes soft in the sunlight.

He placed his hand on her arm gently and asked, "What is your name?"

"Michelle Boudreaux," she replied, choking back tears.

"Michelle, *mes amis* the Mi'Kmaq believe the spirits of Blomidon will eternally provide what they need, and I am going to offer up a prayer that they lift heavy nets today. Would you join me?"

He closed his eyes, bowed his head, and said a blessing for the fishermen as he extended his hand out over the Minas Basin. Michelle stared blankly at him for a moment, then closed her eyes also. The rhythm of his voice comforted her, and when the prayer was over she felt peaceful.

He smiled at her. "My name is Father Siméon Allain and I am a missionary." He turned back in the direction of the water, and Michelle's gaze followed his. "The Mi'Kmaq demi-god, the Great Spirit Glooscap, formed that gigantic pile of red sediment and named it Blomidon." Waving a crooked finger in front of her, he pointed toward the cliffs. "Glooscap topped those cliffs with evergreen forests to protect them from the harsh maritime elements of wind, water, and the highest tides in the world. They believe that a beaver's dam had for years extended from Blomidon to Parrsboro Shore. In one mighty strike of his fist, Glooscap had smashed the beaver's dam, allowing the Bay of Fundy tides to gush into the Basin for the first time."

"Glooscap." Michelle rolled it off her tongue several times. "It's such a strange name for a god."

"Not to *mes amis*." The old man told Michelle a bit about native folklore as he pointed to the boat, now moving toward the other shore. "The Mi'Kmaq raise their young to look to Blomidon for strength, and *la force* is always there, if you seek it. After the mischievous Glooscap created the first Mi'Kmaq from an ash tree, he sometimes changed them back to trees or stones if they misbehaved. Our Lord will never desert us, but the Mi'Kmaq god Glooscap was different. When he found his people making war with each other too many times for his liking, he gave up on them and paddled off in his birch bark canoe. One evening as sunset fell across the Basin, his people watched him row away. He had left them with a grim prophecy: A race of pale-faced men would one day come here, take all their lands, and rule over them."

"I'm from Louisiana," blurted Michelle, "and I'm looking for my cousin Monique LeBlanc. We're actually more like sisters, we're so close. If I don't find her soon, I'll just . . . Have you heard about her?"

"I am from the land of Acadie," replied the old man, "from the parish of St. Charles in the fertile marshlands here. *Les aboiteaux*, they shout to all who listen, We belonged here! It is very sad, the way my people . . ."

"I'm very sorry about your people, but you don't seem to understand. I have to find my cousin Monique! I'm really scared!"

He smiled, glancing down at the fingers of water rushing in the sand toward their feet.

"Please, sir," Michelle pleaded, "have you seen anything suspicious this morning? A girl from Louisiana, my cousin Monique LeBlanc, disappeared from Grand-Pré Park last night. You must have heard something about it!"

The old man placed his hand on her shoulder to balance his legs, which had begun to shake. His eyes were now completely fixed on something behind her. Startled, she turned around. She saw nothing but a large boulder.

"I have to go," she muttered. She slid his hand from her shoulder and held it until he seemed steady again, then turned and ran toward stone steps that led from the beach up to the top of the cliff.

"*Au nom du Père, et du Fils, et de Saint Esprit, ainsi soit-il,*" she heard him saying behind her. When she looked around, she was surprised to see him kneeling in front of the rock and crossing himself over and over. Michelle reached the top of the stairs and glanced behind her one more time. The sun's glare on the large rock was dazzling and caused a stabbing pain over her eyes. She rubbed her temple to ease it.

She stood at the edge of the bluff and called down to him, "Are you OK?" He didn't answer. Suddenly another sharp pain caused her to cry out. She gripped the front of her head with both hands, massaging her temples. Behind her closed eyes she could see a bright orange flash, just like the brightness that remained from a flash bulb when she had gotten her picture taken as a young girl. She blinked her eyes to make it go away, then looked back down at the old man.

There was nothing left but a tattered gray sweater lying on the sand.

Chapter 2

The Forest Primeval

Four Months Earlier
Thursday, April 28

Sultry, late afternoon air pressed down on the LSU campus. In her dorm, Monique lay on her single bed, a book propped up in front of her on a pillow. The room was small, and her roommate Terri's bed was cluttered with clothing. They had done laundry together that morning for the first time since the oppressive heat had arrived a week earlier. Her boyfriend Ted was lying next to her on her bed, drifting in and out of sleep as a small fan whirred on a table nearby. He stirred and rolled over closer. His sticky skin touched hers and she inched away.

"Are you done?" he asked, still half asleep.

"Not even close. I still have to read all this." Monique flipped several pages of Longfellow's poem *Evangeline* to show him.

"Do it later. Let's get out of here." Grabbing the book from her hands, he tossed it on the floor on his side of the bed.

"Wait . . ." But he had already pulled her up and they were soon walking toward the parade ground in the middle of campus. Students often sat under trees or stretched out to look at the stars.

LSU was the place Monique had called home for the past four years. Every day lately she looked at one aspect or another and fought back tears, first in the student center, then the library, and now here on the edge of the parade ground where she and Ted had sat together so many times. They found their favorite spot under a large old cypress.

"I've been thinking we should get engaged this summer," said Ted.

She looked at him, waiting for the grin that always told her when he was teasing. His expression was serious.

"Hmm, I don't know . . . I'm not . . . I don't think . . . I . . . need to think about it."

"Are you kidding? You haven't even thought about it?"

"I guess I have, but I'm not ready yet. I think we have some problems. Can we talk about this another time?"

"Well, here's what I think. We could get engaged after graduation, when we are summering with my parents. They'd love it. Things will be better when we're on the Vineyard."

"I don't know if I want to go there this summer." Monique was feeling nervous about approaching this subject.

"Why not?"

"I need some time with my father. Maybe you and I could spend part of the summer together in Lafayette."

"No, we definitely cannot. Did I tell you my Dad called last night? He signed a purchase and sale agreement on a house in Alexandria that he said would be perfect for me when I go back home to work for him. I told him we'd come up this weekend and check it out. They are giving you a second chance."

"Me a second chance? Your parents were awful to me the last time we went there, Ted, and you know it! They should apologize to me!"

"You just don't get it, do you?" he huffed, his hair flopping across his eyes. He threw his head back angrily. "My father is giving us a chance to have a great life together."

"Do I have a say in this? You don't have a clue what I want!" Monique shouted. She could feel people looking in their direction.

"Calm down," Ted whispered. "What do you want?"

She whispered loudly back. "I need to spend time with my family in Lafayette. I want to go back for the summer and help Dad at the homeless shelter, whether you and your parents like it or not."

"Wow, a shelter job. You're really aiming high, using your degree to feed homeless people!" They stared at each other for a moment, more angry thoughts forming into angry words that remained unsaid. "Let's see if I have this right. You could come with me and have another great summer on Martha's Vineyard, or you could work at a shelter."

Monique jumped up from under the cypress, holding back the urge to wipe the snide grin off his face. Before she was out of earshot, he called out to her, his words hanging in the air.

"You're a stubborn Cajun and always will be!"

Angry tears blurred her vision. She quickened her step in hopes of getting to her room before she completely broke down. Wiping her eyes so she could see the handle of the door more clearly, she threw it open and hurried up the stairs to the second floor.

"You OK?" someone asked on the stairway.

"I will be, thanks," she mumbled back. She ran into her dorm and flopped down on the bed, the springs groaning from the impact. She pictured his grinning face and pounded her pillow, remembering for the first time what her cousin Michelle had said months ago. Monique and Ted had been at Jacques' and Michelle's wedding reception, and Monique had told her cousin they weren't getting along. "Ted Jones is wrong for you," Michelle had spoken in her gentle voice. Monique had not accepted her opinion at the time and had tucked it away, until now. .

Edward Jones, Jr. was Monique's first and only college boyfriend. She had spent so much time in her dorm room the first year, her roommate Terri teased her about being a hermit. By her sophomore year Terri persuaded her to join drama club, where she had met Ted. She thought he was cute, and he was very outgoing and friendly from the first. He was assistant treasurer, and her job was to organize and move props and give praise and encouragement to her more gregarious roommate's dramatics on stage.

Terri made fun of Ted quite often, especially the way he flashed his cash and credit card around. Ted Jones came from a wealthy family of Central Louisiana land developers, and he couldn't resist bragging about their acquisitions. Terri would often mimic him. Sometimes it irritated Monique, and Terri would apologize. Other times, they roared with laughter. Terri's nickname for Ted was "Tedward."

Monique had confided to her roommate a month ago that she and Ted had become intimate. Terri's almost-sarcastic response had been "Finally." As usual, Terri had asked for details. Monique told her he had been clumsy and rushed, but she had decided that probably they just needed to get used to this new part of their relationship.

This week she'd been determined to prove to herself that she could get what she needed if they had the time together. She invited Ted to her room, knowing that Terri would be out all evening. She had initiated the sex, but before it was over, Ted's cell phone rang. "It's Jon," he had said, and then proceeded to talk. She had left the room and gone up the hall to the common room to cry, just like she was doing now. A knock at the door startled her, and before she could say "Come in," Terri did.

"I just saw Tedward at the club and he wants you to come down," Terri said as she pulled an overnight bag from under her bed and unzipped it. "Is everything all right between the two of you? He acted funny."

Monique didn't reply. When the silence was unbroken, Terri turned and looked at her.

"What's wrong?" she asked. She walked to the fan and turned the dial to increase the speed, then sat down beside Monique and began rubbing her shoulder. Monique finally sat up cross-legged, wiping her nose with a well-used tissue.

"I tried to tell him what I want to do this summer and he just kept talking about going on vacation with his parents."

"I don't know how you did it this long," said Terri. "His parents don't appreciate you at all, Monique, and neither does Ted. I hope you don't go down to the club."

"I'm not. I don't want to see him until I figure out what to do."

Terri got up and moved her overnight bag over to the bottom of Monique's bed to continue packing.

"Remember when Mrs. Jones said that comment about *vin ordinaire* never appearing at their dining room table that time you decided to take the Cajun wine to their place?"

Monique remembered. Terri had wished her luck on Friday when left for Alexandria with Ted, taking a bottle of Cajun Country wine her father had recommended. Then she had consoled her on Sunday night when she came back in tears. Monique had told Terri how Ted's father took a sip at dinner and jumped up from the table, running from the dining room to the kitchen sink, claiming after he returned that it had fermented too much. Ted and his mother had chuckled together behind matching cloth napkins.

"His parents were so snobby about the Cajun wine," Terri was now shouting from the bathroom down the hall. "They think they're so refined, but if you ask me, they have no manners. Why haven't they ever asked to meet your father?"

Terri walked back into the room, imitating Ted's mother. "Oh Edward, darling, give little Edward Junior a big wad of cash to put in his wallet so he can flash it around campus in front of all his friends," she said in a high-pitched voice with a southern accent. "I only met that woman once. What's her name, Buffy?"

"Tabby." Monique giggled.

"Tabby, Tabby," repeated Terri as she strutted around the room imitating a woman walking in three-inch heels. "Have you ever seen her in sandals, or slippers, or how about flipflops?"

"No."

"Well, poor Tedward, he must be sitting at the bar and thinking that because he asked for you, you will show up. He didn't stick up for you at all when you took up the CD to show them last weekend."

Monique recounted that story once more. When she and Ted had gone to Alexandria last weekend, she had taken the CD that her cousin Michelle and her new husband Jacques had just recently cut. As they had sat in the great room listening to the first song, Ted sat slumped in his chair behind a newspaper. The parents made no comments, and Monique had gotten up and shut the music off.

"I really let Ted have it, right in front of them. I told him he was a spoiled brat. And when his mother said to be quiet, I told her she and Mr. Jones were rude and disrespectful toward me. I don't know where I got the nerve to say those things!"

"I know just where you got the nerve, *cher*," said Terri. "You're Cajun! And then what did Tabby say?"

Monique repeated the story one more time. "She said, 'Edward Junior, you tell your girlfriend to settle down this instant! Just because we have more classical tastes in music . . . and for heaven's sake, stop letting her call you Ted!' Stupid Ted didn't say a word to defend me. Of course, I had just called him a spoiled brat." She paused to take a breath.

"And he tells me tonight they're going to give me a second chance! I might not give them a second chance. I guess when he asked about getting engaged things came to a head."

"He *what*?"

"He mentioned getting engaged after graduation."

"What did you say?" Terri came over closer to get every detail.

"I said I wasn't ready."

"Oh thank God!" exclaimed Terri, then, "I'm sorry. It's a hard decision to make, whether to stay in a relationship or not. Maybe I'm too hard on Ted. It's just that I don't think he appreciates you enough. I started to think that if you ended up with him, I wouldn't be able to keep in touch. I couldn't stand those parents of his."

"Well, how does visiting me in Lafayette this summer sound?"

"I would love to," said Terri happily as she zipped up the bag crammed full. "I love your father." She gestured as though she was stirring a big pot of food and sampling it. "'Terri, Honey,'" she said as she imitated Monique's father in the deepest voice she could muster, "'let's celebrate your graduation. I'll cook you some nice, spicy shrimp that will burn off your tongue!'" The girls both laughed and hugged.

"Have a great time in Lafayette and see you Sunday night!" Terri shouted as she ran out the door. Suddenly Monique realized that their dorm life together would also be ending soon. She had been really lucky. She dabbed at a few tears, and then her cell phone rang.

"Hello?" said Monique, tentatively. She hadn't checked to see who was calling and didn't want it to be Ted.

"Hi, Honey," said the loud male voice on the other end. "What's the matter?"

"Nothing, Daddy."

"Are you sure? Oh well, maybe this will cheer you up. I'm having a real *bal de maison* for your Uncle Bill's birthday tomorrow night. Can you two come here for the weekend?"

"I will. Ted will be busy."

"Oh, damn, there's somebody at the door. Can I call you back?" asked her father. "I'll call you back, honey, I promise."

The line went dead and Monique set the cell phone on the desk.

Broussard's class was her first tomorrow, so there wouldn't be time in the morning to get the assignment done. She brought up a blank Word document and wrote her name and tomorrow's date. She found the book on the floor where Ted had dropped it. With a glance at the first lines of the poem *Evangeline*, she decided that reading the poetry aloud would help her concentrate.

"This is the forest primeval . . ." Monique stopped and studied the question she'd written in her notebook during yesterday's class. "Why does Longfellow begin the story this way?" Professor Broussard had assigned the reading of the first five pages of the poem, along with a written answer to his question. She read on, then tapped her thoughts out on the keyboard.

An hour later, her assignment finished, Monique looked at the small clock on her bed table. It was 11 P.M. She threw on a nightshirt and brushed her teeth, carrying the cellphone with her to the bathroom next door. Jumping with surprise when the phone played its familiar ring tone in her fingers, she hurried back to her room, shut the door and climbed on her bed.

"Hello, *ma petite*," said her father. "Are you two able to come? I forget where we left off."

"Just me." She tried to be lighthearted.

"Wonderful!"

"Are you cooking crawfish?"

"Shrimp gumbo. In fact, I'm making it right now." He paused, slurped, and made a smacking sound. "Mmm, good. I found a new sausage to put in that gives it some zing. Actually, Pépé delivered them earlier. That's who was at the door. He said to say Hi."

"Oh, good. Dad, your gumbo already has lots of zing."

"Ah, but this one has even more," he exclaimed. "You will have to wash it down with a garden hose full of cold water." Monique forced a laugh.

"What's wrong, honey?"

She sighed, and confided to him what had happened earlier. "Let it out, *cher*," he said. Her father had been two parents to her since she was a little girl, even helping her sew prom gowns. "Your mama would want me to do this," was what he always said. Other than that comment, he rarely spoke about his deceased wife. The last time she had tried, the conversation had not gone on long before he changed the subject.

"Where do you get the energy to be cooking at this time of night? It's almost midnight. Go to bed!"

"I'll just finish this up tonight so I can do some baking tomorrow." She could hear a spoon clanking on the sides of a pot. "And gumbo is better if you let it rest overnight, anyway."

"It smells good from here."

"Thanks. By the way, what are you learning about these days?"

"Well, tonight I was actually working on an assignment for Historical Fiction class."

"That sounds interesting."

"It is. It's about *Evangeline,* the poem by Henry Wadsworth Longfellow."

"Oh!" her father exclaimed. "That's the story your mother loved!"

"Did she tell you that?"

"Yes, she read it, and before she died . . ." Her father stopped, took another slurp of his culinary creation, and continued. "Before she died, she started going to festivals and telling stories about the Acadians. We traced both our ancestries back to *Le Grand Dérangement* from Nova Scotia, back in the 1800's."

"Actually, Daddy, it was the mid-1700s."

"That's right, that's right. Your *Gra'mere* LeBlanc was a Gaudet before she and your grandfather, *Grand-père* LeBlanc, got married. And on your mother's side, your *Mémère* Mélanson was a Babin before she got married. I believe your mother said all our family names go back to the Acadians who came from France to North America."

"I miss *Mémère* Melanson." She longed to add, "and Mama." When her father didn't say anything, she asked, "Could we talk about this a little when I come home?"

"Yeah, it's probably time. I'll see you tomorrow night, and oh, I forgot to tell you that Michelle and Jacques will be here."

After they exchanged *bonsoirs*, Monique clicked the cell phone shut.

She closed her eyes and tried to remember the rambling garden behind her house that Michelle's mother had described to her many times after her mother's death. Aunt Marguerite had been upset to see the back yard become thick with overgrowth. Michelle told Monique one night that her mother had also complained about the terrible curtains that Uncle Joe put up on the windows, and how she had asked Uncle Bill to talk to Joe about them. It was several years later when Monique was in grade school that the drab curtains finally came down, returning the house to the light-filled home Catherine had tended.

She felt guilty about how much she had neglected her father over the past year. During the winter months she'd cancelled her car insurance to save money, and trips away from campus were only when she went with Ted to visit his family.

I'm coming to Lafayette, Daddy, she thought, and a *bal de maison* is just what I need.

Monique crawled into bed and closed her eyes. She pictured Michelle and Jacques, and wondered if she would ever have what they had together. Jacques was ragged around the edges, a big, burly, and hairy contrast to her cousin's willowy frame, but she had also come to realize that he was a jewel. He listened with intense interest when the two cousins reminisced about their childhood exploits. Monique had told him at their wedding how his new bride's talent had blossomed since they met. The first time Monique could recall Michelle trying out the accordion was at Michelle's mother's fortieth birthday party. Uncle Bill had showed his daughter the notes to a simple song, and Michelle had struggled to get her small arms around it. Dressed in a lacy dress, ringlets dangling around the accordion, she mastered the song before the party was over to the delight of family members who applauded and cheered.

Now Michelle and Jacques jammed with the best there was on the Cajun-Zydeco circuit. Michelle's sweet soprano and Jacques' baritone harmonies, combined with her accordion and his fiddle, were now attracting fans from both coasts. Since the Lafayette Duo had performed at the Newport Folk Festival last June, they were getting more attention from the East Coast.

As she began to relax and drift into sleep, she was on the way to the party . . . the music . . . Daddy . . . .

"Wait here while I ask Michel to play our song," said the young man standing beside her. He let go of her hand to run quickly to a small wooden stage.

"My dear, where is he going?" asked a male voice behind her.

"He is asking Michel to play 'Ciel d'automne,'" she replied to Pierre's father. Pierre ran back, lifted her slightly off her feet while giving his father a nod and a smile, and brought her to the dance floor to sway with him to their favorite fiddle rhythm. She felt the strength in his arms as he held her tightly. The song quickened, causing dancers to bounce off other couples as they attempted to keep up. When it was over, loud hoots of praise rang out.

"Let's go outside," Pierre whispered. They both began to shiver when the brisk salt air hit their heated faces. Pierre pointed in the direction of the Gaspereau River and whispered softly in her ear. "Soon, when we are married, we will be sleeping together on a straw mattress up in the garçonierre of my father's house until the men can get together and build us a house of our own." She felt her face flush with thoughts of them sleeping together. They walked a bit farther, and stood close to the cliffs, watching and listening to the waves washing to shore. Pierre turned and looked at her, and gently lifted his fingers to her face.

"Ma Cherie, tes babines sont si doux!" he whispered as he glided a finger over her lips. The tender moment was abruptly interrupted when Pierre's name was called.

"Yes, father," he answered reluctantly. He removed his finger,

substituting for it a kiss. The sensation sent a rush through her body.
"À demain," he whispered, then turned to his father. A church
bell rang out nearby, and the ringing . . . louder . . . no, beeping alarm
. . . .

Monique reached out to shut it off. The kiss, the dancing, had seemed so real a moment ago, but the bright morning sunlight streaming in woke her to the realization that she had just a few minutes to make it to class. She threw on a pair of jeans and a top, washed her face, brushed her teeth, and grabbed her books. Hurrying down the hill she reached up to her lips, imitating the feel of Pierre's finger caressing them in her dream. She could still feel his kiss, and the excitement that it stirred in her.

Chapter 3

Historical Fiction 401

Friday, April 29

Monique entered the classroom and slipped quietly into her seat. Professor Broussard had his back to her as he walked up the aisle gathering assignments. He turned when he saw her, and she pulled her completed paper out of her binder and handed it to him.

"The next literary work we will study is *Evangeline*, the epic poem by Henry Wadsworth Longfellow," he began. "Until maybe thirty or forty years ago, this poem was studied by school-aged children. How many of you remember ever reading this story?" Two hands went up tentatively. "Good, that's about what I thought. What do you remember from the story?"

A student near the center of the class offered, "I just remember something about a young couple being separated when their families were shipped out."

"Good. Can anyone add to that?"

Monique waited but no one answered, so she raised her hand. Broussard nodded at her. "I think lots of families were separated. They were put on boats and exiled. Eventually they ended up in Louisiana."

"That's right. Over a period of years, thousands of people were forced from their homes, families were separated, and a large number died during this tragic period. Almost a century later, Longfellow published *Evangeline*. It brought the previously unheard-of story of *Le Grand Dérangement* to everyone's awareness, through the characters of Evangeline and Gabriel.

"To some people, the poem is now considered too romanticized. But *Evangeline* allowed Longfellow to tell a story that even today has important implications for many people. In the ill-fated romance of Evangeline and Gabriel, he personified the cruelty of *Le Grand Dérangement*. I have chosen to examine this literary work for two reasons."

Broussard stopped and picked up a marker. He then placed a large *1* on the board.

"First of all, this story has much to say about how political leaders can shape the course of human destiny, for better or worse." Broussard scribbled "Culture and Political Forces."

"When we examined *War and Peace* and *Gone with the Wind*, we saw how Leo Tolstoy and Margaret Mitchell knitted the two elements of history and fiction together. We also discussed their characters and what they symbolized.

"And my second reason:" He wrote a large *2* on the board, then, "My Genealogy." He glanced around at the students. "Is there anyone else here who thinks the story told in this poem is part of their genealogy?" After a few moments, several students raised their hands. "Good, we'll come back to that question later. The main question I will want you to answer by the end of our time together is: Have the authors we're studying combined history and fiction and maintained the integrity of the history?

"I also would like us to discuss whether or not *Le Grand Dérangement* should be studied as an American story. It involved British and Colonial American politics, misguided leadership, and disenfranchisement, and one historian has even called it the first North American ethnic cleansing. We'll talk more about that later.

"A military leader from New England by the name of Colonel John Winslow was given the mission of performing the first deportations at Grand-Pré, having landed his army in this area during the summer of 1755. His journal is the only good record that remains of what took place then. All other information seemed to disappear.

"Once the Acadians were captured and made prisoners that fall, arrangements were made to place them onto transport ships and disperse them to places unknown in the colonies, Europe, and the Indies, with the hopes of destroying their culture and assimilating them. Their homes, barns and churches were burned to the ground, and a complete culture of people who had never known poverty or disease became outcasts of society. After ten years or more searching for a place to call home, hundreds came to Louisiana, and these are my ancestors and perhaps yours as well."

Looking up to see a student's hand raised, Broussard called on him, "Yes, Mr. Miers."

"Doc, it sounds to me like this is every bit as much an American story as Paul Revere and Custer's Last Stand. Why isn't this in our U. S. History books?"

"That's a good question, Rick. But rather than giving you an answer, I would like to hear what you or your classmates have to say about that."

Dennis Cormier responded, "Well, they say the winners write the history books. And in this one, the Acadians lost. They lost everything. So, I guess since this story starts in Canada, and it's a pretty unpleasant chapter as far as our British roots go, it's easier to leave it out. Paul Revere and Custer are much more attractive stories to tell." After a pause, he asked, "Wasn't this covered at all in history books?"

"Yes, Dennis, it was, very briefly. I suppose it's similar to the destruction of the Native American culture. Historians know it happened, but it might be controversial to write about how it happened."

"Let me give you a bit of background about Longfellow, a writer who was able to get the history exposed to millions of people in American and European society about one hundred years after it took place. Longfellow was a New-Englander, an English-speaking person who became inspired to tell this story at a time when the Acadian culture itself had long been spread out and disjointed. A century had passed since the deportations when Longfellow wrote the epic poem of *Evangeline*. The poem did much to educate the world about what a tragedy *Le Grand Dérangement* had been, and although the Acadians continued to struggle, it is important to note that their culture was still very much alive then, and remains so today." The professor smiled.

"As I said, Longfellow was from New England, where a good portion of the colonial military that executed the deportations had come from one hundred years earlier. Longfellow became a professor at Harvard University where he remained for twenty years, and along with *Evangeline,* he wrote the epic poem *The Song of Hiawatha*, among others. He captured native themes of early America, and had the privilege of being a contemporary of other great pioneers of American literature such as Emerson, Hawthorne, Thoreau, and Holmes. He was admired during his own lifetime, and today remains one of the most important figures in 19th Century American literature."

"According to this small regional history book written by a man named John Herbin, Longfellow was having dinner one night with his fellow author and friend, Nathaniel Hawthorne. A guest of Hawthorne's joined them, a minister by the name of Reverend Conolly. A member of his congregation was the aunt of a Nova Scotian author and historian, Thomas Chandler Haliburton. Haliburton had shared with his aunt an Acadian legend surrounding the events of 1755, and she then passed it on to Reverend Conolly, who during the dinner conversation tried to persuade Hawthorne to write about it." Broussard continued to scan the pages of the small book he held, flipping several before continuing.

"Longfellow could not get the legend out of his mind. He decided to approach his friend Nathaniel Hawthorne shortly afterwards to see if he had begun writing yet. Hawthorne had not, and agreed to let Longfellow take a stab at writing a poem about it. Hawthorne gave his friend and fellow author some notes he had kept, and the following is an excerpt from Longfellow's diary showing him trying to decide on the name of *Evangeline*:

> *. . . December 7th . . . I know not what name to give to—not my new baby, but my new poem. Shall it be Gabrielle, or Celestine, or Evangeline?*

"Until Longfellow published *Evangeline*, many readers were not even aware that *Le Grand Dérangement* had taken place. Evangeline's Gabriel died in her arms, after she was separated from him and searched for him over many years. The characters became real in the minds of people all over the world, and inspired a few works of art. In Grand-Pré there is a statue of Evangeline, one side showing an innocent young girl and the other a tragic, saddened woman. In St. Martinville, there is also a statue of her. Perhaps some of you have visited the Acadian Memorial there."

Professor Broussard placed the book on his desk.

"Feel free to borrow this if you'd like," he said, pointing to it. He shuffled a pile of papers and began to distribute them. Monique noticed a smile on his face, an expression she had come to recognize as one that he had when he was about to share something personal with the class. These moments had only happened a few times. During one class he had told them that he was a former student at Louisiana State, and as quarterback he had helped the team win two bowl games. Later on she found out more. He had been the Fighting Tigers' MVP for two years. Another time he told them he was building a log cabin in the Atchafalaya Basin and it was coming along nicely. So now, Monique sat up in her seat and listened intently to what he was about to share with the class.

"I enjoy lecturing on Longfellow's *Evangeline*," he said. "When I attended the Université de Moncton, I did my Master's thesis and went on to write a book about Acadian language, folklore and music. I am descended from Acadians, and I'm sure several of you would discover that you are too if you were to study your genealogies. Mr. Cormier, your name probably is Acadian, and Miss LeBlanc, yours too. You might find it interesting to ask your families what they know." He paused and glanced in the direction of the students he had called by name, and waited momentarily for a response. When none came, he continued, "Miss LeBlanc, one of Longfellow's characters has your last name.

"An Acadian by the name of René LeBlanc moved his family to Grand-Pré in 1675. He was imprisoned at one point during the French and English struggles for power over Acadia. However, over many years he became highly respected by both his fellow Acadians and the British governors, at least until Lieutenant Governor Lawrence came along. René LeBlanc's signature can be seen on some Acadian documents of negotiation with the British colonial governors.

"Acadia was originally owned by France, but became part of a treaty agreement with Britain in 1713. In it, France agreed to give Acadia to the British, and the Acadians were given the choice at that time to either move to an area in Canada under French rule or sign an oath of allegiance to the British Crown if war broke out with France. The British colonial leaders recognized that Acadian farmers traded their crops up and down the coast of America, and Queen Anne of Britain wrote a letter to the governor in 1713 in support of the Acadians."

Broussard paused to review his notes, then read aloud:

. . . Without any molestation, as fully and freely as our other subjects do or may possess their lands or estates . . .

Broussard sighed deeply. He sat back in his chair, placing one foot up on his desk. When a large chunk of hardened mud fell off his sneaker to the floor, he jumped up quickly, picked it up and tossed it in the garbage can. Distracted, he walked up the aisle toward Monique's row.

His black hair was always closely cropped on the sides, the rest in place except for a tousle that dropped down over his eyes occasionally. Monique's eyes drifted down from his face as she observed what he was wearing. His sage-green button-down oxford and Jerry Garcia tie with khaki Dockers looked nice on him. Monique always enjoyed seeing what he had on each time he came into class. But the old sneakers were not his customary footwear. Usually he wore loafers. Caked mud fell off the sneakers as he walked, leaving a small trail here and there in the aisle.

"Let's go to ten years before *Le Grand Dérangement*. It's 1745, and France is fighting one of many battles against the English in the colonies. They want the men of Acadia to help them, so this is what they were told:

We order you to deliver up your arms, ammunition , . and those who contravene these orders shall be punished and delivered into the hands of the Indians, as we cannot refuse the demands these savages make for all those who will not submit themselves . . . .

Broussard shook his head. "Imagine how difficult it would be for them to turn down the wishes of their mother country, which threatened them with retaliation from their brothers and friends, the

Mi'Kmaq. Still, no matter how difficult the situation, the Acadians stayed faithful to their promise to remain neutral, and this was their reply. It was signed by, among others, the notary public René LeBlanc.

> *We live under a mild and tranquil government, and we have all reason to be faithful to it. We hope, therefore, that you will grant us the favor not to plunge us into utter misery. This we hope from your goodness, assuring you that we are, with every much respect, your very humble and obedient servants.*

A hand went up near the door, and Broussard nodded to give the student the floor. "I'm a little confused," said the student. "The British finally shipped them out, but before that, their own mother country France was threatening to throw them to the Indians, who were actually their friends, if they didn't fight with them against the British. Neither side seemed to really care one flip about the Acadians. It just seems like the Acadians were caught in the middle. All they wanted to do was to live their lives the way they had on their own for years, but nobody seemed to be on their side."

Broussard replied, "That is absolutely correct. And it gets worse from there. In 1746, Governor Shirley of Massachusetts writes to England with a proposal to make the Acadians convert to Protestantism or be exiled. He really wants to see the entire eastern coastal colonies become English-speaking. However, Britain's response, coming from the Duke of Newcastle, is to instruct Governor Shirley to 'publicly remove any such ill-grounded suggestions.'

"In 1754, the leadership of Nova Scotia changed suddenly. The governor in power, Hopson, had been sympathetic to the Acadian people, even putting policies in place to protect them, but he became ill and returned to England. He chose as his successor Lieutenant Governor Charles Lawrence, a bad choice for the Acadians. Lawrence wasted no time in writing to London to report that the Acadians possessed the best and largest tracts of land, and in his opinion, the province could not be settled 'with any effect while they remained in this situation.' I'll read you the response from the British Secretary of State." Broussard checked his notes again.

> *It cannot be too much recommended to you to use greatest caution and prudence in your conduct toward these Neutrals.*

Professor Broussard looked around, making eye contact with a few of the students. When no one responded, he continued. "I don't expect you to remember everything I'm telling you, but I would like you to have a working familiarity with the history and politics.

A contemporary historian views *Le Grand Dérangement* as the first 'ethnic cleansing' to take place in North America. You might want to read *A Great and Noble Scheme*, by John Mack Faragher. There has been a great deal of debate about whether or not England knew the deportation would take place. Depending on who you talk to, some researchers believe that England was ultimately accountable for the leaders that they placed in authority in their colonies."

Monique saw an expression on the professor's face that disturbed her. What is it? she wondered. It's his eyes. Usually they were bright blue, dancing with intense interest in the material he was presenting. Right at this moment they were dark, piercing . . . angry?

"Would you like to take a break for a few minutes or keep going and leave a bit early?" he asked. Monique looked at the big clock on the wall over the professor's head. There was an hour left, and she was hoping to get out early and drive to Lafayette. Students in front of her looked left and right and the general consensus was to skip the break and press on.

Broussard nodded. He moved from one side of the room to the other, brushing his misbehaving tousle of hair back from his forehead. Head down, he walked over to his desk, checked his notes, then continued.

"It was no secret to the Acadians that their presence in Nova Scotia was resented," he said. "What they didn't realize was that the newly-appointed lieutenant governor, Charles Lawrence, was devising a plan with Governor Shirley of Massachusetts to make them prisoners of the British Crown. The leaders planned to destroy their culture and replace them with English-speaking settlers.

"Charles Lawrence, in my opinion," stated Professor Brossard as he pounded his fist on his desk, "was a racist, Catholic-hating, son-of-a-bitch!"

Broussard fell back in his chair and rubbed his hand. Except for the sound of someone clicking a pen, the room was silent.

"Professor, you all right?" a male student finally dared to ask. Monique thought it sounded like Dennis Cormier, but she didn't want to turn around to look. The professor shook his head, and more silence followed. Monique looked across the aisle at a young man she'd talked to a few times. She questioned him with her eyes, and he shrugged in response. The pen clicked on. Glancing at the clock again, Monique watched the second hand go around several more times. He shook his hand, his expression a pained one. Finally he spoke.

"I'm very sorry for that outburst you just witnessed. I don't know what to say."

Monique felt bad for Professor Broussard. She wanted to tell him it was OK, but held back. Sometimes she hated her shyness, and this was one of those times.

"When I was a young kid, around ten years old," he said, "I started noticing a picture in the hallway of my family's home. It showed people being forced onto boats by soldiers, and their faces looked afraid and confused. In the background, houses and barns were in flames. Sometimes I'd just stand and look at the picture and wish I could crawl into it and stop whatever was happening. My mother saw me standing in front of it one day when I was, oh, maybe twelve years old, and she told me it was a picture of *Le Grand Dérangement*. She said it happened a long time ago, far from Louisiana, and because of it my ancestors came here to live. She said their lives were much better afterward.

"That picture left a heavy imprint on my soul, in spite of my mother's attempt to give it a happy ending. All the stories I've heard and research I've done has never seemed to relieve what I felt then and still feel now. I don't know if this makes sense to you or not." The professor paused and waited for a response that didn't come.

"Those poor people had nobody to help them," he said, his voice breaking, "nobody to stop it from happening . . ."

"Dr. B, that makes perfect sense to me," said a young man behind Monique. "I'm not Acadian or Cajun. But just listening to you talk about how these people were mistreated over and over again by two different governments started to make me mad too, right up to the point when you scared the hell out of us." Giggles followed the broken tension. "So don't feel bad about getting emotional about this. If I'd done as much reading and research on this as you have, I'd be mad as hell too."

Professor Broussard pulled a tissue from a box on his desk and wiped his forehead and eyes. He nodded at the student who had just spoken and managed a slight smile. "I hate to talk about these leaders, but I have to. Some historians depict Lieutenant-Governor Charles Lawrence, who governed Acadia during this awful period, as a military leader who was doing his job to win the power struggle between France and Britain. Governor Shirley of Massachusetts could be viewed in the same way. And Colonel John Winslow, who led the army that carried out the expulsion in Grand-Pré, could be seen as an honorable soldier obeying his orders. I see them all as greedy, self-serving, and hateful, and I admit that this is a very biased opinion. Obviously, I can't be objective in educating you people on this material, and that makes me question my ethics in lecturing on it." The professor looked directly at Monique, his eyes communicating disappointment in himself. She tried to look sympathetic and smiled as supportively as she could.

Someone, Monique thought it was Rick Miers, said, "Doc, I'm no expert on ethics, but it seems to me that you're being straight with us about what happened, since you're reading from lots of sources. And you're being honest with us about your own feelings, so everything is good. I can't speak for anybody else, but you have sure gotten me interested in what I thought was going to be a stuffy old story from the olden days." More giggles and some expressions of agreement came from around the room.

"In that case, I'll try to continue," Broussard replied with a smile. "And I'll try not to scare you." After a glance at his notes, he began to speak again.

"These Acadians were unarmed farmers, not an army. And I agree with Farragher, that this was ethnic cleansing of an entire culture of people! Just imagine, would you ever conceive that someone would want to drive you out of your home, burn it down, and ship you off to someplace far from home, never allowing you to come back? My ex-wife used to say, 'It was so many generations ago, get over it!' I knew she was right, but I couldn't."

Broussard laughed for the first time, and his students laughed nervously too, a display of collective confusion about how to respond to their professor. "On the sixth of June, 1755," he continued, "one hundred English-speaking soldiers came to the Minas Basin, supposedly to do some fishing. They billeted themselves into the homes of Acadians, two soldiers in each one. In the middle of the night they left the homes of their hosts carrying as many firearms as they could find, and later seized the rest. Then they captured the farmers' boats. The Acadian people were shocked to wake up one morning and find their firearms and boats gone, and appealed to the Halifax government for help with getting them back. One hundred of the most respected leaders of Acadia were delegated to draft a petition to Governor Lawrence, in which they stated that they needed their boats for fishing and their guns for protecting their families from wildlife. One of these was René LeBlanc. In the petition, they stated their allegiance, saying that it would not be removal of guns that would keep them true to their promise of neutrality, but their own consciences.

"Then, in July, 1755, fifteen of the hundred delegates were summoned to appear before Governor Lawrence and his council. They were reprimanded harshly for their insolence. They were asked once more to take an unconditional oath of allegiance to England, and in desperation they gave in to the request. Governor Lawrence said that it was now too late. The fifteen leaders were taken prisoner. More Acadian men were summoned, and more taken prisoner, including priests. Abbé Daudin, the priest at *Saint-Joseph-de-la-Rivière-aux Canards,* a few miles from Grand-Pré, wrote in his journal, giving us quite a dramatic portrayal of the events of that time:

After taking off the priests, the English raised their flag about the churches and made the latter into barracks when their troops passed there . . . the missionaries reached Halifax with this fine accompaniment, drums beating.

"Colonel John Winslow received his orders from Governor Shirley of Massachusetts to go to Acadie. The Acadian French, with the help of their Mi'Kmaq brothers, far outnumbered the English, and the Mi'Kmaq had military power in the colony. English speakers were in constant fear of being scalped. Attempts by the government to start other English settlements were unsuccessful, and they resented that the Acadian farmers thrived. Colonel Winslow came from Marshfield, Massachusetts with two thousand New England troops and received his orders from Massachusetts Governor Shirley in late summer to conduct the deportation of Acadians from des Mines in the fall of 1755 during harvest time.

"A proclamation was drafted on September 2nd and sent to Grand-Pré. On September 5, four hundred and eighteen men and boys over the age of ten were to be summoned into the St. Charles des Mines church under orders from the King of England. The poem *Evangeline* begins just before that day."

Professor Broussard picked up a book from his desk, flipping several pages. "By the way, an ancestor on my father's side is Joseph Broussard, who was from the New Brunswick area of Acadia. He was nicknamed 'Beausoleil' and fought against the British, hoping to one day bring his people back from exile. His family remained in hiding in Acadia for many years, fighting a guerrilla type of warfare. Many of them died. He was a warrior who was feared and respected by his enemies, the British, and in his later years he led one of the first groups of Acadians here to begin the colony in Louisiana."

Professor Broussard paused, flipping more pages of the book and holding a spot with his finger. His demeanor was calm now, and he actually began to smile. He enjoyed reading excerpts of literary works to his classes. Some students didn't like it; she'd heard comments from others about being treated like third-graders. But Monique loved it. She watched as the professor adopted his familiar stance beside his desk, book held in one hand and the other free to wave around for effect.

"'This is the forest primeval . . . '" he began, projecting his voice in a way that caused several students to snicker.

"Is something funny, Cormier?" he asked, half-serious and half in fun. Monique turned around. Dennis Cormier apologized, looking embarrassed.

"This is the forest primeval," he again stated, this time glancing around to see if everyone was listening.

The murmuring pines and the hemlocks
Bearded with moss, and in garments green, indistinct in the twilight,

Stand like Druids of eld, with voices sad and prophetic,
Stand like harpers hoar, with beards that rest on their bosoms.
Loud from its rocky caverns, the deep-voiced neighboring ocean

Speaks, and in accents disconsolate answers the wail of the forest.
This is the forest primeval; but where are the hearts that beneath it
Leaped like the roe, when he hears in the woodland the voice of
*   the huntsman*
Where is the thatch-roofed village, the home of Acadian
*   farmers,—*
Men whose lives glided on like rivers that water the woodlands,
Darkened by shadows of earth, but reflecting an image of heaven?
Waste are those pleasant farms, and the farmers forever departed!
Scattered like dust and leaves, when the mighty blasts of October
Seize them, and whirl them aloft, and sprinkle them far o'er the
*   ocean.*
Naught but tradition remains of the beautiful village of Grand-Pré.
Ye who believe in affection that hopes, and endures, and is patient,
Ye who believe in the beauty and strength of woman's devotion,
List to the mournful tradition still sung by the pines of the forest;
List to a Tale of Love in Acadie, home of the happy.

PART THE FIRST.
In the Acadian land, on the shores of the Basin of Minas,
Distant, secluded, still the little village of Grand-Pré
Lay in the fruitful valley. Vast meadows stretched to the eastward,
Dikes, that the hands of the farmers had raised with labor
*   incessant,*
Shut out the turbulent tides; but at stated season the flood-gates
Opened and welcomed the sea to wander at will o'er the meadows.
West and south there were fields of flax, and orchards and
*   cornfields*
Spreading afar and unfenced o'er the plain; and way to the
*   northward*
Blomidon rose, and the forests old, and aloft on the mountains
Sea-fogs pitched their tents, and mists from the mighty Atlantic
Looked on the happy valley, but ne'er from their station
*   descended . . . .*

Professor Broussard looked much more relaxed now, finally, thought Monique. She lingered on his face as he read, taking in the tanned skin that was weathering to maturity after thirty-some years. She thought he was handsome, his short sideburns with a hint of gray around the temples giving him a distinguished look. His blue eyes under dark brows sparkled enthusiastically when he lectured, and when he did manage a smile, Monique thought it lit up the room. He also had a way of making students comfortable in his class. She liked how he used student participation during his lectures.

However, Monique had heard long before she entered his classroom that when he was unhappy with a student, he would single them out and ask to see them after class. At these times, he could be intimidating. It was well known on campus that he hated plagiarism and laziness, and nobody took his class for the easy way out. What was not known was what went on in his personal life. Female students did know he was divorced, but there was no other information to be had on the subject of his personal business. Well, once in a while he gave a glimpse of his life outside the halls . . . what does he do for fun . . . she'd have fun this weekend . . . get away from Ted . . . what a nice dream I had last night . . . why couldn't Ted be like the man in my dream . . . I have to pay attention . . . .

Reverend walked he among them; and up rose matrons and maidens,
Hailing his slow approach with words of affectionate welcome . . .

. . . I can't wait to get out of here . . . it's so hot . . . when I get home, I'll stop at the store and say hi to Pépé . . . . Monique jumped, startled to discover that all eyes, including the professor's, were on her.

"Miss LeBlanc, I asked if you would you like to read," spoke the professor. Heat rose in Monique's face. Broussard continued to stare at her, waiting for an answer.

"OK," she squeaked. She cleared her throat and looked down at her book, flipping over to the next page, hand trembling. "I'm sorry. I can't find the last line you read. Can you repeat it please?"

"Nice try, Monique," laughed the professor. "What were you daydreaming about, something you can share with us?"

She froze, and could not believe the words that popped from her mouth. "I was thinking about a dream I had last night."

"What kind of dream? I enjoy studying dreams, as a matter of fact." A few snickers could be heard from the other students.

Monique wanted to crawl away. Professor Broussard was waiting for her to tell the class what she had dreamed about. She struggled to remember it, her heart thumping in her left ear.

"Well, umm," she stammered, "Let's see . . . I was dancing in a hall with someone, it was like a barn there, I could smell hay . . ." She felt her face burning, and thought she heard a snicker. Struggling to keep her voice from shaking, she tried to remember. "I heard fiddle music, and the person I was with, he was my age, took me outside and we walked down to some cliffs. He pointed out toward the ocean and said that in the darkness, something . . . *les platins* . . . I think he said, glistened in the moonlight."

"What word did you just say?" asked Broussard.

"*Les platins?*" she said, trying to pronounce in the French accent she had heard in her dream.

"How do you know that word?"

"I don't know. It must be in the poem."

"It's not," he said with certainty. "It is an old Acadian word for "mudflats" that can be seen when the tide goes out. They are particularly noticeable in eastern Canada, where the tides are the highest in the world. The water rises about fifty feet, and when the tide is low the water goes out quite a distance." Broussard continued to look at her, but now she didn't mind. The self-conscious moments were over and students were chatting informally waiting for their imminent dismissal. He dismissed class, then asked Monique, "Do you have a few minutes?"

"Sure." The professor walked down the aisle and sat on the desk in front of her.

"Monique, I'm curious about your dream. Can you remember anything else?"

"Hmm, let's see. I remember what I was wearing in the dream, because it was so different from anything I've ever seen," she continued after thinking a moment. "I had on a long, black dress with a white apron over it, and a thin cloth, like a veil, over my hair. Pierre, the man in my dream, wore short pants, what are they called . . . breeches? We were dressed very old fashioned, and the house he pointed to was old fashioned. The air was cold and I could hear waves splashing far in the distance."

"It's funny you had that dream. It seems to describe the sights and sounds of Acadia," Broussard said excitedly. "This could mean something. Do you believe in paranormal experiences?"

Monique shivered and shook her head.

"I think you might have had one." His eyes were wide with excitement now.

Monique's teeth began to chatter and goose bumps on her arms made her shiver and hug herself. She felt embarrassed again and glanced down at her books. "Oh, I don't think so. Anyway, it scares me to death, the idea of ghosts and stuff like that. My cousin Michelle saw a ghost in the bathtub once, and it terrifies me to think about it. The ghost talked to her, and even though I don't believe ghosts talk to people, my cousin told me what it said and she doesn't lie, so I have to believe that it really happened."

"What did the ghost say?"

"It, or she, said that she was her Great-Gra'mère." Monique shivered again. "My cousin Michelle was only ten at the time. I was nine and I was staying over at her house for a couple of nights because my father was at the hospital with my mother. Michelle got up to go to the bathroom in the night and came back screaming. We sat up with the light on all night. She said that while she was washing her hands the ghost appeared in the tub. She was so scared, and so was I when she told me." Monique glanced up at the clock. "I'm sorry, I have to drive to Lafayette."

The professor's blue eyes were searching her face, making her uncomfortable. She could feel herself blushing. "Can I tell you something quickly, and then I'll let you get going?" She nodded in the affirmative.

"When I was doing research at Grand-Pré, something in the realm of the paranormal happened to me along the same lines as what happened to your cousin. I went to the chapel there late one night, and met someone, an old man, who spoke to me. He called me Beausoleil."

"Your ancestor you told us about today?"

"Yes," he replied, looking pleased that she had listened in class.

"So what made you think something was strange about that?"

"He vanished right after we spoke."

Monique shivered again, embarrassed that she couldn't control it better. The professor laughed, then apologized for frightening her. She hoped she wouldn't dream about this conversation tonight.

"Do you know anything about your family history?" Broussard asked.

"I do," said Monique apologetically. "I'm sorry I wasn't able to mention it during class. Sometimes I get afraid to speak up. But I talked to my father about it on the phone last night after he asked what I was studying. My mother and father apparently did some research on their Acadian ancestors before my mother passed away."

"Sorry about your mother," he said sympathetically, "and I want to apologize for putting you on the spot in front of the class today, especially if you get a little anxious about it. I'm glad we had this conversation, though, and I still think your dream means something. Maybe when you learn more about your own history, we can talk again sometime."

Monique nodded and left the classroom. She heard Professor Broussard calling out to have a nice weekend in Lafayette. Remembering that she hadn't heard from Ted since last night, she suddenly felt an empty feeling inside.

Chapter 4

Laissez Les Bon Temps Rouler

Outside the stuffy walls of the classroom, the air was moist and hot. The sun's glare reflected off car roofs in the parking lot and Monique squinted to shade her eyes as she walked. Once they adjusted, her sights fell on Ted walking up toward her. He waved to get her attention, and she suddenly felt confined by the sun's heat.

"Hi." A pain shot through her stomach.

"Where you going?"

"I'm going to Lafayette." She moved away from him to show she was in a hurry.

"I'm going home too," He came closer, bending his knees to make better eye contact with her. "I'm sorry about last night. I guess I was in a strange mood."

"What do you mean?"

"You know, asking you to get engaged."

"What if I had said yes?"

"I'm so glad you didn't." He laughed, pounding his fist to his chest as he said it. Monique couldn't believe what she was hearing. She fought to keep her anger down.

"What's going on in Lafayette?" he continued.

"*Un bal de maison.*"

"In English?"

"A party . . . for my uncle." Her tone was edgy, and she fought the urge to explode at him. He sensed her mood and responded antagonistically.

"Is your accordion-playing cousin going to be there?"

"Michelle? I thought you didn't like her."

"Oh, I think she's hot, it's just that music." He made a face at Monique and grinned.

"Well, she has lots of fans, and she doesn't need you! I have to go . . ."

"Wait, I don't want to fight. Let's not make a big deal out of last night. I'll tell my folks you're coming up next weekend, OK?"

"No, nothing's OK. I need time to think about things."

"Fine then," He held his head high, flipping his hair out of his eyes with one hand. "While you're thinking about things, why don't we just see other people!"

Once Ted could no longer see her, Monique ran quickly to her dorm. Packing in a hurry, she didn't care what she was throwing into her small duffle. Her eyes were blurred with tears that she fought back, and her head pounded. She walked in a trance to the lot behind her dorm where her old green Mustang was parked. She couldn't wait to get away from here. Merging into traffic on I-10 as it crossed the Mississippi River, she replaced the Coldplay CD in her player with a new one she had borrowed from Michelle. Lennie Gallant's voice guided her into a more relaxed place, away from Ted and school. Tears still nudged on the edge of her thoughts as she glanced in her rear-view mirror at the reflection of her own face, the face of a sad little girl who needed her mother. She didn't like that picture of herself one bit.

It will be OK, she imagined her mother saying. Go home to your papa.

Gradually, she sank into the melodies of the music and the staccato rhythms of the tires on the pavement as she sped toward Lafayette. Her Papa would be so happy to see her. She wondered if he was wishing her mother was still alive to celebrate her graduation.

Bayous on both sides fell away on the drive over the Atchafalaya, birds swooping overhead. Soon she would be back home, where she could sleep in the bed she'd grown up in.

Before she knew it, the elevated portion of the highway over the wetlands had ended, and she was looking for the exit that would take her home. As she approached the old neighborhood, Monique pressed the stop button on her CD player. A pleasant surge of energy came from a mysterious place in her body and she was actually surprised to discover she felt ready to join the world again. Her father would hug and kiss her as though she'd been away for years instead of months.

The neighborhood seemed so peaceful. Everything was the same as she'd left it months earlier. The only thing different was the way she felt, what she had learned, the way she'd changed. This place held a life she'd lived before college. Her life at LSU felt completely different. In a way, leaving had made her appreciate what she was coming back to, and she decided to drop in and see Pépé at the local grocery store. Pépé was one of those people around her age who had stayed in Lafayette, and it seemed unlikely to her that he would ever leave. Still, it was nice when she opened the door and he greeted her happily. They caught up on the local news and she was surprised how many of their high school friends were married, one or two with a child already.

When she reached her street a little later, Monique steered her car slowly into a lone empty spot at the end of her driveway. Cars formed a line along one side of the street and up around the next corner. The sound of live music filtered out onto the street and Monique could hear her father laughing at something. The front door was open, a ceiling fan on the porch humming. The smells of gumbo and barbeque hit her nose, and she took a deep breath of it. Opening the screen door, Monique was greeted by a kiss from her Uncle Bill. Aunt Marguerite stood next to him, her arm in his, and she removed it to give Monique a hug. Her father grabbed her duffle bag from her and threw it on the hallway chair, then extended his arms in his usual style. He embraced his daughter in a huge, hairy-armed bear hug that squashed her up against his chest, followed by the usual cascade of kisses. Lastly, he held her face in his big hands and said, "*Ma cherie,* I'm so happy to see you!" His arm lingered on her shoulder while he bellowed out for someone to bring her a drink of something. Michelle appeared from behind her father with a glass filled with ice cold water and handed it to her.

"Hey, I'm not the guest of honor here," she laughed, squeezing Uncle Bill's arm. She reached out for Michelle's hand and allowed her to lead the way to the living room couch, where they plopped down together.

"Where's Jacques?" Monique asked, and her cousin pointed to the dining room. "I'll get us some wine," said Michelle as she walked away. Monique recognized the fiddle music cranking up in the dining room. At parties like this, her father moved the dining room table out to the back porch and lined the walls with chairs, turning the large room into a place to sit and sing, get up and dance, or pull a chair over and join a conversation. She noticed that her father had also pulled the curtains back. It felt airy, and a memory from somewhere inside her brought a sensation of lightness to Monique's body. She sighed as her eyes drifted to the window. A neatly mowed lawn beckoned. Maybe she and her father could go this weekend and get some flowers to plant there.

Rob Lejeune, a high school senior who lived next door, came over to Monique with two bottles of water. She took one and thanked him. He smiled and drifted on to find another potential partner for the two-step that Jacques was now playing.

Michelle had returned with two glasses of wine.

"Thanks. I'll stick with the water," said Monique, holding up the glass Michelle had given her earlier and refilling it from the bottle Rob had given her. "I haven't had anything alcoholic since your wedding."

Michelle placed the wine on a small end table. "That's not a bad thing," she replied, her face wrinkled in a disgusted expression. "When we perform some people get so plastered I wonder if they come out to see us or just want another excuse to drink."

Monique brushed a strand of her cousin's hair with her fingers. "I love your hair this way. Did you get it cut or something?"

"Thanks. I did get it cut a little differently for the summer. It gets hot on stage. You look good, but just a little tired. Have you been studying a lot?"

"Yes, finals are coming up, and I didn't sleep great last night. I broke up with Ted today."

"I'm sorry."

The cousins looked at each other. Michelle was holding back on any comments about Ted for now, and Monique appreciated her restraint.

"Here comes Jacques," said Michelle, a wide smile showing a dimple on each cheek.

"Glad you could come," said Jacques. He and Monique exchanged a hug, and he sat down beside his wife. Michelle took his hand and told Monique about a song they had practiced for later on.

"It's an old Acadian song called '*Mon Pére A Fait Batir Maison.*' We're working on it for *Le Festival Acadien* in Nova Scotia this August. We're the featured performers there. Imagine that!" Suddenly Michelle's eyes grew wide. "You have to come with us!"

"Well, now that I'm not going to Martha's Vineyard, maybe I will. I do have money in savings I could use."

"We'd love to have you along," added Jacques. "If you want to help as a roadie, we could even pay you some. Then you wouldn't have to use all your savings." Michelle rewarded Jacques' idea with a kiss on his cheek.

"Jacques, Michelle, *vien voir ici* and give us the 'Lafayette Breakdown,'" shouted someone from the next room, and Monique joined the crowd listening and dancing as the Lafayette Duo sang their signature piece. Rob Lejeune extended a hand to Monique and they crowded in, bumping into people as they kept up with the raucous rhythms. Drenched in sweat and completely out of breath at the end of the song, they walked into the kitchen to check out the spread of food on the counter. They loaded up plates while catching up on each other's news, then drifted in different directions. Monique went back to her spot on the couch and her father sat down beside her.

"I think everyone has found the food," he said, wiping his forehead with his apron. "Are you having a good time, honey?" She nodded, mouth full of gumbo.

Jacques and Michelle came out to the living room along with Uncle Bill and they sang requests for the next hour or so, filling the house with the familiar Cajun songs. One person asked for "*Allons a Lafayette,*" and another's favorite was "*Jolie Blonde.*" Jacques and Michelle took the opportunity to rehearse *La Porte d'en Arriere* by D. L. Menard, and the party wound down with the Lafayette Duo performing original songs they had recorded on their CD, *Coeur D'Acadie*.

Uncle Bill and Aunt Marguerite were the last to leave at around one a.m., after thanking Joe several times for making it such a wonderful birthday party for him. Monique began cleaning up, but her father motioned for her to stop.

"We'll do this tomorrow," he said as he beckoned her to sit with him at their small kitchen table. "Honey," he said tenderly, "it's great to have you home."

Monique looked in his eyes. "It's good to be here, Dad. I was wondering," she said tentatively, "do you think we could look at Mama's things sometime this weekend?"

Joe took a slow, deep breath and exhaled. "For a long time it was hard for me to deal with losing your mother. It's still not easy at times after all these years. But, when you started to ask about her more, I remembered something. After she died, I packed away some of her things for safe-keeping until you were older. I had kind of forgotten about those things, but now I think it might be a good time for us to look through them. I know there are things in her cedar chest that she wanted you to have."

"I would love to open it this weekend."

"I'll get it down tomorrow from the attic." Joe paused for a moment. "Tonight when we were singing I felt that your mother was here with us."

Monique shifted in her chair. She thought about her conversation with Professor Broussard earlier in the day.

"I know what you are thinking about, Honey. You're probably remembering the time that Michelle saw Great-*Gra'mere* in the tub. I believe she came to bring us comfort when your mother was dying, and that she was here to take her to Heaven. I've felt Catherine's presence often lately, and I wonder if she is around because you are graduating. I made a promise to her in my prayers this week that I would honor her memory by sharing her journal and things with you."

"Thank you, Papa."

With a kiss to his daughter's forehead, Joe LeBlanc bid her goodnight and retired to sleep in a cot on the veranda. Monique went to her room upstairs, changed into a nightshirt, and fell between the sheets of her childhood bed. She pushed away thoughts of ghosts and spirits and fell gently to sleep.

The next morning, Monique was only half-awake as she lumbered into the kitchen and poured herself a cup of coffee. She felt herself come to life with the caffeine from the rich, dark brew, and smiled as she watched her father at the stove cooking them breakfast. He asked about Ted, and she told him.

"Something has been missing," her father said. He looked at the eggs he was scrambling.

"What do you mean?" she asked.

"When I met your mother it was magical!" He flipped the spatula in the air and specks of egg spattered on the floor. "I don't think you have experienced real love yet."

Monique groaned and got up to get a paper towel to scoop up the mess.

"Dad."

"It's OK, you are still young."

"Dad! I'm twenty-one years old. And it was magical with Ted, sort of."

"*Non, non, ma cherie,* it cannot be sort of magical," said her father, shaking his head. "It is totally wonderful, and you feel it right in here!" He thumped his chest. "When I met your mother, I thought she was the most beautiful woman I'd ever set eyes on. And as time went on, our love grew even deeper. That's when you know it's the real thing, my darling, and you deserve the real thing. You are a beautiful woman, inside and out. Don't settle for anything less."

"Dad, I'm not beautiful," Monique lamented. "Michelle is beautiful, I'm just average looking."

"What? That is simply not true!" exclaimed her father. He turned off the burner, pulled her up from her chair, and led her to the big front hall mirror. "Look." He stood behind her and held her head, turning it left and then right. "Look at your complexion," he said as he guided the back of his large hand over her cheek. "It has a magnificent tone, and your nose, it is a French girl's nose." Monique laughed, but she kept looking and listening.

"Ahh, and your eyes, *ma belle fille,* they are a satiny brown, like your mother's. And your figure is like hers, *aussi.*"

"Look at my hips, they're huge!"

"You are built like a woman, my dear, not like a skinny rail. Women are not meant to be beanpoles; they are meant to have lower body strength for carrying hampers full of laundry and a child on each hip!" Joe LeBlanc roared at his own comment, and his eyes twinkled.

"Daddy!" Monique cried, and they both laughed and hugged. She wanted to ask, tried to push it away, then blurted it. "Do I remind you a lot of Mama?"

"Yes, you do. I suppose I never really told you in what ways before. Besides your physical features, your personality is similar as well. She had the same natural curiosity about life and lots of love inside, just like you. And she could be very stubborn, like you."

"Yeah, right Dad, nobody could ever call you stubborn," Monique shot back. "That reminds me. When I argued with Ted he said 'You're a stubborn Cajun and always will be.' It hurt my feelings, but I suppose I am stubborn at times."

"I think being stubborn is a good quality if you believe you are doing the right thing," said Joe thoughtfully. "However, if you are not . . . well, then it can be a bad quality. For Catherine, it was a good one because she would persist in what she believed in. I loved that about her. There was only once I got angry at her stubbornness. She didn't want any more cancer treatments a few months before her death, and I didn't like that choice at the time. I felt she should keep trying. Now I realize she was tired and they had already taken a lot out of her."

Joe LeBlanc paused for a moment. Monique wanted to ask so many questions, but she also didn't want to push her father. He took her hand and they walked back to the kitchen. He served up the eggs and made some more toast.

"She would have loved last night's party! She would have been singing and dancing too, and learning the Acadian songs that Michelle and Jacques are practicing. Before she got sick, she became interested in the history. She and Aunt Marguerite talked about taking you and Michelle for a vacation up to Nova Scotia to see where the deportation occurred. Your mother studied the stories and retold them."

"Where?"

"Oh, mostly at family gatherings, but then she got her big opportunity!" Joe was animated, a beaming smile on his face as he paused to recall. "At a St. John's Acadiana Festival she told a couple of her stories and the people loved them! She called her presentation *Catherine's Cadeau* because her stories were a gift from her heart to theirs. She was invited to come the following year, when was it, around 1988? But by then she was too . . . sick."

"Oh, Papa," Monique cried, throwing her arms around her father's neck. She was shocked at first that he was sobbing. She had not seen him cry for many years. She had caught him reading sympathy cards and crying once, but after that he did not show his emotions in front of her. Thinking about it, she realized that he had gone on with everyday life for her sake, to make a normal life for her. Feeling his head resting against hers, the ache welled up and she broke down along with him.

"I hope . . . your mother knows . . . you will be graduating," he said through gasps of breath. "She . . . would be so proud . . . ."

Joe slowly stood up, walked to a closet, and removed a box. "I took these things from your mama's cedar chest. I think it's time for you to have them." He lifted up what looked like a journal, some news articles, and very carefully, several pages from a very old book and a small baby's quilt.

"What's this?"

"Your mama told me this quilt had been passed down for many generations in her family. She wasn't even sure how old it really is."

"It's so beautiful! And some parts of it seem very old." She hugged it close to her and, closing her eyes, breathed in its scents. Then, she carefully replaced it in the cardboard box. She lifted loose pages of an ancient book. She wondered who had owned the book, and why it had been passed down. The words were nearly illegible, and she could see they were written in an old style of French, on the subject of religion. She placed the pages back into the box, being careful with the edges that had begun to crumble away.

Monique then glided her fingers over the journal her mother would have held, and read aloud the surnames Mama had written: "Brasseaux, Bourque, LeJeune, Boutte, Bernard, Martin, Broussard, Mouton, Arceneaux, Comeaux, Thibodeaux, Cormier, Boudreaux, LeBlanc, Leger, Chaisson, Doucet, Hebert, Poirrier, Mélanson, Babin, Dupuis."

"My professor's name is David Broussard," she noted, "and there is a guy in my class named Dennis Cormier. You'd like Professor Broussard. He's a good teacher and I'm learning a lot about the Acadian culture in his class."

Her father didn't answer, and she looked over at him. "My God, look at this Monique! It is a folk tale your mother wrote." They pulled their chairs closer together and Monique read:

Once there was a beautiful young woman who lived in a small parish. She was very devoted to her faith, and was reaching the age of betrothal. Several young men in the village had hopes that she would be their wife, but she had plans to become a nun. This made them all very sad.

One day the young woman, Mariette, was walking in the forest and a thunderstorm came. A very large tree branch fell on her leg and she was stuck there. She was very afraid that a wolf would find her, and her greatest fear came true when a wolf came out from behind a tree and strolled right up. He growled at her a little bit, then began licking her shoes. To her surprise he spoke.

"If you will marry me,' he said, 'I will let you live."

"But I am about to become a Sister of Mercy," she cried.

You will not become anything if I have you for my supper,' answered the wolf.

The beautiful young woman had no choice but to agree to marry him, and the wolf grinned happily. In an instant, he turned into a very handsome young man with muscles that nearly burst out of his shirt sleeves. He lifted the very heavy branch off Mariette and carried her out of the forest. On the way, she wrapped her arms around his neck and decided that marrying him might be better than entering the convent after all, since it was the will of God that she should be rescued.

Father and daughter sat silently, looking at the handwritten story.

"She loved to entertain," said her father, blowing his nose again. "She would have gotten on the Internet. It's so much easier now to find information. She probably would have had her own web page."

"Catherine's Cadeau," they both said simultaneously.

"Dad, I'd like to live here for awhile, and I can help you at the shelter if you want. Can you use some help?"

"I could. I'm very worried that social services is going to close it next year. I've heard rumors. You could help me with organizing the paperwork to send to the state. I am not good with computers."

"Whatever you need. You are such a good father, and I know it wasn't easy for you, losing Mama. It's my turn to do something for you." Her father jumped up from his chair and embraced her so tightly she had to catch her breath. At St. Charles Church later on, Monique stood beside her father as he boisterously sang the hymns.

Chapter 5

Bachelor of Arts–History

Late May

The last three weeks of school flew by. At least once a day Monique saw Ted with a blonde girl who was in her sociology class. The girl, Monique observed, wore caked-on make-up and tops that were too low-cut. The first few times she saw them together, she had returned to the dorm and seethed. But the anger soon gave way to the realization that she was the lucky one. Terri was always willing to listen. One day Monique sat alone in the Tiger's Den having lunch and the girl came toward her.

"Are you Monique LeBlanc?" the girl asked tentatively.

"Yes."

"My name's Stacy Sozinski." The girl pulled out the chair opposite Monique and sat down. "You're Edward's old girlfriend, right? We're in Sociology class together . . . and like . . . I thought I should introduce myself. Edward said to say 'Hi.' I hope this isn't awkward or anything."

Monique was speechless. She felt more awkward than she could remember, and she looked around to see if Ted was lurking somewhere. Most of the students had already left for classes.

"O.K., well . . . I . . . like . . . told Edward I didn't understand one of the readings we got assigned and he said you're really smart and could probably help me . . . and . . ."

"I'm sorry, Stacy, I'm already late," blurted Monique as she packed up her books. "Don't you think it's strange my old boyfriend would tell you to come to me for help?"

Stacy looked back with a puzzled expression, as though she was still trying to decide if Monique was saying yes or no to her plea. "Edward just thought . . ."

"Edward . . . ." Monique shook her head and walked away. She was so angry she thought she might have to ditch classes for the rest of the day. Fifteen minutes later she was laughing hysterically with

Terri back in the dorm, as Terri in her usual form mimicked Ted's mother meeting Stacy and giving her make-up instructions.

The last day of Historical Fiction class came, and when she took her seat for the final time she felt a deep sadness that the class was ending. The professor was late. Students eyed the clock, counting down the minutes. The ten-minute rule was moot when Broussard came in after nine minutes, and Monique smiled while others groaned. She noticed that he was wearing an indigo-blue denim shirt with a silk tie she'd seen before. His chalk-white pants were spattered in mud and he was sporting the old sneakers again.

"Sorry I'm late," he mumbled, unloading a pile of books and papers onto his desk that spilled everywhere. When he looked up at the class, there was a collective gasp and one of the male students exclaimed, "What the Hell?" Monique was stunned to see that her professor had a freshly swollen black eye.

"Don't ask!" Professor Broussard shot back, with a hint of a self-conscious smile. He proceeded to pick up papers and walk down each aisle distributing them.

"Today I want to talk a bit about the North American leaders who arranged the deportation of Acadians. I want the class to think about the works we've studied this term and write a three-page paper double-spaced. Think about *War and Peace, Gone With The Wind,* and *Evangeline,* and give your personal reflections on leadership. Use current examples of present-day leaders in your assignment if you choose.

"Those who were instrumental in the deportation were Governor William Shirley of Massachusetts, Governor Charles Lawrence of what is now Nova Scotia, and Colonel John Winslow who carried it out. They all were military men," he stated as he placed a paper on each desk. Monique reached for hers as he walked by.

"I find it interesting to note that Governor Shirley, who hated the French so much, went to Europe at one point and returned with a young French bride. Perhaps he wanted to take the focus off any criticism he would encounter from New Englanders by turning their attention on Acadian farmers.

"Governor Charles Lawrence was also a military man, following in the footsteps of his father, a British general who led battles against the French in Europe. Charles was born in Plymouth, England in 1709, and by the age of 20 was in North America. Lawrence became Lieutenant Governor of Nova Scotia in 1754, and was a hateful . . . well, you already know what I think of him." Several students tried to muffle giggles.

"As you can plainly see," the professor commented with a sigh, "I cannot seem to teach this material without getting riled up again. I feel like I have failed you all."

There was momentary quiet, and then a voice. Monique was startled to realize it was hers.

"You haven't failed us," she said. "This has been one of the best classes I've had."

"Thanks, Monique," he replied sadly.

"Can I say something, Professor?" asked another student.

"Yes, of course, Dennis."

"In a way, showing us your personal feelings about *Le Grand Dérangement* makes it real. It really happened, and even after hundreds of years it still affects you. I've been talking about it with my parents, and now I can really appreciate why they've been so interested in knowing their history."

"Dennis is right," agreed a student who had raised her hand. "I'm not Cajun, but I'm glad to know how y'all got here. It's an interesting story, even if it's sad. And it's gotten me thinking how leaders can misuse their power. It still happens, even in modern times. I guess the people who wrote our own constitution really put lots of thought into how to prevent a few people from getting lots of power and hurting others with it. But even so, it sure doesn't always work out that way."

Another student raised his hand and the professor nodded. "I've taken so many classes over the last four years and at times I've wondered, 'What am I doing here, learning this stuff?' This class wasn't like that. It certainly has been lively, Professor Broussard. You are not a boring teacher, I'll say that much!"

The students broke out in laughter and applause. David Broussard smiled, waving his hand for them to stop.

"Thank you, ladies and gentlemen," he said humbly. "By the way, I've been thinking about something else I wanted to share with you. Not to make excuses for myself, but I'm not the only descendant of Beausoleil, who has strong feelings. Another descendant of Beausoleil, Warren Perrin, lives in Lafayette. Maybe some of you have heard his name before. He's an attorney, and used his knowledge of the law and his love for his own culture to begin legal action against the British Monarchy for a formal apology to the Acadian people. Even though many generations have passed since *Le Grand Dérangement,* he wanted to make Britain accountable for the actions of its leaders. He petitioned on behalf of the Acadians to get the apology they deserved, and it took awhile but the Queen of England accepted the petition and proclaimed a day called Acadian Day. It is commemorated annually on August 15.

"Leave your reflective papers in the mailbox outside my door within the next three days. Thank you, ladies and gentlemen, for all I have learned from you."

A stream of students left the classroom, and Broussard quickly gathered up his books. Monique approached him.

"I'm sorry, Miss LeBlanc," he said pointing to his eye, "I'm going to have to attend to my injury."

"Could I meet with you sometime tomorrow? I'd like to talk to you about another dream I had."

"How about noon?"

She answered with a nod yes.

"In the Tiger's Den?" got another nod from Monique.

"Great. Thanks. I'll see you tomorrow, then."

Monique felt a little excitement at the anticipation of the meeting. She left to go back to her dorm and jot down the main points of a dream she'd had last night, while it was still vivid.

"Again, we were standing down by the beach," Monique said the following day as she carefully ate her salad. Chewing self-consciously, she swallowed and wiped her mouth with a napkin. The Tiger's Den was nearly empty. The professor's eye was still badly swollen, and she tried hard not to stare at it.

"My surroundings were so vivid," she told the professor. "Pierre stands beside me again, and he says he cannot wait until he can carry me on our wedding night, to his house, to the *parement*." I didn't know what that meant, but I thought you'd know. What is a *parement*?"

"*Parement* is an old Acadian word for 'doorway.' In this case, it probably referred to him carrying you over the threshold, as his new bride. Anything else you remember?"

"Yes. This happened in my other dream too, but I wasn't going to talk about it in class. I was embarrassed enough already. Pierre kissed me and said, '*Tes babines sont si doux.*'"

"'*Babines.*' I think that's an old Acadian word for lips. The word still exists, just in a little different context."

"Yes, I almost forgot about this, but when he said it he touched my lips."

"That young man sure knows how to be romantic. And you, young lady, certainly do have interesting dreams!" David Broussard hesitated as though he was thinking about how to say something. "You know, I would like to keep in touch with you. I know people say these things all the time and it doesn't happen, but I really mean it."

"I'll look for you after the graduation ceremony. I'd like my father to meet you. You mentioned the Atchafalaya Basin one time in class, and my father used to fish there. He had a boat and he and my uncle had a crawfish business there for quite a few years. It was a good business; the crawfish were plentiful back then."

"Yes," Broussard agreed, "they used to be. My family made a good living there too before . . . I guess I have something in common with your father. And definitely look for me after graduation. I'll look for you too. See you soon."

Monique watched him walk away from her. She wondered about

his divorce. The gossip mill had reported that his ex-wife now had a gay partner, and that he and she were still friends.

She looked forward to meeting up with him after graduation, and her thoughts went to Ted. She had always pictured them celebrating graduation together. Monique wondered if she'd see Ted and his family at the ceremony.

A few days later, just outside of Assembly Center, she introduced her father to Professor Broussard, who looked relaxed and attractive as usual in a crisp, white shirt and black dress pants. Joe pointed to his black tie adorned with tiny red crawfish hardly visible to the eye.

"I like that," he said with a smile.

"I told Professor Broussard you fished the Basin," said Monique to her father. "He has a log cabin there."

"Not the same as it used to be," Joe said.

"That's for sure," agreed David. "Like Monique told you, I have a cabin there and am having some problems, legal ones. A developer from Alexandria, Jones is his name, thinks he owns my land, and I guess I'm going to have to fight him in court. My grandfather knew every inch of the Basin and my father too. We have the deed, but . . ."

"Did the legal problems have anything to do with your shiner Monique told me about?" bellowed her father as he nudged his new friend. Monique wanted to sink into the grass, but was immediately relieved to see her former professor laugh at her father's comment.

"Absolutely!" exclaimed David. "He's getting his shots in, but I'll win the war! Why don't you and Monique come up and visit me this summer? I'm sure you know some secret froggin' spots, and I'd love to show you the place I've built."

"Could we take Monique out froggin' with us?" asked her father.

"I'll dig out my hip waders," she teased.

"No, you won't need those," explained David. "We catch frogs from the bow of my boat. Your father and I could take turns steering. Why don't you plan to come over in July?"

He shook her father's hand, then hers, holding on for a few seconds more as her father wrote down his phone number.

"You have a lovely daughter. You certainly raised her right, and I don't imagine it was easy . . . alone."

"It wasn't. Monique is a good girl and lost her mother Catherine at four years old . . . may she rest in peace."

They said good-bye and Monique and her father left to load her belongings into her car and his old truck. A few minutes later she merged into traffic on I-10 behind her father. By then any sadness she felt about leaving had been replaced with happiness that she was following her father back home to Lafayette.

Chapter 6

Atchafalaya

Friday, August 5

"Bobby asked about you today," said Monique's father. It was a humid summer night as they sat together on the front porch.

"Not interested," his daughter waved without looking up from the book she was reading.

"It would be good if you allow yourself a date with a young man sometime."

"When do you want to go out?"

Her father chuckled. "Oh, by the way, your professor called today and invited us up this weekend."

Monique set the book down and got up from her chair. "This weekend?"

"Yes, we can leave right after I finish work on Friday afternoon."

"Good."

The phone rang in the house and she ran in to answer it. Her father followed.

"What's wrong?" she asked in a startled voice. Her father looked over at her and she motioned as she rolled her eyes at him that everything was okay.

"Oh, Monique, it's awful," Tabby Jones was saying on the other end. "Edward Junior had an accident and he needs you." Monique listened to Jeff's mother with an occasional "oh" or "uh-huh" and ended the conversation by saying that she'd talk it over with her father and call back the next morning.

"What was that all about?" asked Joe after Monique hung up.

"Ted's mother said that he and Stacy were sailing with Ted's parents and when Stacy tacked the boat, the boom struck Ted in the head and he fell overboard. They pulled him out and he was unconscious all day yesterday. When he finally came around this morning, he asked for me."

"What about Stacy?"

"Ted's mother said they sent her back to where she came from." She attempted to imitate Tabby Jones' high-pitched, snobby voice, but admitted to her father that she couldn't pull it off the way Terri could.

"She actually said it like that?"

"She said those exact words," Monique replied more seriously. "Oh yes, and then she said, 'Stacy doesn't have class. She's a Polish girl and just didn't fit in with us.'"

"Hmm."

"I know. But maybe this accident changed Ted. I'm not sure how I feel . . . ."

Her father invited her for an evening walk in the back yard, and she was glad for the opportunity to ask about planting flowers. Later on, they drove to a nursery to pick out some new additions to the garden, and then made plans to spend part of tomorrow afternoon planting them.

The next morning Monique dialed the number tentatively as her father left the room. She asked Mrs. Jones as politely as she could if she could please talk to her son. Mrs. Jones argued, saying that she could talk to Ted when she got there. Monique stammered a bit.

"I cannot accept that," Ted's mother had replied sternly. "Edward needs you, and his father and I have already arranged for our chauffeur to pick you up at the airport."

"May I speak with Ted?" Tabbi Jones let out a sigh and there was silence on the phone for a moment.

"Hello?" came the familiar voice. "Hi. I guess my Mom told you what happened. I have this gigantic bump on the top of my head. You should see it. By the way, Stacy and I broke up. She was completely a rebound thing, and I hope you know that I didn't care about her like I do you."

"Ted, I've missed you too. Maybe we did break it off too quickly, before we could talk some things out. I guess we both needed time away . . ."

"Yeah. You probably just needed to suffer without me for awhile," he said with a laugh. "Dad has bought me the most awesome house, with a horse barn and tennis court, and a place to dig a swimming pool. And you should see the new mansion my parents live in now. We have a chef, and . . . just a sec . . . what, Dad? Oh, he's saying we can use the yacht anytime we want. Come on, this is your big chance!"

Monique felt her face flush. "You know what, Ted? I'm going to stay here and help Dad, then go up to Canada with Michelle and Jacques at the end of the summer. I really want to support them in promoting their new CD, *Coeur d'Acadie.*"

"What? Say that again in English? Canada? Why?" Ted shouted back at her.

There was a pause, then her voice: "Good-bye, Ted."

"Wait!" She clicked the button on the phone and hung up the receiver. When it rang immediately afterward, she felt a twinge of guilt, then relief as she let the answering machine pick up. She glanced at her father who was standing at the door between the kitchen and living room, and pushed the "delete" button before listening to the message.

"They are not nice people," Joe said. "I just remembered that your professor Broussard said that he was in a lawsuit with someone named Jones, a developer in Alexandria. Do you think it could be Ted's father?"

"I guess we'll find out when we go," replied Monique.

Later, after planting, watering, and admiring the new flowers in the garden out back, they got on the highway to David's place. Driving through Breaux Bridge, Joe told her a story about his days on the Atchafalaya.

"One night out froggin', my friend T-Boy Leger caught the biggest frog we'd ever seen! Well, almost. Honestly, I think its eyes were as big as quarters. I managed to catch it by one leg, and then T-Boy grabbed it and caught the other leg, and we tried to pull it into the boat. But it slipped away from us and disappeared under the water, then came back up and looked at us like it was taunting us to go after it again. I made another grab at it, but when I did, some muddy water flew up in my eyes and I couldn't see a thing. But by then, we were laughing so hard, when T-Boy tried to grab at it, he fell head-first into the bayou. Once I got him back into the pirogue, we decided to call it quits. But we never forgot that night. Poor T-Boy, he died a few years ago. His boat burned in a fire and he was never the same after that. We ate lots of frogs him and me, real good eatin'."

"I don't eat frogs," said Monique.

"Have you ever tried one?" asked her father, already knowing the answer to his own question. Monique made a face, and her father laughed. "Ah, when I fished out here we made many a meal out of froglegs."

She was glad to change the subject. "I think David said his log cabin was down this next road on the left. It's called Cypress Bend Road." They drove onto a very bumpy dirt road, then stopped at the end. "Wow, that's a log mansion!" exclaimed Monique. Before them was a two-story cypress log home with wrap-around porches on both levels. Dark green shingles accented the gabled roof. Beyond where the lane circled in front of the house, stood an ancient tree at the edge of a quiet bend in the bayou. Hanging from one of its branches, a chair-swing like the one on her front porch rocked slightly in the breeze. Close behind the log house the woods stood untouched, the noonday shadows of tree foliage dancing on the roof.

Atchafalaya Frogging

"Here we are," declared her father as he beeped the horn. David Broussard, in t-shirt and cargo shorts, burst forth through the front screen door to greet them warmly and help them bring in overnight bags. His bare feet showed the white skin where his sandals had left their mark.

Walking inside, Monique looked around in awe. "This is beautiful! You actually built this yourself?"

"Thanks," said David. "I guess I must have mentioned that in class."

Monique nodded and smiled.

"I'll give you a quick tour." He walked his guests around the great room, showing them the cathedral ceilings and the stone fireplace that was built right up the wall to the ceiling.

"I didn't build the fireplace, my friend did. I did put this in," he said, pointing to a log beam that extended the length of the room between the first and second floor. "One day I was sitting here reading and it cracked. See right here? It runs the complete length. I thought I'd been shot!"

"This is nice too," said Joe, pointing to a large window that looked out onto the swamp beyond. He sat down in a cushy chair in front of it. "I would just sit here for hours at night, just watching the gators and the birds."

"I do that sometimes," laughed David. "Come, I'll show you my room where you can sleep tonight, Monique. You can put your bags in there. Joe, you can have the guest room up in the loft if you like."

"I'd love it. But where are you going to sleep?"

"Don't worry about me. I'll put out a cot and sleep right down here."

Monique and her father followed David through a set of French doors into his bedroom.

He brushed his hand along the wooden headboard. "A friend made this from birch," he said. "Actually he's my cousin. Lives out beyond St. Martinville."

Monique looked around the room and set her bags on the bed. "It's beautiful," she said. Then, after Joe had left the room, "Thank you for inviting us here. This is so good for my father. He's missed fishing."

David smiled. "Glad to do it," he said as they rejoined Joe.

"You have a beautiful home!" Joe exclaimed, tapping the arms of the easy chair. "I would be embarrassed to invite you to ours now."

"Oh, no, please don't say that," replied David. "I decided after my divorce that I was going to give myself this rustic place, that it was my dream to put something really nice on the Broussard property. But it's not a shrine or a place to show off. It's my haven from the world. I'd give away the furniture tomorrow, sleep on that cot over there, and be just as content. I'm sure you have a wonderful home. After all, you raised a lovely daughter there." Monique blushed, and Joe beamed.

"I do love the cabin I've built," continued David, "but only for sentimental value. That make sense?"

"Yes. And I would love to cook some jambalaya for you at the LeBlanc house sometime. You can come for *Festivals Acadiens* in Lafayette next October. Do you like music festivals?"

"I do, and I'll hold you to that," replied David.

"You seem to have lots of privacy here," remarked Monique, who recalled the day in class when Broussard had walked in with a black eye, and the time before that when he'd worn sneakers caked with mud.

"I did, but as your father so directly pointed out at your graduation, I got my shiner from something that's been happening over the past couple of months. There's a developer interested in taking my property away from me. He wants to chop down all the woods behind me and take this area as well as fifty acres adjacent to it to build an upscale recreational resort for sport fishermen. It's now in court, but I'm worried because the developer has contacts with government officials. I own a very old deed showing the land has been in the Broussard family for generations. My lawyer seems to think it's enough for my case, which reminds me, I have it in the lock box and need to take it in to him this week." He waved for them to follow. "Let me show you some things outside."

Monique did not want to miss the chance to ask. "Is the developer's last name Jones?'"

"Yeah, how'd you know?"

"I mentioned it to her," Joe chimed in. "You said something about it graduation day when we met. Is it Ed Jones?"

"Yes, that's right. How do you know him?"

Joe and Monique exchanged glances.

"I just broke up with his son," she said. "Don't worry. I won't be talking to them again. Ted's mother . . . ." Monique's voice trailed off.

"All I know is that the father thinks he's going to buy up the Atchafalaya and build high-end camps for rich people, and he's not going to take my neighbor's land to do it," said David. By now, the three of them were by the tree with the swing. As Monique and Joe sat and began gently swinging, David said, "This cypress tree is over two hundred years old. I love sitting out here as the sun goes down."

Joe replied, "I sure understand why." The three friends enjoyed the idyllic setting, watching the sky and the shadows begin to darken as the daylight faded.

Later, David grilled some hamburgers and Joe made a salad while Monique set the table. Monique's father began moving his head from left to right and massaging his neck.

"You OK Dad?" asked his daughter.

"Just a little headache. It started bothering me on the ride here."

"Go lay down for a few minutes, Joe," offered David. "Monique and I can finish our coffee out on the porch." Joe nodded and went up the stairs to the loft, and Monique and David moved out to the front porch.

"I picked up a froglight for you," he said to her.

"What?" she asked with a laugh. Broussard handed her a large light on a wide circular elastic band connected with a wire to a large battery pack. He used his to demonstrate for her how he positioned the headlamp atop his head over his old, worn LSU ball cap.

"Froglights. For when we go frogging. We'll all go out after dark and when we shine the lights along the shoreline, the light catches their eyes and blinds them."

"I don't know how to do that," she said, trying to keep the aversion from showing in her tone.

"Here, hold out your hand, right here," he said as he reached for her hand and placed it in mid-air between them.

"Pretend your hand is the frog in the water. Ready?"

"For what?"

He made a lightning-fast grab at her wrist. "Now, try to get away," he teased, maintaining a strong grip. Monique tried to pull her hand back, feeling silly that an instant ago she had just jumped and screeched.

"There is no way I can do that," she said, shaking her head and hoping he would change his mind about taking her out. David laughed and reassured her that she would soon get the hang of it.

Joe LeBlanc came out of the loft later on, around dusk, and said that he still didn't feel great.

"Good, we'll do the froggin' next time," said Monique.

"Oh no," answered David. "You didn't come up here to miss the best part. Joe, you just relax back here while we're gone. I'll give a call to my neighbor, Louis Benoit, and he'll steer for us."

With froglights in place, Monique and David later had their positions in the bow of his boat as David's friend Louie directed it slowly into the murky corners of the Atchafalaya. The night was clear, the moon nearly full, and they inched along with their three lights beaming across the muddy waters probing the shallow waters along the shore.

"Over there," said the professor, pointing to a set of eyes. He lay on his stomach at the front of the boat to make grabbing the prospective prey easier. "As you get closer, you can see their bodies," he whispered. Monique stared but was unable to make anything out but the frozen eyes staring into the light beams. He invited her to get into the same position as he was in and when she did, he reminded her to be perfectly quiet as they neared their target. David had his hands beside hers. They were silent for quite some time, until the boat was almost on top of the frog. He quickly grabbed behind the eyes, resulting in a great thrashing in the water.

"Grab on," he said, and she tried but the slippery surface of the frog repulsed her. He kept his grip and pulled a large frog into the boat. He directed Monique to open the sack below their feet, then lowered their squirming catch into the darkness.

"Good one," shouted Louie from the stern.

"Ready?" David asked again, and she nodded into the darkness. His eyes twinkled with the reflection of the boat light, and his excitement reminded her of the way he looked when he was teaching. His hand briefly brushed against hers as they continued to glide along in the shadows of the Basin. David pointed to the shadowy shape of an alligator.

"See there? Those eyes are a little too far apart for us." When the gator moved, allowing Monique to see what it was, she quickly pulled her hands back into the boat.

"Don't worry," he reassured her, "I'd warn you in plenty of time." As they repeated the process a few more times only losing one frog to the brown waters of the Basin, she was surprised that she lost most of her revulsion and became more comfortable with it all. She even began to enjoy being part of the teamwork involved.

Monique's mind drifted into the murk before her. She wondered about him, who he saw, when he had been with a woman last, what it was like to make love with him. She could hardly believe she was having these thoughts.

"Let's start heading back," he called out to Louie, and then laughed when Monique jumped with fright.

"I'm sorry, did I scare you? Keep an eye out for more frogs." He pushed himself up to a sitting position and crawled back to the stern to talk to Louie about turning the boat around in this narrow slough. Monique tried to concentrate on watching the water.

David returned and she pointed out a new set of eyes on the bank ahead. This time, Monique had her hands ready. Just before the boat ran aground, she plunged them into the water. She made contact with a slippery surface and tried to hang on. As she lifted the bullfrog up and over the side of the boat, David hooted. At the sound, the frog's squirming became more violent, and David reached to help Monique maintain her hold of the writhing creature. Suddenly, the frog broke free, flew through the air, and landed on her shoulder. She screamed, and David lunged to regain control of the creature. They wrestled with it, bodies twisting around each other to capture it. The frog won the battle and hopped back into the water, disappearing in the murk. The two froggers collapsed in laughter and Louie joined in, tears streaming down his face.

"Nice try," David said proudly, planting a kiss squarely on her cheek. "Wait until I tell your Dad you almost got 'im." Monique could feel heat in her face from all the excitement and was grateful for the darkness that hid it.

"Thanks," she said. She was jolted when the boat came up against a submerged cypress stump, and David reached out with an arm to push them free.

"Got to keep away from these. Some sport fishermen who come down here don't know that going slow prevents their boat from being damaged from things like this. They either learn fast, or end up in the water themselves and maybe a hole in their boat."

Back at the cabin a half hour later, David excitedly told Joe what had happened. When David asked Louie if he was hungry and got an affirmative answer, Joe jumped up and swung into action. In no time, he had the frogs they'd caught in a pan and on their way to becoming a delicious frog sauce piquant. It had been years since Joe had made this delicacy, one of his very favorites.

Monique excused herself for the night, not wanting to watch as they ate or to be coaxed into trying some, thinking to herself, I'm not quite ready for that yet. Listening from her room as David bragged about her frogging skills, she tossed and turned trying to calm down, adrenalin still pumping from the wrestling match she and David had had with the frog.

As she tried to relax, she could hear her former professor talking in the way she remembered from her Historical Fiction class. He was telling the other men about how the rise in Acadian and Cajun pride over the last half century had sparked the building of an Historic Site in Grand-Pré, Nova Scotia, where the statue of Evangeline stood outside the chapel. On the grounds, he said, there was also a statue of Longfellow, and there were new plans to expand this site as well as others in the Maritimes.

"A man named J.F. Herbin, whose mother was an Acadian, erected a stone cross that marks the site of the Acadian church cemetery in the Saint-Charles-des-Mines parish at Grand-Pré," he said. "And you might have heard of the Deportation Cross, an iron cross erected in 1924 and located in a farmer's field down where a creek bed used to be. I walked down the railroad tracks to that place once, and when it was placed there it was believed that the Acadians were taken out to the ships from that spot."

"And there's the memorial at St. Martinville," added Louis Benoit. "The mural and the wall of names really made me realize how many of our ancestors came here to Louisiana, and what they went through beforehand. A replica of the iron cross you saw is also at St. Martinsville, and a replica of the mural was placed in France somewhere. There's a place there where some of the deported Acadians created a settlement for a period of time."

"Nantes, France," responded Broussard. "Nantes is a place near the Atlantic coast where a colony of Acadians lived for a time after they were exiled. The colony was called Poitou, and the remaining houses can actually be seen at *La Ligne Acadienne* in the area of Poitou. All those Acadians came back to Louisiana. Imagine that? An artist by the name of Robert Dafford painted the mural in St. Martinsville, and another one like it is in Nantes."

"You sure know a lot about our history," said Joe LeBlanc. "My wife took a big interest in these things too a few years before she died. She wanted to teach Monique everything about it, and never got the chance. Luckily she took your class, David, and she has passed that information on to me. Catherine was asked to attend an Acadiana festival as a storyteller a few years back, but she got too sick to go. She was able to do our complete genealogies though, and Monique and I have studied them this summer."

Joe paused a moment, then gave his new friend Louie a

jovial slap on the knee and asked, "By the way, Benoit, who is your daddy?"

"Marcel Benoit," answered Louis proudly. "He was a farmer and swamper. Raised ten children, with my mother of course. I was the youngest and when we moved here I wasn't born yet. We came from about twenty miles from here and moved after the flood of '27. My parents and brothers and sister were rescued from the roof of our house, and thankfully some relatives of ours took us in. My uncle and aunt owned the house I live in now and my cousin sold it to me in 1972. My father died the year before and I took over the business. Mom has stayed with us since Dad died, and still talks about how they were rescued just in time by their neighbor who had a boat."

"It was a hard year," said Joe. "I think I remember Marcel. Didn't he have a small restaurant near here? There was an old Victrola in the place and there was always music playing."

"That was my Dad. He and Mom were both music lovers, Cajun and Zydeco—then they called it 'la la.' It was one of the things we did as a family, singing the songs together on many a Saturday night, all our cousins and everybody."

"My folks liked the music too, and my mother got involved in a local group that researched our genealogy," said David. "I've had an interest in it almost as long as I can remember. I had a hard time teaching the material this term, as I'm sure you've heard, and the experience and the way my students responded to it taught me quite a bit."

Joe smiled and nodded. "Monique not only learned about Acadia," he said with a loud and hearty laugh, "she learned that Cajuns, even when they are professors, still have the old fighting spirit!"

Monique stirred in her bed at the sound of her father's boisterous laugh. She could hear the men talking about their love for the Atchafalaya Basin as she drifted in and out of sleep.

"It really scares me that we're losing so much of the marsh these days," she heard her father say.

"Yeah, Joe, I wonder the same thing," Louis chimed in. "I have buddies who work the wetlands in St. Bernard and in Lafourche parishes and they say it's getting harder and harder to find good habitat every year."

David finished his last sip of coffee. "This is such a unique and beautiful area, we have to try to save it. Our people have been fighting with their very lives to keep their land in one way or another for over 300 years, so I think there's still hope. If there's anything we can say about us Cajuns, it's that we're stubborn bastards."

The laughter from the other room roused Monique for an instant before she drifted off again as the fishermen continued to spin tales of their exploits in the Atchafalaya Basin well into the early morning hours.

David had breakfast ready for them when they got up close to noon the next day. The men made plans to get together again in a couple of months to do some fishing. David said that he would contact other members of the family to come out if they wanted to. Standing in the driveway, David gave his new friend Joe a pat on the back, and Joe thanked David Broussard for a wonderful weekend. Monique extended her hand to David and smiled, feeling the heat rising in her cheeks. He opened the truck door and gestured for her to climb in, then shut it afterward. To her surprise, he leaned through the open window and kissed her on the cheek, and the heat from his lips lingered there as she and her father drove out of the driveway and down the road. Distracted, she had not heard her father recount a witty comment David had said the evening before that caused him to roar with laughter. She decided not to ask him to repeat it and just laughed along with him.

Back in Lafayette a few hours later, Joe went back up to the attic and brought down more of Catherine's papers. They sifted through them several times, discovering new things Monique had never known and things her father had all but forgotten. Joe showed Monique more historical information about his family that her mother had worked on. He pointed out again how the large page of names they'd found traced several generations back to the 1700s in Grand-Pré. Catherine's side of the family went back to another village on the Minas Basin called *Rivière aux Canards*. Joe searched through the papers for the name of Mariette, a woman he said her mother had mentioned a few times.

"I know she told me that this ancestor began one of the first schools for girls in Louisiana during the resettlements, up near St. Gabriel," he explained. "I guess those papers will turn up sometime. It's funny they're not here with the rest . . ."

"Dad, can I keep this picture of Mama?"

"Yes, *ma cherie.*"

Monique held the picture and made a decision. "Dad, I've decided to go to Nova Scotia with Michelle and Jacques at the end of the summer. I can use money in my savings account, and I want to do something before I go back to school again."

"Are you thinking about a master's degree?" her father asked.

"Yeah," she replied. "I've come this far, and I might as well go back to LSU, maybe during the spring. But first, at the end of the month, Michelle and Jacques invited me to go with them to Halifax for *Le Festival Acadien.*"

"I'll help you. I have a little money put away. I think graduate school is a great idea, and the same goes for your trip to Nova Scotia. I want to help you with that too, because, who knows, maybe you will be able to go visit Grand-Pré!"

"I think Michelle said *Le Festival Acadien* will be held at the Halifax waterfront," Monique said, excitement rising in her voice. "I looked at a map, and Halifax doesn't look like it's that far away from Grand Pré. I hate to leave you here by yourself though. Do you want to come too?"

"*Mais cher,* I am used to being alone, and I want you to go and have a good time. While you're there, I'll go up to David's and we'll go out fishing. I've missed being on the water. I might even buy myself a boat!" Joe LeBlanc leaped up from his chair to embrace his daughter. "We're having a great summer together, aren't we?"

"The best!" answered Monique as she wrapped her arms around him.

Chapter 7

Nova Scotia Bound

Wednesday, August 24

Jacques Boudreaux was listening to his father-in-law. Uncle Bill stood beside Joe, who had driven the group to the airport. Joe had invited Bill to join him for the ride, and to stay over in New Orleans for the night.

"I want to take Bill to this restaurant that serves the best crawfish *étouffee* he has ever tasted," said Joe.

Jacques' right hand held Michelle's and his left arm was draped around Monique's shoulder as Joe described the details of the roux-based sauce that gave the crawfish at this place a particular flavor which, so far, he had been unable to duplicate. The three younger people were awaiting their departure from the Louis Armstrong New Orleans International Airport, and Jacques' shoulder-length curly brown hair was damp with sweat as he reached up to brush it away from his eyes. In a t-shirt, cargo shorts, and sneakers, he stood in burly and disheveled contrast to his wife Michelle and Monique. Both young women were dressed fashionably in skirts, tops, and sandals. Monique had straightened her hair earlier in the day and had it in a ponytail, and Michelle's auburn hair in its short cut was adorned with a barrette.

"You take care of my two favorite girls," said Joe LeBlanc to Jacques.

"I sure will," Jacques replied. "Believe me, the three of us flying up to Canada will be a hell of a lot easier than going up with the band. The bus will get up there, oh, probably Friday, and this way Michelle and I can figure out how we're gonna set up the equipment. Besides," he laughed, "they offered to pay for it, so why not?"

Joe extended his hand to Jacques. "I know you and Michelle will knock them dead! You go up there and give them some good Cajun music," he said, kissing his niece and embracing his daughter in a final good-bye.

As the threesome walked toward security, Monique looked back to where her father and uncle were still standing. She gave her father one more cheery wave before she could no longer see him. Inside, she felt a sinking feeling of sadness and anxiety that he hadn't decided to come too. She comforted herself with the realization that she would be back home in just a few days.

Making the connection to Halifax went smoothly, and after watching the lights of Boston disappear behind a layer of wispy clouds at dusk, they settled in for the shorter flight.

"What's Canada like anyway?" Monique asked. "Is it as civilized as where we live?"

"That's a terrible thing to say," scolded her cousin. "Canada is a great place, and Halifax is a really cosmopolitan city. In fact, Americans should make a point of learning more about Canadians because they often resent Americans who come up there and act like they're superior."

"OK, OK, I was only asking . . . ," answered Monique.

"I'm sorry, I guess I just want to be careful not to come across as an arrogant American." Michelle paused for a moment. "You know what? I'm really nervous they won't like our performance."

"Forgiven," said Monique with a smile, "and relax. You're good and you deserve this break. They'll love the Lafayette Duo.*"

"Monique's right," added her husband supportively. "I used to spend summers in New Brunswick, Canada, and the people love music. There's lots of French people who are probably even related to us somehow. Don't worry about it, *cher,* just give em' what you got."

"Thanks, guys. I guess I have performance anxiety."

"And I promise not to act like an arrogant American," said Monique. Michelle and Jacques both chuckled.

"You don't have an arrogant bone in that little Cajun body of yours," said Jacques.

The group of three unfastened tables and reclined chairs as far as they would go. A snack was served, and Michelle looked through a magazine she had picked up at the airport. Jacques leaned as close to the window as he could comfortably get and dozed off. Monique found a brochure tucked into a slot in the back of the seat in front of her and began browsing through it.

Scenes of picturesque harbors and villages caught her eye and imagination. Rolling hillsides with farms on them, a bustling city waterfront, and sandy beaches piqued her interest in the place where they would soon land. It seemed so different from the flat lands she was used to. She saw a small picture of a chapel with a statue of a woman in front of it, and held it close to see the details.

"Is Nova Scotia a reasonably safe place to travel alone?" she asked Michelle.

"I believe it is," said Michelle, "but I'm not sure I want you wandering around too much."

"OK, mother. Ask Jacques what he thinks."

"Is Nova Scotia a safe place?" she asked with a nudge to her husband.

"Umph," Jacques mumbled, shifting position against the window.

"Jacques says it's safe," Michelle replied with a giggle.

"I know where this is. My professor in Historical Fiction told me he went to college around here. He knew quite a bit about this chapel, and I think it's the National Park in Grand-Pré."

"I know where that is too," said Michelle. "Jacques has a cousin André who goes to college near there."

"What college?"

"Acadia, I think. Isn't that right, Honey?" Michelle looked at Jacques for confirmation, and when he didn't respond he received another nudge. He responded with another mumble.

"Jacques said 'right,'" The girls giggled like adolescents again.

Jacques was now waking up and making a face at them.

"What?" he said. In a daze, he reached for Michelle's soft drink and guzzled it down.

"Your cousin André goes to college in Nova Scotia, doesn't he?" asked Michelle again.

"Yeah, Acadia. André and I get in touch every so often," said Jacques, now ready to join the conversation. "He'll be done next May, and wants to spend some time as a roadie. He actually knows some stuff about sound engineering."

"How are you related again?" asked Monique.

"My family has relatives in Shediac, New Brunswick," explained Jacques. "We went up there quite a few summers when I was younger, and me and André hung out all the time, drivin' and swimmin' and fishin' all around there in his boat. He loves to go fast, and our folks always had to get after us to slow down. Once they took the boat away and gave us a rowboat," he laughed. "André was so mad!"

"Maybe André would be around to show Monique some of the sights," said Michelle.

"Yeah, maybe . . . I guess I can ask him while we're there. He's comin' to the festival I think," Jacques said with a searching look, as though he was trying to recall the last conversation they'd had. "It's just that . . . like I said, he drives too fast, so if you drove with him Monique, you'd have to tell him to slow the hell down!" Jacques paused, still trying to remember what else his cousin had told him lately. "Oh yeah, he said he and his girlfriend were fightin', so I don't know how that would work out with him drivin' you around and all."

The group was now distracted from further conversation by

the sight of foggy grayness that completely enveloped the plane. The twinkle of runway lights showed the travelers they were just about to touch down, and before long they were hearing over the loudspeaker that the plane had landed at Halifax International Airport where it fog was settling in and the temperature was fifteen degrees.

"Whoa!" exclaimed Monique as the three waited in the line of passengers getting off the plane, "we're gonna freeze!"

"That's Celsius," explained Michelle to her cousin. "It's about seventy degrees Fahrenheit. Still cool, but not freezing." The three travelers went through customs, and Jacques' luggage was checked, after which the girls chastised him for not dressing better.

"Sorry," he said, and Michelle and Monique each grabbed one of his arms in instant forgiveness. They proceeded to the car rental, gave the name of the agency who was paying, and were soon headed to the parking lot to pick up their car. The air was damp and chilly for August, and the fog was getting thicker.

"Where're we staying again?" asked Jacques.

"I have the directions," said Michelle through chattering teeth. "Let's just get in the car and look at them."

They studied the map by the inside light of the car and began driving. After getting lost once, they stopped talking and concentrated on following the directions. They pulled into the driveway of a condo complex on Tower Road, found the parking lot, and checked to see the number of the place designated as theirs for the week. Upon finding it, Monique was pleased to see the outside light was on and a lamp glowed inside the living room window, presenting a homey and welcoming sight for weary travelers walking through the front door. On the table, they found a complementary basket of fruit and bottle of wine with a note from the festival promoters.

"Can you believe this is ours for a whole week!" exclaimed Michelle as she spun around in the living room. She threw her arm around Monique and they went from room to room scouting out the place. Jacques carried in all the suitcases and asked the girls what rooms they wanted them in. Monique settled into her bedroom while the others unpacked in theirs. She opened her suitcase and took out her mother's framed picture.

"We're here," she whispered, kissing the picture and placing it on the table beside her bed. Gathering what she needed for the night, she turned down the cover on her bed. She wondered if she would be hot with that cover, then decided she could roll it down if she were. The bed was suddenly so inviting she was tempted to crawl in for the night. She changed into a nightgown and washed up.

"How about a glass of wine, Monique?" asked Michelle from down the hall, and Monique shouted a "sure," and threw on a robe. She slid into a big recliner near her cousin, who was curled up on a comfortable couch next to it with her husband. Jacques had taken a quick shower before throwing on a shirt and sweatpants, and his curly mass of hair clung to his head. Michelle had on a mint-green linen nightgown, and Jacques was handing her the glass of wine he'd just poured. He picked up another wineglass and gestured toward Monique.

"Please," she said, and after he poured one for himself, Monique offered a toast.

"To the Lafayette Duo," she announced.

"Or maybe the Lafayette Trio," Jacques suggested, to which Michelle lifted her glass in agreement. "You do have a good voice and your harmonies blend with mine," said her cousin.

"Thanks for the compliment," laughed Monique. "I'd love to have even a little bit of the talent you two have." She took a sip of wine. The fruity flavor in her mouth reminded her of the night of Michelle and Jacques' wedding, when she had overdone it.

"A toast to the bride and groom," she said. "What a night that was!"

Michelle beamed. "It was wonderful, wasn't it."

"It was beautiful, and everybody had a great time," said Monique, adding, "well, everybody except Ted."

"Yeah," agreed Jacques, "thank Heavens you got away from Ted. Hey, why don't I call Andrè." The girls waited while he held the receiver to his ear. "No answer," he mumbled, then put it back on the hook only to pick it up again a few seconds later and dial again.

"Who are you calling now, Hon?" Michelle asked.

"André."

"You just said there was no answer," she replied.

"There wasn't," he stated matter-of-factly.

"Then why are you calling again?"

"Because when I call his dorm, I have to let the phone ring and somebody around there will pick it up sooner or later. I keep telling him to get a damn cell phone . . . . Hi, André? Yeah, it's Jacques."

The girls watched and listened to the conversation.

"Yeah, we just got in, oh, about a half hour ago . . . it was good, the girls wouldn't let me sleep . . . what? . . . . Oh, Michelle's cousin came with us . . . . Good looking? Yep, she is . . . want to talk to her?"

Before Monique had time to think, the phone receiver was passed to her.

"Say hello," coaxed Jacques.

"Hello," said Monique shyly, feeling the heat come to her face.

"Hi," said a friendly male voice. "I'm Jacques' cousin and I guess I'll meet you sometime this week. I was planning on coming down to the waterfront to see Jacques and Michelle perform. I wanted to come to the wedding but couldn't make it."

There was a pause, and Monique stammered to fill it.

"It was . . . a good . . . I mean a really nice wedding."

"Yeah, Jacques finally found a woman who's good for him. Actually, I'm kidding. He's a great guy, and an awesome musician. I can't wait to hear them together at the concert."

"Me too," said Monique, growing more embarrassed with her inability to think of anything better to add to the conversation. Jacques reached out to take the phone, and she passed it to him.

"André," he asked, "are you still seeing that girl you told me about?"

The girls were once again listening, trying to figure out what the response was by what Jacques would say next.

"Aw, that stinks," said Jacques. "What? Two weeks ago . . . just like that, huh? Hey, why don't you come down tomorrow?"

Michelle waved to her husband. "Ask him how far away he is from Grand-Pré. See if he could pick Monique up."

"He's only about a mile away from Grand Pré, I think," said Jacques, and his cousin confirmed his estimate. "Hey, instead of coming here, why don't you pick Monique up at the Wolfville bus stop and show her around Grand-Pré? She has a couple of days before the festival begins." Monique could feel her blush deepening. But now she was very interested in the other half of the conversation. "André says he can meet you at the bus. It stops right in town and he can take you to Grand-Pré for the day if you want."

Monique replied, "Sure, I guess so."

"What?" Jacques was listening again. "André says his friend is the manager at Blomidon Cottages and would probably give you a room for the night if you wanted to stay over. Then he can drive you back to Halifax the day after. But not too fast!" Jacques shouted into the phone.

"Actually, that might be more fun for you than sticking around here and waiting for us to finish the business we have here tomorrow," suggested Michelle. "Besides, I think André is pretty cute. Isn't he cute, Jacques?"

Jacques was waving to Michelle and making a face while trying to continue the phone conversation. He got the bus drop-off times from André and wrote them down on the pad by the phone.

"Thanks, André. Hey and listen, I promised Monique's father I'd take good care of Monique, so you better do the same or your ass is grass, got it amigo? Good."

Jacques put the receiver back on the phone cradle and took a big swig of wine, emptying the glass. He poured himself another one while he told Monique more about his cousin.

"He's a good swimmer," said Jacques. "When we were kids, he'd swim across the lake and think nothing of it. I started out with him one time, and honest to God, I got to the middle of the lake and didn't know how I'd make it the rest of the way. I never did that again. He just made it look so easy! Damn!"

"What's his major?" asked Monique.

"Engineering, I think. He's talked about going on our tour with us next year, but I told the dude he has to finish school."

"Well, I'm turning in," yawned Michelle.

"Good idea," said Jacques.

The three friends said good-night and Monique snuggled into her bed for the night. The air was cooling down, and the warm comforter felt wonderful. Tomorrow, she would pack a small bag and take her mother's picture to the place where her ancestors had been expelled ten generations ago.

"Good-night Mama," she said.

"*Bon soir, mon petite chou,*" said her mother as she tucked in the blanket placed lovingly over her daughter. "Two days from now you will be married, and I cannot believe you have grown up so fast. We have a busy day ahead, so rest well. *Je t'aime.*"

"I love you too, Mama," whispered Monique as she descended into sleep. "I love you too."

Chapter 8

The Evangeline Trail

Thursday, August 25

"Wake up," said the familiar voice. "Today's a busy day."

Monique opened her eyes wide and blinked several times. She sat up, and her cousin slowly came into focus.

"What's the matter?" Michelle asked. She placed a cup of Tim Horton's coffee on the bedside table next to the picture of her Aunt Catherine.

"Nothing, I was dreaming," yawned Monique. She picked the coffee up, fumbled with the opening, and took a drink. "I dreamt I was with my mother. Well, it was my mother in the dream but she didn't look like my mother. Come to think of it, Michelle," she said sadly, "as hard as I try, I really can't recall what Mama looked like. I have her picture, and that helps, and I close my eyes and try really hard to see her but I can't see her face."

"I don't remember what she looked like either," admitted Michelle. "I sort of recall her voice, the way she laughed especially. If Aunt Catherine was laughing at something, you couldn't help laughing too. Remember?"

"No," said Monique. "I can feel her though, like the way she tucked me in to bed and sang a song or said a prayer. It was so gentle and made me feel safe as a small girl. That's the feeling I like to remember about her. In my dream, I think my mother was kissing me goodnight and saying that two days from now would be my wedding day."

"I wonder what that dream means," said Michelle, her curiosity peaked. "Dreams do have meanings, I believe. Maybe this one means that coming here is a new beginning for you and your mother is trying to tell you that. I just remembered that I had one before you broke up with Ted, and in it you were telling me you ended it. When you actually did tell me, it was like *déjà vu*."

"That's why you didn't seem surprised. I thought you were just being kind."

"Well, it was both I suppose. But like I said, it was as if it had already happened."

The women heard a door open and left the bedroom together to greet Jacques, who had gone to meet with the promoters of their Nova Scotia performance. He was not looking happy.

"I went to see John McConnell from Entertainment City," he said, "and I looked over the equipment he leased. The drums are an old set and the guy who planned to play them during tomorrow's rehearsal thinks he has the flu. I'm calling the boys to stop in Nashville and borrow a set of drums from Dooney's band. I knew we should bring all our own stuff. And the mixer we have to rehearse with cut out three times! We've gotta have a drummer. Damn, every time we're on the road . . . why can't things fall into place for once?"

"Can't you insist that they get a better set of drums?" Michelle asked, stroking his hand. "If the back-up band stops in Tennessee, they'll be cutting it really close for Saturday, Jacques."

"You're right, Michelle. I'm callin' 'em right now to get the best set of drums in this city, and a drummer that's healthy who can start with us today. And a keyboard—the one they have looks like a kid's Christmas toy. It's crap."

"Just relax, Jacques. We can rehearse without back-up if we have to." Michelle looked at Monique, lost for any more words to help calm her husband. Monique offered a suggestion.

"Why don't I just get a taxi to the bus station? It can't be that far from here."

"No way!" Jacques exclaimed. "Let's forget about all this bullshit for awhile and go see Halifax."

They left their temporary digs and took a drive down to the waterfront. The air was fresh, just slightly warm with a sea breeze. Sailboats in the harbor moved along slowly and steadily in gray-green water that was as clear as glass. The Halifax Citadel was covered in lush green lawn and flower gardens were placed esthetically. Tourists strolled the grounds or sat on the lawn and enjoyed the sailboats in Halifax Harbour.

"Maybe sometime before we leave we can come and tour the Citadel," said Michelle, glancing over at Jacques. Monique was the one to respond.

"This was a fortress when the city was first established," she said, remembering back to her Historical Fiction class. "Professor Broussard said that once Halifax was established in the war between the French and British to control the colonies, the Acadians were even more threatened by the British influence."

The three friends left the waterfront a few minutes later and drove to the bus terminal. Jacques and Michelle waited while Monique got her ticket.

"Are you sure you want to stay there overnight?" asked Michelle.

"Oh, yeah, I completely forgot to tell you this," exclaimed Jacques as he patted his head with his hand. "André called my cell phone this morning and he said he got the room for free. Don't worry about a thing, Monique. He's a reliable guy and will be there waiting for you, I guarantee it. I told him if he didn't take good care of you, I'd throw him in the Bay of Fundy. I swam in that water before, and it's cold enough to freeze your . . ."

"Jacques!" said Michelle. "I think the bus is here!"

Monique waved to Michelle and Jacques as she pulled out of the station. Jacques looked much nicer today, she noticed. He had broken with his usual shorts and t-shirts and had on a short-sleeve shirt and tie with a pair of jeans. The tie had a guitar running down the length of it, which made Monique smile. His hair was neatly combed, and he was handsome as he stood holding hands with her *petite cousine*. He wrapped his arm around her small waist, pulling her in closer to him. They waved until Monique could no longer see them.

The bus made its way through the city streets and to the outskirts, circling a long exit lane to merge into highway traffic. The noise of the airbrakes went away when they got on Highway 101, and she glanced at road signs with names of places she'd never heard of. She looked out the large window of the bus as it passed rocky crags of cliffs along the highway.

The scenery became rural and rolling, grassy green with pastures. Cows grazed as though they had all the time in the world, and as the bus approached larger towns, there were billboards advertising lodging or restaurants. Irving Gas Stations dotted the landscape. The bus drove through the little town of Avonport, and Monique checked her map. She picked up her bags to move closer to the front of the bus. A large, jutting bluff appeared on the horizon and she thought it was one of the most beautiful sights she'd ever seen.

"Are you a student?" she asked a young man sitting across the aisle.

"Yes," he replied.

"What is that called?"

"Oh, that? Blomidon." She noticed he said it with no more feeling about it than if she had pointed to a cow.

"Do you live around here?" she asked.

"Yup, right in Wolfville where we'll be stopping." As though reading her mind he added, "I'm from here, so I guess I take the scenery for granted."

"It's beautiful," she said. She giggled at the way he had pronounced Wolfville as "Wooffel." "You don't call it Wolfe-ville?"

"No," he replied, adding a snicker of his own.

The bus drove into the small town of Wolfville and stopped on a back street in front of a row of stores. Once the bus pulled away, she spotted a small restaurant by the bus stop and stopped in to buy a drink of water and use the ladies room. Coming back outside shortly after, she observed a young man walking toward her. He had dark eyes and dirty blonde hair that was covered by a baseball cap with a large "A" inscribed on it.

"Hi, Monique?" His smile helped calm the nervousness she was starting to feel, and he reached out to take her overnight bag. Their hands brushed, and she felt herself blush.

"Hi," she replied.

"I'm glad you made it. Did you have a decent ride on the bus? Sometimes the air conditioning is too cold or doesn't work. I don't use the buses but some of my friends do. Are you hungry?"

"A little." She was worried that her shyness would take over and she'd be lost for words, but she asked about how close in relation André and Jacques were, and André was more than happy to tell Monique about his boyhood days with Jacques in Shediac, New Brunswick.

"I'm glad he found a good woman," said André. "He used to be a little on the wild side, but he's got a heart of gold."

"That's funny. He said the same about you!"

"He said I'm wild?" asked André incredulously.

"He said you like speed."

"Speed as in going fast, I hope you mean, because I stay away from the amphetamines."

"Yes, speed as in going fast."

"Guilty as charged."

"I love Jacques," said Monique. "He is certainly opposite to Michelle in many ways, but musically they are stunning, and when he dresses up he is really quite handsome."

"He's smarter than he seems too," said his proud cousin. "One time when I was about ten and he was around twelve, my family took a trip to Louisiana for a week to visit Jacques' family. While we were there, we went to a music festival and camped over for the weekend. Some of the fiddlers had a 'fiddlers in the round' where they all sit around and take turns playing part of a song. Jacques sat with them and he could keep up with just about every song they played!"

"Who else was in the circle?"

"I didn't know it at the time, but they're really well-known Cajun musicians. There was Michael Doucet, for one. He sat right beside Jacques. And Dewey Balfa, and Varise Connor. I'll never forget when Mr. Connor shuffled his messy hair and told him he was goin' places. I was happy to be just sitting there listening. It was awesome."

"Yeah, Jacques seems like he could find a way to fit in anywhere."

"And another thing I admire about him is the way he manages the band," said André. "They love him and are totally loyal, because he takes care of them. Some guys in his position act like they're something special, and the band gets fed up after awhile. Not Jacques. I don't think his ego would ever take over. That's why I really want to work for him and every once in a while I get fed up with college and just want to do something different. But he keeps on me to finish my degree."

"Are you looking forward to *Le Festival Acadien*?" she asked.

"Yeah, definitely. Jacques said he and Michelle learned some old Acadian songs and put a more contemporary folk sound to them."

"Do you know any Acadian songs?" she asked.

"I should," André said with a laugh. "My folks raised me on Acadian songs and stories that have been passed down. My grandparents didn't speak any English at all." He paused, then spoke more quietly, almost timidly. "I like your name, Monique. I've never known a girl by that name."

Monique felt a strange flutter when he said he liked her name. He was sweet, and she was growing comfortable in his company. They walked down through the small university town. The streets were filled with college students walking on both sides of the street, and when they came to a quaint restaurant with a small patio out front they made their way over to a table and sat down. Their waitress, a student that André knew, came to take their order, and within moments Monique had an iced tea and a crisp tossed salad. André had ordered an Italian sub, and when he only ate half, Monique offered to finish the other half. She asked him if he was involved in sports, and André told her that he was captain of the swim team and they had won the conference championship last year. When she asked if they could win another one this year, he seemed less than enthusiastic about their chances.

After they finished lunch, André pointed to the Blomidon Cottages and said they should walk down and check in. When they got to the office, André opened the door, gestured for Monique to enter first, and introduced her to his friend, Bill.

"She's a looker, André," Bill teased, "but did you have to go all the way down to Louisiana to find a girl who'd go out with you?"

"Actually she hasn't said she'd go out with me yet," replied André with a mischievous grin, "and don't jinx it for me, Bill!"

Bill laughed and handed Monique the key to her room.

"Enjoy yourself here, Monique, and y'all come back often," he said in a feeble attempt at a southern drawl. "We like pretty Southern girls around here."

"Bill is a big flirt," said André as they walked toward her cottage.

"He's OK, though. He's married with three kids and loves his wife, so I know he just thinks you're pretty and wants to give me a hard time."

They stopped outside her cottage, number twelve. She wondered if she should invite him in, and quickly decided that it would be the polite thing to do.

"Come on in for a few minutes, I want to show you something," she said. He stood inside the door while she placed her small luggage bag on the counter and took out her mother's picture. "I don't want you to think I'm crazy when we go to Grand-Pré, so I want to explain something. This is a picture I recently found of my mother. She died when I was a young girl, and I'm taking this with me when we go to the park. Mama always wanted to bring me there, but now I'm bringing her instead, so don't be surprised if we walk around Grand-Pré and I talk to her, OK?"

"No problem. I'm sorry about your mother," he said. "It must have been tough to lose her."

"It was. But I have a great Dad, so I'm grateful for that."

"Listen, I don't mean to rush off, but I have an Art Appreciation class in a few minutes and I have to get back to campus. I decided to get this course in during the summer. Hey, do you want to come?"

She nodded, placing the picture on the counter and locking the door behind them. Within minutes they were across town on campus and André was leading her toward two empty seats in a dimly lit amphitheater. The long rows of chairs descended to the floor below, where a woman stood by a lit podium.

"*Bonjour, classe,*" said the professor. Monique's eyes slowly adjusted to the darkness, as she squinted at a professor who seemed to be smiling at her own attempt to speak French. Picking up a stack of papers from a small table beside the podium, she moved to the front row and handed them to a student who took one and passed the stack to the student next to him. The professor returned to the podium.

"I am pleased to introduce the curator of the Acadian Exhibit which is presently at the Art Museum in Halifax," she said, making a loud, hollow noise as she twisted the microphone closer. "Mme. Lillian Leger has brought slides of Acadian art and photographs, and I'm sure you will all listen attentively as she gives us her presentation. Without further ado, Mme. Leger."

A younger woman came and stood in front of the podium, and the lights were dimmed down so that she was barely visible. Nearly simultaneously a very large screen at the front lit up, and a clicking sound brought up a slide. A close-up of a sculpture of Evangeline struck Monique's vision so dramatically that she coughed to stifle a gasp and was grateful for the darkness as she swiped at a tear rolling down her cheek. With the hint of a French accent, the speaker explained that this statue was located in front of the chapel just a short distance away, at Grand-Pré Park. She said that the artist had deliberately sculpted a young woman, who when viewed from the side displayed by the slide, appeared innocent and full of the promise of life. The following slide showed the sculpture when viewed from another perspective, and the speaker asked the students to take a moment and look at the difference as she clicked from one to the other several times.

"As you can observe," said Mme. Leger, "in the second view of the statue, Evangeline appears older and filled with the despair of *Le Grand Dérangement*. She has lost her lover, her family, and the life she cherished has been completely destroyed, as though it never existed in the first place."

Mme. Leger paused for a moment. The next slide that came up showed a longer view of the statue and chapel behind it.

"That's what I came here to visit," Monique whispered to André excitedly. She was surprised when he reached for her hand.

"And I will take you there," he said as he squeezed her hand and let it go again.

The curator quickly clicked through other renderings of Evangeline and historic Acadia. By now, the much-thinner stack of papers had reached them, and André handed one to her, then took one himself before passing them on. Monique held the paper close and realized it was a list of all the works of art and the artists who had created them.

Mme. Leger paused and waited for the next slide. "Here you see Acadian art by Camille Cormier from Shediac, New Brunswick. His depictions capture our imaginations with what everyday life was in the Acadian farm villages."

"He's from my home town," André whispered to Monique. She was pleased to see the statue at St. Martinville, Louisiana come up next on the large screen.

"And that's from where I live," she whispered to André.

"This next picture is of the mural at the Historic Park in St. Martinville, Louisiana," said the curator. "There is one similar to it in Nantes, France, both painted by American artist Robert Dafford. A stunning photograph of the iron cross at Grand-Pré against a dark and stormy sky is one of my personal favorites. John B. Webb from Nova Scotia is the photographer who took it, entitling it *Angry Sky*. Claude Picard, an artist from New Brunswick, painted the pictures found in the chapel at Grand-Pré. Acadian art, as you can see, is still very much alive, and Cajun artistry is still thriving in the contemporary works of Cajun artists Elton Louviere, George Rodrigue, and others. In fact, I have met Mr. Rodrique personally and am hoping the hurricane does not do damage to his studio in New Orleans this weekend."

"What hurricane?" whispered Monique.

"I heard about it. A Category three or four," replied André.

"Really? When?"

"Not sure. A couple of days from now. I only caught a little bit about it on the car radio."

"My Dad's there. I'd better call him tonight."

"Is he in New Orleans?" whispered André.

"Lafayette."

"I think the storm is supposed to go east of there, more towards Mississippi."

"Oh." Someone behind them made a "shh" noise, and they glanced at each other and smiled. They remained silent as the speaker finished up the lecture by saying that the Acadian Exhibit would be in Halifax for the summer months.

The class ended and the doors were forced open by students streaming outside. They strolled in the warm sunshine up through town again toward Tim Horton's. When they got there, André held the door, allowing Monique to walk in first. He got them each a cup of coffee and they walked back to the Blomidon Cottages.

"Do you have a boyfriend who let you come all the way up here without him?" André asked.

"I did have, but we broke up at the beginning of the summer," Monique replied. "What about you, do you have a girlfriend?"

"I did have for the past year, but she liked to party more than I did. I didn't mind her having a good time, but when I didn't go with her, my friends would tell me afterwards that she'd had a few drinks and came on to them, things like that. I don't think she meant to hurt me, at least she said she didn't. I believed her at first, but I reached my limit and that was it."

"What's her name?"

"Lauri. We still say hi to each other, but that's about it."

"I broke up with my boyfriend just before graduation," Monique said. "I didn't feel like he respected my feelings in some ways either. My father says you know when it's the real thing, but I never felt very sure that Ted was the one for me."

"Well, I guess if you were still with him you might not have come here, and I'm really glad Jacques gave me the chance to get to know you. Would you like to go down to Grand-Pré Park tonight for awhile?"

By this time, they had reached her cottage. Monique unlocked the door, and they both entered.

"I would love to. I need to get some rest first though, if that's OK."

"Sure. Just give me a call at the dorm, and remember to call twice, OK?" said André. "I wanted to get out of there and get an apartment this year, but couldn't make it work out. My cell phone doesn't work and my folks said they'd buy me a new one, but I hate to ask them for money. I've had a summer job managing a swim team, but won't get the stipend until mid-September. Then maybe I'll be able to get one and call you in Louisiana."

Monique suddenly detected a sparkle in André's eyes. She could feel herself blush, and wanted to say something in reply but no words were coming. André's face showed his disappointment.

"So, would you like my dorm number, or would you prefer to be alone? I was supposed to go out with a couple of friends, but if you still want to see Grand-Pré, I'll take you."

"Yes, I'd like to go," Monique said, cursing her shyness.

André jotted down his number and handed it to her.

"Call twice, OK?"

"I will."

She watched André walk back to his car and heard the engine start as she closed the door to the cottage. The guilt about not responding to his invitation to stay connected gnawed at her. Here was a tall, handsome, nice guy, and he was obviously interested in her. She already liked him a lot, but he was leaving thinking that she had just blown him off. She could not let her shyness ruin this chance.

Monique threw open the screen door and shouted his name once, twice. The brake lights told her that he had heard her. She ran to the car as he pulled it to a stop at the end of the parking lot. He opened the door and stood to meet her, and she put her arms out to him.

"I would love for you to call me in Louisiana," she said. "I had a really wonderful time with you this afternoon."

Smiling, he bent down and kissed her, a slow, lingering kiss on the lips. Feeling his arms wrapping around her waist, she raised to her tiptoes as she reached up to clasp her hands behind his neck. His muscles felt strong and certain, holding her in a way that said clearly that he already cared for her. She looked in his eyes, telling him with her own that she had feelings for him too.

"I know this doesn't make sense, but this feels so comfortable, almost familiar. This is the first time we've kissed, right?" Monique teased.

"Well, unless you've dreamt it or something, it definitely is. But it feels pretty comfortable to me too. Why, are you feeling like it's *déjà vu?*"

"Yeah, I think so." Monique set her head on his shoulder, closed her eyes, and enjoyed the tender embrace.

After savoring a few more moments together he said, "I'd better go and let you rest awhile." She agreed, and they said hesitant good-byes, glancing back at each other as each went in opposite directions.

Inside the cottage again, Monique removed her sundress and put on a tank top and shorts. She flopped down on the bed and let out a deep sigh as maritime breezes blew gently in through the open window of her room. Each new one drifted across her body, and she was in a dream again. In a small room with a strongly metallic smell, she knelt in prayer with Pierre. Monique felt very scared. He held his arm around her, trying to comfort her.

She woke abruptly and sat up. Groggy and disoriented, it took her a few seconds to remember where she was. She stared at the orange light of dusk streaming in through the window and rubbed her arms to warm them. The air had turned chilly. She jumped up to shut the window and could see that, in the street, the trees were shadows. A couple walked along holding hands. She noted that there was no fog like there had been the night before.

Shuffling off to the bathroom and then out to the kitchenette, she made herself a cup of green tea, then reached for the paper André had written his number on and read his full name that he'd written. "André Legere," it said. She dialed the number, let it ring a couple of times, then hung up and dialed again. A male voice on the other end said "hi."

"Is André there?' she asked.

"I dunno. Where's André?" the person on the other end asked anyone nearby.

Monique could hear muffled tones of other voices, and the speaker came back to the phone again. "André's out, maybe with Lauri. Can I give him a message?"

"No, no message thanks," Monique answered, hanging up the phone. Why would André go out with Lauri? she wondered. He had said he was thinking of going out with friends, but that was before they'd kissed. Maybe the person who answered the phone didn't know they'd broken up. She had to admit she felt let down and confused, but soon decided she'd ask him when she saw him next. Her dream was really disturbing her right now, and she had really looked forward to going to the chapel tonight. It seemed a waste of time to sit here all evening, so she considered going to the park alone. Who would know the closing hour of the park?

David Broussard popped into her mind, and she recalled the news about a hurricane that she could also ask him about. She searched in her wallet for his card he had given her before they left Breaux Bridge. Finding it, she dialed his home number.

"Hello?" said the familiar voice.

"Hi, it's Monique." she stated tentatively. "Am I calling at a bad time?

"No, of course not. Your father's coming up here tomorrow and we had planned to go out fishing for the day but there's a hurricane coming so we'll see what happens. Maybe we'll hang around here and I can get your father to give me some fish recipes for a party I'm having. Oh, yeah, I remember. He told me you took a trip to Nova Scotia with your cousin. Is everything OK?"

"Yes, fine, and I'm glad you'll be spending time with Dad. I just wondered if you happen to know what time the park at Grand-Pré closes at night?"

"I don't know. What time is it there? Hmm, a little late. I would think it would be closed by now. Do you have someone to go with you?" he asked in a protective tone.

"Yes, well, I did but now I don't."

"Where are you now?"

"I'm at Blomidon Cottages. Do you know where they are?"

"Yes, a mile or so away from the park, too far to walk," he said. "And I think you should wait until tomorrow. It's probably closed by now."

"Are you worried I'll see the ghost?"

"Very funny. No, I'm not worried about ghosts. I'm worried about you wandering around alone. I know your father wouldn't like that either so just hang tight at the cottage and watch TV or something until morning."

"O.K, Dad," she joked again. "I will."

"Promise?"

"Promise."

They said good-bye and Monique hung up the phone. She sank into the old couch and picked up the remote. There was nothing of interest on. Checking the time she saw that it was just past eight o'clock, and she opened the door to see what the air was like outside. She slid on pants and a sweatshirt. Sorry, David, she said as she clicked off the TV.

Flipping through the pages of a phone book laying by the phone, she found "Taxis" in the yellow pages. Her finger rested on "Annapolis Taxi," and she dialed. Within twenty minutes she stood alone in Grand-Pré Park, thanking Jack, the taxi driver. She asked him to return in a half-hour before reaching into her purse to pay him.

"You can jest pay me when I come to git ya. I trust ya."

Monique smiled and thanked him, then tucked her wallet back into her purse right beside the framed picture of her mother. The park was smaller than she had imagined. She walked along the lawn, and noticed a line of majestic willows. The shadows danced along under the branches as they swayed with the breeze. She approached the statue of Evangeline and stood under it. Taking out the picture of her mother, she sat beneath it for a few moments, closing her eyes and imagining her mother here with her. Sadness came. Afterward, she strolled around the grounds more, then finally chose a quiet spot on the grass beside a willow tree.

She shivered, aware for the first time that there was nobody else around. She decided to take her mother's picture out again and say a prayer. After that, she would be ready to go back to the parking lot and wait for the taxi. She set the picture down and knelt.

"Thank you, Father, for bringing me to this blessed place. It is so peaceful here. I know my mother dreamed of coming to this very spot. Thank-you for giving me a loving mother and father . . . ."

Monique turned toward a rustling sound in the grass. Someone was moving slowly toward her in the shadows, and before she could become too frightened she realized the person was stooped and having difficulty walking. However, she stood up, just to be cautious.

Fateful Meeting in the Willows

"Hello?" she called.
"Hello. Monique?"
"Yes. André?"
"*Non*. My name is Father Siméon Allain, and I am from here, from Acadie. I hope I did not frighten you."

"No, well yeah, a little bit." The old man stood nearby, looking carefully at the willow tree she sat under. He smiled at her. She wondered if she'd met him before. His coat had holes where it was worn and tattered.

"*Je suis un* missionary," he said, still looking at the tree.

"Oh."

"*Oui.* Ah, this tree has grown for such a long time. It is beautiful, isn't it?"

Monique shivered when a chilly sea breeze seemed to sweep by her face.

"How did you know my name?" she asked. "Did the cab driver say it when he dropped me off? I didn't see anyone out here."

"*Oui. Qui est* in the picture?" He pointed a finger toward her hand.

"My mother. She died." Monique lifted the picture toward him and he moved toward her, struggling to walk. He took the picture in one hand and moved it so that the moonlight fell on it.

"You look very much like her. What was her name?"

"Catherine. She passed away when I was four. She always wanted to bring me here to show me where her ancestors were deported from, but didn't live to make the trip. She and my aunt always planned to bring my cousin Michelle and me here. They thought it was important to know our ancestry. I brought her picture with me on my visit here from Louisiana so that I could feel she's with me." Monique suddenly felt embarrassed. "I suppose it sounds silly . . ."

"*Non*, not at all. I feel she really is here with you. And she even looks like Louise a little."

"Who's Louise?"

"When I knew you before, *ta mère*, she was Louise."

"What? Oh, I'm not from here, so we've never met." She shifted her focus from the old man to the road beyond, watching for the taxi.

"Oh, but we have. You see, your mother and you both lived right here in 1755," said Father Allain, his voice brimming over with excitement. "*Ta mère*, she was Louise, *et ton père*, François. Do you understand? You did not lose your mother at that time, not even during the exile!"

"Oh?" She felt a cold draft on her neck. "May I have my picture back? My taxi's coming back soon."

"*Oui.* You do not believe me," he said with a shake of his head. The smile remained, but his eyes looked sad as he handed the picture back to Monique. He spoke so lovingly, like a grandfather she thought, and she decided to spare his feelings.

"I'm sorry, I just don't quite understand what you're talking about," she said gently. "I hope you have a nice evening, but I have to go now."

"As I said, I was a missionary here in Grand-Pré," he continued, speaking louder as she moved slowly away. "The priests had all been taken, but I was able to stay to continue my work with the Mi'Kmaq. You and I traveled together during *Le Grand Dérangement.*"

Monique knew it was far-fetched, but she was becoming a little interested in his fantasy. She moved back toward him just to see where this story went. It was safer to wait here than to stand out there alone by the side of the road. He seemed harmless enough, too frail to hurt anyone. He probably just wanted someone to talk to.

"Where did we go?"

"*Nous* . . . we went to Boston."

"Did we come back?"

"*Non,* we were forbidden. We stayed in Boston for awhile, some for the rest of their lives. Others went on to Louisiana. Pierre was imprisoned with Beausoleil, who was trying to win back Acadie. But he was released and . . ."

"Who?" Monique's ears perked up at the mention of the name "Pierre." It was an interesting coincidence. She pressed on. "And my mother, what happened to her?"

"She lived a long life. She and your Aunt Cecilia, they stayed together after your father died, *dans un ville en* Massachusetts. They were fortunate in that the town cared about their wellbeing. Beausoleil led a group of Acadians to settlements in Louisiana."

"You should write a story about this," she said, realizing immediately by his expression that he was offended.

"This is not a made-up story," he insisted. "It really did happen, when you lived as Monique Mélanson right here in the village of Grand-Pré." The old man seemed to be growing a little frustrated, and she felt the connection she had established with him unraveling.

Where is the damn taxi? she wondered. She was ready to go back to her cottage for the night. "I really did enjoy meeting you, *Monsieur* Allain," she remarked, extending her hand to his.

"*Oui.*" He reached out to receive it. A curtain of blackness fell across her face for a brief second, and her stomach felt as though it had hit the ground with a thud. In the next moment, she opened her eyes and blinked them several times to clear away a foggy blur. Expecting to see the old man standing above her, instead she saw a much younger man in the black robes of a priest. He grasped her hand tightly in his.

"She is coming to," he said. "Praise God, Louise, she has only fainted!"

Monique blinked her eyes several more times and raised her head. Kneeling at her side, a man more handsome than she could ever have dreamed was smiling at her. His straight black hair hung to his shoulders, and soft eyes of chocolate brown looked into hers as he bathed her face with a cool, damp cloth. The eyes looked extraordinarily familiar.

"What happened?" she asked.

"You just fainted, that is all." A woman appeared behind the man, holding a cloth bag. She passed it near Monique's nose, and it emitted such a strong smell it nearly made her gag. She coughed and sat up.

"My dear daughter, you must have been overcome," said the woman. "Someone bring Monique a drink of water! Is she going to be all right, Father Allain?"

"*Oui,* I think she will be fine. Her color is beginning to return." Monique took in her surroundings. She was in a small kitchen, lying on a wooden floor. She heard voices of women and children in the kitchen, and the clicking sounds of knitting needles. A loud creak of a heavy wooden door was followed by the sound of footsteps in her direction.

"I ran to the beach and got this for you, Monique." A young girl reached across to Monique with a cloth rag dripping with ice-cold water. Monique cried out in surprise when the liquid splashed her in the face.

"Mariette!" she exclaimed.

"The water is cold today, see? My hand is turning blue. And the tide is nearly up to the cliffs!"

"Thank you," said Father Allain quietly, smiling at the young girl. "You are very helpful, and this other cloth was already getting too warm." He wrung the dripping one out in a small pot that someone had set down beside him, and placed it on Monique's forehead. "Mariette, did you pick blueberries this morning?" he asked.

"Why, no, I did not. But I did help Mama make some blueberry pies."

"Then your hand is blue from that. The water at the beach is not that cold today," smiled Father Allain. Some of the others present found his observation amusing, but Monique noticed that her mother looked pale and fearful. She also observed that she and Mama were both dressed the same, in long, wool skirts with aprons over them. A pair of wooden shoes peeked out from under Mama's dress.

"Thank-you Father for helping me," she said. "My darling, you scared your poor mother to death!"

"Perhaps she was overcome at the thought of marrying Pierre," said Mariette, which received a few giggles from the other young girls present.

Monique reached for her head in reaction to a sharp pain above her brow, and she found she was back in Grand-Pré, standing by the tree with the old man again.

"What happened?"

"*Un miracle,*" smiled the old man, full of excitement. "Now, listen carefully. You may return to 1755 if you wish to learn more about our people. You will experience some terrible hardships, but I will stay at your side. You also need to understand that those who love you in your present life will search for you, enduring great distress."

The old man was now struggling to stand, and his breath was labored. "I have little time left. I tried to give this gift to Beausoleil," he sighed, "but he was not ready. Perhaps you are not either . . . ."

Monique backed away from Father Allain, and ran as fast as she could toward the road. Her heart raced, and her legs were unsteady. She stood at the shoulder of the pavement, listening for the taxi. "Please hurry, please hurry," she whispered. Anxiety crept up through her stomach and into her neck, and she sucked in gulps of cool air to try and calm herself. She felt faint, and sweat beads wet her forehead, making her shiver in the chilly breeze. How could this be happening? What would Michelle say if she knew? Would she believe it?

Monique could hear the sound of a car engine growing louder, and around the corner came the car she was hoping to see, a "taxi" light over its roof. Whatever just happened, it seemed as real as the old priest who still stood over in the shadow of the willow, waiting. The woman who bent over her was her mother, and the man? He had the same eyes, the same gentle voice as Father Allain. He *was* a younger Father Allain. The eyes, voice, they both were the same. She looked up the road again at the approaching taxi, then over at the old man under the willow tree.

Monique found herself moving away from the pavement and back toward the park. She thought again about her mother Catherine, and the gifts she made sure were preserved after her death. The picture, the small quilt, and her journal all seemed to be meant just for Monique. Most importantly, her mother instilled in her daughter a deep longing to visit Nova Scotia and come to this park tonight. Slowly she began to walk toward Father Allain, to make her way back toward her past.

Seconds later, Jack pulled his taxi to a stop in the parking lot where he had left Monique. She was not waiting at the chosen spot by the road. From the willow tree to Evangeline's statue to the chapel and surrounding grounds, there was no one. Jus' my luck, he thought. She sure was some nice girl to talk to on the way here, I jus' didn't think she'd jump ship. He radioed dispatch to report that the pickup wasn't there.

"Sure didn't strike me as the kind to stiff a fella' on a fare," he said to the dispatcher. "Oh, well . . . ." After waiting a few more minutes just in case, he left the parking lot, headed back to the taxi stand. The willow tree swaying in the breeze was the only movement in the empty park.

Chapter 9

The Present Is Opened

Wednesday, September 3, 1755

Monique glanced around the room, then up at Father Allain. From the floor she saw many pairs of legs, some young, some old, and all of various shapes. By the sound of Angeline's voice Monique could tell she was worried, but her neighbor's face was blocked from Monique's view by her very large stomach. She stood directly above Monique, offering another fresh damp cloth to Father Allain. He took it, then stood up and held out his other hand to Monique. He pulled her gently to her feet, and he and Louise guided her on either side to a wooden chair. When she told them she still felt faint, Father Allain requested that she lean forward, and he placed the cool cloth on the back of her neck. Her mother sat on the other side of her and both stared vigilantly to make sure she did not pass out again.

"What happened?" Monique asked after a moment.

"I do not know, my darling," said her mother. "I looked up and greeted you when you walked in here, and you just looked at me and said 'Mama.' After that you turned as white as a ghost and sank to the floor like a dishrag. Are you bruised?"

"I think not," replied Monique, holding out her own arms and legs to quickly examine them. "I feel fine now. May I sit up and do some needlework?"

"Thankfully Father Allain was knocking at the door," continued her mother. "I was nearly overcome myself." Louise made the sign of the cross and folded her hands in front of her in a short prayer. "In the name of the Father, the Son, and the Holy Spirit," she said, after which she turned to the other women present. "Please pray with me," she demanded anxiously.

"May I sit up, Mama?" Monique asked again after the prayer was over. Her mother continued talking and did not respond. After several more moments leaning over with the cloth on her neck, she moaned.

"The cloth is warm now and is doing no good anyway. I must sit up or I will get a headache!"

"Yes, dear. I will remove the cloth," said Father Allain. He took it away and Monique opened her eyes, twisting her neck this way and that. Father Allain was looking at her and smiling brightly.

"Your color has returned," he said, "so I shall leave now and go assist your father on the Mélanson farm. I will set these cloths outside in the sun to dry. May we have a prayer before I depart?"

The women in the circle set down their sewing and bowed their heads as Father Allain began, "Dear God, thank you for sparing Monique from injury and affliction. Please send your grace on all these women present. I ask you to bring Angeline a healthy baby, and for Your guidance to help her neighbors and loved ones to know the best ways to support her in the months ahead."

"Amen," came a chorus of voices at the end of the prayer. Father Allain waved good-bye and left.

"We wanted it to be a surprise for you, but now is the time to tell you what we have been doing," said Angeline. "The lace work we have nearly completed today is for your wedding the day after tomorrow!"

Monique gasped with surprise and looked at each woman's lap. Her neighbor Hélène smiled and held up a doily, and Hélène's daughters each held up one also. Her mother, sitting beside her, held up a bureau scarf.

"It will be the perfect size for a small table your Papa and I are giving you," she said happily. Angeline held up an apron bordered in lace, and Aunt Cecile lifted a corner of a blanket.

"When we have completed them," said her mother, "you can store them in the pine chest your father built for you."

"I too have a surprise," said Monique. "I have nearly completed a baby blanket for Angeline." She looked at her own lap and saw that she did not have the blanket with her. "Did I leave it at home?" she wondered aloud. Mariette, Monique's cousin from le Canard, asked if she could run and get it, and Monique gave her a nod "yes."

"Just think, mother, someday I will be crocheting lacework on top of a large shelf such as that of Angeline," she whispered, so that the children could not hear.

"Are the relatives all coming from le Canard?" asked some-one.

"Oh, yes, it will be a glorious day," replied Louise. "My little girl has grown to be a woman!" She leapt from her chair to give her daughter a kiss. Monique closed her eyes and tears came.

"Oh Monique, why do you cry?" her mother asked.

"I've missed you, Mama," Monique replied.

"Are you certain you feel well?" asked her mother, her expression puzzled.

"Yes, Mama. Father Allain even said my color was back."

"Yes, he did, but why did you say you missed me? We have not been apart."

"I don't know why. Perhaps I meant I will miss you after Pierre and I are married. Where has Father Allain gone? I wanted to ask him something."

"He went to talk to your father. He said he would meet us back at the farm later on."

The other women had silenced their conversations with each other to listen in on theirs. The whereabouts of Father Allain was always a subject of interest in the village.

"Will Father Allain be staying for supper at your farm?" asked Madelaine, a young woman Monique's age and the daughter of Hélene.

"Yes, I did invite him," answered Louise, giving Madelaine a look that implied it was not really her business.

"Monique," asked Madelaine, "were you surprised to wake up and see Father Allain leaning over you and wiping your face with the cloth?" This question elicited some giggles from other adolescent girls, and Monique understood full well the meaning of it. Father Allain was admired by the young girls of the village, as well as by 'most everyone else. Every spring when he returned to Grand-Pré and made camp at the edge of the village, it was a happy occasion.

The group of women began to rise from their chairs and pack up their needlework for the day. It was time to return to their homes and attend to the evening meal. Soon the men would be back from work in the fields and orchards. With the corn in and left outside to dry out from the rain, the last few sunny days had been perfect for storing it in the barns. There was still much work to be done in the next few weeks to get ready for winter.

"This will be the last time for awhile that we will come together for a sewing circle," said Angeline. "Once grain harvest is over, I will invite you all back and we can resume work on last spring's quilt. This autumn I will be unable to join you in the fields, as my midwife has said I am about to deliver any day now."

"May we see the quilt?" asked Mariette.

Angeline got up from her chair slowly and disappeared behind a curtain. She came back and held up her handiwork for all to see, just five large squares completed.

"See how pretty it is already?" she said proudly. "By next spring, we will have a beautiful work of art to exhibit at the St. Charles Des Mines picnic."

"Let us plan to resume work on it after the *grènier* is gathered," said Louise as they dispersed from Angeline's kitchen. Monique glanced at her with a puzzled look. "*Grènier*," her mother laughed. "For mercy's sake, Monique, you know what that is!"

Monique and Louise walked the short distance down the narrow dirt road to the Mélanson farm. From the road they could hear the pounding of nails at the encampment where the New England soldiers were. The churchyard had been taken over by them, and Monique's mother cast an irritated look toward the noise. "We cannot even see our own church," she muttered to her daughter.

Once they were back in the quiet of their own kitchen, Louise lit a fire in the fireplace. The women peeled carrots, and François brought in six salted herring. He had traded apples in the village for this delicacy, and hummed to himself as he found a pot to heat them in. Louise went outside to gather more wood, and Monique stood on the blue-slated hearth and stirred a large pot filled with water, potatoes and an onion. François dropped the cleaned herring gently into the pot suspended in the circular oven. Soon the aromas of its contents filled the kitchen. Monique bent over the pot and breathed deeply. She turned toward the open door and could see her father, François, as he stood at the washing trough scrubbing his arms and hands. Monique glanced up at the sound of footsteps out front, the familiar steps of Father Allain joining Papa. She averted her eyes, staring blankly at the fieldstones that framed the large fireplace. She knew that Father Allain would be removing his black robe and folding it carefully as he always did, before placing it next to him on a nearby fence. She glanced back again. Water gushed as her father poured more water from a wooden bucket into the trough. Both men, their shirts removed, proceeded to scrub with lye soap as they discussed the progress that had been made today in the apple orchards. With fifty barrels picked by the women, François and Louise Mélanson were both pleased to say that the harvest had been plentiful.

Monique looked up suddenly when her mother came in from outside. She pretended to look at Mama, all the while focusing instead on the activity outside the door. She observed Father Allain's deeply tanned back. His muscles were taut as he bent over the trough to rinse off.

"Set the table, dear," said Louise as she pushed the door shut with one foot and unloaded the wood onto the hearth. Monique obeyed sheepishly, walking over to the wooden cupboard and opening a drawer. She placed forks at each setting, still straining to hear the conversation between the men outside. They were talking about some villagers at Habitant who had been asked to provide food to the soldiers. Monique heard her father say that he would prefer to share his harvest with his own countrymen. Father Allain cautioned him that if they were asked on orders from the Lieutenant Governor, they would have to comply whether they liked it or not.

Monique suddenly realized that bowls would be needed for the salt herring and carrots, and she reached quietly up into the open cabinet to get them, placing them carefully at each person's place setting.

"My dear Uncle René LeBlanc will be visiting us tomorrow evening," her father was saying to Father Allain as they walked into the kitchen. "He will bring the marriage papers for Pierre and Monique, and Jean Doucet and I will sign them. It is very unfortunate that we cannot have the wedding in the church. What do you think about the soldiers making camp for the entire winter here in the parish of St. Charles?"

"Between us," said Father Allain, "I do not care to see the colors of the British flag flying over our beloved church. I do not know if it is true or just a rumor, but I heard that an Acadian was requested to assist in translating an announcement which will be given to us tomorrow. You must not breathe this to anyone, François and Louise, or you either, Monique. I was told that it will direct the old and young men, as well as boys ten years and over who are inhabitants of Grand-Pré, Mines River, le Canard, and places adjacent, to come to the church at Grand Pré this Friday at three o'clock in the afternoon.

"But that is during our wedding celebration! For what purpose?" asked Louise.

"I do not know any details about what they are going to communicate to us."

"Who are the orders from?" asked François.

"I'm not certain," replied Father Allain. "From what I understand, they will be delivered by Colonel John Winslow, commander of the New England troops here."

"Yes," said François. "I know who he is. I have seen Colonel Winslow parading around our village with his soldiers. My cousin from le Canard saw a group marching along the Riviere Canard several days ago with their drums beating, and Pierre, my daughter's betrothed, saw a large group of fifty or more marching down through Mélanson, along the Rivière Gaspereau. They seem to be enjoying the scenery here, and why should they not? This is indeed God's country!" François raised his arms in a gesture of gratitude to the Almighty.

"We are most fortunate to have this beautiful place as our home," said Louise. "And on Friday, Pierre and Monique will say their vows to one another. It will be a glorious day for all of us! But, François, I must tell you what happened this afternoon. Monique fainted when we were at Angeline's farm doing needlework. I thought I would be frightened to death. Thankfully, Father Allain was there or I do not know what I would have done." Louise stopped long enough to give Father Allain a loving smile, then turned back to Monique. "Perhaps you worked too hard this morning, my darling. Which reminds me—did you notice the loaves of bread we baked in the oven today,

François?" Monique saw her father open his mouth to say something, but Louise continued on with barely a pause.

"Monique kneaded the dough, and it rose wonderfully. When she removed the bread, she placed it on the table outside and covered it with a dishcloth to let it cool. You should have seen the villagers and even some of the soldiers who stopped to smell the aroma of it. Perhaps it is a sin to say so, but I believe that Hélène was a little envious that her daughter Madelaine cannot bake bread as fine as Monique's."

"You will make a capable wife for Pierre," said Monique's father proudly. "He is very lucky. And I know he loves you, because I have seen it in his eyes." Her father pointed to his own eyes to emphasize his words. "His eyes tell how sincere he is, just like his father, and his grandfather. They have all been very noble men, and we are blessed to unite our families."

"And the love of the Virgin Mary will also bless your marriage," added Father Allain. "Shall we now say grace?"

When supper was over, the family continued to linger at the table awhile. They prayed for good weather for the wedding ceremony. Louise and Monique picked up the dishes, and the men went outside to attend to some evening chores. When they returned, they stood outside and talked about the tall wooden fence the soldiers had built around the church at Grand-Pré. Monique strained to hear what they were saying as her mother talked on about the wedding tomorrow. She could hear Father Allain telling of his concern for the priests of Acadie, and she heard him say that he had heard the Mi'Kmaq speak of other villages which had encampments of English speaking soldiers in their churchyards also.

Their voices grew louder, and the door opened.

"Do not worry, Father Allain," said François. "From what Uncle René has told me, the British won at Fort Beauséjour this summer and are probably just basking in their victory for a few months before returning back to their New England farms."

The men continued their conversation, and Louise invited Monique for an evening stroll. Down the dirt road they went, arm-in-arm toward their favorite spot on a small wooden bench beneath a willow tree.

"What a lovely night," said her mother. "I will miss our evenings together."

"Oh, Mama, we will still have many evenings together," answered Monique affectionately as she took her mother's hand in hers.

"I fear things will be different," said Louise sadly. "I have had a dream several times that I have lost you and don't know where you are, and this afternoon when you said you had missed me it gave me a very strange feeling."

"I'm sorry, Mama, I think I was confused from fainting. And besides, things will not be that different," laughed Monique. "I will be living in the next village. And just imagine this! We can bring your grandchildren to visit."

"Oh, yes, that is something to look forward to," said her mother as she patted her daughter on the hand.

After watching the sun set over le Canard, the women strolled along together back up the dirt road. They retired to the small farmhouse kitchen where François and Father Allain still sat at the table, enjoying a laugh over something that had happened earlier in the day. The women cut a few slices of cooled bread and spread it with molasses that François had traded for harvested apples. After enjoying a few slices together, François went out to the barn and returned with a few tools.

"Is this a good time to repair the kitchen wall?" François asked his friend, and with an affirmative nod from Father Allain, he placed the tools on the table.

"We don't want any holes in our wall when the wedding guests arrive," said François, smiling at his daughter. Monique watched her father as he mixed up a thick substance and he and Father Allain packed the mixture into the hole in the wall by the table.

"What is that?" she asked curiously.

"It is called *machekoui*," replied her father.

"Oui, *machekoui*," agreed Father Allain. "It will serve as very good insulation against the winter cold if you put it in all the small cracks also." After François had smoothed the thick substance with a knife, he then spread it over some smaller open areas on the wall where small sprigs of hay had begun to show through. Father Allain proceeded to smooth each spot down even more.

Seeing how Monique was looking at the freshly-repaired wall, François explained, "When it is dry, it will look much better, so do not worry. Father Allain taught me how to do this a few years ago."

"And I learned how to make *machekoui* from my Mi'Kmaq family," offered Father Allain. "They showed me, and I taught your father how to make it. It comes from the bark of the birch tree. They agreed to allow me to pass their secret to your father in exchange for some of the *herring ancine* he and your mother prepare and salt just the way they prefer."

"I have never heard you say before that the Mi'Kmaq people are your family," said Monique curiously.

Father Allain suddenly seemed surprised, and his complexion reddened. "They became my family when I was a boy," he said quietly.

"Come Father Allain," said François after completing the final touch-ups. "I will walk back to your camp with you. *Bonsoir, ma* cherie," he added gently as he kissed his daughter on the top of her head. Father Allain kissed her head also, then opened the door and beckoned for his older friend to go ahead of him.

"*Bonsoir*, Papa, *Bonsoir*, Father Allain," said Monique. Sitting alone in the kitchen, she quietly hummed a hymn they had sung some time ago at an evening Mass. She missed the masses. Soon after their priest had been taken away, their church had become a camp for the soldiers. She did not like the way some of them looked at her and the other village girls, and she wished that they were not making camp in their sacred church, but she dared not say it out loud. Sometimes when she saw them on the path, she would turn around and go the other way. Colonel Winslow had recently forbidden the soldiers to roam the villages, and she was glad about that.

Louise had already gone to the bed she shared with François in the small room beyond the kitchen to the west side of the Mélanson farmhouse. Monique had the room on the east side, so that it would get the sun's warmth first. She stood up and walked toward it, pushing back a curtain. Beads dyed with indigo decorated the side, and it was one of her favorite things. It divided her room from the main living area. Her father had traded twenty bushels of apples for the curtain, which had come from somewhere down south. Monique felt the heavy texture of it in her hands and put it up to her cheek. In one day from now, she would no longer slip behind it to get ready for bed. The curtain not only provided privacy, it also held in the warmth generated by the kitchen stove on a cold winter night. She wondered about her new sleeping quarters with Pierre and what they would be like. Undressing, she slid into a nightgown, then crawled into her bed. She drifted off, awakening briefly to the sound of her mother's voice close to her face and the feel of her blanket being tucked in around her shoulders.

"Good-night, *ma cherie*," said her mother. "Tomorrow you will be married, and I cannot believe you have grown up so fast. We have a busy day ahead, so rest well. *Je t'aime.*"

"I love you too, Mama," whispered Monique as she descended back into sleep. "I love you too."

Thursday, September 4, 1755

The following morning, Louise woke Monique early, immediately after François had left for the fields. Louise was excited to show Monique the chicken he had killed and cleaned. They cut the chicken into pieces and scrubbed freshly harvested onions and carrots. Monique had learned from her mother how to cook *poulet fricot*, and some of the neighbors around Grand-Pré were certain it helped to calm their digestive systems. Her mother put in salt pork, barley, and certain herbs that she kept a secret from all but her daughter. She had made Monique promise to guard this knowledge carefully, as it had been passed down over four generations of grandmothers. As Monique cut up all the vegetables, Louise tended the heavy wrought-iron pot filled with water that was in the oven.

Monique brought the vegetables to the fireplace, dropped them in the pot, and watched as her mother added the chicken and herbs. Her job was to tend the stew as it simmered in the cauldron, while Louise sat at a small table next to her scrubbing some clothing to hang up on a rope line outside. They talked about the wedding and in particular about Father Allain being present to do the ceremony.

"I think something is bothering Father Allain," said Monique.

"Oh, Monique," her mother reassured her, "Father Allain would have told François if something was wrong. I am certain he is probably just preoccupied with his duties. He will be packing up soon to follow the Mi'Kmaq inland for the winter months, and perhaps he is sad to go. Let us take some stew over to him later on."

"Mama," laughed Monique. "You think *poulet fricot* is the cure for all ills."

"I am not alone in that belief. Besides, my mother always said that anything prepared lovingly has healing qualities. Father Allain is part of our family, and if indeed he is feeling a little troubled this will be good for him."

Louise recalled the time when Father Allain had come to Grand-Pré village for his first visit. Monique had been a baby. He had almost immediately become a close friend of François, who had commented many times about how the missionary had held Monique in his arms and said a prayer for her to be protected from disease and harm. He had looked at her as though she was his own child, and over the years the friendship between Father Allain and the Mélanson family had grown deeper. François and he both revered their friendship with the Mi'Kmaq, and Louise and Monique knew that Father Allain had spent some years among the native tribe. He occasionally told them happy stories of his life in Mi'Kmaq camps before entering the seminary.

Everyone in Grand-Pré and the villages beyond had heard that Father Allain could both write and speak the native language fluently. When natives came across the Basin of Minas or down the Riviere Gaspereau and dragged their birch bark canoes onshore, one of the children would be called upon to run to Father Allain's small hut on the edge of the village and bring him back to translate.

In conversation, especially after a glass of ale at the Mélanson household during a peaceful evening, he occasionally said a Mi'Kmaq word instead of his usual French. If he received a puzzled look, he would realize his mistake and correct it, to everyone's amusement.

It was never spoken aloud, but admissions of attraction for the Jesuit missionary were whispered in secret and sealed with a pact for it to remain so. He was physically appealing, with shoulders that were broad and strong. He towered over all of the women and most of the men, and the villagers looked up to him in both the physical and the spiritual sense. Dressed in his black Jesuit robe with his long, black hair hanging to his shoulders, he carried himself in a regal fashion. Many Mi'Kmaq following in the footsteps of their beloved Chief Membertou were converted to the Catholic faith by the gentle persuasive faith and strong stature of Father Allain.

As natural as it was to see him clothed in his robe, it was equally so to see him in work clothes around the village. Side by side with the farmers of Grand-Pré, Father Siméon Allain picked apples at harvest each fall, helped with barn building, planted in the spring, and joined the other men in dyke repairs when called upon to do so. He had a good understanding of the engineering principles of building *aboiteaux* that would keep out the ferocious Baye Française tides, and a strong love for the marshland soil.

Each time the men repaired the *aboiteaux*, François would tell his wife and daughter how his friend the missionary had requested that the men cease their work so that he could hold his traditional ceremony. Over the years, it had begun to feel like another Roman Catholic sacrament. Father Allain would reach down in the soil and scoop enough to fill his cupped hands, as though it were communion bread. Then he would break it and, looking up at the sky, praise God for the rich nutrients held by the red mud brought in off the ocean floor and mixed with the marshland grasses and roots of the rivers and creeks.

"Father God, we give thanks for your bounty," he would say, "for this beautiful, fertile soil you have given us. Just as it is knitted together with the elements of the earth, so our Acadie is knitted with the love we have for each other as well as for our native Mi'Kmaq brethren." The men would end the ceremony with an "Amen," cross themselves, and resume their work shoveling and packing the *aboiteaux* before the next high tide.

Monique continued to wonder about Father Allain's childhood as she stirred the stew that simmered in the fireplace. It was not something he talked about, not even to those with whom he shared many hours of conversation. Monique was surprised he had given a hint about it last night. His life with the Mi'Kmaq was held close to his heart, in both a sacred and sorrowful way, it seemed to her.

By the time the sun was high over the dykes, the stew was ready. Monique used a ladle to pour a bowl for her mother and herself, then sliced some of the bread made the night before and set the table. She got another wooden bowl and scooped some to bring to Father

Allain. The two women ate quickly, then walked over to his tiny cabin and knocked on the door. He answered and extended an invitation to come in and rest for a few moments.

"Monique and Louise, it is delightful to have a visit from you! And thank you kindly for this wonderful food," he exclaimed happily. He took the stew offered to him, and found a small metal spoon. The three of them sat in his kitchen at a small pine table that wobbled as he stirred the stew to cool it down.

"This is the best *poulet fricot* I have had in a very long time," he said.

"You need your strength, Father Siméon Allain," said Louise in a self-satisfied tone. She rarely used his first name, and it was an indication to Monique that she was truly concerned about his wellbeing.

"Are you ready for your wedding, *mon petit chou*?" he asked Monique affectionately.

"Yes, Father Allain. I am nervous, though."

"Well, there is rarely a new bride or groom who is not. It is a big step you take before God and your parents, getting married. One should be nervous."

"Father Allain," said Louise, "Monique is a little worried about you, and I hope she does not mind that I speak on her behalf. Is everything all right?"

"No, it is not, Louise," Father Allain answered after thinking a moment. "Everything is not all right, and there is nothing to be done about it at this time. I hesitate to even speak of it, but I must ask that you pray for the Acadian priests who are encountering great difficulties. It has been described to me by my Mi'Kmaq brothers and sisters that they observe priests in many villages being dragged out of their churches and British flags raised over the rooftops. I do not know what it means for our parish, with our priest gone and the British colors flying. I have been asked to assist them by passing messages on to the Mi'Kmaq. I ask you not to speak to anyone else about our conversation, at least for now."

"Perhaps it would be helpful if you talk to François," said Louise.

"You are free to pass my concern on to him, but we must all keep our own counsel for the present, and be guided through prayer. In time, God's will is always made clear. He watches over the birds of the air, and the fish in the ocean. His loving hand created everything around us, and we all have a divine purpose to fulfill."

Awhile after, Monique and her mother walked back down the path toward their farm. They did not speak, and Monique wondered about what Father Allain had said but was fearful of upsetting her mother. Passing the church, Monique tried to avert her eyes. She stole several glances, enough to see that soldiers stood guard and marched back and forth in front of the gate. They could see nothing behind the tall wooden fence, and ocean breezes muffled the voices inside. All Monique could hear was the ominous flapping of the flag above the church.

When they were back at the farm, each woman took a side of the heavy soup cauldron and carried it back out to the fire to warm it before François would return for supper.

As Monique lingered in the kitchen afterward and hummed a hymn she liked to sing, she dropped her dishcloth. Smiling to herself, she picked it up and held it up to her cheek. According to Acadian tradition, dropping a dishcloth was an indication of a visitor. Perhaps the special visitor today would be Pierre.

She went to her bed and gathered up the wedding gown that Angeline had made. There was still a hem to be sewed into it, and she and her mother would work on it this afternoon. She took it to the kitchen, placed it on the loom, and got thread and needle to begin the handiwork.

When her father returned from the fields, the three Mélansons sat down at the table together. Louise served more of the hot and delicious *poulet fricot,* and while it cooled Monique's father talked about the barrels of apples that would have to be picked up in a hay wagon tomorrow. He said the corn was nearly in, and he was glad the rain had stopped. Louise told François that she and Monique had taken stew over to Father Allain earlier, and that Monique had been concerned about his health.

"I asked if he was troubled and he confided to us that he was worried about the parish priests. Why do you suppose he said that? Are they being harmed?"

"I do not know for certain," answered François, "but there has been some talk that all the priests of Acadie were taken prisoner by the government. Some say they are on Ile George. I believe that the only reason they are allowing Father Allain to remain is so they can use him to convey messages to the Mi'Kmaq and warn them to stay away.

"Listen, we have had our problems with those who have governed us for the past forty years, since the treaty that gave Acadie to the British. I trust our leaders, including our Uncle René LeBlanc, to continue using diplomacy to solve any disagreements. Your uncle knows those who govern, and they trust him. He and the elders have told them many times we are just simple farmers who want to stay out of the business of government. Uncle René and others have assured them that we will not take up arms against the British, and that we wish to remain true to our promise to be neutral in all matters between Britain and France. As a matter of fact, Uncle René knows

Colonel John Winslow quite well. If he is concerned, he will tell us when he visits, and he will certainly be able to give us the latest news. Oh, speaking of news, they have posted a notice that we are to meet at the church tomorrow at three o'clock for an announcement."

"Yes, François, Father Allain did say they were expecting him to relay messages to the Mi'Kmaq. And he also mentioned just yesterday that there will be an announcement," recalled Louise. "Should we be concerned about this?"

"I see no need," responded François. "There are no Acadians from here who have been disloyal to our promise to remain neutral. I heard of one man from Piziquid who went to fight at Louisburg, but I did not know him personally. I also heard somewhere that a ship from France went down in the Atlantic Ocean and scalping knives were found onboard. I do not know of any in our villages who would be capable of scalping even a fly! So . . . do not worry, and let us say grace now."

The family of three bowed their heads and joined in a prayer for the priests of Acadie. They also added a prayer that Father Allain's anxiety would diminish by tomorrow once the announcement was made. "And Lord, we are filled with love and gratitude for Father Allain who will give the marriage ceremony tomorrow. We are thankful you have given him the strength to overcome great obstacles in his life. We ask your blessing on our prayer, Amen."

Monique and Louise looked at each other, both wondering who would ask the question.

"To what obstacles are you referring, Father?" Monique asked sweetly as she blew on her stew to cool it down.

"I must be more careful," answered her father. "I promised him I would never divulge this information. Just know that Father Allain has withstood great trials, and I pray that his most bitter ones are now over. Perhaps I should have kept this prayer to myself, for now I have made you and your mother curious about it. However, I must be true to the promise I made to him never to betray his confidence."

"Yes, you must," responded Louise. "Monique?"

"Yes, Mama?"

"Do not press your father anymore. If Father Allain chooses to talk to us about it, he has already indicated that he will decide the time."

"Yes, Mama." Monique looked down at her lap.

"My dear daughter," said her father, "I can say this about it. Father Allain told me things that would cause both you and your mother great heartache, and he implored me to keep them to myself."

Monique could see in her father's expression that he too suffered for knowing. She took some comfort in the fact that Father Allain had trusted her father and he would be true to that trust. She also liked it that he treated her as a woman and not as a child.

A knock at the door brought her thoughts back to earlier when she had dropped the dishcloth. She jumped up to open the narrow wooden door of their house, and then peeked through the opening in an effort to keep out the chilly air of early evening.

"Monique, hello, it's me," said the familiar male voice on the other side. She welcomed Pierre in and beckoned for him to sit at the table. Monique watched as Pierre sat down and shyly searched for something to say. She continued to gaze at him, wishing she could sit closer, trying to break the awkward silence herself but unwilling to attract attention to her face. She reached up to see if it was heated on the outside as well as the inside.

"Monsieur Mélanson," Pierre said after a long silence, "the apples are juicy this year."

"Yes, Pierre, it is a very good year for juicy apples," responded François. The table fell silent again.

"Madame Mélanson," said Pierre after a few more moments, "my mother saw you and Monique go toward Father Allain's camp today. She was going to invite you to come to our house but you seemed in a hurry."

"We were," replied Louise. "We were taking warm *poulet fricot* over to him."

"And how is he today?"

"He is fine," Monique answered, smiling shyly at Pierre.

"Would you like some bread, Pierre?" asked Louise.

"Yes, please."

Louise rose from the table and sliced several pieces of bread, bringing them over and placing them in front of Pierre. While he looked longingly at the food in front of him, Monique quickly scooped up her wedding dress and ran from the kitchen, swiftly tossing the beaded curtain back and laying the dress out carefully on her bed.

When she returned a moment later, her mother had placed a bottle filled with molasses beside the bread she had offered Pierre. He picked up one slice and drew in a deep breath to take in the smell of it. Monique quietly giggled at this quirk of his she'd seen several times before, then watched him pour molasses on it and take a bite. He closed his eyes as though he hadn't eaten for weeks, his dimpled chin dripping with the molasses that was pouring down from the bread. Some landed on his shirt, but he did not notice.

"Delicious!" he exclaimed. "You are a wonderful cook, Madame Mélanson."

Monique noticed that Louise smiled at her future son-in-law with love in her eyes.

"Actually," she said proudly, "Monique baked this bread. " She offered Pierre another slice of bread and he accepted happily, smiling at Monique.

"Where is your Papa this evening?" asked François. "I told him that the Notary Public would be coming over to seal the marriage papers."

"He was chopping wood when I left. He and I are trying to get as much chopped as we can so it will have time to dry out before winter. I offered to help him but he said to run along and tell you he would be here presently." Pierre grinned at Monique, the sticky syrup residue from the bread glistening off his lower lip. He licked it, and Monique felt herself blush. She glanced down at her hands in her lap.

Another knock at the door was a welcome excuse for her to leave the table for a moment and get another breath of fresh air.

"Hello, my friends," said Jean Doucet, bursting in the door and immediately commanding attention from everyone present. A tall and heavy-set man, he bent over slightly when he entered, placing a kiss on Monique's cheek. Passing Pierre's chair, he planted a hearty slap on his son's back.

"You just had your supper, young man! Where do you put the food? Monique, I am glad you love to cook, because you have lots of work ahead of you."

Jean took a large chair that was off to the side of the room and slid it next to François. Monique noticed that the two older men were almost immediately involved in a serious conversation that she could barely hear. She heard the words "summons" and "tomorrow." Louise had gone to get water from the well, and Pierre beckoned to Monique to join him on a bench outside the door.

As soon as they sat down, he sneaked in a quick kiss on the lips of his bride-to-be. His lips were warm and still sweet from the molasses. When he whispered that she looked pretty tonight, his words and his breath were sweet also. They held hands as they looked out toward the Basin, where the night moon shimmered off the water. He brushed his thumb lightly over the palm of her hand, and his touch sent a sensation of excitement through her. She longed for more time alone with him, to feel his body against hers.

"Pierre," said Monique, "remember the night we danced together all evening when we first met?"

"I remember the day we met. It was when you were picking blueberries," he answered.

"No, that was a few years ago. This was one night last fall, when you invited me to the harvest festival."

"I do not recall that night," Pierre said, looking puzzled.

"Pierre! Remember you asked Michel to play a song and we danced, then we sneaked away outside to look at the stars? I could hear the waves against the shore. When I got a chill, you put your arm around me. Oh, Pierre, it was such a beautiful night, how could you forget? You must recall how you pointed to your house and told me that we could sleep in the *garçonierre* together after we were married? And you spoke about *les platins*, the mudflats, how they glistened in the moonlight. That was the night when you first told me that you loved me!"

"Oh, *les platins!* Yes, of course I remember now. Actually, I have been spending many hours in the *garçonierre,* cleaning it and building . . ."

"Building what?" she asked.

"I wanted it to be a surprise for you, but now my embarrassment is making me talk too much. I will not tell you any more about how I have prepared it for us!"

"Pierre! Please tell me."

"No, Monique. It will spoil the surprise."

"Very well. Let us talk about the harvest festival this year. I would very much like you to escort me to it as your new bride," said Monique.

Pierre knelt down in front of her. "Monique Mélanson, soon to be Monique Doucet, would you kindly accompany me to the harvest dance?"

"Yes!" she exclaimed, wrapping her arms around his neck. "This is another beautiful night, Pierre, the night before our wedding."

"Yes, the waters are calm tonight," he commented as he moved to sit back down beside her. "Last night it was not so, and neither was it one night last week. I saw the phantom ship right over there on the high tide." Pierre pointed toward the bluffs.

"You did?" She knew the legend well, although nobody she knew had ever actually seen it.

"Yes, I really did, I swear!" It was over there to the northeast, near Gros Ile. I was down on the beach that night swimming at high tide and I saw the ship burning brightly. I could hear sounds coming from it too."

"What sounds?"

"People crying in grave pain, just like others have claimed to hear."

"Were you alone?" She shivered at the thought of it.

"Yes. When I looked around to see if anyone else was present to witness it, I turned back to look at it again and it had vanished, just like this." Pierre snapped his fingers. "It was right out there."

Monique followed where his finger pointed. There was nothing but darkness and yellow moonlight across the Minas Basin.

Chapter 10

La Préparation

A few minutes later, Monique heard a rustling sound out by the road. She gripped Pierre's arm.

"What is it?" asked Pierre.

"Can you hear something?" Her momentary nervousness changed to joy when she recognized the familiar silhouette. "Uncle René," she called out affectionately to the Notary Public. Her hand still holding Pierre's, she pulled him up to come and help her elderly uncle with the papers that were slipping from underneath his arm. The two young people accompanied the old man to the door, and Pierre opened it for him.

"Come in, come in, Uncle René," beckoned François, who had heard the commotion. He moved a chair to the head of the table. Monique's mother entered and after kissing Uncle René's cheek, she quickly left again with a smile to her husband and a promise she would be right back. François nodded his understanding.

The group made small talk about the weather being good for harvest. René LeBlanc set the papers on the table to get them ready for the required signatures. The others watched him, remaining quiet out of respect for the Notary Public's duties. A knock at the door caused François to excuse himself from the table and open it for his wife, who struggled to push a small wheel barrow over the threshold and into the kitchen. It held a large jug of ale, and François wheeled it toward the table, lifting off the heavy jug while Louise took down the ceramic mugs. Monique knew it was a special night, because the ceramic mugs sent from France were rarely used. Her father proudly announced that the batch they'd made this time was a tasty one, and ale was poured for all, including a small taste for Monique and Pierre so that they too could participate in a grand toast to their wedding.

"To the wedding of our children tomorrow," said François, and he and Jean joyfully clinked mugs together. Jean drank his down rapidly, then lifted the heavy jug again to pour another. His tanned biceps flexed as he held it aloft for François to replenish his as well.

He was greatly admired for the muscles he had retained after forty years as a blacksmith, and he beamed with pride whenever his strength was mentioned.

Papers were signed, and the Notary Public affixed his seal, setting them aside to dry. He then addressed the young couple seated next to him.

"Father Allain will marry you children tomorrow afternoon," he said solemnly. "He is a good missionary and a man filled with the Holy Spirit. We must offer up prayers for Father Chauvreulx, however, and pray that Father Allain remains safely with us."

"Uncle René, Monique and I took *poulet fricot* to Father Allain today and he talked to us a little bit about that. What did happen to Father Chauvreulx?" asked Louise.

René LeBlanc's face fell, a look of indignation replacing the joy that had been there a moment before. "When the soldiers were billeted into our homes," he said, "one of them stayed at the rectory with Father Chauvreulx. Father Allain, thankfully, was with him at that time. Father Chauvreulx, according to Father Allain, took the conditional oath of allegiance to the British Crown many years ago, yet they did not trust him because he performed sacraments for some Acadians who fought over at Louisburg. They captured him, and at the time, Father Allain was in danger of being captured also. A soldier who had made his acquaintance took the commander aside and declared that Father Allain was neither a priest nor a missionary and had not taken part in those ceremonies. Luckily, at the time, Father Allain was assisting with a barn building and was dressed just as you or I." Uncle René paused to take a sip of ale. "I believe Father Chauvreulx expressed unhappiness about the British flags flying on our churches," he continued. "As a result, they carted him off like a common criminal."

The Notary Public scratched a long, fading scar on his face, one that had many times accompanied the story of his capture by the Mi'kmaq a few years before. They had staged an attack against the British at Minas, and René had spent several years in grim conditions.

René glanced from one person to another at the table, his expression very serious and his voice low. "Please keep our conversation from others in the village," he said. "I fear for Father Allain. They may mistrust him as time goes on because he is fluent in Mi'Kmaq. His seminary teacher was Father Maillard, did you know that? Do you remember when Father Maillard visited our parish and delivered several homilies?"

"Yes," answered François. "I recall a service of worship at which Father Maillard preached about the perils of trading brandy to our Mi'Kmaq brothers, because of the immorality of it. I think it was around the year 1748."

"Yes," nodded René. "Father Maillard learned Mi'Kmaq while living among them for many years. He created a Mi'Kmaq alphabet and has since then published some books in Mi'Kmaq. The British suspect him of assisting in Mi'Kmaq raids against them, although Father Allain does not think it is true and neither do I. Regardless of what is true, Father Maillard has been captured also and is now a prisoner on Ile George. The British are very afraid of the Mi'Kmaq, because the French from our mother country are trying to use them to war against the British. I have heard that a few months ago a French military ship sank in the Atlantic, and hundreds of scalping knives were found amongst the wreckage. Some say the knives were meant for the Chief in Shubenakadie, and for Beausoleil Broussard. I do not know if this is true or not. It is often difficult to know what to believe. However, I do know that none of us is capable of such violence."

"Do you think the announcement tomorrow will be about our priests being returned?" asked François.

"I do not know," answered René. "Colonel Winslow has given no indication of that. I did inquire as to why they have built the wooden fortifications, and he said it was to protect themselves from the harsh weather. They certainly cannot be here to harm us, since they have previously removed all our arms from our homes. But there has been so much political strain, everyone vying for our lands and our allegiances."

Jean pounded his fist on the table, startling everyone. "My musket was taken away," he shouted loudly, "and I am very angry at these British-led troops who try to intimidate us. Must we always look for reasons?" he bellowed, his large arms now flailing wildly around the heads of those sitting next to him. "Is might indeed the right of the strongest?"

"Father," admonished Pierre.

"I've seen men exert power over one another unjustly many times in my life," agreed René. "That is why we must trust in the Lord to be just. We have tried throughout the years to conduct our business fairly and with diplomacy. We have also kept our Catholic faith. If we continue to stand steadfast to our promise to remain neutral during times of war between the French and English, we should not have anything to fear."

"There is something I do not understand," said Pierre. "When Acadie was given back to the British back in 1713, why did our leaders insist on having a conditional oath of allegiance instead of an unconditional one? What is the difference?"

"That is a very good question, my son," answered René. "I do not think many younger people understand this. An unconditional oath of allegiance would have meant that we would be obligated to bear arms for the British in times of war. Young Acadiens such as you would have been recruited to fight the British wars. We felt that it was the will of God that we remain steadfast in our friendship with our brothers the Mi'Kmaq and true to our connection with the mother country, short of taking up arms for France. So we agreed to a conditional oath, which committed us to remaining neutral in any conflicts like the ones that are going on during the present days. We have remained true to our promise, to our friendship with the Mi'Kmaq, and to our faith."

Expressing a talent he had honed for many, many years, René LeBlanc began to sing softly and soothingly in a tenor that age and wisdom had only enhanced:

> *C'est Dieu le createur*
> *Qui decid le destin*
> *De ceux qui sont pecheurs,*
> *Et qui devienn'nt marins.*
> *C'est lui qui commande*
> *Dans les entrailles amies,*
> *Cinq hommes en ce monde,*
> *Pecheurs de Sormany.*

The cherry wood table around which the family of Acadians was congregated now felt to Monique as sacred as the sanctuary of the church they were being denied. She felt the blessing of the Virgin Mary on them, and when she looked at Uncle René, he exuded a glow of holiness she had witnessed before a few times. All eyes were on him lovingly, as though each word he sang reached down into their souls.

Afterward, the silence was broken when Louise searched in her apron pocket for a handkerchief and dotted tears from her eyes.

"Thank you, Uncle René," she said, crossing herself.

"You are welcome my dear Louise. And now, to complete the business at hand," he stated, turning his attention back to the papers. "The seal is now dry, and the dowry is, as you wished, set at two horses, a cow, and one hundred pieces of silver."

"I am giving you Pauline, my milking cow," said François to Pierre.

"*Merci*, Monsieur Mélanson. Monique and I will treat Pauline well."

"And now," said the Notary Public, "I must depart." He took a final sip of ale and made a strange face as he rose from the bench.

"What is it?" asked Louise. "Do you not like the taste?"

"The ale is delicious," he said. "It is my arthritis that is disagreeable."

"I have herbs to help. Do not leave yet, *mon cher*; I will get them." Louise rose from the table. "Perhaps while you wait you will search the archives of your memory for a story about a new bride and groom."

"Oh, now let me see," said the Notary, a pensive expression on his face. "I cannot think of one at the moment."

"I know one," said Monique, raising her hand. The group turned toward her nearly simultaneously, and she was immediately embarrassed.

"Monique, have you had more ale than the portion you were given?" asked her mother suspiciously.

"No, Mama, I have not," she replied in an offended tone. "I, as the new bride, feel it is my turn to tell a story, that is all."

"Please tell us then, and accept my apology for accusing you of taking more ale," said Louise.

"Very well," she began.

Once there was a young and beautiful girl named Catherine who lived in a small parish just like this one. The girl was very faithful to her church, and boys would come to Mass just to see her. Many of them hoped to be the one she would choose to marry, but all were disappointed when she turned them down. Her reason was that she wanted to become a Sister of Mercy.

Early one morning she was coming home from Mass and a thunderstorm came up suddenly. The lightning snapped a huge branch from a tree above her, which landed on her leg. It did not hurt her but she was stuck, unable to move an inch. She sat there and grew increasingly fearful that nobody would find her. Twilight came, and she knew the wolves would be coming out to seek food. Surely she would be attacked and eaten. A big wolf then appeared from behind a spruce tree.

"Please do not eat me," she begged.

"I will not, if you promise to marry me," he answered.

"But how can I marry a wolf?" she asked.

"Would it not be better than being my supper?" he reasoned.

"Yes, it would, except I have made a vow to the stars tonight that I will enter the convent tomorrow if I am allowed to live," she cried, tears streaming down her cheeks.

"Well," replied the wolf with a devilish grin, "I will give you a moment to pray for the stars to reconsider your destiny." He then moved a bit closer and licked her wooden clogs.

"I will marry you," she said, immediately after hearing his teeth click against her shoe. Instantly, the wolf changed into a very handsome and strong young woodsman with a broad smile on his face. His muscles rippled as he lifted the branch away effortlessly and carried her back to her parish. On the way, she wrapped her arms around his neck and snuggled close to him for warmth from the brisk

wind that rustled through the trees. She silently thanked the stars above for granting her this new destiny.

Monique was pleased and relieved when all those seated around the table burst into applause.

"Monique," exclaimed her mother, "wherever did you hear that tale?"

"I don't know."

"I have to admit, that is one even I have never heard before," said Uncle René. "And you, just as the young woman in the story you told, have as your destiny a life with a strong and handsome young man who will take care of you."

Pierre smiled and looked at François. "I will take very good care of Monique," he said proudly.

"How did you meet each other?" asked René. He sat down on the bench again, nodding in response to Jean's unspoken offer of a fresh mug of ale.

"I first saw Pierre in le Canard one day when my aunt invited Mama and me over to pick blueberries," she said. "We sailed across to le Canard where we met Pierre's father, who took us on a hay wagon to where the women were. I was so happy to go with them! I seldom get the chance to go all the way to le Canard. I began picking the blueberry bushes along la Riviere des Vieux Habitants with my cousin Mariette. I remember Aunt Cecile and Mama being just a short distance from us. I wanted to spend time with Mariette before she was sent to Port Royal to live with the nuns for several months."

The group smiled and nodded their understanding of what Monique was telling them. Everyone had heard that Mariette's parents had sought the help of the church for their daughter's incorrigible behavior, and she had been sent to Annapolis, to a boarding school run by the Order of St. Ursula.

"Mariette and I noticed the men repairing an *aboiteau* just below us," Monique continued. "There were, oh, perhaps eight of them working there, and I watched as they built it higher and higher, and very wide. By the time they were finished the tide was nearly half way up the *aboiteau*, and a boy dove down into the water to check something . . ."

"The sluice," said Pierre. Monique smiled at him warmly, then continued

"This boy, who was Pierre of course, stayed down so long that the men began to shout loudly, especially Jean, who was there also."

"I was just trying to see if the clapper valve was working properly," explained Pierre.

"I saw Jean tear off his shirt and dive into the water, then come up several times," continued Monique. "The men grew frantic, several more diving in. Mariette and I were very afraid the boy had drowned, and we held hands helplessly and prayed! Just then, we saw his head pop out of the water. He was winded, but not struggling for air as you would expect. The men embraced him, particularly Jean." Monique reached up and stroked Pierre's face tenderly, causing him to blush in front of the other men. Jean placed a large arm around his son.

"I remember it as though it happened yesterday," he said. "Now, I do not get frightened if he is under the water for a couple of minutes. He is the best in Acadie for staying under and checking for problems."

Pierre joined in with the story. "It was a good day for me. On the way home in the wagon, the others congratulated me, and a pretty girl sat beside me, her dear little cousin resting her head on her lap. Mariette had fallen asleep, and Monique and I had a chance to talk to each other." This memory caused everyone present to laugh, especially when Pierre added affectionately, "She is a dear when she's asleep."

"She is," agreed Monique. "So that is the first time I saw Pierre, and I have loved him ever since." She leaned closer to him and grasped his arm affectionately.

"Well, I have had a wonderful time with you, my friends," Uncle René said as he rose from his chair slowly, "but it is time for these weary bones to get some rest." Louise jumped up quickly to fetch him some herbs from the cellar, then escorted him out to the path. She stood in the cool night air, wrapped in a shawl and watching René's labored walk down the road. Gazing up into the starry sky, she whispered a short prayer that he would safely arrive home for the night.

The wooden fence around the churchyard was now dark except for a flickering light through the wooden fence and the smell of tobacco smoke. Several soldiers stood guard outside the gate and Louise strained to hear their conversation, but a rustle distracted her.

"Mama." Monique spoke softly, linking her arm in her mother's. "It has been a wonderful evening." The two women strolled toward the large willow tree to sit at their favorite spot and gaze at the stars one more time before bed.

Back inside the house, Jean and Pierre assisted François with picking up the ale mugs.

"Your apple barrels are quickly filling," said Jean.

"Yes," replied François, "it is a good harvest this year and there will be plenty to feed our guests tomorrow. And soon, *patés des pommes!*"

"My son," François teased as he placed a hand on Pierre's shoulder, "will you and Monique give us a grandchild or two? I am growing older, and someday I would like to sit at the beach and watch my grandchild play in the water. Perhaps he will become as fine a swimmer as yourself."

"I desire that also, François," said Pierre.

"I have said that we can have the village men reconstruct the shop into a bigger house if they have a large brood," said Jean as he laughed heartily. "Regardless, it will be nice to have a woman in the house again."

"Isobel, God rest her soul, was a good woman, Jean," said François sympathetically. "But we would not wish her to be here now, as sick as she was at the end."

"My darling Isobel, may she rest in peace. She would be so happy to see Pierre marry Monique. She baked such delicious bread! Pierre, when he was a young boy, would hold it to his nose and breathe in the fresh-baked aroma, and she would laugh with such pride. And the dances, she loved the dances. I will teach our grandchildren how to dance to Michel's fiddle in her honor!" he said as he began to dance a jig right there in the kitchen.

"Come on, Papa," said Pierre as he shook his head and pulled on his father's arm. "It is time for me to take you home so you can sleep off your ale consumption." Jean gave his son a hearty slap on the shoulder and extended a large hand to his friend François, who shook it affectionately. He quickly grabbed his son's arm for balance when he nearly lost his footing. "I guess it is time I go home to bed!" he roared with laughter. "François, my friend, we will have much to celebrate tomorrow, for Isobel, for you and me and your wonderful Louise, and for all our relatives and neighbors!"

Chapter 11

Acadia University

Thursday, August 25

Back in the dorm it was 10:30 P.M., and André was feeling that old familiar disappointment. His luck with women hadn't been good since Lauri, and Monique hadn't called. He sat on his bed feeling stupid. It was a bad idea to come back from New Brunswick this month, he thought. He had been bored there, but things were not better here. Probably he should have looked for an apartment by now instead of coming back to the dorm. He hated the phones here. Why did he always read women wrong?

He got up and walked out into the hallway. Triggs, a math major everyone went to for help, was standing there reading the *New York Times*.

"Hey Triggs," said André, "you didn't happen to answer the phone tonight, did you?"

"Um, let me think. Yeah, actually I did," he said finally.

"Did somebody call and ask for me?"

"Um . . . hmm . . . I'm trying to remember," said Triggs. "Was that last night or tonight? Oh yeah, it was tonight, 'cause I was on my way to the library to study for my calculus exam. Then the phone rang so I put down my books . . ."

"Who was it?" asked André. He waited until Triggs finished reading and glanced back up from his newspaper. The only response was a blank look.

"Who was it?" he repeated.

"A girl," Triggs finally answered, gesturing with his index finger.

"Triggs, help me here, please. What did she want?"

Triggs folded the paper, wrestling with the pages that wouldn't fold correctly. When he was done, he placed it on a small table beside him. "She just asked if you were here, and I said you were out with Lauri."

"No way!" said André.

Triggs looked puzzled. "Yes," he said, "it was definitely a female voice . . . why? Oh, sorry, did I screw up?"

"Big time," replied André. "Didn't you know I broke up with Lauri?"

"No, man, nobody told me," said Triggs, developing a whine he always had when he felt left out. "I'm really sorry, nobody told me. Maybe her number is on the . . ."

Triggs continued to whine apologies as André ran at breakneck speed down the hall. He waved back to his dormmate that he wasn't mad and nearly tripped over his own feet going down three flights of stairs to the ground floor exit door. Out in the parking lot he jumped in his car and sped down through Main Street. The sight of a police car coming up behind him made him apply the brakes so he wouldn't get pulled over, and he stepped on the gas again after the police car turned. He raced toward Blomidon Cottages and roared into the small parking lot. He knocked on Monique's door four times, but there was no answer. Only one small light was on, and it was too dark to see into the bedroom.

He ran to the office to get Bill, but he was not behind the desk. Back in his car, André drove up and down the street, hoping he would find Monique going for a walk. Stopping again at the cottages, he knocked on the door and called out Monique's name. The office door was open and André could see through the screen door that Bill was back behind the desk. André called in to ask if he had an extra key to the cottage.

"You can't do that," said Bill. "You'd be invading a guest's privacy."

"I just need to know that she's there. I promised her brother-in-law I'd take care of her. I was supposed to go to the park with her tonight but when she called the dorm, one of the guys . . . stupid Triggs! Just let me look and see if she's there. I don't even care if she's mad. I'll explain . . ."

"Relax, man. Let's go knock on her door again."

The two men walked toward the cottage and Bill knocked on the door. André called out Monique's name, but there was no answer. "I'm going to the park. I'll be back," he said to his friend as he ran to his car. In Grand-Pré the park was closed, and there was no sign of anyone on the grounds.

"Damn," he muttered to himself, "damn, where is she?" A rolled up paper drifted across the lawn, and he bent over to pick it up. As he unrolled it, a feeling of fear swept up his back. It was the program from this afternoon's art appreciation class. He ran back through the park to the parking lot, then raced his car back up through the winding back roads to Blomidon Cottages. Pulling up right in front of the office he ran in through the screen door that slammed behind him.

"Bill," he said as he panted for breath, "call the taxi place and see if they picked her up." Bill hesitated. "Please, call now!" he demanded. Bill shook his head. "You're pissing me off, pal. She was here, at your cottages, and now I can't find her anywhere. And I found this, which means she was there. This is the program from my art appreciation class this afternoon. I found it at the park."

"So?"

"Don't you think in some way you're accountable for her whereabouts?"

"Well, you know, André," said Bill sarcastically, "she is a grown-up."

André heard his friend still mumbling as he stormed out of the office. He raced down the street to the tiny "Annapolis Taxi" office wedged between two restaurants. Inside, he had to wait in line behind two people who did not seem to have the correct address for where they were going and had to make a call.

"Where you goin'?" a middle-aged man at the counter finally asked him.

"No . . . nowhere," replied André. "Did anybody pick up a girl who's staying at Blomidon Cottages? Her name's Monique LeBlanc."

"What's the matter?" another younger man asked, picking up on the urgency in André's voice.

"Well, Smitty," the man behind the counter said, "this guy is asking about a run we made tonight. We got a call from Blomidon Cottages, from a girl who needed a ride to Grand-Pré Park. It's right here in the book, at 9:30 P.M. Her friend here says he can't find her. Jack was supposed to go back and get her but there's no record that he made the return pick-up."

"Let's get Jack out here and see what he says—OK, Frank?" said Smitty.

"OK, Boss," replied Frank, who called out back and told someone that he was needed out front right away.

"My name's Dave Smith, but you can call me Smitty, since everybody else does," he said as he reached out to shake hands with André. A door in back of the counter opened, and a scrawny older man with a wrinkled face came out holding a cup of coffee in his hand. A cigarette dangled from his mouth.

"Hi, I'm Jack," he said, his leathery hand extended to André, who shook it absently. Jack took the cigarette from his mouth and stuck it in an empty soda can on the counter. "It was me that picked that girl up. I drove 'er down to Grand-Pré Park. A real nice girl, said she's from Loosiana and visitin' here for a couple days. I told her my wife has cancer an' all . . . she said she was real sorry. Said her mother died of cancer. She asked me to come back an' pick 'er up in a half an hour but when I do, she ain't around. I got out an' walked around . . . just in case . . . called her name . . . whistled like this . . ." Jack put two fingers in his mouth and emitted a deafening whistle, then smiled proudly. "Ain't too many people who can't hear that."

"Why didn't you report that she was missing?" asked André.

"Well . . . 'cause . . . well I told 'er I didn't like leavin' 'er alone at night . . . but college women . . . they can be right independent and I didn't want to insult 'er. Like my niece, Cindy . . . same age . . . smart as a whip . . . she comes over an' helps my wife when I'm workin', on account of her cancer . . . she can't do much these days . . ."

"Jack," said André, "please think . . . did you see anything suspicious when you went back?"

"Nothin' at all. I waited in the taxi a few more minutes, then gave one more whistle." Jack lifted his fingers for another demonstration, but was directed by his boss to hold off. He thought for a second, then continued. "By then I had another run so had to go."

"Call the cottages again and see if she came back," said Smitty, "and if she didn't we probably should notify the police."

André called Bill, apologized for snapping at him, and asked if he'd heard from Monique. Bill had just gotten back from checking her cottage again and said she still wasn't there. André left for the cottages while Smitty called the police. When André joined Bill, they went back into her cottage again, and this time André noticed an open phone book. When he scanned down the page he saw "Taxis." There was a card by the phone, the name of a professor David Broussard in Louisiana, and on the other side was André's name and number on the piece of paper he'd given to her earlier.

Within minutes, an officer arrived and André followed him back to the taxi place.

"Hello, Officer Pete," said Jack, who proceeded to tell the policeman what had happened. "I ain't in trouble, am I?" he asked.

"No Jack, you're not in trouble. But we will have to get a written report from you and from André. We'll need to know what she was wearing when you dropped her off. And we can try to get DNA from the paper she dropped. Of course, yours should be on it too. Just set it on the counter and I'll get something to place it in."

André paced nervously. "I was supposed to bring her there tonight. This is all my fault. If I had a damn cell phone she could have called me instead of a taxi."

"Look here, young feller," said Jack to André. "Don't think I don't feel guilty too. I drove away from there and I was wond'rin' all the way what happened to 'er. I even called my wife when I got back here to tell her about it. I've been drivin' taxi for nearly forty years . . . wait, has it been that long . . . gee wankers, it has! Anyways, it always makes me nervous when people aren't where they s'posed to be. She's a real nice girl and I hope . . . I mean . . . I'm sorry I didn't . . . ."

"It's OK, Jack," said the officer as he placed a hand on Jack's shoulder in an attempt to reassure him. He turned toward André. "I'm Sergeant Pete Williamson from the RCMP. We can't put an APB out on her yet because she's considered an adult. But I'll get more information from you in case she doesn't come back within forty-eight hours. And I would recommend you notify next-of-kin just to let them know what's going on."

"Oh, God," André moaned helplessly. "Her cousin Michelle . . . her husband Jacques is my cousin. They're in Halifax this week, performing at a festival, *Le Festival Acadien.* Damn . . . can we just look for her again before I call them?"

"I'd call now," said the officer firmly. "Then you and I can take another drive to Grand-Pré and do a search. I'll get a couple more cruisers down there right away."

André checked his watch. Eleven o'clock. He dialed the number and sat down. He'd been offered a seat at a desk covered in papers and leftover coffee cups, and he pushed them aside nervously.

"Hello?" said Jacques.

"Hi, Jacques," he said, clearing his throat to talk.

"What's up?" Jacques was happy to hear from his friend. "How are you and Monique getting along? You didn't get in an accident, did you?" André told him what had happened, and then held the phone away from his ear.

"She's what? What the Hell? That's not funny, André."

"I wish I was kidding. The RCMP is here and we're going back to look for her again. Believe me, I'm going to look all night until I find her. Not much crime happens around here, so she's probably all right, OK? Maybe she walked down to the beach. I'll look there. I'll find her, don't worry."

"Oh my God, how'm I gonna break this to Michelle? She'll die. I'm not tellin' her yet. I'll call you back on your cell phone. Damn it! You don't have a damn cell phone! Call me back at midnight, on my cell phone, OK? And you better have good news!"

André said a quick good-bye, then rode with Sgt. Williamson back down to the park. When they pulled into the parking lot there were already two empty cruisers there. Sgt. Williamson and André met the officers inside the park grounds, but they had no news and said they had found no sign of foul play. André and the Sergeant went down to search the beach, and finding nothing they returned to the park grounds to check in with the other two officers again. They all stood by a large willow tree, updating each other.

"Anything besides the program André found earlier?" Williamson asked.

"Just one item," replied one of the officers. "We found this picture. Do you recognize this, André?"

André groaned and fought back nausea. "Monique showed me this picture of her mother this afternoon. She said her mother passed away a few years ago and she planned to bring this with her when we visited here tonight."

Chapter 12

Ciel D'automne

Friday, September 5, 1755

Under a clear blue autumn sky, Louise Mélanson stood on the small front porch of her farm, putting the finishing touches on the wedding decorations that she had made. She stopped to watch some fishing boats sailing toward shore on the incoming tide. The fragrance of sweet grass in the morning breezes struck her senses, and she paused to take in a few breaths. The sun shone brightly on Cape Blomidon, its cliffs reflected in the waters beneath. What a beautiful day, she thought.

She and Monique had completed the early morning chores of gathering eggs and milking cows, and then they had helped François to move barrels of apples off a cart that sat in the back yard. By noon the work had stopped, and the wedding was the only thing the two women were talking about as they prepared a meal together in the kitchen. Their excitement over the celebration was soon tempered by Louise's serious expression when Monique mentioned the beginning of her married life with Pierre in the *garçonierre* of his house.

"Monique," said her mother, "there is something . . . I would like to say to you about that."

"Yes, Mama. What is it?"

"Well, I would like to tell you some things about the marriage bed."

"Oh, Mama!" Monique felt herself flush with embarrassment, and raised her hand to her face.

"Yes, my dear, it is a very difficult subject to discuss, but very important. Are you not wondering what will happen tonight?"

"Yes, Mama. I try not to think about it, because there is so much I do not know."

"Then let me explain some things, the way my own mother told them to me the very day of my wedding. The love of a wife for her husband is expressed in many forms, and one of those is child-bearing. When a wife has marital relations with her husband, a child is very often the result. You have seen how Angeline is about to bear her first child. Often at night, in the marital bed, the husband has desires. It is the duty of the wife to allow him this, unless she is ill. If she is, she must tell him. As the man and woman lie together in bed, the man will get on top."

"On top of what?"

"On top of the woman."

"Oh."

"Yes. And it is considered proper for a woman to lie very still while her husband is on top of her."

"But Mama, how can anyone breathe with another person on top of them?"

"The husband is strong enough to support himself so that he does not crush her. The act also requires that he move, but again, the wife does not. This is how women of honor behave in the marital bed. Do you understand?"

"Yes, Mama. Mama?"

"Yes, Monique?"

"Angeline spoke of the man putting a private part of his body into his wife's body. She whispered it to me, and giggled so much when she said it that I could hardly understand what she was saying. It made me very afraid. Does it hurt?"

"The first few times perhaps, but not after awhile. And Monique."

"Yes, Mama?"

"A husband and wife get used to each other, and then it does not hurt at all. When a woman has a baby, there is pain, but the joy of motherhood makes the pain of labor very worthwhile."

"Thank-you Mama for this talk," said Monique. "May I go outside now?"

"In just a moment. I want to share with you something very personal, something my Aunt Matilde told me. I have told you before that Aunt Matilde lived in Paris and led a very interesting life. Shortly after I was married, I received a letter from her. I was not able to read it, but your Aunt Cecile found a teacher who sometimes read things for others. She agreed to come to Aunt Cecile's one day and I brought the letter there.

The teacher read it several times, so that we could all fully understand everything Aunt Matilde was trying to tell me. She said some things that were different than what my mother had told me, and I feel that this is the proper time for me to share them with you. I have preserved the letter in a secret place among my souvenirs, and will give these things to you someday."

Louise led her daughter to the table, beckoning for her to sit. The older woman sat down facing the younger one, and began to speak very softly. Monique noticed that her mother kept an eye on the closed door for a few moments. Then she began, looking intently at Monique.

"Aunt Matilde told me never to tell my mother that she had written the letter, and so you must promise to keep this a secret."

"I promise, Mama."

"Aunt Matilde talked about her life in Paris, and said that she had heard it was possible for a woman to find pleasure in marital relations. She had known of courtesans who gave as well as received pleasure in the act of . . . well, I am embarrassed to be telling you this."

"Go on, Mama."

"Aunt Matilde, you must understand, was bold in comparison to most women. She did not want to settle for life in the country, or staying with my mother and the rest of her family in the settlement here in Acadie. She craved the excitement of Paris, and soon became part of high society there. Her letter—oh, it smelled so wonderful when I first opened it—the French perfume! I remember breathing in the wonderful fragrance. She stated that with her new husband, she had allowed herself to move a little bit in the marriage bed, and that she found this very pleasurable. I was shocked when I read some other things she said, and cannot even speak of them! Perhaps when Mariette is older, I can give you the letter and you can have her read it. What I am saying is this: if in time, you discover that it is a pleasurable experience in the marital bed, do not think something is wrong with you. However, it is essential that you keep this knowledge to yourself, because it is considered dishonorable to have such feelings. Do you understand?"

"I am trying to, Mama, but truly, I do not. I am only feeling trepidation about Pierre and I . . . Mama, I have never even seen a man with no clothes on!"

"And that is as it should be. You have saved your body for your husband, and he for you. Marriage is about many aspects—love, caring for each other throughout your days and years until old age, and raising children together. And in your marriage vows you promise to keep yourself only for your husband for as long as you both live.

"May I ask you a question, Mama?"

"Why, yes."

"If bearing children is one of the duties of a married couple, why did you not have more children? I have often looked at my aunts and uncles, and the number of cousins they produced. Olivier has eleven sisters and brothers. Why is it I have none?"

"I did not ever speak of this to you before, because I feared you would feel somehow responsible. When I gave birth to you, I had great difficulty and . . . well, your father worried for several weeks that I would not survive. My mother had a similar affliction, and she knew some medicinal treatments that she administered to me. She gave birth to two children, your Uncle Jean-Baptiste and me, but she also lost two other *enfants*. This caused her much grief. She worked very hard to keep you cared for and give me the medicines I needed in those first few weeks of your life, and your father told me he shed some tears, fearing that he would lose us both. Your Papa and I have always been grateful that we were blessed with one healthy child. Come now, let us go outside together and see where your father is."

François was out back by the barn, checking the apples in his barrels again, more out of concern than pride. He had found two soldiers standing on the cart earlier, looking into the barrels. François had stood alongside Pauline as he put her out to pasture, and watched as the soldiers held up the apples and admired them, all the while speaking to each other in English. He had not enjoyed their appreciation of his crops, and had marched quickly toward them with the intention of asking what they were doing. They disappeared into the woods behind his property before he had the chance.

Several days ago, François noticed another soldier walking past his pasture with one of his comrades and commenting in English as he pointed to the livestock grazing in the pasture. The soldier had looked at the animals and patted his stomach, as though he were talking about what a good meal they would make. François saw the other soldier stop to write something down. He had heard that other Acadians were providing the troops with food from the harvest, but he was not inclined to offer anything. He had always saved his to share with his fellow villagers or his Mi'Kmaq friends, and unless he was told to do so he had no plans to give any away to these English-speaking soldiers.

Everywhere he looked these days, they were marching around. When they had first made their encampment, they mulled around the villages after dusk, but now they seemed to be restricted to daytime marches. He was glad this was the case. He had a wife and daughter to protect.

François' unpleasant thoughts were quickly replaced with the joy of hearing his wife's voice, calling him in to join them for a midday meal in the kitchen. Monique had sliced fresh bread, and there were quartered apples and cooked eggs to eat.

Relatives slowly began coming up the road to the farm on horse carts, chatting and carrying wedding gifts and baked sweets to add to the afternoon feast. François helped his cousin from Habitant as he untied his horse from the cart, then walked with him down to the fenced-in field. He opened the fence to let the horse roam free for the afternoon, and the two men walked back to the house.

Children began to cluster together and amuse themselves with games on the grass, running to the barrels to pick out juicy red apples to eat. When they saw the village fiddler, they ran toward him excitedly. Michel Boudro, a lanky young fisherman from the village, was also a welcome sight to François, who held out his arms to his young friend as he sauntered along the grass. He pulled his fiddle from under his arm, and when the children saw it they ran alongside him pleading for a jig.

Jean Doucet, dressed in woolen pants and vest and topped with a black brimmed hat, hurried up the path to join François and hear the music. He took out a handkerchief to mop beads of sweat from his brow, then shook hands with the bride's father. The three older men sat together on the small wooden porch watching with delight as children crowded near Michel excitedly, trying to get in step with the rhythm.

Before long, Jean rose from his chair on the porch. Peeling off his vest he soon picked up the beat until he was step-dancing on the wooden floor without noticing that he had an audience. Everyone had turned to watch him, and they began clapping in time. Jean's face grew redder and redder, and Michel laughed and played the song faster, stopping every few measures to allow Jean's clicking on the wooden floor to keep rhythm, then picking it up again until it ended abruptly, to everyone's sheer delight. There were loud cheers for Jean, who gave everyone a wave before lumbering breathlessly back to his chair again, sweat pouring off his forehead.

"Oh my," he sighed, "I am not young anymore!" Jean removed the handkerchief from his pocket and mopped his face again.

"At least you are still alive, my good friend," laughed François. "If I were to do that, I would be lying on the ground dead now." François pounded his chest for emphasis.

"I am certain you would not be. You still do heavy work in the orchards, lifting the large barrels onto wagons after the women pick the apples."

"No more than I can help," admitted François. "I supervise the younger men who have strong backs."

The men stopped their conversation and sat together listening to Michel play a local favorite, *Ciel d'automne*. Young and old paired together to dance as he played under an archway that was decorated with ribbons and beads. Michel had prepared a special piece for accompaniment at the moment when the bride and her father would walk forward together and stand here in front of Father Allain. He played a few notes of it for the father of the bride, and received a hearty pat on the back.

Down the road a short ways at Monique's and her mother's favorite spot, Pierre and his cousin Olivier sat on the bench by the willow tree. Olivier, his best man, lived at the next farm over from the Doucet men in Gaspereau, and his whole family except for his twin brother was here to attend the wedding. Pierre was jittery and began to complain of being hungry, and soon a young girl waiting for the opportunity to talk to Olivier brought over a basket containing bread. She offered Olivier a few slices along with a very pretty smile, and he accepted gratefully. Pierre was offered one as well and accepted. He smelled his and promptly ate it, while Olivier seemed to prefer conversing with the young lady and held his in his lap for the time being.

At Angeline's house, three of the bride's aunts were ceremoniously sliding the wedding gown over her head and down her body. They smoothed out the wrinkles, and everyone present gushed with sheer delight over her beauty. One cousin began pinning her hair up, and another powdered her face. Angeline, stretched out on a cot in the corner of the kitchen, lamented loudly about having to stay in bed today. She had been overdue for a week, and her midwife was insistent that she was to remain off her feet.

"Is it not bad enough I have to miss the wedding?" cried Angeline. "At least I should be able to see the bride in the wedding gown I sewed for her! You are all blocking my view!"

The circle of females immediately opened so that she could see Monique, causing Angeline to burst into tears, then suddenly grip her large belly as though she was about to die from the pain. With all eyes on her, she waved after a few moments to indicate that the pain had subsided.

"Be careful," cautioned the midwife. "You will knock the garlic off your stomach."

"It is doing no good," growled Angeline. "And I feel so silly holding it there."

"Do not worry about looking silly. It will help you to deliver."

The women made various attempts to offer kind and comforting remarks without saying the word "baby" or "labor" in front of the children. Their chatter was interrupted suddenly when the door opened with a bang and Monique's cousin, Mariette Trahan, burst in with a large bouquet of flowers.

"Here," she said to her older cousin as she handed them to her. "I picked them from the cemetery." The women gasped, and Monique flushed with embarrassment.

"Mariette," she scolded, "you are not allowed to pick flowers from the cemetery. How did you get in there? The soldiers guard the cemetery."

"I know, but I asked one of them in English if I could please go in and visit my grandmother's grave, and I guess he liked me because he let me in. And I cannot very well put them back now." There was no hint of apology in her tone, and she had already turned her attention to the saucer of garlic that balanced itself precariously on Angeline's extended belly.

"Are you having a baby today?" she asked, and more gasps came forth. "I've asked where they come out, but nobody has told me. Tell me, Monique, where do they come out?" When Monique froze in disbelief, Mariette continued. "If you don't know yet, you need to find out pretty soon!"

The room fell completely silent. Monique was shocked, then stifled a laugh when she looked around at the other faces, some stern, some stunned. "Sit still, Monique," cried her Aunt Cecile. "I am still trying to fix your hair." Monique tried, but she could not hold back, and burst into laughter, holding on to her sides helplessly. Seeing the bride laugh, others could not resist joining in, and the older women held their hands over their mouths as they too laughed. The younger ones followed suit when they perceived it would be acceptable to do so, and whispered to each other as they tried to understand what the joke had been. Tears of pained release flowed down Angeline's face and she rolled around awkwardly, trying to hold on to the saucer that threatened to slide off her belly.

"How old are you?" asked Angeline after she caught her breath.

"Ten," replied Mariette.

"Oh, dear, Oh my, Oh Lord," repeated Angeline, shaking her head back and forth until another labor pain caused her to cry out loudly again.

Monique decided it was time for Mariette to leave.

"I must take Mariette back to the farm," she said.

"In one moment," replied Madelaine. "I want to brush a bit of color on your beautiful, radiant skin. Does Monique not have the most wonderful complexion?" A chorus of affirmations came from the women present.

"It is lovely."

"Glowing."

"Beautiful as any in Acadie."

"She's a beautiful girl, Louise," said Angeline, causing Monique's Mama to beam with pride.

Monique rose, kissed both her mother and Angeline, then waved to the others and said she'd see them at the wedding. She led her young cousin by the hand out the door. Monique was certain that there would be gossip about how naughty her Trahan cousin had been. There always had been that gossip, as long as she could remember. Nobody understood her cousin as well as she did. She looked at Mariette's face, the face of a child whose mind was far ahead of anyone she had ever known. In time, Mariette would learn how to curb her own impulses better. Monique was quite certain of that.

She and Mariette talked quietly as they walked the short distance up the dirt road. Monique had lifted her dress so that the dirt and puddles in the road would not get the hem of her dress dirty, and Mariette reached out to help her with one side of it, placing the cemetery flowers in her other hand.

"Mariette," said Monique as she stepped gingerly along, "you look very pretty today. I am glad I chose you for my flower girl."

"Mama brushed my hair so much, my head hurts." The younger girl rubbed her skull and winced. "She says it had so many snarls she wondered if a squirrel lived there."

"Well, she certainly made it look nice. You have such lovely braids." Monique stopped to fix one of them that had become a little undone. Each one was adorned at the end with a bright yellow ribbon. "I think the boys will notice you this afternoon. Did your mother make your pretty apron?"

"Yes, she did, and I told her to put a pocket in it big enough to hold a book," said Mariette happily. "And look! When I stopped to see Father Allain, he was packing up some of his books in a crate and he gave this one to me from the St. Charles des Mines library. He said it was given to him by Father Chauvreulx." Mariette let go of Monique's bridal gown and reached into her pocket for the book, which she held up excitedly. Monique took it and looked at the cover. She had a momentary feeling of embarrassment that she could not read it very well.

"What is the title of it?"

"Father Allain said it is about religion and being a faithful Catholic," explained Mariette, who read the cover to her older cousin. "The author's first name is François, just like Uncle François, and his last name is spelled S-A-L-E-S." She pointed to each letter as she said it. "It is called *Introduction to the Devout Life*, and Father Allain said that François Sales was educated by the Jesuits, just like he was. Father Allain looked a bit sad when he gave it to me. He told me it was a special book for a special girl and that the book teaches love for God and other people, and hu . . . mil . . . humility. He said we can all become better Christians, with God's help." Mariette paused. "Monique," she said, "do you suppose that God thinks I'm a bad girl? Father Allain said today that he loves me and I should always remember that God loves me too. He said that he trusts me to take good care of this book and return it to him when I finish reading it."

"You are a very special girl, Mariette, and I love you too," said Monique. "And I believe that you will try with all your might to take care of the book. However, sometimes things happen that we do not expect, so I hope Father Allain will not be too disappointed if the book meets with unfortunate circumstances."

Monique had hardly gotten the words out when Mariette tripped over a branch sticking out of the ground and fell face-first into a mud puddle in the road. She stood up quickly, her dress dripping

with muddy water and splotches of mud. The cemetery flowers had
landed all over the road in front of her, and she scooped up the two
that were the least damaged. Monique expected her young cousin to
cry, but instead she quickly reached in to pull the book out of her
apron pocket, wiping the water off it with her sleeve.

"See, it is fine!"

"Oh, Mariette! I do not have time to take you home and get
new clothes for you."

"My dress will soon dry in the hot sun and I'll scrape the pieces
of mud off then. I am hungry though. When can we eat?"

"After the wedding, we will go into our kitchen. We have fresh
blueberry preserves waiting there, and many delicious loaves of bread
that have been brought to us today."

By now they were near the farm, and Monique could see that
relatives had already gathered in front of the farmhouse. She heard
her father announce the reminder that the men and boys over the age
of ten had been summoned to the church for an announcement at
three o'clock, after which they would promptly return and continue
the wedding celebration. He asked the women to kindly wait for them,
and jokingly added that they should not enter the kitchen to eat until
their return.

"My two girls," he announced with pride as Monique and
Mariette joined the family gathering. Monique wrapped an arm around
her father and kissed his cheek, and François gently touched Mariette
on her head.

"Can I go inside and eat?" whined Mariette. "I am so
hungry!"

"Well, we should wait," whispered Monique, hesitantly. She could
tell that Mariette did not seem to plan anything of the sort by the way
her cousin was inching her way toward the porch door.

Monique followed her. Food was spread everywhere on the
wooden kitchen table: loaves of bread, fresh blueberry preserves, a
small but delicious looking wheel of cheese which had been ordered
from New England, and salt pork. Fresh water stood in jugs, along
with ale for the men and fresh apple juice. Monique cut a slice of
bread for Mariette, then walked around the kitchen. She lingered for
some time on the sights and smells of the home she loved. A crucifix
nailed to the wall was a gift her father had made for her mother when
they were first married. In the middle of the driftwood cross was a
yellow stone, and she suddenly decided she would like to hold the
cross when the time came to say her wedding vows. She removed it
from the nail where it was hooked and held it to her heart, saying a
brief prayer for the Lord to bless her wedding.

When she and Mariette stepped back outside, Father Allain
was already standing in the spot under the archway where he would

administer the vows. Wrapped around his neck and descending down the front of his black robe was a long, colorful scarf made from beaded cloth, and Monique recognized it as Mi'Kmaq ceremonial attire. Father Allain smiled at her with all the love of a proud uncle.

Monique led Mariette down the grass a little ways, and her father quickly joined them. "There you are. It's time," said François as he motioned to Father Allain. With a nod from Father Allain, Michel began playing and the ceremony had begun. Monique and her father walked arm in arm to the rhythm of the lilting music, slowly moving toward the missionary priest. Mariette paraded in front of them smiling brightly and carrying her book and the two drooped flowers. François squeezed the arm of his daughter affectionately, and when she glanced at him she saw that his eyes were moist with tears. Pierre, Olivier, and Jean Doucet stood at their places in a half-circle, Father Allain in the middle.

When Monique reached Pierre, her father let go of her arm and gave Pierre a nod. Pierre held out his arm, which Monique linked in hers, and Michel took his cue to play more softly during the recitation of the marriage vows. Monique held the driftwood cross close to calm her nervousness. The ceremony was completed a few minutes later, and the groom finally kissed his bride after Father Allain pronounced them man and wife. Father Allain leaned forward to give her a quick embrace also.

Family members greeted the new couple and mingled outside and in the kitchen, enjoying the feast of breads, cheese, and homemade sweets that had been brought by the guests. Michel resumed his place on the lawn amidst the dancing and singing that drifted up into the village skies. After a few songs, François walked over to Michel to ask him to announce that they would have to leave for a few moments.

"I will be back shortly," said Pierre to Monique as the men and boys gathered to go to the church.

"I shall be waiting." She reluctantly let go of his hand and waved to him as he joined the others headed down the path. Monique turned back to the celebration that was continuing, now with a somewhat subdued tone.

She tried to keep her mind away from worrying about Pierre and the rest of the men by talking to many of her neighbors who had joined them for the wedding. Her friends and cousins helped to distract her from her worries with compliments on her gown, and how beautiful she looked today.

"Your hair, it is so silky this afternoon," said one of her cousins. "I love the way Angeline made your dress," said another. "Are you going to save it? Perhaps when I am wed I may borrow it."

"Perhaps," said Monique. "I will be placing it in my pine chest after today, and maybe . . ."

"They're not coming back," came the cry of a young boy who was hurrying up the path toward the farm. He stopped in front of one of the women and gasped, trying to get enough breath to talk. "Papa . . . sent me . . . back to tell you, Mama . . ."

"Tell me what?" asked his mother.

"Tell you . . . they are not allowed to leave the church."

"Oh, my dear Jacques, you must be mistaken. Where did you see Papa?"

"I knocked on the door, and then I tried to open it but it was locked. The soldier shouted, 'Whose boy is this?' Papa called out to me to tell you they are prisoners of the Crown."

"What does that mean?" They looked from one to another, stunned faces hoping for an answer.

Monique watched her mother leave the group and hurry down the path. She looked beyond to see Father Allain, his robe removed, running up toward them. Monique lifted her skirts and ran quickly toward them with Mariette in tow.

"I fear they have made a grave error. François, René LeBlanc and several others are with Colonel Winslow at the priest's house right now," he explained, trying to catch his breath. "I am certain they will be able to convince the Colonel he is mistaken. We must remain calm until this is resolved."

"Until what is resolved?" asked Louise.

"Colonel Winslow has declared today that all Acadians are now prisoners of the British Crown and will be removed from here!" Father Allain's usually calm voice broke. There were gasps of surprise from the women, followed by cries of anguish. "I am going there at once!" exclaimed Louise, who promptly proceeded down the road, hiking her skirts and marching along in righteous indignation. Monique followed, and when they reached the front gate of the wooden enclosure, she let her mother go on ahead, while she ran up to the fence to try and get a glimpse inside. Through the wooden slats she could make out that a few of the men were standing near the church doors and being guarded by soldiers with bayonets drawn. Suddenly she thought she could hear Jean shouting, so she called his name.

"May I talk to someone?" she asked a soldier at the gate.

"For just a moment," he said, "then you must leave."

Monique ran inside the gate and up the church steps. "Jean," she gasped when she saw his bruised face. "What happened to you?"

"*Les cauchons*, one of them struck me," he shouted, shaking his fist. "These bastard soldiers have come to our village and told us we are to be sent away as prisoners!"

"Jean, please control your temper," whispered Monique. "What do you mean?"

Jean lowered his voice, but the rage was palpable. "Their leader told us that we would be sent away from here as prisoners of the British Crown!" Jean's voice was rising once again, and Monique felt a deep fear in her stomach. She could see from the corner of her eye that a soldier was watching them, and she struggled to hold back tears.

"Please be careful," she whispered.

"Your father has gone to Colonel Winslow's quarters along with some of the others. The Notary Public René LeBlanc is there also. They will take care of this before the day is out, and if not, I will kill the soldier who struck me, I swear. How dare they! Go and look for Pierre, Monique. He is with Olivier."

"I'll look for them. Please do not get into any more trouble. Your face is very swollen already."

"I know. I can hardly see out of this eye. They can try and kill me, but I will gouge their eyes out before I die!"

"Shhh," she admonished him. "I will find Mama and come back later." Women were now coming up the road in large groups, crying and pleading with the soldiers to let them in to see their husbands, sons and fathers. Monique found her mother holding hands with Mariette and trying to calm her. The little girl cried and called for her mother.

"Please watch Mariette until Aunt Cecile comes back," said Louise. "I am going back into the church right now to speak to the Colonel himself. They forbade me to earlier, but this time, I will insist and will not leave until I can see him face-to face!"

"Be careful, Mama," said her daughter. "I just found Jean and he said there was an announcement that we are prisoners of the British Crown for some reason. What did we do wrong?"

"I assure you we did nothing wrong," said her mother. "They are wrong, and I am certain that your father and others like your Uncle René can negotiate our release from this ridiculous order. I spoke with Father Allain about it and he is confident also. I must go now. Please take care of my sweet Mariette." Louise stroked the child's cheek, then walked up the stairs and into the church. Monique found some children playing quietly nearby and soon one of them had invited Mariette to sit and play a game with her. Monique stood silently and watched Mariette and her new friend Joseph, her thoughts going in a thousand directions.

"Monique," said a familiar voice behind her, startling her out of a daze. "Pierre!" exclaimed Monique as she rushed to embrace him. "Have you been freed?"

"Only long enough to tell you what has happened. In exchange, I had to agree to bring back Olivier's twin brother Joseph, who went to le Canard today to repair a dyke. They gave Father Allain permission to come out also, so that he can tell the women to bring food for the men. They will be expecting me back at this hour tomorrow. We have been declared prisoners."

"By this hour tomorrow, perhaps they will realize they have made a terrible mistake," said Monique. "I saw your father."

"Where? Can you take me to him?"

Monique turned to her young cousin, who now appeared to be totally content to play with her new friend Joseph. "Mariette," she said, "promise me you will stay right here until I come back for you in a few minutes."

"I promise," replied Mariette.

"It is very important."

"I promise."

Monique took Pierre's hand and led him to the fence near the guard's quarters, where his father was still standing. "I have to warn you, Pierre, your father's face is very swollen and still bleeding.

"I was there when it happened," said Pierre sadly. "Papa shouted at Colonel Winslow and called him a name I cannot repeat. It was in French so I hoped they would not understand, but they could plainly see that my father is a powerful man. A soldier standing guard struck him down with the butt of his gun to make an example of him. When Papa stood back up he had blood all over his face and running down his shirt. He looked at me as though he wanted to fight back and I shook my head; otherwise, I think he would be . . . I hate to think of what would have happened next."

"Try and keep him calm," said Monique. "Tell him my mother has gone into the church to find my father and this will be straightened out soon enough."

"I will try and calm him, but it will not be easy."

Monique hurried back to check on Mariette. On the way, she ran into Father Allain.

"Have you seen my mother?" she asked him.

"Yes. She is waiting outside the priest's quarters for your father to come out. They will not permit her inside, and she was giving them a piece of her mind when I left. She was telling them in no uncertain terms that they should hang their heads in shame for the way they are treating the Acadian people."

Monique could not help but feel proud. "They will regret making my mother cross."

Monique was relieved to find Mariette still sitting in the same spot where she had left her before. However, by now she did not look happy and complained of being hungry.

"Come," said Monique, "we can go back to the farm and get something to eat."

"I went into the cemetery again," said the young girl.

"You did?"

"Yes, *Tante* Louise took me over to the cemetery, and had me ask if they would let us inside to place the two flowers on grandmother's grave. When the soldier on guard was not looking, *Tante* Louise had me run over to the priest's house to see if Colonel Winslow was in there. He was, and I could see Uncle François, Father René and his sons, and some other men in there speaking to him. He is a fat man in a red uniform with a funny wig on his head. He did not look very tough to me, and I do not like him sleeping in the house where our priest lives."

"I know," said Monique. "And then what happened?"

"*Tante* Louise took my hand and walked over to the door. She had me ask Colonel Winslow in English to come over to speak to my aunt, and he stopped talking to the others and came over. She had me tell him she would like to meet with him tomorrow at noon."

"And?"

"He said for us to come over at twelve o'clock tomorrow."

Chapter 13

Gathering Storm Clouds

Wednesday, September 10, 1755

Monique had been sitting by the creek since the sunrise over Gaspereau. It seemed so long ago that the terrible summons was read in her church, and still so hard to believe it was now a prison for the husbands, fathers and sons of her village. She had seen Colonel Winslow stand here yesterday and call out the names of twenty married men, then order Uncle René's son Pierre to lead several soldiers into the woods so they could capture and bring back the younger men that were still missing. The Colonel had read their names, all one hundred-nine of them. She had not seen her Pierre for the past five days and had broken down crying when his name was read. Father Allain was reminded of his strict orders to tell the Mi'Kmaq to stay away from Grand-Pré, and he replied that he had gotten the message to them and their promise.

She sat in silence, thinking about her father. He had received permission to leave the prison compound and come back to their farm until a cut on his foot healed. For the first few hours it seemed easy to pretend nothing had changed. Mama and Papa were there, with Mariette curled up in a corner under a blanket. But Papa's breathing became labored, and he had lain down on a cot that her mother made up in the kitchen.

Mama talked nearly constantly about her arguments with Colonel Winslow, and how she planned to visit him each day from now on, just as she had the first day when this terrible announcement had been made. She felt quite sure the Colonel was taking her verbal petition seriously and would appeal to his superiors on their behalf.

François went over and over the events at the church last Friday, especially his friend Jean's outrage and his punishment for speaking up. He hoped Jean would be careful. He was also worried about Uncle René, who had been very distressed by Winslow's announcement. But what he feared most was that Father Allain would be captured and sent to where the other priests were imprisoned if he did not cooperate.

"Uncle René begged on his knees for the opportunity to agree to an unconditional oath of allegiance to the British Government," Papa said, then shook his head to indicate a denial of their request. "Colonel Winslow said it was now too late, that we should have agreed to this many years ago. The Colonel refers to René as 'friend' and 'neighbor,' but who treats his neighbor as he is treating us? He told us arrangements have been made to send us to the colonies, that we will be welcomed there and will have new lives. He said he would take particular care of Uncle René. I told him our lives are here. Oh, Louise, we belong here! I pray to God that our mother country hears of this terrible thing and comes to our aid."

"I still do not think Colonel Winslow has the heart for making us leave here even though he has been ordered to do so," said Louise. "I asked him how he could take on such a mission and sleep at night. He replied it is not his choice, that it is the will of His Majesty, that he is but an obedient and humble servant."

"I think that their provisions will run out before long," said Monique. "Perhaps they will be convinced to go back to New England to their own families then. After all, they have been away since the summer. Their wives and children must be wondering when they will be coming back to tend their farms."

"I wish you both were right," said François, "but yesterday Colonel Winslow talked of his communications with other commanders at Chignecto and Annapolis Royal. At some villages, the French and Indians have fought against the soldiers and killed some, making their commanders very nervous and more determined about their mission. Tomorrow the Colonel will be choosing twenty more of our men to go out and find those who ran into the woods. One of these who are captured could be our own Pierre, who was granted permission after the announcement to leave for a day and find Olivier's twin brother. Many have not returned, and their women and children weep and are growing very hungry."

"We have to take Mariette back home tomorrow, François, and I am not certain if someone we know will be going to le Canard." Louise glanced over at her little niece. "Without Mariette, I can no longer talk to Colonel Winslow in English. He told me that he would arrange for a soldier to take Mariette home, but I will not hear of it. I have heard that, at night, some of Winslow's soldiers have beaten our villagers." Monique and her mother both looked toward Mariette, not wanting her to hear the fear in their voices. The young girl was completely oblivious to the conversation, nestled in a large chair under a blanket and reading the book Father Allain had given to her.

"Mariette," Louise asked, "When you finish your chapter, could you come and sit over here at the table and write more on our petition? I would like to have it ready to take to Colonel Winslow tomorrow."

Mariette looked up without smiling. "May I also write that the Colonel looks like a fat old woman in his powdered wig, Aunt Louise?"

"Oh, Mariette," said Louise, laughing for the first time in days.

"Perhaps we should also ask that they let us move somewhere else after we are given the winter months to prepare," said François. "I would like to be able to get in my complete harvest and trade as much as possible. Then I would be in a position to help more family members move."

"François, you are such a caring and generous man!" said his wife. "If the soldiers stay here the winter, they can help us in the spring. Our elders and sick will need the means to be moved so that they do not suffer more than is necessary. And young mothers, like Angeline, will need assistance with their babies. It is also essential that we be allowed to worship as Roman Catholics."

Monique recalled that Mariette had written everything down. The next morning, Louise had promised to take it to the prison compound at the church. She got signatures or an "X" from as many villagers as possible and on her return, told Monique that the Colonel had spoken most kindly to her, referring to her as "my friend Louise." He promised to send their petition on.

Monique was abruptly brought back to the present by the sound of shouting. She stood up in the marshland grass. Long lines of prisoners proceeded down the slope toward the creek, escorted by many blue-uniformed soldiers on either side. Bayonets flashed, reflecting the sun's light.

Mothers, sisters, wives, and grandmothers that she recognized ran alongside, falling on the grass, crossing themselves and weeping, pleading for their loved ones to be released. Some of the women tried to give food and blankets to their men and slumped to the ground, overcome by their own distress.

Monique noticed the long line to the far left was made up of the youngest men. It was also the most heavily escorted by soldiers. She ran toward this group being shoved forcefully along toward the riverbank. Out of breath, she hurried alongside, scanning them for a glimpse of Pierre. When she spotted him, she shouted out his name as loud as her panicked voice would allow. He turned, his eyes blazing with anger. She called out again, and he called back for her to move away from the soldiers. One of them pushed him roughly in a physical demand for his silence. Pierre knocked against another man, and they both fell to the ground, then scrambled to get back up.

Monique kept pace with the tragic procession. Boys called out for their fathers, and fathers shouted back to keep moving. Reaching the mouth of the Gaspereau River, they were ordered to halt. Numbers of twenty were counted out and crowded onto small boats, then rowed out into the river and loaded onto the decks of the transport ships at anchor there.

She sat by the river with the other women of her village, weeping and watching as the ship filled with young Acadian men sailed out into the Basin. Just before sunset, she was surprised to see Father Allain walk down to the riverbank. He did not have his robe on. Her mother had told her earlier that Father Allain had buried it beneath their cellar.

Father Allain told everyone to pray that their petition was read. He led evening prayers. She refused, keeping her eyes open. The sun was setting, and she stared at the orange-red reflection of it on the mud flats at low tide. Pools of water settled between the flats, the brightest ones in a straight line from the sun to where she was standing. She had the sensation of a curtain coming down as the sun disappeared beneath the horizon. The mudflats darkened, and the air chilled. She hurried back up toward the road while Father Allain was still leading evening vespers. Her mind was on Jean. Back at her farm a few minutes later, she checked to see if her mother or father had a message for her to take to him, and her Mama helped pack some bread, water, and cheese into a basket for him.

"Jean Doucet?" she called out at the gate. He came to meet her just inside the wooden fence. "I have seen Pierre. He is now out in the Basin on board a ship. Jean, I do not know what is going to happen to him."

"I think they are taking the younger men out there so that they will be easier to control. Some have escaped to the woods, and others have tried to fight the soldiers. Did Pierre look injured?"

"No. Perhaps they will all be brought back when things are resolved."

"I don't know. And your father, how is he?"

"Still not well. I fear his foot is getting worse. He has lain on a cot in our kitchen. Mariette helped Mama and Papa write a petition for our release, and Mama took it to Colonel Winslow. They are so worried about you!"

Jean shook his head in despair. "And I too am worried about all of you. I hope that Colonel Winslow listens to our petition. I can see it is no use for us to band together to fight them. They are well-equipped with ammunition and I have seen at least three men beaten in front of my eyes for attempting to fight. Some of these soldiers hate us and will use any opportunity to hurt us. They call us 'dirty papists.' Colonel Winslow warns them of the consequences of being violent toward us, but at night when he is in bed, some terrible things happen."

Monique shivered. She reached out to her father-in-law and held his hand for a moment.

"Is Father Allain on one of the transports?" he asked.

"No. They have ordered him to find Mi'Kmaq brothers and tell them to stay away from here."

"Could you ask him to visit me tomorrow?"

"Yes, I will, Jean."

Monique left, walking back to the farm in the darkness. The warmth that struck her when she opened the front door immediately tempered the chill from the bay winds she had struggled against on the way. Her mother sat in the kitchen, her father lying beside her on his cot. He told Monique that Uncle René LeBlanc had paid them a visit while she was gone, and he said some villagers would be sent out to another transport tomorrow. Uncle René had also spoken to Father Allain tonight.

"As you know, Father Allain has buried his robe in a safe place," said Papa. "He also recommended that we bury anything else we do not want them to destroy. He told us something horrible, and it grieves me to say it aloud. Father Allain heard that they might burn down our houses . . . ." François paused, resting his face in his hands for a few moments. Monique looked over at her mother, searching her eyes for help.

"I think that this is a good time for us to pray and sing the 'Ave Maris Stella' together," said Louise. "We must keep our hopes up that a miracle will happen for our people." She began to sing:

Ave Maris Stella,
Etoile d'Acadie,
Protégé tes fidèles
Qui levent leurs voix vers toi
Qui levent leurs voix vers toi

Acadie, ma patrie,
Tu vis dans mon coeur,
Où que je me retrouve
Mon âme est Acadienne
Mon âme est Acadienne.

Monique sang through her sobs. Mariette came over from her usual spot to sit on her lap. Time stood still in their kitchen as they prayed for Pierre and Jean, for Father Allain, for the villagers and their many relatives. When Monique finally left her mother and father together in the kitchen to go back to her bed, she wondered if there would be any restful sleep until this was over. She tossed and turned and drifted into a fitful dream.

Monique, I have made a promise that I will keep you safe. Here, put on my sweater. It will keep you warm in the swells of the violent ocean and in the slums of the shameless city . . . .

Monique awoke suddenly and sat up in her bed. It was pitch black, and there was a loud chopping noise outside her room.

At the sound of a crash, she leapt out of bed and pulled back the curtain between her bed and the kitchen. The door to the outside was in pieces on the floor, and two soldiers, guns drawn, stood in the kitchen with Mama and Papa. Papa was struggling to stand up. One of the soldiers saw Monique and went toward her, violently pushing her toward her father. She lost her balance and fell against him, knocking him to the ground.

"Molasses," said the other soldier. "And bread." He picked up half of a loaf that was on the table and shone a lantern on the table and into cupboards.

"Where is the ale?"

"Where are your coins kept?" asked his comrade. "Give me your lantern and forget about food for a moment," he shouted. The blue-uniformed soldier took the lantern and shone it in François' face. "How many acres do you have, Acadian? And how many bullocks? When you are gone . . . ," he said with a covetous grin. The Mélansons looked on silently, François angry and the others terrified, only Mariette able to comprehend anything their tormentors were saying. The soldiers spent several minutes eating and drinking and peering threateningly at the Acadians while they stayed huddled together in the corner of the main room.

Suddenly, there was a sharp, lightning-like blast just outside, and the blade of an axe thrust through the thick pine door. Colonel Winslow himself climbed over the door split in half. He held a lantern up to the faces of the two soldiers. Although he was dressed in nightwear, he was terrifying to behold as he held his musket. Behind him followed a guard detail in full uniform with muskets drawn and bayonets fixed.

"You are ordered to the guardhouse, and you, Captain Townsend, are also ordered to the guardhouse," he shouted. "MOVE!" The two intruding soldiers lowered their weapons and handed them over. Colonel Winslow turned to François and Louise. "I will post a guard outside your door," he said in broken French. Touching the brim of his hat, he muttered a "*Bonsoir*" and stepped over the broken door into the night.

There were several stunned moments of silence before François moaned in pain. "My foot, it hurts," he cried. Louise and Mariette lifted him onto his cot as Monique hurried to find something that would serve as a bandage. They huddled together, waiting for the illusion of safety that daylight would bring.

Chapter 14

Historic Park

Friday, August 26

"Where the hell is she, André?" shouted Jacques into the other end of the receiver. She's been gone nearly twelve hours!"

"I don't know!" André yelled back just as loudly. "Why don't you get your butt up here to help me look?"

André could hear Michelle in the background, speaking gently to Jacques, trying to calm him down. He took a deep breath and another gulp of strong coffee.

"Michelle's been calling Monique's father," said Jacques. "We haven't been able to find him. He was going fishing somewhere, and . . . what? Michelle says there's a hurricane coming there. She says to tell you she got permission to announce Monique's disappearance tomorrow at the festival, to get more people helping."

"I'm surprised you guys are still doing the show," said André.

"It's funny because I called the promoters in Boston late last night and again this morning. Guess what? They're Acadians. The last name of the head guy is Poirier, and he said that it's up to us, that if we have to cancel he'll understand. But, he said if we do want to do it, we can dedicate *Le Festival Acadien* to her if she hasn't shown up by then. Hopefully she will, and all this won't matter anyway. The guy I talked to, Jean-Paul, has a friend pretty high up in the CBC who's also Acadian. His name is, just a sec, I wrote it down here, Pierre Cormier. Jean-Paul's gonna call him today and propose doing a live broadcast of both days of *Le Festival Acadien* on all the major stations in the Maritimes if she's not found by then. He said that she's one of our own and he's pretty sure this guy Cormier will do it. God, though, I hate to think that on Sunday we still might not know where she is."

"I know. I can't think about it either. Still, it's nice to know people care that much."

"Yeah, Michelle and I are still pretty much in shock but we're gonna do this," replied Jacques. "We have to."

"I do have some other news," said André. "The police said that a guy from Grand-Pré was walking his dog down the street Thursday night and saw a man on the park grounds. His description of him was that he was an old geezer who could hardly walk. He had a big heavy sweater on, which struck the guy as strange because it wasn't cold that night. And there was something else, I can't remember what, damn it, I forget."

"Hey, André, Michelle just said we're gonna have a quick rehearsal with the band in fifteen minutes. Then we'll get on the road for there. How 'bout you meet us at the park around, oh, 10:30 this morning?"

"Great . . . oh yeah, I know what the other thing was I wanted to tell you. When the guy walked back up the road he saw a car with a taxi sign on top pulling into the parking lot. He said he heard a loud whistle. I know that Jack, the guy driving the taxi, said he whistled for Monique. Then the guy who was walking saw it leave shortly after. He was close enough to notice that nobody got in. So Jack the taxi man didn't see her, which means something happened just before he got there. But there was no sign of foul play, according to the police. And you wouldn't think an old man could overpower a young woman, would you Jacques?"

"You wouldn't think so. Was there any sign that she fought him off? I think Monique might try and put up a fight, don't you Michelle? Yeah, me too. Michelle says that Monique took a course in self-defense, and would have been able to protect herself, especially from an old man. So maybe she ran away from him into the woods or something. Anyway, we're gonna call Blomidon Cottages and pay for the room for a couple more days, in case. And you can stay there too if it'll be easier."

"Actually, I might. My bed at the dorm is covered in dirty laundry, and I can grab a quick shower in the morning without having to wait in line for the bathroom. And maybe Michelle could leave Monique's dad a message to call the cottage so I can give him the latest news."

"I'll tell her. Gotta go!"

André hung up and drove down through town to Blomidon Cottages. He talked to Bill for a few minutes, then drove the rest of the way to the park and down to the beach, where he sat beside a large gray boulder. He called Monique's name a few times until he saw a person farther down and felt stupid yelling.

After he left there, he drove back up the road to the chapel. It was open by now, and there were a few tourists mingling around. André walked around the inside of the chapel, then back out on the grounds. He stood by the willow tree and closed his eyes. What had happened here? The breeze betrayed nothing as it cooled his face and rustled the drooping branches.

He walked back to his car in the parking lot. Restless in his own skin, he decided to drive down to the beach again. Walking slowly down the stairs from the top of the bluff to the beach, he found a spot in the sand to sit down for a few moments. It was low tide, and he impulsively took off his shoes and socks and ran out to the mud flats. The sun was glistening off them and as he got up close, the ochre-colored ooze sprang up between his toes and over his feet, making a sucking sound with each step he took. It reminded him of his boyhood days at Shediac, walking through the muck with his cousin Jacques. He thought about the day they had learned the hard way that walking out to the flats in sneakers would get two kids in trouble. The mud hadn't come out, no matter how long they scrubbed, and their parents had not been pleased to throw away what had been perfectly good sneakers.

André looked up as a small boat made its way across the Basin toward Horton Landing. What if Monique had gone swimming here the other night and drowned? Was anybody searching the Basin for her? André decided that his next stop would be the police station, where he would hopefully find out when the news of her disappearance would be on the radio and TV. He picked up his shoes and socks and suddenly realized that there was no place to clean his feet, so he sat back down to wait for the mud to dry.

The boat came closer, and André could see there were two men in it, one with a line in the water. He had never taken to fishing, and some of his relatives thought there was something wrong with him. As he had grown into his lanky body, he was redeemed by his ability to swim well and maneuver a boat in the water. Feeling a strong urge to call home and talk to his mother, he decided to get in touch from the cottage tonight.

A young couple holding hands met him on the stone steps going up from the beach. They said "Hello," and André suddenly wished Monique was here to hold hands with him. He wanted to protect her, and had failed.

André drove barefoot on the back road from Grand-Pré back to Wolfville. His feet were still slippery so he drove slower than usual. He had a key to the cottage Bill gave him earlier, and after pulling in and parking he went in and showered, then left for the RCMP headquarters in New Minas.

"Tell me again why you didn't put out an APB on her before this?" asked André, trying but failing to hide his frustration.

"She is an adult, so the laws are different than for someone under eighteen," explained Sgt. Williamson. "What we're going to do now though, and I've already called for it today, is to get it on the radio. It's been on since early this morning . . . a missing-persons bulletin."

"Good, finally."

"Have you been able to contact her next-of-kin?"

"I can't get hold of her father."

"Why not?"

"He lives in South Louisiana, and a hurricane's coming."

"I heard. Communication could get more difficult. Do you want me to try through the police department to contact him?"

"Sure. And my cousin Jacques and I will try too. Jacques is married to Monique's cousin Michelle and they're the ones Monique came up here with. Michelle has Monique's father's number. They'll be here in about an hour. I have to get back down to the park to meet them."

"I really don't know what else to tell you at this point," said the officer. "I've seen a number of crime scenes though, and I can tell you this definitely does not look like one. There is absolutely not one piece of evidence that indicates a crime. No blood or fluids, and nothing on the picture except finger prints. Just another thought though: Have Michelle bring up Monique's hairbrush, so we have a DNA sample."

"What about the woods, are you searching them?"

"We've had search and rescue parties in the wooded areas all around there in the past couple of hours. We have a good team on this."

André thanked Sgt. Williamson for his time and drove back toward the park, stopping at Tim's for a coffee. The shop was alive with tourists and students returned to classes for the fall semester. He sat with two friends who came into Tim's at the same time, and they told him to call if he wanted help looking. He took their numbers and arranged to meet them at the park later. He'd feel better if he did a search of the surrounding woods himself. There was still the matter of the Basin, but the RCMP said that they had it covered and nothing had been found.

He drove back down to Evangeline Beach and wandered around, then went back to the park again to wait for Jacques and Michelle. Not long after, they pulled into the parking lot and right up beside his Honda. When he got out to meet them, he fought back tears, and he could see that Jacques was doing the same. Michelle's face was so red and her eyes so swollen, he thought that she had done enough crying for all three of them. They talked about what to do next, and Michelle said she was too upset to listen to what the police would say. André and Jacques got into André's car, and Michelle leaned against the side of the car beside her husband's open window.

She said she wanted to walk around the park. André gave her directions to the beach. Before Jacques and André drove away in the Honda, André also pointed Michelle in the direction of the willow tree where the police had found evidence of Monique's disappearance last night. She walked toward it waving a teary good-bye, and sat underneath it for awhile.

After a few minutes, she thought that visiting the nearby beach might calm her nerves. She walked back to the rental car and drove the short distance. Sitting by a large, gray boulder, she looked out toward the red bluffs beyond and watched the seagulls circle above. Rehearsal had been impossible this morning, and she was glad to hear from Jacques that Jean-Paul had been supportive about them taking the day and coming up here. The sound engineers were another matter; they were unhappy to have to wait until tonight. What would it be like to try and sing when her cousin was lost? Her only hope was dedicating the show to Monique.

She watched a person make his way slowly up the beach toward her. He came closer, and she could see he was a very old man. He looked frail standing at the shore in front of her. When he made the sign of the cross she went over to talk to him. Maybe he had heard about Monique, she thought. As they talked, she got a strong sense that she'd seen him somewhere before. He said how beautiful Evangeline Beach was, and she agreed. It was beautiful and peaceful here, not the sort of place that a loved one should disappear from, she thought.

The old man said he was a missionary, and referred to "his people," the Acadians. When she had asked him if he'd heard about Monique, his lack of interest offended her. He had treated her like a child who was missing the point.

But then . . . how could she tell even Jacques that he vanished, leaving only an old coat or something on the sand? Later, she sat in her car back in the parking lot, pondering it. She felt panicked and tried to breathe deeply. She'd had her share of ghost sightings, and was almost used to them, but never had an apparition left an item of clothing behind. She wondered if her anxiety over Monique was making her a little delusional. Her hands had shaken so badly this morning, she wasn't able to play the accordion, and now she was seeing things. She tried to still her mind, and asked God for help.

It was a relief to see Jacques and André pull into the parking lot soon afterward. She embraced Jacques, who assured Michelle that the RCMP were checking everywhere along the shore, up the coast into Cumberland County and back down the coast to Digby County.

"Sgt. Williamson will be on the case night and day now," said Jacques as he held his wife tightly, "and he told André that Jack from Annapolis Taxi called this morning to say he organized a group of his friends and neighbors to search the woods for Monique.

Apparently he knows the woods really well from living here all his life."

André offered to go to the café to buy some sandwiches and

apples, and on his return the three friends walked over to sit under the willow tree for a few minutes. Jacques checked his watch. They'd need to leave in a half-hour in order to get back for a four o'clock rehearsal.

"I know, Hon, it's the last thing I want to do too," said Jacques, responding to his wife's heavy sigh. "But this is what we've got to do to get the word out."

Michelle hesitantly told Jacques and André about the old man she'd talked to at the beach, how he looked so lonely and cold in his old woolen sweater. She noticed André staring at her.

"What's wrong?" she asked.

"I guess it's a coincidence but this woolen sweater thing . . ."

"What do you mean?" asked Jacques.

"Well, I'm just hearing that people saw an old man with a gray sweater . . . Michelle, what's wrong?"

"Honey, you have that 'deer in the headlights' look again," said Jacques. "What happened?"

"I left the beach this morning because I asked the old man about Monique and he ignored me. He kept talking about the past, about the native tribe and 'his people,' the Acadians. Maybe he was trying to tell me something, but I don't know what. He acted like he could see something that I couldn't see and then he started praying so I just decided to leave him alone. When I got to the top of the stairs . . . do you know what stairs I mean, André?" Receiving an affirmative nod, she continued. "I turned around to look at him and got a sharp pain right here, in my temple. It really hurt, in fact it still does a little bit." Michelle paused for an instant to rub her head.

"So then what happened, Hon?"

"The old man vanished; I swear he wasn't there anymore. There was only an old gray sweater on the sand. Don't look at me like that you two, I'm serious, and you know what, guys? I'm beginning to wonder if the old man was a ghost. What if he met Monique the other night and she went with him somewhere? He *was* telling me something, I know he was. In fact, I even feel something right now, like a presence, right here with us. Do you feel it?"

"A presence?" asked Jacques.

"Don't you feel it?"

"Yeah, I feel like you're present, and André's present, and I'm present."

"Jacques, don't make fun of me! I feel something, and I really believe she's still alive. I'd know if she was dead."

"Michelle, you're scarin' me. André, what about you? Do you feel a presence?"

"Nope, I'm sorry Michelle but I'm not feeling it."

"Well I am. She's around here somewhere, and we'll find her."

She shrugged her shoulders at her husband and friend, who were both looking at her skeptically.

"Call me crazy."

"Crazy!" said Jacques. "But I've seen your crazy feelings before, and the damn things turn out right. Except this time your psychic luck might have run out."

"I don't think so," she said definitively.

Chapter 15

Preparing for Exile

Monday, October 6, 1755

Monique visited Jean shortly after sunrise. He was growing thin, and told her that any food brought by villagers was usually taken from the prisoners and given to the soldiers. Her mother told her to stand with Jean and watch him eat and drink. Monique could not help but notice that Jean's once powerful arms were thinner than hers.

The soldiers grew used to seeing her, and she discovered that it was easy to board the transport ship at the mouth of the Gaspereau River and bring food to Pierre. She carefully confided the older man's thoughts to the younger man, and it became obvious they were making a plan. She was terrified, and passed each man's news reluctantly.

Yesterday had been a beautiful October morning when she boarded the ship with baked wheat bread and a fresh jug of water. She also carried a bag containing a dress and a bonnet, at Pierre's request. When she went down into the hold of the ship, Pierre whisked her into a small storage compartment barely big enough for the two of them to fit, and there in the darkness he stripped off his breeches and dressed himself in the women's clothes.

It had been almost too easy for the two of them to leave the ship along with the other women. Once on shore, they walked slowly up the road. Monique wanted to run, and had been cautioned by Pierre not to look around, that this would attract the attention of soldiers. She giggled at the sight of Pierre in a large bonnet, momentarily forgetting her fear.

When they reached the Doucets' blacksmith shop, Pierre led her behind a horse stall and took off the dress, then barred the door. He scooped Monique up in his arms and carried her to a safe hiding place inside a small storage room where his father placed the newly-forged horseshoes.

"Listen, Monique, please listen very carefully to what I am telling you. I am going into the forest today after you visit my father."

"No!"

"I have to. I have to find Beausoleil and his men. I met him when I went to find Olivier's brother. I heard Beausoleil and some others were captured by the British and imprisoned at Fort Lawrence. But they escaped during a storm a few days ago. He is a strong leader. Right now, he is with some Mi'Kmaq and one of them is Eyes of Black Bear, a runner. Eyes of Black Bear has spied on many villages all over Acadie, and the same thing is happening with Acadians everywhere. They are all being taken as prisoners. Everywhere our people are herded like cattle and put on ships. They could separate us from our families and our land here forever, and I will not sit back and let them do it! When Eyes of Black Bear told Beausoleil who my father is, he asked for our help. He said that we can fight the British and win if we all use every opportunity possible. I know how to use the tools in my father's shop to make weaponry, and Beausoleil has convinced us that with ammunition we can defeat the enemy. Do you understand why I have to do this?"

"No."

"Please, Monique. I beg you to try and understand. I cannot bear the thought that they will take our life together away from us. Now that I have met Beausoleil, I believe that we have the chance to defeat them, and so does Papa."

"Oh, Pierre, I do not know. Mama has said that Colonel Winslow promised her our whole family would be placed on the same ship. I think it is dangerous to go to the woods. They will try to kill you if you join Beausoleil. He is a warrior, and I do not believe you would kill anyone. They would kill you first. I do not like Beausoleil for talking to you about such things. How did you meet him in the first place?"

"I was on the road to Gaspereau when two soldiers came by in a wagon. They ordered me to ride with them, but soon after I climbed on, the wagon was ambushed by some Acadians. The soldiers holding the reins tried to outrun them, but the wagon flipped over and I rolled down the embankment. It knocked me out at first, but then I came to and began running along on the edge of the river as fast as I could. I thought I had been recaptured when I fell and a musket appeared in front of my face, but it turned out to be Beausoleil himself. Have you ever seen him? He is fierce-looking, with coal black hair and blue eyes that seem to pierce through a man's soul. At first I thought he might kill me, but Eyes of Black Bear told him I was Jean Doucet's son and he laughed and held out his hand to shake mine."

"Go on."

"Well, then Beausoleil told me to wait in the woods and track the soldiers who guard the edge of the forest behind their camp. He wanted me to kill one and take his gun. I could not kill him, so I was captured."

"See? They could have killed you."

"I was thrown back into the church with men my age, and our hands were bound behind our backs. The soldiers guarding us all seemed very nervous, and then Marcel, whose father is a miller, told me that he heard the British were attacked by French and Mi'Kmaq in one of the other villages. It was after that they decided to put us on the transports so we would not rise up against them, and that is when I saw you. I wanted you to see that I am fine and ready to fight for Acadie."

"Pierre, what if instead we both go to the church and speak to Colonel Winslow? I will bake bread to offer to the soldiers, and plead with the Colonel to let your father go. Then we can find Mama and Father Allain and Mariette and her family. We will ask Colonel Winslow to place us together on the same transport. And poor Angeline too, she needs our help . . . . Do you know anything about her husband, Claude? Oh, please, Pierre, do not look at me that way. I am very, very afraid you will be taken away from me in a transport or killed if you go into the woods. I could not bear it! Please say a little prayer with me."

The two young people knelt on the hard floor, praying for strength and hope to get through the ordeal in front of them. Monique appealed to Mother Mary to guide their direction. She breathed in the iron smells of the blacksmith shop.

After the prayer was over, Monique reached out to touch Pierre. Her hands were warm from being nestled in her apron pockets earlier, and she placed them on his face. Brushing the hair back from her forehead, he leaned to kiss her, the tender kiss of a new bridegroom. They embraced, and his arms wound around her waist to pull her closer.

"I made up a rhyme for you, and drew a picture," he said, reaching into his pocket. "I asked Mariette to write it down and I memorized it to say to you. Now seems like the right time."

"I did not know you were a poet."

"I am not. Only a simple farmer who loves a wonderful girl named Monique Mélanson. She has become my wife, Monique Doucet." He kissed her cheek and began:

I fell in love one day at des Mines shore.
I saw a girl Monique, with skin so pure,
A brown-eyed beauty, oh, and when she smiled
My heart from then on, with hers did abide.

"Pierre . . . what a beautiful poem."

"Are you afraid, Monique, to be alone with me for the first time? I mean . . . ."

Her answer was in the way she reached for him and pulled him closer. His gaze melded with hers, her mouth with his, and hands drifted toward buttons, unfastening, peeling off the layers of restraint that were no longer necessary. He glided her toward the floor until her back was flat against it, then eased himself down until his body was alongside hers. The dusty hardness of the floor beneath her, at first uncomfortable, disappeared from her mind when his arm moved beneath her back. He spread his jacket out underneath her, looked into her eyes, then down toward her body beside him, her clothing peeled away and surrounding her.

Pierre reached across her body and slid his hand up the side of her leg, then further to the curve of her hip. His eyes following his hand, he glided it over her smooth white stomach and up to cradle her breast. Monique covered his hand with her own, continuing to gaze into his dark eyes. With her other hand, she caressed the taut muscle of his arm, then lingered on his shoulder and down his back. The hard muscles beneath his velvety smooth skin were filling her with emotions she had never known before tonight. He moved closer and they kissed. Warm skin touched skin and she gave in, trusting, sinking into the rhythm of the ocean waves that came to shore, one after another.

"Oh, Monique."

"Je t'aime, Pierre."

He brushed her hair back gently and whispered that he would never hurt her, and she knew from this moment that she could trust him completely. She glided her fingers across his shoulders and down his back again, and they shared one more kiss.

"You are so beautiful tonight," he said.

They lay together and enjoyed the feel of their bodies touching and the peace and joy of their first union.

"Did you hear that?" Pierre whispered suddenly.

"I hear the ocean."

"I hear that too, my love, but I thought I heard the sound of the whippoorwill. It could be a signal."

"A signal?"

"Eyes of Black Bear."

Pierre stood up and listened again, one finger over his lips, the other hand reaching to fasten his breeches. He silently cracked open the door to the shop, and both remained silent. Pierre's eyes said to be still, then indicated that he had heard what she had heard, the faint sound of a door opening. Pierre stood behind the door hunched over, preparing to lunge. The repeating sound of a whippoorwill on the other side of the door brought a look of relief to his face.

"Eyes of Black Bear?" he whispered.

"I am here," replied the voice on the other side in broken French.

"Wait a moment," Pierre said, giving Monique time to gather herself. He then ushered his friend in and closed the door.

"I hear thunder of boots," Eyes of Black Bear said in a warning. "You must leave quickly, now."

Eyes of Black Bear led the way out through a back window into the trees beyond, beckoning for the other two to tread carefully and quietly. Pierre placed his feet exactly where Eyes of Black Bear had placed his, and Monique tried her hardest to do the same. Soon they were out of sight of the shop.

Pierre turned and stood silently. He sucked in his breath, and Monique wondered why. He pointed, and she gasped and cried out at the sight of flames in the distance. Pierre shook his head at her, an unspoken bid for silence.

"I saw soldiers . . . ," whispered Eyes of Black Bear. "They bring Jean down road to your house before, throw fire on thatched roof."

"Why?" asked Pierre.

"We leave now?" Eyes of Black Bear asked in his native Mi'Kmaq.

"Yes, we leave now."

Monique looked up at her husband, her eyes filling with tears.

"Good-bye, my love," whispered Pierre in Monique's ear. "I promise I will fight hard to win back Acadie."

"Monique, pick wildflowers for awhile," warned Eyes of Black Bear. Monique wept as she lingered at the edge of the forest, picking small pieces of pine to boil for tea. When a soldier spotted her, he soon turned away again. She held her tears until she was back up the road to the Mélanson farm. Now starving, she found a crust of bread and walked back to the prison grounds to find Jean. She met a guard there, and requested to speak to Colonel Winslow. She told Colonel Winslow that her father was injured and had asked to see his friend, Jean. Colonel Winslow refused. Jean, he said, was a prisoner. She pleaded with him, saying that her mother was worried about him and told her to promise the Colonel she would escort him back herself tomorrow. The Colonel gave in.

"Thank-you Monique," said Jean as the two of them walked toward the Mélanson farm. "I am so sorry they have done this to your father."

"And he is sorry for what they have done to you." They walked silently for a few minutes while Jean ate the small portion of bread crusts she had brought.

"I have been so hungry," he said. "They do not have enough food for us, and some days we get only water."

"I know. They have taken all our food."

Monique told him some more news about Acadian men who were running into the woods, and how the soldiers were ordered to go and capture them. She did not mention Pierre specifically, but knew that Jean would understand her cryptic reference.

"Beausoleil is a very clever warrior," he said. "He and his army will hide well, with the help of the Mi'Kmaq. And they will win."

"I hope so."

"I know you are very worried, but I must tell you that if I were a younger man I would kill for my countrymen."

As they had reached the path leading up to the farm, Jean scouted out the area around and began to speak more directly. "Try not to worry too much. I think they will win with Beausoleil as their leader, and I am glad to be able to help them. Do you know that when the Winslow's soldiers discovered Pierre was missing from the ship this afternoon, they tried to question me about it? They did not believe me when I said I knew nothing, so they dragged me to my house and burned it to the ground in front of me. I denied them the satisfaction of showing any anger. They did not burn the shop, which was very stupid of them. Perhaps they plan to save it to threaten me with another day, but before they do, Beausoleil will take everything from it that he needs to kill them all."

There was nobody at the farm, so the two continued to walk farther, where a group of other villagers had gathered.

"*Gloire au Pére et au Fils et au Saint-Esprit...*" Father Allain was praying. The villagers began to sing the "Ave Maria" after the prayer, and their voices echoed across the mudflats to the beach below.

Monique noticed Colonel Winslow standing nearby. He seemed to be observing them. She watched from the corner of her eye as he walked back up the road in the direction of his quarters.

Back at the fortified church yard a few minutes later, Colonel Winslow closed the door of the rectory behind him and sat at his desk. He reached for his pen in the inkwell and opened the journal in front of him. Turning the pages back, he read what he had written about his accomplishments over the past few weeks. He studied again the inventory of Acadian possessions, pleased to see that he had documented everything. Their animals as well as their goods, their acreage, and their farming equipment were all there.

The harvest was now nearly completed by the women, and there was no time to spare in getting all the Acadians on the transports to Boston, Philadelphia, and the other colonial cities. By his calculations, not enough transports had arrived as yet to send his neighbors off to their destinations without overcrowding the ships. However, he had done all he could for them, and would need to move them away to protect his own soldiers from being attacked. They were out-numbered, and if things got out of control . . . .

He thought about his return to Marshfield, Massachusetts. He missed his wife. Perhaps he would ask again about taking his old friend René LeBlanc back to Marshfield with him. Governor Lawrence had dismissed the idea without even a discussion of it the first time he asked.

The Colonel was proud of the discipline he had demanded from his New England soldiers, and felt that the Governor owed him something. He hoped to be rewarded with a more prestigious mission in the future, or a military honor. To own some of this land would be a fitting reward as well. He had certainly proved himself to be a seasoned leader of men. While some of the other military leaders had left themselves vulnerable, his fortified camp had not been invaded by Mi'Kmaq. When that problem arose in the Mélanson house, he had ordered the court martial of the two offending soldiers after a brisk lashing and a few hours on the wooden horse. Soldiers feared the wooden horse, not only for the physical pain they endured, but also for the humiliation of having their arms and legs locked into it for days on end. He simply would not tolerate any molestation of the Acadians.

He had gone over the rules with his soldiers again today. Families would be allowed to get on the ships together, and the letters from Lieutenant Governor Lawrence to colonial governors would ensure that the prisoners were treated well when they arrived at their destinations. Colonel Winslow wrote down the day's events, then retired to his bed for the night, hoping that he would get a better night's sleep than he had for the last week.

At two in the morning, after much tossing in his bed, he got up, lit a candle, then walked to his desk. He took out a piece of stationery, his hand moving slowly and thoughtfully across the page as he wrote to a friend back in Massachusetts:

I know they deserve all and more than they feel; yet it hurts me to hear their weeping and wailing and gnashing of teeth. I am in hopes our affairs will soon put on another face, and we get transports, and I rid of the worst piece of service that ever I was in.

Down the road a short distance, Monique still sat with Father Allain. "Was I wrong, Father?" Monique asked the missionary through sobs as they sat together.

"There was nothing you could do, because his mind was made up. We will pray for his safety. I spoke to Jean myself tonight, and it is good that his shop was not destroyed. We must continue to have faith that God is with us. There are more than a few young men who are now in the woods, and they came to me in secret for a blessing before they left. Would you like to say a prayer with me now?"

Monique wept during the prayer, and Father Allain wrapped a strong arm around her. "Much is expected from the women during these times," he said, trying to comfort her. "You are being ordered to bring in the harvest and prepare food for the men who are all prisoners. You are expected to remain strong. So much of the food is taken from us to feed soldiers and you women bear the guilt, even though it is not within your control to change the fact that you cannot do more. We see soldiers looking healthy, while our men get weaker every day. Every morning I see the women and many children go to the fields weeping. It is a terrible sight, and I weep myself as I pray for all of us to be delivered from this awful trial. I have been ordered to tend to the animals, and some animals have run into the woods, where soldiers search for them. Soldiers have stolen horses that they prize. Promise me you will not tell this to anyone, but I have freed some horses of Louis Cormier, so that the soldiers cannot claim them."

"Father!"

"I sought repentance from God." In the moonlight Monique could see a glimmer of mischief in his eyes. She knew that she too had disobeyed once or twice. She thought about Pierre in a bonnet, and a smile drifted across her face. Then she recalled their intimate moments in the blacksmith shop, and she averted her eyes from Father Allain's.

When they decided it was time to get some rest, Father Allain accompanied Monique back to the farm and continued on to his camp. Louise, unable to sleep, greeted her daughter at the door and they shared a cup of ale together. Monique retired to her bed and her mother to her place beside her husband in the kitchen, nestling into a chair next to his cot for the night.

Tuesday, October 7, 1755

Monique and Louise rose early the next morning, milking the cows and gathering eggs. They had been instructed to bring the eggs and milk to the prison camp. Monique took the driftwood cross she had held on her wedding day and carried it up the road with her. Having it gave her something she needed. Perhaps it was hope for a better day ahead. Mother and daughter walked reluctantly up the road toward the church, past their favorite bench under the willow tree. They made plans to sit here tonight.

A wagon came toward them, drawn by two horses they recognized as Jean's. As it got closer, they could see that two soldiers were driving it and two more were seated in the wagon. It rode up beside them.

"You," demanded the officer in charge who stood in the wagon, "stay here. You, get on." The women looked at each other, unable to distinguish where he was pointing.

"*Qui?*" asked Monique.

"Yes, you get on."

"*Pourquoi? Moi?*" Monique said as she was pulled up and into the wagon.

Louise ran alongside them until she was ordered to stop. "Hold on to the crucifix," she cried, tears streaming down her face.

Monique was knocked to the hard wooden floor of the wagon as it rode through the wooden fence surrounding the encampment and down a narrow road.

"You, come," said the soldier in English when the wagon stopped. His expression was devoid of emotion, and she had to hurry along just to keep up with him. Horrified and weak from lack of food, she kept pace until they reached a small shed at the back of the grounds, and after she was shoved inside he barred the door, calling out something she did not understand. Then he locked it and left.

Dusk fell, and she still sat on the dirt floor of the shed. She had never felt this frightened before, and prayed as hard as she could, holding the driftwood cross close to her chest. Was she here because of Pierre? She worried that they were both now in great danger, and thirst consumed her. She cried out in fear a few moments later when the bar to the windowless shed was slid away. There was still enough light for her to see that a soldier dressed in a blue uniform stood at the wide-open door, gun in hand. He placed a pot of water on the floor.

"Where is Jean?" he asked, holding his gun in front of the iron pot so that she could not take it. In the shadow she could see another man wearing regular clothes standing beside him. The other man began translating his questions and her answers. She thought his voice sounded like the son of Pierre LeBlanc, Uncle René's grandson.

"*Je ne sais pas.*"

"She does not know," the other man stated to the soldier.

"Where is Jean?" The soldier demanded again, waving his gun threateningly. She burst into tears.

"I do not know where he is. Please let me drink." She moved toward the pot of water.

"She is thirsty," said the interpreter, "and she says she does not know the whereabouts of Jean."

"Tell her there are tools missing from his shop, and axes," shouted the soldier in English.

"He says there are tools and axes missing from his shop," said the French speaker. "Please," he spoke in French, "I do not wish harm to come to you."

Monique stared at the Frenchman looking at her with a shocked expression. She reached for the water and was thrown back by a sharp crash to the left side of her head. She laid on the floor, blinking her eyes in an effort to see.

"Please stop," the interpreter called out.

Another sharp blow and Monique collapsed into the darkness. Hours later, she opened her eyes to the glare of daylight streaming in a hole in the shed roof, and groaned in pain when she touched the swollen left side of her head. She reached up to her hair. It was crusted with dried blood. Rolling to her side would help to relieve the pain, and when she did she came face to face with someone lying next to her. Father Allain, his face bruised and swollen like hers, smiled at her.

Chapter 16

Le Grand Dérangement

Wednesday, October 8, 1755

Just as Monique opened her mouth to ask Father Allain how he got there, she was interrupted by a familiar voice shouting outside the door of the small shed.

"*Allons!*"

"René?" Father Allain called out.

"*Oui. Allons . . . .*"

The door swung open, and blinding sunlight that streamed in forced Monique to close her eyes. A hand reached down to pull her by the arm up from the floor, and she reached for the crucifix. She was led out of the shed, her eyes now adjusting to the daylight enough to see soldiers all around them. They were moving out through the gates of the encampment and to the road.

"René!" repeated Father Allain. Her Uncle René was being carted in a small wheelbarrow by one soldier, with Father Allain right behind them followed by another soldier who seemed to be in charge. Monique was startled to see that a bayonet flashed over Father Allain's right shoulder. They were led silently down the road to a landing place at the mouth of the river, and once there, tossed into a waiting boat. Her neighbor Angeline groaned in pain and attempted to shield her baby from the bodies of her neighbors that were crowding in all around her. Monique noticed she had him wrapped in the five squares of the quilt she had shown them a few weeks before.

Monique tried to console Angeline.

"My baby is hungry," she said. "I have nothing for him. I do not know where Claude is. I fear he has joined his Métis brothers in the fight."

"Have you seen my mother?" she asked her neighbor.

Angeline shook her head, and Monique searched the crowds of people on shore hoping to see her mother and father. Other mothers and fathers came hand-in-hand with their youngsters and pushing wheelbarrows carrying sickly and older family members. Soldiers directed people into this boat or that, but not before they tore away the keepsakes in their hands and tossed them into a burning fire. Monique gasped with shock when a soldier reached into the boat and grabbed up her crucifix. She watched as he flung it into the air, and saw it land in the middle of the flames. She could see a fiddle, half-burned. The soldier stared at her with such contempt, she quickly turned away.

Acadians of all ages were rowed out to the many transport ships that waited for their loads. Some who were too weak to care wailed in sorrow and pleaded to be allowed to stay on the river bank until they died. Her eyes were desperately fixed on the shore as she hoped for a glimpse of her father or mother. The shore got farther away, until they were out to the mouth of the Gaspereau River, where a transport ship waited..

Time seemed to slow down, and Monique pleaded with God to stop this from happening. There were no words from anyone, only cries, moans, and terrified stares into each other's faces as the prisoners were directed across the deck of their transport ship and down into the hold. When the door shut, there was darkness. Deafening screams and groans caused a searing pain in Monique's chest, and the smell of vomit brought her to her knees on the hard, wooden floor. Once her eyes adjusted to the dim light that shone in under the door of the hold, shadowy faces of terror were all she could see.

The door to the hold opened periodically throughout the rest of the morning, and prisoners were forced to press more tightly together. It was impossible to stand up. They shifted around, trying to find a small space, and some pushed their fellow cargo in resistance. Some got on their knees to give older ones a space to sit or lay down. Monique gasped for fresh air every time the door opened. Her eyes would grow accustomed to the dark, and the sudden sharp daylight stung them each time, making it difficult to see who was being forced in.

As daylight waned, she and Father Allain found a space to rest together, comforting one another as best they could. They had decided to try to inch their way closer to the opening, and when the door opened the next time, Monique begged to be let out for air. The soldier on guard motioned with his gun for them to go, telling them in French they had one half-hour.

"Father Allain, look! We are still in the Basin!" They were surprised to see that their transport had left the mouth of the Gaspereau River, only to be anchored offshore from their village. Monique wondered if perhaps they were not going to have to leave after all. Before she could convey her thoughts to Father Allain, they were both swept up by the crowd of prisoners on deck as everyone moved quickly to the port side of the ship. A collective gasp went up.

"Oh Dear God no," shouted Monique. "Look!"

Father Allain crossed himself and leaned against the side of the ship, unable to stop the tears that rolled down his face. She reached for his hand as she watched the dance of flames in the sky above the Mélanson farm. Black smoke drifted around the flames until the

Virgin and Fires

patches of it from each barn and house up and down the road mingled together and mushroomed out over the dykes in their direction.

"*Mon Dieu!*" whispered Father Allain, and Monique followed where his finger pointed. Standing on a large boulder on the beach was a woman. Her garments shimmered in white and blue, and her face was surrounded in rainbow colors that shot out in every direction. Monique noticed a sensation in her left hand as it held tightly to Father Allain's. It was so heavy she could not have moved it away if she tried. A tingling sensation arose from her hand up her arm to her shoulder, and she felt afraid. When tears overcame her, the woman reached her outstretched arms in the direction of their ship. Time had frozen. The tingling continued to move through her shoulder and into her chest, but now she was not afraid anymore.

The vision vanished in a few moments, and the only thing left to see were the red flames, licking up into the sky, melting the landscape of Acadie. She put her head down, and Father Allain squeezed her hand.

"Did you see The Virgin Mother?" he whispered.

"Yes."

The soldier approached them and said it was time to go back. She walked in a daze behind Father Allain into the hold of the ship. They found a place to lie down next to each other, and Monique tried to sleep, to escape the cries of help from hungry children and the occasional panicked cry of someone seeing a loved one dying.

October 9, 1755

When Monique opened her eyes after a brief and fitful sleep, she felt a sharp pain in the pit of her stomach. She was lying curled up, and pushed away a heavy boot wedged into her abdomen. A sea of people lay on all sides of her. The door to the hold was opened, letting in a hint of a new day beginning. The smell of excrement filled the air in the hold, and she fought back nausea. She sat up and looked for Father Allain. He had rolled away from her, and she climbed over sleeping bodies to get back to him again.

"Father Allain," she whispered. He did not respond to her. She said his name again. He crossed himself and opened his eyes.

"*Oui.* I was praying for God to deliver us. I feel the Baye Française currents swelling under our ship. The sea gives life, and the sea takes life. It does both with no sentiment. We are of the earth and return to it, often in peace and sometimes in torment. Monique, I am a little frightened, because I feel that the sea is angry. Do you know that I love you like a daughter? I must say this, in case we perish today."

"Father Allain, please do not say such things! Do you not have faith that we will be returned to our village soon?"

"Monique, our village is no longer there. Did you see the flames yesterday?"

"Yes, Father. And I saw the Virgin Mary," she blurted. She had promised herself not to speak again about what she'd seen, for fear she was losing her mind.

"Yes, yes, I too saw the vision. Did you hear her ask me to take care of you?"

"She spoke to you, Father? I heard nothing, but she smiled as though she knew me. She was so beautiful. Do you think she is with us now?"

"Yes, and she does know us both, and all who are here, as her own children. However, I also fear she was delivering the message that we will not survive this."

"Oh, Father Allain, I am more frightened than I have ever been. I do not have the strength to get through this. I know it is a sin to speak of it, but I would rather die. I do not know what happened to my mother, to Papa, to Mariette. I want to die and I pray to be taken gently by Mother Mary!"

The ship had begun to rock as waves pounded against it. Monique felt bile in her throat and gasped for air. She thought about the last time she had eaten, yesterday. She pushed the person next to her away to get more space, and heard a groan. He was burning hot, and she took off her sweater to fan him, then tried to remove his shirt. She did not recognize his voice as he begged her for water. She had none, and quietly moved away from him.

The waves crashed harder now, and the ship rocked side to side and from front to back with no rhythm to its movements. It rose on a mountainous wave and crashed back down, pounding the human cargo against its wooden belly. The noise of the waves smashing the boat was deafening and filled all her senses. A body slammed up against hers, and she cried out for Father Allain. She could not hear the sound of her own voice. All was lost, then a small miracle.

"I am here, Monique." She scrambled to follow the sound of his voice and held on to his hand. Once again she had the sensation their clasped hands were bound together, that they would not come apart. She did not want them to come apart. The tingling returned, making its way up her arm and into her chest. Father Allain's hand was all there was to hold on to at this moment. She remembered the beauty of Mother Mary.

"Please, Virgin Mother," prayed Monique, "please spare us from this Hell."

Monique waited, expecting that at any second the boat would break apart and they would be floating in the frigid Atlantic. She shivered on the cold floor, and Father Allain seemed to sense it. She felt his arm around her. The sea was settling some, and the cries of those in agony and fear were rising over the ocean's roar.

"Pray for peace, pray for peace," Father Allain began to say. His voice grew louder, so that those nearby could hear. "We must all pray for the peace that comes from our faith. Pray with me:

Notre Pere, qui es aux cieux,
que ton nom soit sanctifié,
que ton regne vienne,
que ta volunté soit faite
sur la terre comme au ciel . . . .

Monique heard voices in unison, reciting the Lord's Prayer. After it was over, Father Allain shouted: "The ocean is calming. We will live another day. Our lives are a precious gift, are they not? The Blessed Virgin has indeed traveled with us."

Monique closed her eyes, listening to the voices of Acadie as they recited the Rosary together several more times. The occasional wave still caused them to lurch forward and back, but gradually the sea calmed. She fell asleep, her hand still in Father Allain's.

Chapter 17

The Search Continues

Friday, August 26

After Jacques and Michelle left early Friday afternoon, André went back to Blomidon Cottages, talked to Bill awhile, then went to his Art Appreciation class. Restless from sitting for two hours, he jumped into his car and drove to the liquor commission, picked up a six-pack and drank most of it, then crashed on the bed in his cottage. He thought about Monique and how she had probably taken a nap in this very spot a few nights before. Sleeping fitfully, he rolled out in the early evening and walked up the street to the Pizza Place, still half-awake. The lights seemed brighter than usual, but he chalked it up to being a little hung over. Returning to Blomidon Cottages, he suddenly got the urge to go back to the Park and try to get into the church. Parking his car in the parking lot, he crossed the road to the Historic Park, passed the statue of Longfellow and the dimly-lit information plaques about the Acadian farmers building aboiteaux. He walked up the steps to the chapel and pushed the large, creaky door open.

"Son of a bitch, you scared me!" exclaimed a heavy-set man wearing overalls.

"I'm sorry," André said, feeling an adrenalin rush of his own.

"Who're you?"

"I'm a tourist. Do you talk like this to all the tourists?"

"No, 'cause tourists don't come aroun' this time a night. You ain't supposed to be here."

"I'm a friend of the missing girl, Monique LeBlanc. Did you hear about her on the news?"

"'Course I did, but don't expect me to know nothin'," the man grumbled as he hastily dusted a display case. "The police already been around here, down at the house, askin' me questions, and I already told 'em I didn't see nothin'. I came in that night around nine, cleaned up the place, then went home."

"Well, I'll just get out of your way so you can finish up your work."

"Good," grumbled the man as he turned away.

The lights were so dim in here, André wondered how the custodian could even see enough to clean. He walked out, letting the door slam shut behind him.

Damn, that guy's creepy, he thought, feeling goose bumps going up his arms. When he went back to Blomidon Cottages, he drank another beer and fell asleep watching the news. Monique's disappearance and *Le Festival Acadien* were the local news headliners.

Saturday, August 27

At 8:30 A.M. on Saturday morning, André had already been up for hours. Jolted awake at four by a bad dream, he appreciated a hot shower that he didn't have to wait in line to get. After calling his mother in Shediac at 6 a.m. to tell her what was going on, he watched the morning news and fell back to sleep. Monique's picture flashed on the TV, and he dreamed about it, waking up irritable afterwards.

He searched through his pockets for a piece of paper with a name and number on it. The girl who worked in reception at the park had looked up the number in the phone book for him in exchange, she said, for a cup of coffee at Tim's. He had been nice to her, but his mind was consumed with finding Monique, and he had told her so. She replied that she understood.

He sped up the street to the dorm and searched for the paper there. Where had he put it? Rummaging through the clothes piled on his bed, he realized that he hadn't done a single bit of laundry lately. The blue shirt, had he worn that one when she gave him the piece of paper? André began heaving items of clothing around the room. Hearing a rustling sound in the pocket of a pair of jeans, he pulled out paper only to find that it was a receipt. He swore, then grabbed a pair of shorts and found it.

The phone rang out in the hall, stopped, and started again.

"It's Jacques," said Triggs from outside André's door.

André ran out into the hall and picked up the dangling receiver.

"Anything?" asked Jacques.

"No," replied André. He held the phone on his shoulder so he could smooth out the piece of paper. "I have to go, I'll call you later," he said.

"Wait . . . why?"

"I have to call a number in my hand."

"You wrote a number in your hand? What's it for, something about Monique?"

"No. Yes. I have a piece of paper in my hand that someone gave me and it has the name of a person and their number on it that I have to call right now. I'll call you back."

André had just hung up on Jacques, and he knew he'd have to listen to his wrath later on. But right now, he dialed the number on the paper. After only one ring, a man picked up.

"Hello?"

"Hello. Is this Mr. Daigle? My name is André Légere and I'm sorry to be bothering you this early, but I'm calling about Monique LeBlanc, the girl who's missing."

"Hello, André. It's no bother at all. I told the girl at the reception desk at the park to tell the missing girl's friends I gave the police a report about what I saw that night."

"I know you gave the police a report, but I hope you don't mind me calling you myself. Can you tell me anything else about the man you saw at the park Thursday night?"

"Not much, but I did some checking on my own this morning about who he could be, and I actually haven't called this in to the police yet."

André grabbed a pen and paper. "What's that?"

"I wanted to see what the custodian looked like, and when I saw him I knew he wasn't the man I saw in the park that night. The police didn't think he was important to the case, even though I have to admit he's a strange one. At any rate, the man I saw Thursday night was awfully old, could have been in his nineties, with droopy shoulders, you know, pretty hunched over. He had on a heavy sweater that was full of holes, a gray color from what I could see. It was getting dark out. Nobody around Grand-Pré seems to have a clue about who the man is, and we all pretty much know each other around here. This really doesn't tell you much, does it?"

"Anything's a help. Thank you Mr. Daigle."

"Call me back if you have any more questions."

André said a polite good-bye and hung up. Something Gerald Daigle said was bugging him and he didn't know what it was. The custodian at the chapel was a strange one, he agreed with that. But the police didn't consider him a suspect.

André told Jacques about the conversation with Mr. Daigle.

"No offense, pal, but I don't think that helps," grumbled Jacques.

"Yeah, I guess I'm really grabbing at straws now."

"Can't blame ya. But I have some good news. Michelle and I are definitely psyched to do the show today, 'cause it'll be on cable TV and we want to get all the Maritimes involved in finding Monique. We got permission to dedicate the festival to her and put her picture up and a police number to call. Jean-Paul Poirier is flyin' in here from

Boston tonight and will crash at our place after the show. He's actually a hell of a guy, and says his parents helped to form a group of some kind in New England to study the history of the Acadian people. He wants to donate some of the proceeds from the festival to help the police find Monique. He had a theory that maybe she was abducted by somebody. It's creepy and I hope he's wrong."

"I don't think she was abducted. Mr. Daigle gave a good description of the old man and what time he saw the taxi. And he didn't see anybody else. It's like she just vanished into thin air, unless the old man was some kind of a decoy. But things like that just don't happen, do they?"

"I dunno, Cuz."

"Any word about Monique's father?"

"Michelle called her own parents. Her father Bill is Joe LeBlanc's brother, and I guess Joe went to see a friend of his by the name of Broussard and they haven't heard from him since. The guy lives up near Breaux Bridge so he's not near the hurricane, but they don't have the guy's number so they can't call him."

"Broussard? David Broussard? I remember seeing his business card by the phone at the cottage," said André, a little excited to be able to offer something. "I think Monique may have called him. I'll call you back when I get down there in a few minutes."

"Good. Michelle says she needs Uncle Joe here for the festival. She thinks if he talks to the people, you know, being Monique's father . . . ."

"I wonder why she called that David Broussard guy?"

"No idea," said Jacques absently.

"She told me he was her professor at LSU," André remembered. "He taught a class about the Acadians, and Monique said she learned about her genealogy in his class. But why would she call him then?"

"Honey," Jacques called out to his wife, "why would Monique call that guy David Broussard the night she disappeared?" Jacques waited for a response, but none came.

"Hmm, she didn't answer so she must be out of earshot. Maybe Monique called to see if her father was there or something?"

"Yeah. Who knows?"

"Yeah. I just hope we can get holda Joe before the storm hits. I saw some pictures of it on the weather channel.

"I haven't been paying much attention to the news," said André.

"Hey, Cuz, why don't you come down here for the show this afternoon! You've been running back and forth like a maniac there. Let the cops do it, just for a day."

"I'll think about it. Right now I have to go to the Laundromat, then check in with the RCMP again. They're getting sick of me asking what they plan to do next. I did hear about Monique on the news though."

"I saw it on TV this morning, on the Halifax channel." After a brief silence, he said he had to wrap up their conversation and get to the park for the show. "Please come down, André," Jacques once more coaxed his cousin, "I really need ya here, man."

Chapter 18

Le Bateau de Horreur

Wednesday, October 15, 1755

The morning after the storm, the door to the hold was opened early. Bright sunlight shone directly into Monique's face, startling her awake. She shielded her eyes, making out the silhouette of a man in uniform, his shoulder buttons flashing. He was shouting an announcement in English. She crawled over closer to Father Allain.

"What did he say?" she asked.

"I heard the word 'bread.' Perhaps they will give us food today."

A few prisoners were permitted to leave and then the door slammed shut without pity. The rest of the starving souls were left to cry and moan in pain. Children wailed loudly, and parents were forced to listen, adding to the din many cries of their own. Monique tried to get on her knees, to see if she could see anyone she recognized in the ocean of bodies around her. Her legs buckled, and she sank down on the cold floor again, pain shooting up her leg and into her hip. She hoped she would be able to stand when her turn came to go up on deck.

Monique and Father Allain heard their names called later, and they held on to each other, crawling around others out into the cold, crisp air. They quickly ate the small ration they were offered.

"Father Allain," Monique said afterward. "I feel strong enough to walk a bit. Perhaps we will recognize some neighbors among those who are here on deck at the same time."

"Come, we will see." They slowly walked the side of the ship, gripping the wooden railing for support.

Oh, please God, Monique thought, let Mama and Papa be here somewhere. An old woman reached out for Monique's hand. "Help me, I have lost my husband."

"Where is he?" Monique asked.

"He is dead, still in the cargo hold, he does not breathe . . . . I have nobody . . . ." Father Allain bent down to touch her hand.

"What is your name?" he asked.

"Clotilde," she whispered, kissing his hand. "What is yours, Father?"

"I am Father Siméon Allain. I am a missionary."

"I know. I have seen you, at St. Charles des Mines Parish. Please pray for me," she begged, and Father Alain and Clotilde prayed the "Hail Mary" together. Clotilde wept, and Monique felt her heart ache for the poor elderly woman. So many broken people, she thought.

"And your husband's name?"

"Charles. Charles Comeau, from le Canard. Our children . . . we do not know . . . I do not know . . . . My Charles is dead. I am alone and Father, I have sinned against God."

"God forgives all," said Father Allain.

"Oh, Father, you do not understand what I have done. Charles was in great pain. He was sick before we came on the boat, and he struggled to breathe during the storm. He had been in terrible pain for so long. Yesterday, he cried out so, pleading for help, that I put my coat over his face until he stopped moving and . . . Do you understand, Father, I killed my Charles to end his pain. I believed that we would all be drowned during the storm . . . . I did not want to live . . . . Blessed Virgin please forgive me! Please forgive me, Charles, for taking your life," she wailed as she knelt and raised her arms to the Heavens over and over, then heaved herself on the deck. Father Allain sat down next to her.

"I believe the Blessed Virgin does hear your pain today," he whispered. "Clotilde, before they take us back down, I want to find you so that you can be with us until the voyage is over. Would you please just stay here, while Monique and I look around the ship for her parents? I promise I will return for you when they call us back down." Clotilde nodded.

"Angeline!" Monique called out. She had laid eyes on her neighbor, who was walking toward them holding her baby. Monique's delight quickly dissolved to shock when she looked at the infant she cuddled close to her. He was gray and seemed lifeless.

"What is his name?" asked Monique.

"Michel. He is very cold, and I have no milk to give him. I have been starved until just now, when they gave us bread and pork. The water I drank in the hold tasted terrible, and I fear it made my baby sick. He hardly even cries."

Monique recognized the small quilt he was wrapped in. "Please do not get discouraged. I will get my ration of water for you and Michel."

Father Allain and Monique walked slowly up and down the deck with Angeline, trying in vain to find a kind face among the uniformed guards. They received nothing but blank stares. Father Allain lifted the blanket when Angeline began to moan in despair, and his dark eyes showed sadness. He told Angeline it was time to perform the last rites on the small infant, and they prayed together as Michel drew in his last shallow breaths.

Angeline stood silently gazing at her dead son, patting his head and humming a lullaby. The three reached the stern of the ship where Angeline stopped and kissed Monique.

"I have cherished our friendship," she whispered. The new mother looked into the wake. Monique looked too, realizing too late that Angeline had deliberately leaned far over the side. Her balance lost, she fell headfirst into the ocean, gripping Michel tightly in her arms.

Screams of horror pierced Monique's ears from all directions, deafening the sound of her own. A soldier appeared on the spot where Angeline had stood a few seconds before, and was swiftly unfastening his uniform in a desperate attempt to rescue her.

"Cease! They are gone!" commanded his superior.

Monique watched in shock as Angeline, still clutching Michel tightly to her breast, disappeared into the waves splashing against the vessel. The wind had caught the small quilt and was blowing it back toward the ship. It fluttered and flew . . . up, up toward Monique and Father Allain. He reached out and captured it, as if by doing so, the last moments would reverse themselves. Father Allain held it, and Monique touched the wet fringes of lace. It was all that was left of Angeline who was forever lost in the whitecaps of the ocean that enveloped her.

"Most Holy Father . . . ." Father Allain prayed, between gasps of air. "Please forgive our sister Angeline for taking her own life today. We pray, Father, that you will meet her and her son Michel in paradise and she will find peace in your most merciful embrace."

Monique reached for Father Allain's hand, and they stood together silently. She held the quilt up to her cheek, making a promise to carry it with her when they returned to Acadie. She would bury it herself, on Angeline and Claude's farm.

The prisoners on deck went back to the freezing hold of the ship when they were ordered. Another long day in cramped darkness tested their endurance, and throughout the night, those that had the strength sang the hymns of Acadie for their more unfortunate friends who suffered from cold and disease. There would be little sleep on the rough seas, and the smell of excrement kept Monique heaving onto the floor throughout the night.

The following morning, Monique heard whispers among the prisoners.

"Philadelphie ou Boston?" Monique's stomach calmed, and she began to realize that the ship was now gently rocking back and forth on the waves. She lay quietly and listened for any other snippets of information, and sat up when someone farther down toward the door of the hold spoke. She recognized the voice. It was the voice that translated English when the soldier had held her prisoner in the shed back in Grand-Pré. She squinted her eyes to see better, and thought it looked like Uncle René LeBlanc's grandson Pierre talking. She listened more intently, but did not understand. Father Allain leaned toward her.

"Did you hear? Pierre LeBlanc just said we are no longer prisoners of the British Crown."

She lay back down for a moment, looking up toward the wooden ceiling. Grand-Pré—it seemed like a lifetime ago. She was so weak and hungry again and hoped that there would be food for them today. Father Allain sat nearby, crowded in with an old couple and Clotilde, and praying with them all. Monique crawled closer, and after the prayer Father Allain explained to her that the man he sat with had had a seizure during the night. Monique admitted, if only to herself, that she had vaguely heard the commotion but could not bring herself to raise her head from the floor. She looked over at the old man sitting there so meekly. She put her head back down, relieved that he was still alive, that they were all still alive today.

A cry of joy rose from the people still listening to Pierre. Although she did not know why they had cried out, the sound brought a smile to her face.

"Monique," Father Allain called over to her, "did you hear what Pierre LeBlanc said just now?" She shook her head, and the missionary gripped her hand. "He said that we are docked in Boston, and that leaders here will be inspecting our ship. Today we will all be permitted on deck to get food and water, and we will be able to see if your mother and father are on board!"

"But Father Allain, what if we are the only two people we know . . . ."

He placed a finger to her mouth and shook his head. "We are all Acadians, so none of us is alone. I heard that Colonel Winslow said he would try to keep families together, and it is possible he took a special interest in ours. Your mother worked so very hard to convince him he was making a mistake, and I think he truly liked her. While we hesitate to trust the wind that blows our camp away during the hurricane, we must learn to trust it once again to cool us in the summer sun. Perhaps even Colonel Winslow has the capacity to bring something good to us."

Monique and Father Allain bowed their heads together in prayer. The elder man and two women leaned over to indicate they wanted to be part of the devotional. All of them sat silently afterward, waiting. The old couple talked about their farm. They were from la Riviere Habitant, and had been brought on board in wheelbarrows by their grandsons. The man said he was afraid he would be separated from his wife, or even left behind, but Colonel Winslow himself had ordered their departure on this ship together. They were grateful, but wondered how they would manage in this strange place. They hoped they would find their sons and soon return to Acadie.

Hours later, it was their turn to move toward the open door of the hold. They ventured slowly, the younger ones holding up their elders. Once outside, Monique shielded her eyes until they adjusted to the sunlight. The winter winds whipped around Boston Harbor, and they crouched together on the deck in the shelter of the side of the ship. An announcement was made in French that bodies of five dead were stretched out on the deck at the bow, and family members could go and identify them. Father Allain offered to go with Clotilde, and Monique stayed back with the others. When Father Allain and Clotilde returned, Monique confirmed with him something she had noticed.

"Father, there are hardly any soldiers around us. Where do you suppose they went?"

"They have been asked to leave. Someone explained to me that they were replaced by guards the government of Massachusetts has chosen." Men wearing the dignified suits of important officials walked up to them, then wrote things down in black books. When Monique saw Pierre LeBlanc, Father Allain asked him in broken English what was happening.

"There are men here from the legislature of Massachusetts," he explained. "They have heard of us and are conducting an inspection. We were supposed to continue to Philadelphie, but conditions on board were so deplorable that officials here have demanded we stay on board at the dock until their inspection is complete. Apparently, the captain of our ship was given a letter from Governor Lawrence before we left Acadie, and in the letter Governor Lawrence said that we were a danger to the security of Nova Scotia, the British name for our Acadie. Mr. Hutchinson is the gentleman I spoke with, and he is very kind. There he is now!" Pierre beckoned to the man, who waved and walked in their direction.

"Hello," he said, extending a hand. He and Pierre spoke, Pierre struggling to find the words. "You need the little Acadian girl I just met who speaks English," said Mr. Hutchinson. "She was over there eating."

Monique had comprehended the words 'little girl' and 'English.' "What did he say, Pierre?" she said frantically, shaking his arm to command his attention. "Pierre, did he say a little girl who speaks English? *S'il vous plait? Le nom, le nom?*"

"Oh, Monique wants to know the little girl's name."

"I think she said it was Marie, no, it was more like Maria, Marietta, something like that," Mr. Hutchinson said, furrowing his brow in an effort to recall. "She was over there, seated at a table with her mother."

Monique bolted in the direction the gentleman had pointed, pushing through a crowd of people waiting for rations. She tripped over people lying down and walked around excrement on the deck. Suddenly, there was Mariette, seated in a small wooden chair next to a table and chewing on a crust of bread. And beside her stood Aunt Cecile and Mama.

"Mama! Mariette! Aunt Cecile!" She leaped over a child lying on the deck floor doubled in pain, then turned around. She located the child's mother before joining her own. Her mother and Mariette shouted Monique's name. Monique folded her hands in a short but tearful prayer of thanks to Mother Mary before she fell into their arms.

"Oh, Mama, *Tante* Cecile, Mariette," she said. "Papa?" she questioned. Mama's face fell, and she began to shake her head, trying to get the words out between sobs.

"No, Monique, No—he did not . . . make it through the voyage on this awful ship. His foot became infected, and he had a very bad fever. We shared our portion of water with him, but the water did not taste right. He died . . . the night before last, and is at the bow of the ship. We will try and bury him, but where?"

"Oh, Mama. Come, let us find him." Father Allain and his two elderly companions had now joined them.

"A moment, Monique," said Father Allain. "Pierre or Mariette, would you help with translating this? It is a little complicated, so we will speak slowly. Mr. Hutchinson told me he is part of a committee of men who are investigating the conditions on board this ship. They are appaulled by the treatment we have received, the way we have been crammed together worse than cattle would be treated. They will be investigating how this terrible event could have happened, so I now think it is possible for us to petition to return to Acadie, where we can bury François and reclaim our lives. In the meantime, Mr. Hutchinson said he would help to find us shelter in the city of Boston."

"Go with your women and find the body of François," said Mr. Hutchinson. "Tell the person standing guard to speak with me about what to do with those who perished on the way here. The Massachusetts government owns a cold storage morgue very close to the waterfront. It is for statesmen who request to have their remains returned to Britain after they die. In the winter months, it is sometimes better to place them in storage until such time as they can be transported. I can get special permission for these Acadians to be placed there and later buried in a government cemetery, if it is your wish."

"By then perhaps we will be returning to Acadie," added Father Allain.

The message communicated adequately, Father Allain wrapped an arm around each of the women. They walked back to the ship's bow to where bodies were lined up, most covered in a sheet, some with pieces of sail placed over their faces.

"I see him," cried Louise as she ran to one of the covered bodies, kneeling down beside it. Father Allain lifted the blanket off so that they could see the face of François one last time.

"*Au nom de Père.*" His voice broke, and he nodded at Monique, who picked up where he left off. She watched the tears roll down his cheeks, tears he made no attempt to hide. Louise touched François' face as she held tightly to Father Allain's arm.

"I loved you so, I loved you so, my dear husband," she cried to François, whose expression said his pain had ended. "My life was wonderful because of you, and I will see you soon enough. Your spirit will travel with me every step of the way back to Acadie. Father Allain, could we sing "Ave Maris Stella"? It was François' favorite." The three struggled to sing the words, to hold the tune. After a last kiss placed on François' forehead by his wife and then another by his daughter, Father Allain placed the blanket over his face and led both women back to their place on deck. They stood together throughout a long afternoon and into the evening, waiting for Mr. Hutchinson to come back as he had promised to do.

Mr. Hutchinson did indeed arrive with a horse and buggy just before midnight. Mariette translated as he explained that he had gotten permission for the LeBlanc and Mélanson families to live, at least temporarily, in a small, abandoned warehouse near the harbor. It would not be particularly comfortable, he explained, but it would be a shelter at least. The horse and buggy, driven by a man who Hutchinson said was his friend, took the group up a narrow street. Flakes of snow had started to fall, and the Acadians huddled together again to keep warm. Father Allain led them in singing the hymns that had comforted them so many times.

A small group of young men came out of the shadows and began walking behind them. Father Allain, thinking he recognized them as Acadians, beckoned them to come on the wagon.

"Dirty Papists!"

"French vermin."

One of them picked up a rock and threw it at the wagon. It hit the side with a loud thud, and women screamed and shielded terrified children.

A tall, robust young man came up close. Father Allain grabbed the side of the wagon and held on, then kicked one of his long legs as hard as he could, and the man buckled and moaned in pain. He attempted to kick another, but the group fell away from the wagon as they lifted their companion from the ground and dragging him away into the darkness.

"Go, Go!" shouted Father Allain to the driver in the best English he could muster.

"Monique," said Mariette, "I have never seen Father Allain so angry. He is a good kicker."

"Mariette, Shhh . . . ," said Monique, placing a hand over her small cousin's mouth.

In spite of all they'd encountered, the group broke into laughter at Mariette, agreeing that the missionary had shown amazing ability to hit his mark.

"I played lacrosse at the seminary," he said, "and I built up my leg strength. I also learned how to aim well."

The wagon came to a stop some time later in front of a dingy old building. Tired and shivering, the Acadians walked inside. Father Allain made an announcement as the travelers searched for a place on the frigid wooden floor.

"Tomorrow Mr. Hutchinson said he will come by with food and blankets. He also said we are welcome to stay here as long as we have to, and I requested a pen and paper to begin writing a petition to return to Acadie. Let us give thanks to God for keeping us together through this terrible trial, and please try and get some sleep. We must not give up hope." Monique held hands with her mother during the prayer. She felt her mother's hand so completely, the long slim fingers, the slightly wrinkled skin on the back of her hand. She placed it to her lips and kissed it. Her mother was alive, and she must make sure that Mama did not lose the will to survive during this awful time. They would be together tomorrow in this strange land, and the petition to go back would keep their minds occupied. Monique could imagine her father telling her to take care of Mama, and she promised him that they would survive this night. For the sake of her mother and Mariette, Aunt Cecile, for Father Allain, and for Pierre, she had to remain strong.

Chapter 19

Un Pays Etrangé

Mid-November, 1755

"Oh, I experienced Hell once before, when I was a young boy," Father Allain whispered to Monique in response to her question about whether he thought God was teaching them a lesson about what Hell was like. It was late at night, a week after their arrival in the slums of Boston, and it was too cold to sleep. Strange sounds outside all evening had Monique wide-awake. She worried that someone would try and burn down the building where they stayed. They were hated, and every venture out on the streets proved it. Newspapers spoke of the pathetic Neutrals from Acadie, and Mariette translated their foul sentiments daily. Now, long after midnight, Monique and Father Allain were each huddled under a pile of these newspapers. They had given the few blankets and heavier clothing they owned to Mariette and the other women, and Monique and the men had agreed to suffer through this night's freezing temperatures. Moonlight cast shadows on the bodies of the slumbering Acadians. Gusts of wind rattled the windows and tossed branches against them, making a clicking sound that seemed to mock the ones unable settle in for the night.

"I was a five-year-old boy when I saw my mother and father slaughtered in front of my eyes," Father Allain whispered quietly. "I never confided this to a living person except your Papa. On the ship I had nightmares about it."

Monique turned to face the missionary. His eyes, which had sparkled in the reflection of the moonlight a moment ago, now appeared dark and fierce. "I would wake up during the nights on the ocean wanting to scream, but I could not bear to join the screams and moans of the suffering and dying. If I had, I would surely have believed I was going insane. Last night, I dreamed my mother was screaming in terror and I could do nothing to help her. I had forgotten this memory, and in my dream I saw it as though it happened yesterday. I remember now, running through the woods and being captured. I turn toward my enemies, ready to fight, my small fists raised. They have war paint on their faces. I am so terrified, but I also want to kill them all. I run to the one who most terrifies me . . . strike him as hard as I can on his thigh, screaming at the top of my lungs. He picks me up and carries me back to camp. He holds me even as I smash at his face. He tries for many weeks to get me to talk, but I refuse. He sits with me and burns sage each night, and tries to communicate to me that he believes his tribe has made a grave error. They have murdered French *amis*, not the English enemy. I do not understand until later, when I learn his language and become like his own son.

"They take me to the sweat lodge, hold their ceremony for many days, and he names me 'Fights with Fists.' They hold a special burial, wrap the bodies of my mother and father in birch bark, and place them in the sacred burial ground. They mark the spot with a stone marker, and I return to it many times. I will return again before I die. Living through that was Hell, my dear Monique, and this is Hell too. And the worst now is just as it was then; we are living through it rather than being mercifully removed by death. I learned that God brought me through Hell in my childhood. What I endured was not a punishment, but a fulfillment of His divine purpose for me. The Mi'kmaq became my father, mother, brothers and sisters. God takes care of us now also, and will bring us through to fulfill His purpose. Some of us, such as your Papa, have been taken to paradise already and spared further pain."

Monique brushed the missionary's hand as he lay beside her. "I'm so sorry, Father Allain. I am so sorry for what you went through as a little boy. I am very glad you told me about it. Papa said several times that you had a very difficult childhood, but he never said anything more, although I confess that I pressed him once."

"Your father was a great and trustworthy friend, and when our petition is heard and we return to Acadie, I will do something very special in his honor."

"Do you still have hope we will be able to return?"

"I will have hope as long as there is the faintest chance we can go back. Tomorrow Mr. Hutchinson will be returning to bring us some supplies. He told me today that we will be moved to towns outside of Boston for now, and wherever there is a town willing to take a number of us, that is where we will have to go."

"We cannot stay together?"

"I do not know. We have to take what is offered. And Mr. Hutchinson said that our children could be indentured."

"What is indentured?"

"People will hire us to work in their homes. Most will undoubtedly be interested in girls of Mariette's age, who are able-bodied."

"No, Mariette will stay with us. She will not be indentured." She waited for Father Siméon to agree, but he remained silent. Monique lay awake, thoughts of separation and indenture keeping her awake long after everyone else was asleep. She prayed, "Heavenly Father, please protect my family and friends. I know you would not let anything bad happen to Father Allain, or Mariette either. I know you must have special plans for both of them." Finally, Monique began to feel sleepy. Shivering under the newspapers, she refolded her pillow—the small baby blanket that had belonged to Angeline.

The following day, Father Allain held a Mass.

"We will hold our Masses quietly," he explained before beginning his homily. "We find ourselves to be in this strange land, in the midst of Protestant and Puritan brothers and sisters. We wish not to incur their anger, but only to observe our customary traditions, which bring us hope and comfort during these difficult times. I will speak to Mr. Hutchinson about the observance of *les fetes*, particularly Midnight Mass." He preached a homily on forgiveness and, after the Mass, united the Acadians in praying the Rosary.

Mr. Hutchinson returned as he had promised, bringing several other men with him. He entered the building carrying boxes filled with bread and greeted the Acadians warmly. Using Mariette as his interpreter, he introduced the men as "leaders" from towns outside of the city of Boston.

"My dear friends, first of all I apologize for taking so long to come back to see you. I have been talking to many of your countrymen who have been dispersed to many places around the city and beyond, searching desperately for family members they have been separated from during their voyage. Altogether, there are more than a thousand of you in the Boston area who are in the same predicament. A few others in our towns who sympathize with your situation have appealed to their own churches to provide food and blankets. In the meantime, you are suffered to walk the streets and find work or food, but I caution you all to take care not to incur the wrath of those hostile English-speakers you encounter in your travels. Many believe you will rise up against us or steal our possessions. I understand that you are not so inclined, but they do not."

Mr. Hutchinson paused and waited for Mariette to translate. The group of Acadians chuckled, and Mr. Hutchinson smiled his acknowledgement that Mariette had put her own chosen word of translation on the so-called "hostile English-speakers." He turned to Mariette. *"Comprenent-ils?"* Mariette nodded and smiled sweetly, and he continued.

"I have with me today Mr. John Parkhurst from Waltham, Mr. James Cunningham from Medfield, and Dr. Donald Timbull from

Fitchburg. They represent their towns in accepting a number among you, and have already made arrangements as to where you will stay and how you will be provided for in their communities. We at the legislature have made an appeal to the Governor of Nova Scotia to assist us with the costs of relocating you, but as of now we have not received any answer. We will continue in our efforts. After I am finished speaking, please stand beside the man whose town you have been assigned to."

Mr. Hutchinson waited as the men spread out to allow room, then continued. "Your children will most likely be indentured. This means that they will be assigned work as servants. You will still be able to see them . . ." Mr. Hutchinson stopped speaking and looked at Mariette. She was silent, her lower lip curling downward in an angry pout.

"Mariette, why did you stop translating?"

"I do not like that word, 'indenture,'" she replied in her native tongue. "I will not be anyone's slave, Mr. Hutchinson." She stood firm, shoulders back, defiant. "And you will need to find another interpreter," she added in French before walking back in the direction of her mother and wrapping herself tightly in her billowy skirts. An uncomfortable silence followed, and the four men at the front of the room spoke quietly to each other. Father Allain stood up after a few moments, walking to the front of the hall. In very broken English, he spoke to the men.

"Please, our Acadians, *ils sont* very—how you say eet?—*scary*." He wrapped his arms around himself to express fear.

"Yes, of course," acknowledged Mr. Hutchinson. "Of course you are frightened to have to move again, but I assure you this is the beginning of a better situation for all of you."

Mr. Hutchinson began unloading the boxes of food and gestured for the other men to go outside and bring in large jugs of water. Several boxes contained blankets and home-made quilts, and one held hand-made sweaters in colors Monique had never seen before. Another wooden box contained donated books. Immediately upon lifting the cover, Monique called to Mariette. The young girl shouted with glee and took the box to a corner of the room, emptying its contents and sitting in the middle of the pile.

Monique reached into the box of sweaters and pulled out an indigo-colored one for Father Allain, and a green one for herself, then searched deeper for one that would fit Mariette. A white wool sweater with silver buttons caught her eye, and she ran over to Mariette, holding it up to her. Mariette smiled again as she happily put the sweater on. She paraded around the room, receiving hugs and compliments from her family members.

The men stood silently again after all the boxes were unloaded.

They each had a piece of paper with a list of names. Mr. Hutchinson asked that everyone listen. The first one to step forward was Mr. Parkhurst from Waltham. A tall, skinny man with pant-legs that were too short, he looked around awkwardly and cleared his throat.

"We have provided you with husbandry-work materials such as wool and embroidery thread. The sweaters come from a church congregation. They donated them for warmth and protection from the New England winter cold. When you reach Waltham, we will also give you spinning wheels. The women will be expected to do this labor, and the men will have jobs outside the home, helping men of the community with their chores and repairs. No one will receive more than forty shillings for their labor." Mr. Parkhurst paused, rocked back and forth nervously, then cleared his throat and continued.

"The following will be coming with me to Waltham." He read all the names slowly, deliberately, pausing after each one until the person or persons responded and came to the front.

"Cecile Trahan and Mariette.

"Louise Mélanson.

"Monique Mélanson.

"Jean Bourque and his wife Adele.

"Baptiste LeBlanc and his wife Irabelle."

Mr. Parkhurst paused and looked up. Monique waited for him to look down at his paper again and call more names. She waited for him to say Father Siméon Allain, and he did not. He folded his paper and set it on the table beside him. Her heart sank. Mr. Cunningham from Medfield was next, and Monique's mind raced as he read the names on his list. Father Allain's name was not there either. When Mr. Timbull from Fitchburg read his very short list, he called out the name of Siméon Allain. She glanced at the missionary, and her eyes blurred with tears. He looked at her and nodded, then looked away.

"And I also need to inform you," said Mr. Hutchinson, "so that you do not find yourselves in the unfortunate position of being charged a fine, that celebration of Christmas is forbidden in Massachusetts. Our countrymen observe it in only the most solemn of ways. They will take notice if you do not follow this law."

"May we be permitted to hold our Midnight Mass during *les fetes*?" asked Father Allain. "We have little joy this season, being so far away from everything we know and grieving the loss of loved ones, but we would take great comfort in observing our Mass and the midnight supper of *tourtiere*."

"Yes, I understand," said Mr. Hutchinson. "Please be careful to keep your religious ceremonies very quiet. What is tore-tee-air?"

"*Tortierre* is pork pie," answered Mariette. "*Tante* Louise makes the best ones in Grand . . . ." The girl fell silent but caught the eye of her smiling aunt, who spoke next.

"Mr. Hutchinson, you would be most welcome to join us at Midnight supper." Mr. Hutchinson thanked Louise for the invitation, and promised to consider it.

"Come," spoke Mr. Parkhurst to his group, "we will load up our wagon and depart for Waltham." He gestured to the Acadians standing next to him, and the group of eight followed reluctantly as he held the door for them. Monique, her arm around Mariette, whispered in her cousin's ear. "Ask if Father Allain can come with us." Mariette nodded in agreement and approached Mr. Hutchinson.

"Please, Mr. Hutchinson, we require another member of our family to stay with us. Father Allain, over there, could he please come with us to the place . . . how do you say it? Waltam?"

"I'm sorry, Mariette, but these decisions have already been made for us. Mr. Allain may certainly petition to move, if he can find work in Waltham. In the meantime, he will have to go to Fitchburg. A place has been allotted to him there."

Mariette turned to face Father Allain, who had approached them. "It is fine, Mariette, I will be fine and I will indeed petition to come to Waltham. We must follow the rules."

"I will do my best to help you," Hutchinson assured the missionary, offering a handshake.

Hours later, they were out of the city and in the town of Waltham. People had gathered in the churchyard where they were being let off, standing and staring as if they were part of a parade. Monique felt dirty and disgusting. She fought back tears, which made her feel even more wretched. They were a spectacle, and she heard the whispers about the "French neutrals" and "expelled Papists." She looked at her mother, and was shocked. Her mother stood and stared, appearing numb with fear. Her face was white, and her arms and hands quivered. Monique was frightened that Mama would faint at the next moment.

"Mama, come and we will pray together. Papa would want us to be strong." Her mother nodded, but did not respond as they walked into an old church vestry.

"This church has not been used for two years." Mr. Parkhurst. turned to Mariette for help in getting his message across to his new residents, and Mariette rolled her eyes and complied. "You are welcome to stay here as long as you need to, and in the meantime our legislature . . . ." Mr. Parkhurst paused, aware that Mariette had not quite understood. "Our legislature is like our government." She nodded and he continued. "They will be looking at a number of things about your arrival here. There will be a report issued on the terrible conditions you endured on the transport ships, and your government will be expected to send money. We will also look at legislation regarding indenture, so that parents will not have to give up their children."

With the saying of the word "indenture," Mariette had stopped translating. The pout was back, now directed at Mr. Parkhurst. He stopped, awkwardly looked around, then proceeded to the church door and opened it. He motioned for the group to step inside.

"It is warm in here!" exclaimed Mariette. "Mama, feel how warm it is," she repeated as she ran toward the small wood stove and placed her hands above it.

The Acadians would sleep warmly tonight, for the first time in months. There was enough wood to keep a fire burning for two days, and they were promised that more would be forthcoming. They slept by the stove that night, singing, praying, and weeping together.

Chapter 20

Le Festival Acadien

Saturday, August 27

André's Honda had lots of pep, and he had been having fun weaving in and out between the gas-guzzling SUVs on Robie Street until a cop pulled him over and handed him a ticket. Within minutes he was back to speeding his way toward the waterfront, taking full advantage of the slower tourists who were trying to figure out which lane they should be in. He knew where he was headed, and he was in a rush to get there. This was one thing he could control, and it felt good.

As soon as he was inside the gate to the festival, he spotted Jacques and Michelle up on the stage. Jacques was moving a speaker into place and dragging some cables along the stage, and André ran up to help him. He did exactly what Jacques directed him to do, and Jacques seemed pleased have his help.

"Sit right over there with Jean-Paul," he said. "They brought some extra chairs."

André walked down toward the people there, wishing now he had wandered around a bit. Probably some of his acquaintances from Acadia University were here somewhere, and they had undoubtedly brought coolers. By now the sun was high in the sky, and there was no escape from the scorching heat. He changed his mind about sitting there and went to the concession stand to grab a hamburger. On the way, he met a group of people he knew and they showed him where they were very comfortably situated. Lawn chairs with umbrellas sat in a row, with a holder in the arm of the chair to set a can of beer in. He was welcomed to sit down after he returned with his hamburger and water, and put the water on the grass after being handed a beer. The Lafayette Duo was now on stage.

With a count of four, Jacques kicked off a rocking rendition of *"Fier d'etre Cadien"* adding their own twist to the beat. The synchronicity between Michelle and Jacques was so exciting it sent shivers down André's spine. Jacques was a master at getting the best sound out of the equipment, and the band looked thrilled just to be there together. He chuckled at Jacques' dancing around on stage, his large body awkwardly gyrating to the rhythms in sharp contrast to his wife's willowy, graceful movements. Jacques sported a white T-shirt and khaki shorts with work boots, his signature look. Michelle wore a peasant type of dress, bright blue. What a beauty, André thought.

If he didn't know better, he'd swear that not a thing was wrong today. The crowd responded at the end of the song, cheering wildly. Jacques and Michelle clearly had lots of fans on the East Coast of Canada already. André felt more relaxed than he'd been in days. People around him continued clapping, dancing and cheering, and it was apparent to him that most had been waiting for the show long enough to have a substantial amount of alcohol flowing through their blood streams. He was offered another beer and guzzled it, and when a girl grabbed his hand to dance he took the offer. After a few dances in the heat he sat back down to catch his breath, then reached down under his chair to scoop up the bottle of now lukewarm water.

He decided to cut out the alcohol for now and enjoy the music, but a couple of bad singers behind him began to spoil the experience. He said good-bye to his friends and made his way through the crowd back to the front, where he joined Jean-Paul and introduced himself. They offered him a lawn chair and he enjoyed at close range the talent of his best friend and his wife, and the amazing musical chemistry between them. A beer was handed his way and he guzzled again, feeling the rhythms and strains surging through his body. When the Lafayette Duo played a familiar Acadian song, he recalled his grandmother singing it to him when he was a young boy. The Celtic progressions reached into his soul, into his cells, in some kind of mystical way. He felt transported by them, and closing his eyes he drank in the sounds of the accordion, then fiddle, then the bass guitar, then the percussion.

He wished Monique was here with him. She had been so enthusiastic the other day at Art Appreciation class, he knew she would be thrilled to see her cousin today. It was an injustice that she was missing this, and he felt personally cheated. He knew she had gone to Grand-Pré that night with the same childlike longing that he felt listening to the music of his Acadian roots. He thought about how quickly he'd fallen for her.

Michelle shouted *"Bonjour!"* into the microphone, and received a loud, united *"Bonjour"* back from the audience.

"Mes amis, Acadien et Cajun, laissez les bon temps rouler!"

A deafening cheer went up from the crowd, and Michelle and Jacques gave them a big wave, Michelle threw them all a kiss. After introducing Jacques and the band, she introduced herself and said that this afternoon's show was being dedicated to her cousin, Monique.

"Most of you have probably heard by now that Monique LeBlanc disappeared from Grand-Pré last week. Monique is my cousin," she said, pausing when some people gasped with surprise. "She visited Grand-Pré Park last Thursday and disappeared, and up to this point we haven't found her. There are some things about the police investigation I am not permitted to say, but I do want to tell you all that a witness only reported seeing a very old man in the vicinity at the time of her disappearance. If anyone has any information . . ."

Michelle's voice broke, and she turned toward Jacques. He immediately stepped over close to her and wrapped an arm around her waist. A few members of the audience clapped hesitantly, and others joined in until there was a deafening applause for the young couple.

"Monique, This one is for YOU!" shouted Jacques into the microphone. "Come back to your Cajun and Acadian family soon, ya hear?"

With that, Jacques began a fiddle riff and belted out *"Acadie à la Louisiane."* Michelle hesitated, then regained her composure and sang harmony. Then the couple switched off so that she carried the melody and he the harmony. They melded in a dance, she on the accordion and he on the fiddle, and ended the song on a dramatic note by singing *a cappella*. André looked back at the audience behind him. He was elated for his two friends on stage, and for the band, who were experiencing this almost supernatural feeling of warmth and enthusiasm. Suddenly, Jean-Paul jumped to his feet and extended a hand to André. The two men linked arms and spun each other in a circle, Jean-Paul letting out a "Yee-haa" as Jacques grinned at them from the stage.

Dusk brought out candles, flashlights, the smells of bug repellant mixed with beer, and an occasional cloud of smoke from somewhere. Michelle announced the last two songs and introduced Jean-Paul to the audience. She explained that he was taking an active role in the search for Monique.

"We want to dedicate these songs not only to our Monique, but to all the people of Louisiana who are waiting out the storm tonight," she said. *Bonsoir*, everybody! Remember—lots of prayers tonight!"

The Lafayette Duo charmed the audience with the last songs of the evening, announcing that their CD, *Coeur D'Acadie,* would be on sale behind the stage. André strolled over to buy one, but stopped when he heard his name called.

"I know you, I think," he said, trying to place the girl who had called out to him.

"I'm Anne Hebert," she said. "We went to school together in Shediac, but I was one grade behind you, so you probably didn't know me." She extended her hand to him. "I wonder if you could come over and meet my great-grandmother. She might be able to help you with Monique."

André followed Anne Hebert to a spot on the lawn where a whole extended family seemed to be congregated, from toddlers in strollers to one small and fragile woman who sat in a folding chair in the midst of all of them. Wispy gray hair stuck out in sprigs from beneath a wide brimmed straw hat. She smiled at him, a very wrinkled but joy-filled smile.

"She doesn't speak English, but she really wanted to come and hear the music today. When we tried to wheel her into this park in her wheelchair, her wheels didn't move well across the grass so a man who lives nearby offered to go get his wheelbarrow. We padded it with pillows and blankets and wheeled her in here in it. Mémère looked really funny, but she didn't care, as long as she could come. They let her in for free, since she's ninety-two. Come, I'll introduce you to her. What is your father's name?"

"Alphonse, and my mother's is Lillian. Your mother might recognize her nickname, Waterlily. She and my father run one of the tour boats and one of the tourists who comes up every year started calling her that a long time ago. The name sort of stuck."

"Mémère," said Anne in French as she kneeled down closer to her great-grandmother's face, "I have someone here I'd like you to meet. His name is André Legere." The elderly woman raised her head to get a better look at André, and he saw eyes sparkle in a face that was filled with wrinkles as well as with *joie de vivre acadienne.*

"Jacques is my cousin," said André, pointing up to the stage. Anne translated.

"André is from Shediac," she continued to explain to her great-grandmother. "He's the son of Alphonse and Lillian. Waterlily?" Recognition of the nickname registered on the old woman's face, and she nodded at André and studied him a few more moments.

"*Oui.*" She spoke to Anne in a dialect that André recognized as *Chiac,* but he shrugged in apology when she looked at him. "Rue Chesley," she said, and he replied, that, yes, his parents still lived on Rue Chesley. The old woman began to explain something to her great-granddaughter. André waited. From Anne's expression, he could tell she was uncomfortable translating something her grandmother was recounting.

"I know this sounds crazy, but my *Mémère* says that there were legends passed from generation to generation, and there was one she heard about some priests and missionaries who appeared to Acadian people sometimes. Each one had a message to give regarding the terrible *Grand Dérangement* which nearly destroyed our culture. Perhaps someone appeared to Monique and she followed him somewhere. It is not the first time someone has claimed to see these spirits, usually a man but sometimes a woman, and then disappear for a few days. A story was passed down from my mother that a friend of her great-aunt had such an experience. She had said the man's name was Father Allain and he wore an old gray, tattered sweater." André's mind had frozen. He felt a cold chill running up his back to his neck and shivered noticeably.

"André, are you all right?" asked Anne, noticing André's blanched expression.

"It's just weird stuff—strange things happening."

"My Great-grandmother says that as far as she knows, nobody in this legend died or anything like that. *Oui, Mémère*," she said, then turned back to André. "She wants me to tell you that she believes they were angels, and they came to speak to Acadian people occasionally, to heal the wounds they still feel many generations later and to give them hope during hard times. She says to you, "Worry *pas*.""

"Merci," he said as he took the old woman's hand in his own. She smiled back, and in that instant he felt hope that Monique was still alive.

"Would you like to walk back with me and meet Jacques and Michelle?" he asked Anne.

"I would love to!" Anne waved goodbye to her great-grandmother and told her brother she'd be back shortly. The two walked back up toward the front, choosing to take the long way around rather than winding through the hordes of people sitting and laying all over the large grassy park.

"Have you seen the work they've done at Pointe-du-Chene Wharf? It's really looking great. It's my great-grandma's favorite spot. She can sit there for hours."

"I did see it this summer when I was in Shediac for a few weeks," André replied. "The tourists were everywhere. Your great-grandmother still has spunk, from what I see. I'm not sure I believe everything she said, but it's something to think about. I don't rule out any leads these days."

"She believes in the folk medicine and the stories that have been passed down the generations, and she wanted me to tell you what she knew, which I did for her sake. But honestly, I'm not sure I believe all that either. I wish there was more I could do."

"Thanks, and just to know people care about Monique helps. Maybe lots of prayers will bring her back safely. I really am getting scared we are going to find her body somewhere, and I can't stand the thought. Tomorrow it will be three days."

"Is she your girlfriend?"

André hesitated. "Well, I just met her last Wednesday, and this is may soound strange, but I think for me it was love at first sight."

"I do believe in that."

"I guess I do too, now that it happened to me." André could feel himself blushing as he searched the stage for his friends. Jean-Paul was helping Jacques and Michelle pack up the equipment, and Michelle was standing at the other side of the stage, her head down. She held her cell-phone up to one ear, and her finger in the other one. André beckoned for Anne to follow him up on the stage, where he introduced Anne to Jacques and Jean-Paul.

"Hey cousin," said Jacques, "Jean-Paul is staying with us tonight, so why don't you lock up your car here and come over to our place? You can drive back tomorrow after our last set. A bunch of folks are comin' over, Acadians from Church Point and other guys and with their wives and girlfriends who are here from Prince Edward Island."

"Thanks," said André. "My car's already locked up, and maybe Anne would like to come too. Just think, we are all Acadian descendents. Anne and I are both from New Brunswick, Jean-Paul is from Boston, and you two are from Louisiana. The others over there are from PEI. Pretty cool, I think."

"It's amazing," said Jacques. "It's like a big family reunion today. Why don't you come on over, Anne? I'll give you directions." He beckoned his wife over to meet Anne. Michelle came toward them looking exhausted and red-faced, tears streaming down her cheeks.

"I just called Sgt. Williamson, and there's still no word. He said they picked up the sweater that was left on the beach yesterday, but I guess I was hoping for a miracle today."

"I was too, Michelle, I'm so sorry." Jacques spoke gently to his wife, holding her hand and trying to console her. "What did he say?"

"He said that they're still combing the woods down by Gaspereau, a place they haven't spent as much time checking. They're dragging the rivers, and he said he would call and give me an update in the morning. It almost makes me sick just thinking about it."

"Let's just go home, Michelle. We don't have to have anybody over. I'm sure Jean-Paul will understand."

"No, it's OK. I need our friends to come over." Michelle suddenly realized that there was a new person in their midst. "Hi, I'm sorry, I'm Michelle," she said to Anne.

"No need to apologize," said Anne. "I'm so sorry about Monique, and I will keep her in my prayers, as I'm sure everyone out here today will. You have lots of people supporting you through this. My family, especially my great-grandmother, strongly believes that Monique will return. And thank-you so much, Jacques, for inviting me over," replied Anne appreciatively, "but speaking of reunions, my family is having one this weekend. We chose to have it here in Halifax, just because of *Le Festival Acadien*, and we are all having a fantastic time! We've booked some rooms at the Sheraton tonight and are getting together with some relatives in Yarmouth tomorrow. It was awfully nice to meet you all though, and I adore you two. You really are wonderful together."

Anne and Michelle gave each other a hug, with Anne promising Michelle again that she would pray for Monique. She said good-bye to the group and André walked her back to meet up with her family.

"Would you like me to wheelbarrow your great-grandma back out of the park?" he asked.

"Oh, no, thanks. My brother is the designated driver," she added, "but the shape he's in, he might need to be wheeled out himself! I'm sure someone will be able to manage it, though. Bye André, it's been fun seeing you again."

"Bye, Anne," André said as he waved to her, then hurried back the other way to join his friends. He found them sitting around on lawn chairs between open instrument cases having a relaxed jam session, a cooler open in the middle of their circle. Jean-Paul had left to get a limousine.

"Have a seat," said Jacques to André. "Tomorrow we hope to hear from Monique's father."

By the time the limo arrived, the cooler was empty. There was plenty of room, so André crawled into a seat and curled up, his jacket on his chest. He listened to the others as they recapped the events of the day, then slowly drifted off, hearing only voices in the distance. He was in a dream, sitting in the Grand-Pré chapel. Monique sat next to him, a smile on her face. He leaned over to give her a kiss on the cheek, and she said to him in a deep voice, "We're here."

André opened his eyes suddenly and looked around. Jacques was holding the car door open, waiting for him to wake up enough to crawl out.

Chapter 21

Religion, Reality, and Truth

Early January, 1756

"Mariette, you could have gotten us both arrested," scolded Monique one afternoon when she and her cousin returned to the church after being in town. "You must learn to keep your comments to yourself, instead of blurting them out like you do."

Seated at a small wooden table were Adele Bourque, Irabelle LeBlanc, Louise and Cecile. Aunt Cecile gasped and shook her head. The women had spent the afternoon adding to the squares to the quilt that had belonged to Angeline, and they stopped sewing to hear what happened.

"Sit," said her mother.

"Mama, Aunt Cecile, I honestly worry about Mariette," said Monique. She turned to look at her cousin with scorn, but the young girl had already wandered to a far corner of the room and sat there, by all appearances engrossed in a book.

"What happened?" asked Mariette's mother, her misgivings about hearing the truth clearly showing in her expression.

"We were in the center of town, and a man and woman walked toward us on the street. The man was dressed in the black robe of a man of God, and they both carried Bibles. When he got closer to us he seemed appalled by our clothing or something and tried to put more distance between himself and us. I was angry, but certainly did not intend to say anything to a complete stranger."

"And of course, Mariette did," said the young girl's mother.

"Yes, Aunt Cecile, she did. She walked right up to him and shouted, 'Are you a Christian?'"

"And?" the four women said, all eyes now on Monique.

"The minister at first said nothing. I suppose he was shocked that she spoke such good English."

"And did he respond?" asked Monique's mother.

"Yes. He said he was a Christian, and then Mariette said, 'You do not behave as one.'"

Irabelle suppressed a giggle, turning it into a cough. Monique continued, "If you could have seen Mariette, you would agree that she had a look more fierce than the final judgment of the Almighty Himself!"

"Oh, my dear, oh my word!" exclaimed Irabelle.

"And that was not the end of it. A policeman approached us and called the man in the black robe by name, Reverend Wilson. He asked Reverend Wilson if there was a problem with the vagrants."

"And what did he say?" asked Adele.

"Oh, he did not have a chance to speak. Mariette said to the policeman, 'This man is carrying a Bible, and he does not behave as a Christian. Is that a crime here in Massachusetts?'" The group simultaneously inhaled loud gasps, and all eyes drifted toward Mariette. Monique turned around to see that her cousin was still in the corner, her back to their conversation.

"Did she say all these things in English?" asked Louise.

"Yes, plainly and clearly, as far as the policeman was concerned. He looked like he wanted to pick her up, put her under his arm, and cart her right off to the jail. I asked her afterward to tell me everything, so I could understand why the policeman had become so furious."

"He did?" exclaimed Aunt Cecile, fanning herself to keep from growing too anxious. Louise reached over to pat her sister's hand.

"Yes, he did," continued Monique. "He said, 'Young lady, you are one of those peasant neutrals who have come off the filthy boats in Boston to beg in our towns for food and shelter. I will not have you talking to Reverend Wilson in that tone of voice. Perhaps I should arrest you right now, just to teach you a lesson!'"

"Oh Mercy!" exclaimed Aunt Cecile.

"I am sorry to have to tell you Aunt Cecile that I could hardly contain my tears, I was so frightened. I hadn't understood the words, but I certainly had interpreted the emotions. Thank Heavens, the woman who was with the minister spoke up. Whatever she said, it settled the policeman down immediately. I think she must be someone important. The next thing I knew, she was leading Mariette off to a park bench. I followed, relieved to get away from both of those men. The woman, Mrs. Hoskins, talked to Mariette for quite awhile and asked her many questions."

"What did she say?" asked Aunt Cecile.

"I do not know. I did not ask Mariette about that yet because I am still angry with her."

"Mariette," called her mother, "Can you come here, please?"

"Yes, Mama," the young girl answered sweetly. She meandered

across the hall slowly, pausing to look out the window for a moment. A little closer, she stopped again to inspect something on the floor.

"Mariette, sit down," said her mother firmly. "First of all, you have behaved shamefully today and could have gotten both Monique and you into very serious trouble. And second, I would like to know exactly what that woman said to you."

"She said that she is a Quaker minister. She told me she comes to Boston from Newport Society of Friends to preach, and she noticed that I could speak both French and English, which she said I do very well for my age. Let me think . . . ."

Monique knew that Mariette was enjoying the moment, keeping her audience, the people who should now be scolding her, at rapt attention as she told about the mysterious woman who had rescued her. Monique felt her face flush.

"She asked if I was poor," Mariette said after a moment. "I replied that I am now but last year I was not. I lived with my family on our farm, and we had a happy life. I told her I need to go back home, to beautiful Acadie, as soon as possible. The woman said she had heard things about the Acadian people, about how they were made prisoners and sent away from their farms. She also said that I would undoubtedly be indentured, that she herself was indentured as a young girl. She cautioned me about respecting my elders, but I said that I could not respect someone who carried a Bible and treated others unkindly. She said she would speak to Reverend Wilson."

"Well, even so, you will say the wrong thing sometime, Mariette, and be very sorry for it," her mother warned. "I would like you to sit quietly the rest of the evening and stay in tomorrow, to think about your behavior. We are hated here, and it is very difficult . . ." Aunt Cecile broke down into tears, and Mariette sat with her head down.

"I'm sorry to worry you, Mama," she said quietly.

"I know, I know," her mother said, wiping her nose with a ragged cloth handkerchief.

"We are all struggling to hang on," said Louise. "And you, Mariette, you are very smart and we all know it. We just do not speak of it. You are like a wild pony that cannot be broken. Whatever shall we do with you?"

Mariette started to giggle, and soon she was laughing so hard she was on the floor and doubled over, making whinnying sounds. She got back up, then galloped around the room. The women laughed with her, and Monique finally could not resist joining in. Before long she was holding her sides to keep them from aching. For a brief second she was home in her kitchen in Acadie again, sitting at the cherrywood table. She pushed the thought away. It was good to see Mama laughing.

When the men returned shortly after, Monique was asked to tell the story again, and Mariette added her own embellishments. Monique had to marvel at how this child could go from villain to princess in such a short time.

The following morning they were graced with a visit and good news from Mr. Hutchinson. His first order of business was to thank Louise for the delicious *tourtiere* he had enjoyed during Midnight supper. She held his hand and said "God Bless You, Mr. Hutchinson." He had petitioned for Father Allain to move back from Fitchburg to Waltham, as he had promised that first night when he visited, and told Louise about delivering the good news to Father Allain last night. In return, the missionary agreed to assist a friend of Mr. Hutchinson's who lived in Waltham with shoveling snow and chopping wood.

Monique took a chair by the window immediately after he left, and refused to move from her place there except when required by forces of nature. Late in the afternoon, Father Allain came walking through the door with Mr. Hutchinson and another gentleman. She could not believe her eyes.

The missionary's long, black hair was now cropped short, with sprinkles of gray through the temples. He had lost much weight, and she struggled to hide her shock.

"Are you feeling well?" she asked.

"Yes, Monique. I must be shocking to look at. I have been gravely ill with pneumonia for many weeks, and have just recently been strong enough to travel back here. A Jesuit missionary, Father Cormier from Quebec, secretly took me to the home of his aunt in Fitchburg, and he and two Sisters of Mercy were very kind to me. Without them, I do not think I would have survived. Come, let us go outside and talk."

The two went out on the street, down past several stores toward a large stone building. A grassy hill across the street from it looked like a welcoming place to sit, and the air felt like spring had finally come to Waltham. The two friends sat down, and Father Allain took Monique's hand in his.

"I am so happy to be back," he said.

"Oh, Father Allain. I have prayed so hard for your return! I do not know what I would have done if . . . ." She glanced down at his sleeve. "What has happened to your sweater? It has a small hole here," she said, pointing.

"*Oui,* it began to unravel while I was sick," he explained. "The hole will serve to remind me each day of my friendship with Father Cormier. He has offered to help us, which involves great risk to himself. He knows Mi'Kmaq brothers in Tatamagouche, and told me he would try and find out where Pierre and Jean are located . . ."

Their conversation was interrupted when the men of the house came up the street toward them. Father Allain received a warm greeting from Jean Bourque and Baptiste LeBlanc, and Monique excused herself and walked ahead, back to their church home alone. She pondered Father Allain's last words to her. Would it be possible for this Father Cormier to find Pierre? She dared not think of it too much, or her grief would consume her. What if he had been killed?

Inside the church again, she walked up to Mr. Hutchinson, who was speaking in English to the other man. He, in turn was translating his words into French for Aunt Cecile. She appeared very unhappy.

"Indenture, unfortunately, is what we have to do in order for towns to accept the many Neutrals," he tried to explain. "It can be a very good opportunity to gain some employment, and we . . . I will personally insure that Mariette is placed with good people. Please try and explain this to her. I will be sending someone by tomorrow, a doctor in town who is in need of help. The town selectmen of Waltham have already authorized this indenture. I am sorry. I know it is very difficult to be without your child."

Aunt Cecile shook her head at the interpreter, but consented to try and talk to Mariette. Mr. Hutchinson bid everyone a polite *"Bonsoir"* and he and the other man left soon afterward.

"No," Monique heard Mariette say soon afterward, "I will not be an indentured servant, Mama!" All evening, Mariette pouted. Monique tucked her young cousin in to bed later on, thrilled to have Father Allain back, yet worrying that tomorrow she would lose Mariette to strangers somewhere in Waltham.

Chapter 22

Indenture and Connections

Mid-February, 1756

Dr. Joseph Milton seemed very nice when he spoke to Mariette's mother about her indenture the following morning. Dressed impeccably in a black suit, white shirt, and black tie, he looked, in Louise's words "scrubbed clean as a *des Mines carotte*." The women found him charming, but Mariette whispered in French that his white gloves were probably borrowed from his wife. She did not like him, and made no attempt to hide her feelings.

He agreed with Aunt Cecile that he would bring her back for a visit each Sunday. There were smiles that hid intense sadness, and the doctor whisked the young girl away in his horse-drawn carriage. He returned her five days later, saying that he regretted he could not honor the indenture contract because he feared the young girl had a "most serious condition."

Mariette happily translated what he had said as she sat at her family table enjoying fresh milk and bread. She explained to her stunned relatives that she had told him she laid in the hold of the ship for an entire week with a family who had smallpox. They had all died, she told him, but so far she survived. He had donned his white gloves immediately and briskly ushered her into the horse and carriage after placing a large horse blanket on the seat.

The week following, another indenture contract was signed. A tall woman in very wide-brimmed hat came to the church, her nose high in the air as she was introduced to the Acadian women. She showed Aunt Cecile the contract she received from the town selectmen, and after it was duly signed she pulled an angry Mariette by the hand out the door of the church. Two evenings later, just before sunset, the door flew open and Mariette was dragged in smiling, the woman pulling her along with one arm while holding on tightly to her tilted black hat with the other. Her nose even higher in the air, she very self-righteously claimed that the girl was "incorrigible." Mariette, again sitting at the table and again the center of attention, explained what incorrigible meant. She told how the woman had been standing in front of her large hall mirror just an hour earlier, putting on the large hat with a bright orange scarf. Mariette, always the observant child, had told her that in that color, and with "a neck that was as long as a post," she looked like a giraffe.

"I did not desire to stay," said Mariette, after being lectured by her mother for her rudeness to her elders. Before her aunt could add her comments, the door opened and Father Allain burst in.

"I have some news which is bad and yet good," Father Allain announced. "I have spoken to Pierre LeBlanc, Rene's grandson, who is now living in Amesbury, Massachusetts, a town north of here. He informed us that he has received a letter from Joseph Broussard, *dit* Beausoleil, and I am grieved to tell you all that the fight to reclaim Acadia is very difficult, even though Beausoleil has had several victories. He does not think we will be able to go back to our homeland in the near future, and discourages us from thinking so. The good news, Monique, is that Pierre and Jean are alive. Colonel Lawrence is planning to hire Acadians to keep the dykes repaired when the English-speaking settlers from New England are given our lands.

"Jean has been at winter camp with Eyes of Black Bear and his family because he has been very sick all winter. Many Acadians who escaped to the woods have not survived the very harsh winter, having no protection from the elements. Pierre has joined Jean at the Mi'Kmaq winter camp and when spring thaw comes, they will make the journey here on foot. Pierre speaks every day about his bride, according to Beausoleil. When spring comes, there is another part of Acadia near the Northumberland Strait where we can settle and live without fear."

"Oh, that is wonderful news," Monique exclaimed. "May I send a letter back to him?"

"No, I am afraid you may not," replied Father Allain. "It could put their lives at risk, if you do. The letter that came from Beausoleil was delivered through Acadians who can be trusted. We cannot take a chance on your letter falling into untrustworthy hands."

"I can accept that, Father Allain. I am so happy just to know he is alive. And I trust Eyes of Black Bear and his family to take care of him and his father."

"Yes, you can count on him," said Mariette, beaming at the mention of Eyes of Black Bear. "He and I are blood-brother and sister, and we communicate with each other's spirits."

"Oh Mercy," said her mother, "whatever are you talking about now, Mariette?"

"At night, when all is still, I can close my eyes and hear the sound of the whippoorwill, the signal that the spirit of Eyes of Black Bear is close by. He comes, and he looks at me, to be sure I am still alive. And I in turn have gone to him in my dreams. I go to his camp and whisper down like the wind through the top of his wigwam while he sleeps. I say little prayers for his destiny to be fulfilled."

Mariette paused, and seeing that all eyes were transfixed and waiting to hear more, she continued.

"I was sent away from le Canard for awhile by Mama and Papa," she said matter-of-factly. "Monique, remember when I went to a school for girls in Port Royal? I was eight years old, and Mama and Papa thought the nuns at the Order of St. Ursula could manage my behavior. The nuns were very strict, and I was afraid to misbehave because they gave awful punishments, such as cleaning duties and leather strappings on the bare palms of girls' hands."

She paused for a moment to think. "I did like the things they taught. They would read plays by French authors. One of them was Moliere, who wrote *L'Ecole des Maris*. The best thing about the school was the Mi'Kmaq friends I made, and my favorite of course was Eyes of Black Bear. His Christian name was Steven Humblewa. The nuns and missionaries worked hard to convert every Mi'Kmaw child to Christianity, and I felt sorry for the children who were away from their winter camps. They missed their families, just like I missed mine." Mariette's eyes had wandered in the direction of her mother, who was sitting and listening as though she was hearing Mariette's story for the first time. She glanced back at her daughter, then smiled her consent for Mariette to go on.

"Eyes of Black Bear wanted to run away most of the time, and one night when he tried to, they caught him outside the gates and gave him a terrible strapping. The Mi'kmaq names and customs did not matter there, they told him. He was to learn to speak and write English and become a good Roman Catholic." Mariette stopped for a moment. Monique noticed that Aunt Cecile began to sob, dotting her eyes with a handkerchief.

"One night when I did not eat my supper, I was punished, and I told Eyes of Black Bear that I wanted to run away with him. He said we could go that night, so we waited until the nuns were asleep and sneaked out. Eyes of Black Bear covered our tracks in the woods and nobody found us for many weeks. The nuns worried that we had died in the frozen forest, and so did my Mama and Papa. We went back to live with Eyes of Black Bear's family, and I loved living at their winter camp, after I got used to it."

"Mariette, I was so worried about you," said her mother. "I thought you had perished in the snow."

"Did you Mama, did you miss me?"

"Of course, Mariette!"

"Oh Mama, why did you send me so far away! I thought you hated having me as your daughter!"

"Oh no, that was not the case. I loved you, but I did not know how to make you happy. After your brother and father died, I was unable to handle your mischievous behavior. I had six other children besides, and . . . I am so sorry Mariette, I have always loved you."

"Oh, Mama! I know . . . . I am not an easy child. I never meant to . . . be a bad girl, Mama. I am sorry that Henri died . . . and Papa. I am so sorry for everything that has gone wrong for us . . ."

"Oh my darling Mariette," said Monique, "you are certainly not to blame. You are just a little girl." She reached for her small cousin's hand.

"Mariette, you have been such a blessing to all of us during these awful days," said Louise. "You are . . . you are . . . such a blessing from God."

"Really, *Tante* Louise?" smiled Mariette.

"Really!" answered her Aunt, her mother, and Monique in chorus. Cecile leaned over close and kissed her daughter firmly on the cheek.

Mariette beamed with joy, then her face became serious. "I have wondered many times if Eyes of Black Bear is alive, and I am so happy he is. I think . . . perhaps . . . I love him." The young girl blushed at her own admittance of affection for a boy.

"I saw him on the last night I saw Pierre," said Monique, feeling a blush in her own cheeks and lowering her head in the hope that nobody would notice. "He will make a noble Chief someday."

"He will," said Mariette. "He told me stories about Chief Membertou, the Great Chief of the Mi'Kmaq. They believe that all nature is in balance, and if it becomes out of balance, they perform rituals to bring it back again. I like to think about the whole world being connected, all the people, the animals, the plants, birds, fish, even the rocks. The Mi'Kmaq believe we do not own the lands, that we only take care of them for awhile, and must respect them. I do not blame Eyes of Black Bear for being angry that the nuns wanted him to be something he is not. It is wrong to take another person's identity from them, is it not, Father Allain?"

The missionary held her glance for a long moment. "Oh dear, Mariette, your wise words give me pause to reflect on their meaning. I think you are meant for great things."

Chapter 23

Legends & Long-Distance Meetings

Sunday, August 28

André was knocking down books from the shelves of the Vaughan Memorial Library in a frantic search for something, some lead that might help their search for Monique. He stopped to listen for footsteps, then began to pick the books back up and scan the numbers on them to see where they belonged on the shelf. He knew he had to calm down before he was kicked out of the building. He found something that looked like an index of dissertations and theses that had been written about Acadian legends, and carried it with him to the computer. He sat down and typed in "Acadian legends folklore."

Searching the results that came up on the screen, he scanned a title called "Acadian Folk Legends and their Meanings." The author was David Broussard. He thought, this couldn't be the same one. One click verified that it was. There would probably be an email address on the card back at the cottage.

André ran out to his car and roared down the street. There wasn't much traffic, but a cop car came out of a side street and flashed its lights behind him. Damn . . . he pulled over.

"Hi Officer."

"Young man, you were going forty-five in a thirty mile an hour zone, did you know that?"

"I'm sorry. My girlfriend's lost and I'm not paying enough attention."

"Your girlfriend is the one that's missing?"

"Yes," he answered, hoping his white lie was convincing.

"Well, we hope she comes back alive, but anyone in your way this morning wouldn't be alive either, and it's my job to prevent that. Could I see your license and registration please?"

André groaned. He handed over the documents and waited. It seemed to take an hour before the officer walked back to his car.

"I see you were stopped recently," he said. "I'm giving you a

$100 ticket, young man, and you'd better watch your speed, because we'll be watching you!"

"Yes, sir," André replied, trying hard to hide his nervousness. "I'll slow down, I promise."

"Do that. And I wish you good luck finding Monique. I want to be sympathetic, but I also have a job to do, keeping people safe in this town."

"Yes sir." André pulled out slowly and restrained his impulse to step on it the moment the policeman was out of sight. Just slowing down seemed to help. He felt his muscles relax a little, and he looked around.

It was a beautiful sunny day. He shut off the air conditioning and rolled down the window, stuck his hand out and felt the breeze on his upper arm as he drove down through lower Wolfville past historic houses. People were out mowing their lawns, and he eased up on the gas when he passed a church. Cars were parked along the road and people dressed in bright summer clothes walked up the steps and in through the open front door of the church. He drove down along the dykes and turned the corner to go down toward the park. Tourists strolled across from the parking lot to the park grounds— young families with babies in strollers, an older woman on the arm of her daughter, a man with a painting under his arm that he had just purchased. André parked and stopped in at the reception desk.

"No news," said the girl behind the counter. He waved and left again and drove down to the beach. He sat a moment, then turned the car around and drove back up to the cottages. Checking in with Bill at the desk, they soon discovered neither had any news, and he went over to get the business card by the phone. There was an email address on it, so he asked Bill if he could use his computer to send an email from there.

As André sat back in his chair in front of Bill's computer, something hit him. Anne Hebert's great-grandmother had said something about a legend, a ghost or spirit that only Acadians could see. Who had seen the old man? He grabbed an old envelope and a pencil on the desk and tried to think.

Let's see. Michelle had talked about an old man. Gerald Daigle had seen an old man. André wondered if Mr. Daigle was Acadian. A phone call to the Daigle residence confirmed that he was. Michelle had seen the old man disappear, but the sweater had not disappeared. Michelle was descended from Acadians. Daigle had seen the old man wearing the sweater. So the people who could see the old man all seemed to be Acadians.

He sat back, hardly believing he was even considering this angle. He got into his email account and began typing in everything he'd written on the envelope, told Broussard who he was and that they were searching for Monique who had disappeared, asked the professor to reply A.S.A.P, and then pressed "Send."

Bill asked him to tend the office while he went up to Tim's for coffee. A couple came to check in, and he took their names and cell phone number. He asked them to take a walk around and come back in a few minutes.

A "ding" sound indicated there was a new message. André sat back down and read the subject line that he'd written earlier entitled: Looking for Monique.

"David Broussard" <dbroussard@cadienet.com> wrote:

André:

Just received your message. Hurricane Marie is probably destroying our coast as we speak. Joe LeBlanc, Monique's Dad, has left to arrange for food relief at the homeless shelter in Lafayette, where he and Monique both live and work. Before he left, he told me he was relieved that she's out of harm's way. He plans to come back here later today, and in the meantime I'll figure out how we will get out of here tonight. No flights out of Louis Armstrong Airport, so will probably head toward Houston, if the highways aren't crammed. Monique called me the night she disappeared and I cautioned her not to go to the park alone. Wish she had listened. Don't give up, André.

David

Bill walked in the door with an extra coffee, and André took it, said "thanks," then walked out with a quick good-bye. He got on 101 toward Halifax and kept to the right, reminding himself that he had lots of time to get back to the closing of *Le Festival Acadien* and didn't need to speed. Jacques would wonder where he was, and he wished once again that he had a cell phone. In his room in Halifax, he had had a dream about searching the library for information, and had woken up early. The clock had said 4:42, and he'd driven back up to the Valley, hoping the library was open.

He decided to pull over at an Irving Station in Windsor and make a call. Jacques was between sets and yelled into the phone, trying to talk above the audience noise.

"I got in touch with David Broussard," said André excitedly, "and he's going to see Joe LeBlanc later today. Joe went back to Lafayette because of the storm they're getting. Broussard told me he wrote a book on Acadian folklore a few years back which I found in the library, and there is a legend of a ghost who appears to Acadians . . ."

"But is there any news from the world I live in?" yelled Jacques.

"Not really."

"What?"

"NO, Monique has not been found!" André repeated. "If she was, do you think I'd be talking about ghosts and legends?"

"OK, just wanted to make sure you haven't lost your mind. We're coming up later tonight, and Michelle and I have decided to just get a bunch of people together to search the woods ourselves. We want to check every single possibility and we'll probably just hang out there tonight and maybe tomorrow night too. We've borrowed a laptop so we can keep the contact you've established with the professor." Jacques breathed a heavy sigh. "To tell you the truth, André, I'm starting to give up. It's just not like Monique to not get in touch. I hate to think it, but . . ."

"Well, I'll call my friends who have offered to help too. With more of us looking and hounding the police, we might turn up something. And David Broussard said not to give up, so we're not giving up!" André hung up after Jacques responded that he wouldn't either, if only for Michelle's sake. André had surprised himself with how much ferocity was in his last statement.

He decided to get off at the Wolfville exit and go back to check his email again. Back at Blomidon Cottages a half hour later, he walked into the office. Bill was with a customer, and André sat down in the empty seat in front of the computer.

He realized he had forgotten to reply to David Broussard's reply, and he typed one in.

Any news about Monique's father? Michelle and Jacques anxious to get in touch with him.

André

André sat back and waited for a minute, then decided he was hungry. "I'll be right back," he said to Bill. "Is it OK?" he gestured. "I'm waiting for a reply from someone."

"No problem. Anything I can do to help."

A few minutes later, André sat back down at the computer with a half-eaten donut in his hand.

He was happy to see that he had one message in his Inbox. The subject line said: *News from the Basin.*

"David Broussard" <dbroussard@cadienet.com> wrote:

Andre:

Joe just called and I decided not to tell him yet, since he's going the other way toward Jefferson Parish, where his brother Bill's family and his sister's family both live. He wants to make sure they have all the food and supplies they need to ride out this hurricane. I wish he had decided to just come back here, but he didn't. The storm is pounding the Atchafalaya Basin and it's really scary. Lots of people could lose their homes. The roads are jammed all the way into Texas. I'm not really sure how we'll get out of here when Joe does come back.
I wish I could be more helpful. Please keep me posted.

David

Monday, August 29

Sitting at the computer in the Blomidon Cottages office, André wrote:

Hi David:

Sorry I took so long to get back to you. Monique's cousin, Michelle, and her husband Jacques have been here with an unbelievable crew of searchers, and we've combed the woods the past two days. Looked for any sign of Monique. I think we've seen every tree around here. So far, nothing. Any more clues from your research? We're desperate, man.

André looked at the words. They blurred in front of him, and he knew he was exhausted. He took another sip of coffee. He had been consuming about ten cups of coffee daily, just to get through. Every night he and Jacques drank beers until they couldn't think anymore, and Michelle mostly prayed and meditated. Bill had said that other guests were complaining about the noise and traffic in and out, and last night they'd tried hard to be quieter. Michelle said that in one of her meditations she'd seen a vision of the Virgin Mary telling her that Monique would be back.

Today they had talked about being in some strange sort of purgatory, where a person they loved was neither here nor gone. Their only comfort was that so many people had come out to help and were calling and emailing their prayers and hopes that Monique would soon be found. André never realized there were so many Acadians not only in New Brunswick, but elsewhere. They'd come from all over the Maritimes and beyond, and the dedication of *Le Festival Acadien* to Monique had even made international news programs this week. The press was around asking questions, and André had nothing new to say. It all seemed surreal. Jacques and Michelle told him they were basically propping themselves up at five o'clock the past three mornings to be interviewed, trying to look awake enough to talk. They had both looked like hell beforehand, at least to André, but somehow on TV they'd pulled it off. Michelle looked beautiful and poised, and talked so sweetly about her cousin that the whole world couldn't help but sympathize. Jacques was an interesting contrast, remaining quieter than usual and shuffling nervously with the cuff of his pants with one hand. His other arm had hung around Michelle's shoulder, and his love for her was apparent as she explained how the search was going. She had pleaded through the TV screen for Uncle Joe to call them immediately if he saw this program. They performed a song from *Coeur D'Acadie* on one morning talk show, dedicating it to Monique. Michelle had said several times that they had indeed become Le Lafayette Trio on this trip.

A "ding" brought André's mind back to the computer to read the new email message.

"David Broussard"<dbroussard@cadienet.com> wrote:

Hi André:

Any news? I'm still hoping that you find our girl before I have to break it to her father. It will be terribly upsetting for him. She's the most important thing in his life. I'm not sure where he is right now. His brother Bill's wife called to say that he had gone there and they left to check on their sister in Jefferson Parish. His brother is worried sick.

I need to go chop wood or something to calm down. Damn Joe! He'd better get his ass back here today. Get in touch the minute you hear anything.

David

André was warming up to David. He seemed like a regular guy. He decided to keep the news about Joe to himself for the time being. Michelle and Jacques would only worry more.

He headed over to the cottage for a cold one and was surprised to see that Jean-Paul sat at the table with Jacques. André went to the fridge, then spotted the empty carton on the table.

"I'll be right back," he said, waving off the apologies from his friends.

He drove up the street past Tim's, past the college, and down through Greenwich toward New Minas. Pulling over for gas in Greenwich, he looked across the dykes toward Port Williams. After filling up, he drove over the railroad tracks and across the dykes to the bridge at Port Williams and sat looking at the Cornwallis River. This river showed the fifty-foot difference between low and high tide, but he realized he had never observed it. Right now it was low, the water barely up to the small wharf to the right of the bridge. He took a picture and made a mental note to drop by tomorrow and see it at high tide.

With two twelve packs of Keith's Ale safely stowed in the trunk, André drove back through Wolfville to Blomidon Cottages. He thought about Joe trying to make sure his relatives were safe. Joe must be a good guy, he thought. He wondered what Broussard had meant when he had referred to Monique as "our girl." Did the professor have an interest in Monique? André dismissed the idea. Professor Broussard was probably an old married guy.

He stopped in at the office to check for new emails. Bill was there, training a young student at the front desk. He introduced André and they shook hands. "Sorry about your friend," the kid said.

André had no new emails, and he didn't have anything to offer David Broussard except to let him know his thoughts were with him. For now, he decided, that would have to be enough. He typed in the subject line: *Hearing about the storm.*

Andre wrote:

> *No news. Am hearing about the awful situation along the LA coast.*
> *Police still searching, haven't found a thing. Hundreds of people helping makes it a little easier to bear. Jacques and I are frustrated that they can't get more police power on it. We're really worried they're going to lose interest in the case. The best help is regular people who come forward. They've covered more ground in the past days than the police have, I think. One guy, Sgt. Williamson, has been working hard around the clock and we're glad to go to him when we're losing our minds. Thank God for him.*
> *I feel guilty that I didn't stay with Monique that night. I just didn't think she'd go alone.*

André pushed the "Send" button, and found himself wiping moisture from the corner of his eye. He turned his head away so Bill couldn't see him, then put his hands over his eyes and silently cursed himself for letting this terrible thing happen in the first place. How could he live with himself if they found her dead?

"You OK André?" asked Bill. "You alright buddy?"

André felt Bill's hand on his shoulder.

"It's my fault. I'm a damn loser."

"No, André, it's nobody's fault. You would never hurt anyone, I know that about you. You would have been over here to pick her up that night if you'd gotten the message."

Bill's words penetrated through the pain. "Thanks."

"Hey, John and I are going to Tim's for a decaf. Would you like one?"

"No. I'll just go back to the cottage. Thanks though."

Tuesday, August 30

Outside of New Orleans, Joe LeBlanc was driving west on I-10. He was fighting hard to pay attention to the road in front of him. At just after noon, the highway was still crowded with cars, nearly bumper to bumper at times, but moving well. It was no good to get angry, but he was already fighting against panic. He said a prayer, talked and sang to himself, trying to keep the anxiety at bay. Monique could not be missing; that news had to be a mistake. Once he got up there he would find her. Maybe she had decided she was not interested in that boy, and had just left to go back to the city early, to spare his feelings.

He'd been awake since 3 a.m., on the phone with the police trying to locate his sister, and an hour later he and Bill had taken Bill's boat down the streets of Jefferson Parish toward their sister's place.

Joe thought about a woman named Dorothy he met on the way. She had waved to them – not in a nervous way, but as though she spent every day sitting on the roof of her porch. A large golden retriever was her companion, tail wagging as they brought the boat closer. Bill had motioned to her to move closer to the edge, and she had inched her way toward them, being careful not to let go of the dog's leash. Once Joe got into a position to help her, he fully expected the dog to lurch at any instant, sending them both off the roof to a disastrous fall into the debris-filled water.

The woman had giggled as she edged herself toward him, shifting her skirt around to cover any chance of impropriety. Joe was able to grab on to the corner of the roof, and then reach and lift her clear. She tumbled into the boat rather ungracefully and struggled to pull herself together quickly, adjusting her blouse and skirt and patting her hair back in place.

"Is my hair OK?" she had asked him, and he had reached up to smooth out a stray sprig of hair by the side of her face, causing her to smile and give him a kiss on the cheek.

"You saved me," she had purred in his ear. Together they lifted the dog to safety beside her in the boat.

She offered her hand. "My name's Dorothy."

"I'm Joe LeBlanc," he had replied, accepting it. She continued to hold his hand as she said, "I'm worried that Jefferson Parish is ruined forever. I'm a widow with lots of friends in this parish, and I hope they are still alive, especially my aunt who lives in a nursing home nearby. My husband died suddenly six years ago, so it's just me and my dog, George. I lost some friends and gained some new ones. I've been involved in this community all my life. I don't know where I'll go . . . ."

"I run a shelter in Lafayette," Joe had replied. "You're welcome to come up there. I'm sure there will be lots of people who need help. Do you have a piece of paper and a pen? I'll write down the address for you. You might even be able to help out, and we have a spot for George too."

Dorothy seemed delighted, and said she'd meet him there soon. Bill offered to take her the rest of the way to Lafayette after he located their sister and her family.

"Good luck finding Monique," Dorothy had said, as she leaned over and gave Joe a peck on the cheek. "I'll pray for you."

At the boat ramp where Bill and Dorothy dropped Joe off, Joe turned to go toward his truck and noticed a policeman approaching. "I'm looking for Joe LeBlanc."

"That's me."

"David Broussard is trying to reach you. He says it's urgent."

Joe made a very quick call to David on the policeman's phone before heading out toward Breaux Bridge. David confirmed his fears: Monique was missing, which now topped his list of worries. Joe was worried about Monique, as well as what would happen to Dorothy, and if Bill would find Jeanine, their sister, and all her family. It was too much to take in.

He shivered as his thoughts returned to some of the things he had seen today. Two young children had stood crying with fright as their father tried to save their mother. A dog stranded on a piece of the wooden frame of a house torn apart by floodwaters barked, and people with blood on their faces rode by in boats. A policeman in another boat looked like the weight of the world rested on his shoulders. He kept thinking he must be dreaming, that the water their boat was floating on could not possibly be in the same place where streets were. A river of murky, smelly water rose up past the windows of most houses. As Bill steered the boat around huge chunks of destroyed buildings, Joe wondered if maybe the world was ending.

David said he had booked them a flight to Halifax; the whole trip was already paid for. Told him not to argue. Joe pulled over and picked up two hitch-hikers who wanted a ride to the split with I-55. They had no plan after that. Where would they stay tonight, he wondered after he let them off.

Joe reached for a CD and put it in the player. Jambalaya Cajun Band sang "Le Paradis D'Amour," and he cranked it up as loud as he could stand it. He rolled the car window down and sang along, tapping his hand on the side of the car in rhythm. He had to just keep awake, just had to get to David's.

Chapter 24

New Hope, New Beginnings

Mid-April, 1756

Father Allain and Louise Mélanson walked out of the church hall where they were living, and Father Allain commented that it was a beautiful spring morning.

"Look there, a robin," said Louise, pointing to a bird in a nearby tree that held a sprig of grass in its beak. She sighed, then looped her arm through the missionary's. They turned right and proceeded down the stone street toward town. They were on their way to the where Father Allain was working as a farmer's helper, chopping wood and assisting with a building project. Afterward, Father Allain planned to take Louise to a church nearby and say some prayers for the soul of François. He had withheld one part of the morning's plan as a surprise.

"Louise, I would like to tell you something, and I do not want anyone else to know yet." Father Allain looked around. He did not want anyone from their church residence following him and hearing what he was about to tell Louise. He reached into his sweater pocket and pulled out a piece of wrinkled paper. "I have received this letter from my friend Father Cormier in Fitchburg, who has made contact with my Mi'Kmaq winter camp. An Acadian from Piziquid who now lives in Boston visited him recently in Fitchburg. As I have mentioned before, Father Cormier is at risk to be staying in Fitchburg, because Massachusetts does not welcome Roman Catholic priests."

"Yes, go on."

Father Allain was pleased that he had her attention, and his excitement to share the news increased. "I am happy to tell you that Father Cormier has located Pierre and Jean. Jean has been very sick, and will not be able to travel anytime soon. The Mi'Kmaq have worked very hard this winter to keep him alive. Apparently he was badly beaten before the Mi'Kmaq raided the camp and were able to rescue him. Father Cormier was able to get a message to them that we are here, and that Monique is alive. According to the letter, Pierre wept with joy when he heard the news. Father Cormier says he will probably walk here through the woods, with a Mi'Kmaq guide. He said he will contact me if he hears news that Pierre is on his way. Please do not tell Monique. I would like to surprise her when we know for sure."

"Will Pierre stay here?"

"I do not know if he would be able to. He might have to take Monique back into the woods, to the Mi'Kmaq summer camp. They can survive by fishing and in the autumn, by hunting. Unless he could somehow get permission to stay . . . ."

"Is it selfish of me that I will ask God for a miracle in my nightly prayers? I would miss her terribly. We have lost so much, and now I could lose my cherished Monique. Father, I will ask God to forgive me for putting my own desires ahead of those of Monique and Pierre's."

"It is a natural thing for a mother to want to protect her child, even a grown-up child. And you know this also to be true, that a wife's place is with her husband."

"Yes. I will try to face the prospect with joy for my daughter, who will reunite with her husband. Pierre is such a wonderful boy . . . man . . . and he loves my Monique deeply. I will have to find it in my heart to trust that if God brings them together, that He will watch over them. Oh, I am not certain I am capable of saying good-bye to Monique." After a short pause, she spoke more softly, and Father Allain knew she was struggling not to cry. "I daily lose hope that we will ever return to Acadie. It is so painful to wonder about, I can scarcely think it."

"Pierre LeBlanc has submitted a petition on our behalf to the Massachusetts legislature, and he said they are negotiating with Governor Lawrence. I do not want anyone else to know this until we hear back."

"It may sound strange, but I have found a small measure of hope in our situation as it is now. I have you, Monique, Cecile and Mariette, and the others, and we are family to each other. I am beginning to feel that somehow, we will survive if we are together. I suppose I am tired of worrying what will happen next, and my grief for François and all the others who have lost their lives is almost too much to bear sometimes. I cannot stand to think that my François is somewhere in Boston, stored away in a cold morgue until who knows when."

"Louise, I will do my chores later. I would like to take you to Reverend Wilson and see if he can suggest a burial place for François in Waltham. What do you think of that?"

"Oh, François would never want that! No, that will never do. His last words to me were, "We belong there! We belong there!' He cried them out over and over before he passed away on that terrible voyage. Although he was in the throes of delirium, I still believe it was his final wish to return to Acadie, alive or dead."

"Oui," said Father Allain. "I understand your desire to be true to his wishes. To bury his body here in Waltham feels like a sacrilege. Who even knows if we will have to move again? But you said yourself that you are feeling more secure here, and perhaps this will become your permanent home. Would you at least agree to let me ask?"

"Father Siméon Allain, whatever has gotten into you?" Louise asked. She grabbed his arm with her other hand and laughed incredulously. "Why on earth do you think I would ever settle here?"

"Louise, I liked it when you called me Siméon just now. Please continue to do that. You are my sister, as François was my brother."

As they walked, Louise asked, "Is this the same Reverend Wilson that Mariette and Monique encountered and Mariette insulted?"

"Yes, he is the same. I think you will see that he has changed his thinking about our people since he met Mariette that day."

They had reached the front of a large, brick church, and Father Allain let go of Louise's arm to open the door. Inside, he pointed to Reverend Wilson, who was shuffling around at the front of his Episcopalian church sanctuary.

"Reverend Wilson."

"Greetings, Father Allain. May I be of service to you today?"

"We wondered whether *c'est possible* for someone of the Roman Catholic faith to bury a loved one *dans votre* church cemetery," said Father Allain as he glanced over at Louise. Louise's mouth opened in surprise to hear Father Allain's new command of the English language.

"No, no, Siméon, I could not bear to leave François here if our petition was successful and we returned soon to Acadie," she said, giving the missionary a look of scorn that a mother gives a child who has embarrassed them.

Reverend Wilson struggled to speak, choosing words that Father Allain would be able to interpret easily.

"Father Allain is making this suggestion," he said slowly, giving time for him to tell Louise, "because I have a house that is empty at this time. You see, Father Allain has helped to build me a new rectory. We have become friends. I would be honored if you and your family would like to live at my house and take care of it for me." Both men stood looking at Louise, waiting for her response. Her face was flushed, but told them nothing about her reaction. Louise stared into space, and all was silent in the sanctuary. After a few moments, she answered.

"May I see your house?"

Awhile later, Father Allain was holding Louise's arm as she climbed off Reverend Wilson's wagon. She stood amazed. In front of her was a magnificent Georgian colonial, located just up the street from the stores. She looked at the house, then down the street, then back at the house. "*O, Bon Dieu,*" was all she said as Father Allain took her arm and ushered her toward the front door.

"*O, Bon Dieu, Bon Dieu,*" she continued to repeat when they got inside. She left the men and walked from the drawing room to the kitchen, into the dining room and back to the drawing room again. She said to Father Allain, "*Je n'ai pas d' argent.*"

Reverend Wilson understood, and shook his head. "No need to worry," he said. "I want you to keep the house in good repair and make it your home for as long as you need it," he said. Father Allain translated his words, and smiled when Louise began to talk rapidly to him.

"She says that *vous avez* . . . um . . . beautiful furniture," he said. "She says she and Cecile will make *les doilies pour les chaises* . . . chairs, *oui,* Louise, and will hang curtains . . . ."

Louise had already gone up the stairs. The men could hear her walking from one bedroom to another, talking to herself and exclaiming, "*Mon Dieu, Mon Dieu!*" She came back down the stairs a few minutes later, walking like she was on her way to a debutante ball.

They rode in the horse-driven wagon back to the Episcopalian church, and Louise thanked Reverend Wilson several times before she and Father Allain continued on their way.

"Reverend Wilson said he will speak to his parish committee about the burial of François in the cemetery," said Father Allain. "Reverend Wilson said there is a very private area that he thinks would be suitable."

Louise wept, overcome by Reverend Wilson's generosity. "Why would he take a chance with us, when others think we are vagrants, or worse, that we are criminals?"

"Reverend Wilson has spoken to me about this. He has recently believed that it is God's will for his heart to be open to us, and he is obeying as a servant of the Lord. He said that he is very sorry for all we have been through."

"It is so difficult to think about Acadie. At night I lay in bed and thoughts will drift in . . . . I push them away because it is too painful to remember . . ."

"Truthfully, Louise, I have been thinking that we will not go back, at least not this year. Our people are hiding in the woods, afraid to come out and be killed by the British. Others are fighting to regain Acadie. The Governor will not allow us back as long as there is reason to believe we will join with the Mi'Kmaq and rise up. I do not see much hope in a restoration of the Acadie we knew. It is very sad. I will contact Mr. Hutchinson to see what is taking place these days, but I feel that we are fortunate to be where we are, compared to stories I hear of others and the despair they continue to suffer."

"What stories have you heard?"

"Many of our Acadian brothers and sisters who are still alive are in desperate situations. I have heard that our dear friend and your own Uncle René LeBlanc has been separated from many of his family members. He is ill, and was on board a ship docked in Philadelphie for many weeks. They fear he will die soon. I am sorry to tell you this news because I know your heart will ache more."

"Let us offer prayers for Uncle René today at our evening Vespers," said Louise. She paused to think about something. "When the Reverend offered us his house, I heard François' voice as though he was standing right beside me. He said, 'Make it home, make it home.' I was not certain whether he was saying to go back to Acadie, or whether he was talking about Reverend Wilson's house. I decided to look at the house, and when I walked into it I heard him again, saying 'Make it home.' When I went upstairs, I felt as though he was with me, giving his approval of the room where Monique and I will sleep."

They had returned to the door of their present home, and when Father Allain opened it, Monique, Cecile, and Mariette gathered around to greet them.

"Mr. Hutchinson has been here," said Monique. "He said he would return this afternoon and meet with us. He told me that he is on a committee investigating the indenture of children, and they are recommending that forced indenture will no longer be allowed. He said his service on the committee was because of Mariette!"

Mariette blushed with pride. "Mr. Hutchinson said that it pained him to see me separated from my family."

"That is wonderful news, and congratulations! You are very important, helping to change a law!" Father Allain gave her a hug.

"I was also at risk of indenture," said Monique. "One is not considered an adult laborer until the age of twenty-four. I would hate to be sent away, for fear that news would come of Pierre and I would not receive it." Monique paused. She had seen her mother flush when she spoke of Pierre.

"Mama, why do you look so? Are you not feeling well?"

"Oh, well, I was . . . Monique, Father Allain has something to tell you." She glanced over at him, and he had a cross look. Louise smiled. "Reverend Wilson made us a very nice offer today, did he not?"

Father Allain relaxed. "He did indeed. Let us sit and tell everyone about it!"

Later in the day, Mr. Thomas Hutchinson returned. He was welcomed in and served hot tea and offered a plate of freshly baked bread and molasses.

"Mrs. Jane Hoskins will be arriving in a few minutes. Do you know much about her?" When his small audience nodded that they did not, he continued. "I had the opportunity to go and see her preach, and she told us some things about herself. She is a Quaker minister and has traveled to many places, even to Europe. She is a member of the Society of Friends in Newport, Rhode Island. There are many more Quakers in Rhode Island than here, but she has built up a bit of a congregation here in Boston. She was an indentured servant when she was your age, Mariette, and her name was Jane Fenn. An English preacher recognized her talents and felt that she had a calling to do God's work. She was Anglican as a child, but converted to the Quaker religion. Her adopted father was very disappointed that she gave up one set of beliefs for another. Yet she claimed with complete certainty that she was obeying her Heavenly Father, who she said has shown her many times since that He was always guiding her in the direction of His plan for her. It is possible that she sees in you, Mariette, the same thing that someone once saw in her."

"I will not change my religion!" said Mariette.

"Nor would she ever want you to," said Father Allain. "I think she sees what we see, an unusually intelligent girl with strong convictions." Mariette, satisfied that she would not be asked to give up her Catholic beliefs, smiled at the compliment.

"Mrs. Hoskins has a proposal," continued Mr. Hutchinson, "and she has given me permission to discuss it with you and your family before she arrives. Her sister and brother-in-law live in Boston, and they are highly educated. Her brother-in-law is a graduate of Harvard School of Law. Mrs. Hoskins thinks that if Mariette were to go and live with them awhile, it would give her the opportunity to read many of the books in their library and increase her English vocabulary. She would also converse with them on such a variety of subjects that it would broaden her horizons. In return, if they all like each other and enjoy each other's company, Mariette would be able to assist Mrs. Smith with her household duties, not as a servant working long hours, but as a helpmate."

"I do not like to think of Mariette being so far away," said her mother.

"Boston is not that far," said Father Allain. "When I earn more money, perhaps I can purchase a wagon and barter my labor for a horse."

"Our dear Mariette does deserve the opportunity to be educated," said Louise. "She should have this chance for a better future."

"Yes," agreed Cecile. "And perhaps they can help her become less impetuous." She turned to her daughter. "Please do not insult these people and be carted back here, if you are being offered this wonderful chance."

"Mama, I promise to behave," answered Mariette. "And if they are as kind as Mrs. Hoskins is, I am sure we will all get along."

"And they have also offered another wonderful opportunity, Mariette," said Mr. Hutchinson. "The Smiths and Mrs. Hoskins are planning a trip to France later on this year, and they are hoping they can take you along. They have discussed the possibility that they could show you a place in Normandy where the first Acadians left from in the 1600s. You can come back and tell us all what it was like to sit in the very church where your ancestors worshipped before they left everything they knew for the wilderness of North America!"

Chapter 25

David, André, and Joe

Wednesday, August 31

"David Broussard"<dbroussard@cadienet.com> wrote:

Hi André:

I just heard from Joe. I called the Jefferson Parish police to try and find him and have him call me ASAP. He's probably still trying to find his sister. They haven't been able to get the boat out to their place yet. I guess they're rescuing some other survivors on the way.

Anything new on Monique? Please the minute you hear anything, let me know so I can tell him. I've booked a flight for the two of us out of Houston tomorrow at 10:00 a.m.

I told Monique that night not to go alone. She didn't listen, and she's responsible for that, not you and not me. I'm not happy she went alone and I hope I have the chance to get after her for that.

I'm trying to stay optimistic for Joe, but truthfully, it's almost a week and she just isn't the type of person to not get in contact if she could. I'm sick about it and trying not to think about right now.

I had an experience at Grand-Pré that I don't talk about, except I did hint at it with Monique because she was having dreams that seemed to be about historic Acadia, as though she was living in a different time in these dreams. She even recalled words that were used in their language. We got together to talk several times. I told her that one time I went to the park and thought I saw a ghost. He was old and, this might sound even more crazy, but he talked to me. He said "Beausoleil," the name of one of my family's ancestors. It scared me and I got the hell out of there. I thought I was hallucinating from studying too much. It was right before the oral defense of my dissertation. My cell phone's ringing, gotta go.

André read the message several times, then replied:

> *David, what did old man look like? Was he wearing an old gray sweater? It's really weird.*

"André, let's go!" called Jacques from the office door. "The police think they have something . . . ."

André pressed "Send" and followed Jacques out to his car.

"Did they find her?"

"No, they didn't, but they found something."

They drove up through Wolfville and past Acadia University, then down through Greenwich toward New Minas. Looking down across the dykes toward Port Williams, André thought about the Acadian men who had built those dykes so long ago, and how their work was still there over three hundred years later. Would anything he'd build last 300 years? It wasn't likely. He wondered about those men, what they had been like, what they'd think if they came back today.

"What happened after the Acadians were deported from here?"

"It's funny, I haven't been able to pay much attention to anything but the festival and Monique, but Jean-Paul said last night that a bunch of New Englanders, he said around eight thousand of 'em, came up here a few years after the Acadians were kicked out. They took over the land that the Acadians had owned, and that started to really piss me off, man. They just shoved out all those thousands of farmers and burned down their damn houses. Then they moved English-speaking people from New England up there to start over, like the Acadians never even existed! Jean-Paul said they didn't know a thing about the dykeland farming, so they got Acadians who stuck around to help them with it for awhile. Imagine having to help the people who took your land from you. I guess the engineering wasn't as easy as those English buggers thought."

They had arrived in the parking lot at the RCMP Headquarters. Inside, Jacques asked to see Sgt. Williamson. He was paged, and he came out shortly after.

"Come on in, boys," said the officer. "We've discovered footprints down by the railroad tracks that look like they fit the shoes Monique was wearing that night. A team is out there right now with dogs, trying to track them. We're really glad to have this lead."

"Did the footprints have any other sets of prints with them?" asked André.

"No. And that's another reason to be relieved. We've all worried that she was abducted, and there are of course cases where young women disappear without a trace, but it's never happened around these parts. It's usually in big metropolitan areas. However, I have to remind myself that things happen in small towns too, and people say 'We never thought anything like this could happen here.' I really have to believe she's still alive, but for some reason, hasn't gotten in touch yet. It's a hunch, but that's what my gut says about this case."

"My wife feels like that too," said Jacques. "Will you let us know as soon as you hear anything new?"

"Tomorrow morning I will give you a call and give you an update. I'll be in by 5 or so. I've been waking up every morning at 4 a.m., and I just shower and go to work. If I don't call you, feel free to call here."

Jacques and André felt happier than they had in a week. Sgt. Williamson had finally been able to throw them a bone, and Jacques couldn't wait to tell Michelle that the policeman's gut feeling was the same as hers. Since she'd begun meditating, she'd become even more sure that Monique would come back.

Jacques wanted to talk to Michelle at the cottage, so André asked to be dropped off at the office to check the computer for new messages. He found another one from David with the subject line: What happened?

David Broussard <dbroussard@cadienet.com> wrote:

> *You left in the middle of a sentence. Is everything all right there?*
>
> *In answer to your question, yes, the old man was wearing a tattered old gray sweater. Why?*

André answered:

Hi David:

> *The gray sweater thing is happening all over the place. Michelle saw an old man who disappeared wearing one, another guy who lives in Grand-Pré saw him in the park the night Monique disappeared. It's wicked weird. An old woman at* Le Festival Acadien *told her granddaughter Anne and Anne told me that there is an old folk legend about this. In fact, that's how I first found out that you did research on this because I looked it up at* Acadia Library.
>
> *We went to the Police Station just now and they have a footprint that they think might belong to Monique. Do you want me to pick you and Monique's father up at the airport tomorrow afternoon? Is your wife coming with you?*

André

Before André could find a distraction on the net, the reply came:

David Broussard<dbroussard@cadienet.com> wrote:

André:
I'm divorced, so it will just be Joe and me. That would be great. Our flight is due in at 5:30 p.m. I just heard from Joe's brother Bill's wife. She said that their sister and her family are OK. Some damage to their house. At least I'll be able to relieve his mind on that one.

Yes, I'm familiar with that folk legend. That's why it still scares me to think about meeting up with that old man in the park.

As the legend goes, an elderly missionary appeared at different times to Acadian people after the deportation and he gave them messages. It seemed to be sort of a religious experience, and the people who experienced it told of it like it came from God. I've never been a religious person myself, so when he appeared to me . . . well, I just didn't know what to do so I booked it out of there. It was just too spooky. The bad part is, it has stayed with me ever since and even affected my marriage.

David

André replied:

You can stay here at Blomidon Cottages if you want. I'll go book a room for you. See you tonight. Tell me what you look like and I'll watch for you.

David Broussard<dbroussard@cadienet.com> wrote:

Andre:

I'm 5' 11", with short, black hair. Joe is stocky, a bit shorter, and has a round face, less hair. He's almost always smiling, but probably won't be this time. I'll wear a blue polo shirt and my LSU hat for identification purposes. See you then.

André sat back. It would be a long day. He walked back to his cottage, said "hi" to Jacques and Michelle who were seated at the table holding hands, and went to his bedroom.

Thursday, September 1

It was 4:55 p.m. André stood at the gate where David Broussard and Joe LeBlanc were due to arrive from Newark. Weary travelers rode down an escalator after picking up baggage and going through customs. Some were young, some old, some with babies, several young couples with families, and a few alone. He spotted a man in a blue polo shirt with a cap on, and a more heavy-set older man who didn't seem to know what they were doing next. He knew right away that he was looking at the professor and Monique's father. André walked toward them.

"Hello," said André. "Are you Professor Broussard?"

"Yes," said David, extending his hand. "Call me David. And this is Monique's dad, Joe LeBlanc."

"Pleased to meet you," said André, shaking hands with both men. "Can I help with your luggage?" André took Joe's big suitcase in one hand and extended the other to Broussard, who smiled.

"I travel light," said the professor, pointing to a duffle bag that hung from his shoulder. "I do need to use the men's room though," he added. "I'll be right back."

André set the bags down and looked at Joe, who appeared to be both exhausted and distraught.

"We got some news today," he said, trying to offer some encouragement. "I don't want you to get your hopes up, but we might have a good lead. They found footprints in the mud down around the railroad tracks in Grand-Pré."

Joe barely nodded. André tried to think of other conversation topics.

"Did you know that Monique took a picture with her when she went to the park that night?"

"Monique took a picture of herself to Grand-Pré? That is strange."

"No, it was a picture of her mother. She showed it to me the afternoon she came up to the Valley."

"Ah, now I understand. Monique brought the picture of her Mama that I gave her last spring. Of course, that makes perfect sense. But my daughter would not leave it behind. I think that perhaps someone has taken her somewhere. But where?"

"Let's sit down over here," André said. "I only met Monique the day she disappeared, but I really care for her. We're going to keep looking until we find her, and we have lots of help."

"Jacques' parents told me you are a fine young man and would never hurt my daughter. You see, I called them when I learned from Michelle that Monique had gone to meet you in Grand-Pré. They said wonderful things about your character. It's just that . . . ." The older man stopped, a heavy sigh prefacing his distress. "Oh, I think I am just at my wit's end. My daughter's missing, my beautiful Louisiana is an awful mess!" Joe's voice echoed throughout the open expanse of the terminal, and André was thankful there was nobody in the immediate vicinity of where they were sitting.

Broussard now walked down toward them, and André made eye contact with him. He glanced from the young man to the older one, nodding his assessment of the situation.

"Come on, Joe," he said as he reached for the older man's arm. "Let's get out of here and go to the Valley where we can get some answers."

A few minutes later they were back on 101. André could see that the professor really liked Joe and Monique. From the back seat, he was trying hard to make conversation with Joe that would keep his spirits up.

"We had a great time that weekend we went froggin,' didn't we?"

"I did not go that time, remember?" answered the older man. "I had such a headache that night, I just sat around at your log cabin, or as Monique called it, the 'log mansion.' Monique had a good time with you, though, even though she would not eat the frogs after I cooked them." He chuckled at the memory. "Oh André, you should see David's home. He built it himself!"

A long silence followed, and David tried again. "I know they have to do it, but the security is such a pain to get through. It really wears on your nerves."

"It does. I remember when Monique left to go through security, she turned and looked back at me. I should have gone. I should have."

David said, "Now, Joe, don't be so hard on yourself."

After a silence, he asked André, "Have you traveled anywhere in the U.S. lately?"

"I've only been out of Canada once," replied André, suddenly feeling like a country bumpkin.

"Where have you been outside Canada?"

"Well, I went to Louisiana one time with my family, to visit Jacques and his family. We're related. And I went to Quebec City once on a student exchange trip in high school. And I've made the trip from Shediac to Wolfville quite a few times since I've been at Acadia. That's about it."

"If you've seen the Maritimes and Louisiana, you've seen the best part of the world."

André was grateful that the professor hadn't made fun of him for his lack of travel experience. "Yeah, I'm hoping to go south sometime again."

"Come back to Louisiana," said Joe, who still struggled to contain his sadness. "If Monique was here, she and I would be making plans to feed everybody who's homeless. There are so many people who don't know where to turn! I helped a lady off her roof today, and now my back is killing me. But she was stranded there, with her dog. Bill said he would make sure she got to Lafayette. What are all these people ever going to do, David?"

"I don't know, my friend," David said from the back seat. The group remained silent for a long time. David struggled to think of words of comfort, but there were none.

"Mr. LeBlanc, would you like me to stop anywhere? Are you hungry?" asked André.

"Please call me Joe," he said, "and tell me everything that has happened regarding the search for Monique."

André filled both men in on all the events of the past few days. He said several times how bad he felt that he hadn't gotten Monique's phone call the night of her disappearance. He related to them how he'd gone back in his mind a million times and replayed it the way he wished it had happened, with him there to take Monique to the park the way they'd planned.

David spoke up in support. "Like I told you by email, André, she called me on the phone that night. She went, and what happened afterward is out of our hands. It's a lousy feeling, and I know what you're going through."

"I too wish I had come here with her," said Joe. "I had a funny feeling when she went out of sight, but I just thought I was being silly. It was like a premonition or something, I think."

"Joe," said David, "you probably thought the same as I did, that she was going to one of the safest places there is. And I still believe that. She will probably turn up tomorrow. Maybe she walked off into the woods to go to the bathroom or something and got lost. The weather's warm, and the searchers will find her. They're pretty certain they've found her footprints."

David paused for a moment, then continued. "She really wanted to go to Grand-Pré after learning about her own family backgound. I have to admit, she was my favorite student in that Historical Fiction Class. It was a great class, and when she told me about a dream she'd had one day, I was blown away by it. She said words that came from old Acadia. It's so puzzling, the dreams she was having . . . You know, I had a funny experience at Grand-Pré quite a few years back, and she was having dreams about Acadia; somehow I think it all ties in, I just can't figure out how."

"Do you know the poem *Evangeline*?" Joe had directed his question to André.

"Ah, yeah, I do. I would be surprised if there's an Acadian school kid anywhere in the Maritimes who doesn't know about it. From what I understand, Longfellow never visited the Minas Basin, but he still described it with amazing accuracy. But, why do you ask?"

"I don't know, I was just thinking about how David taught the class, and that is when Monique and I began to talk about her heritage, and her mother's interest in where she came from. Catherine, God rest her soul, if she had lived, would have still been telling stories at the Acadiana festivals. Her stories kept it all alive for Cajun people wanting to know about their ancestors."

"That's absolutely correct," said David. "Some people think that the story of the deportation was passed down through written documents, but most of what we know was passed by word of mouth, and recorded in small historical accounts here and there, and of course in the fictional characters of Evangeline and Gabriel. The truth is, there is very little written documentation to be found. Some historians now believe that the records were expunged to hide the shame of it all. There were no ship manifests either."

"Yeah, and I saw last weekend and all this week what Acadians can do when they get together," said André. "One of the managers of *Le Festival Acadien* is Acadian, and he got CBC-TV involved in publicizing Monique's disappearance. People came from all over, and nearly every single one was Acadian. I wonder why the Acadians back in the 1700s didn't gang together and fight those guys."

"They tried," replied David. "My ancestor, Joseph Broussard, who was called Beausoleil, led a militia of Acadian men in a number of battles against the British military, but they were never able to reclaim Acadie. Joseph ended up bringing a group of settlers to Louisiana a few years after. Say, André, could you slow down a bit?"

"Sorry about that."

"No problem."

"Does either of you have a cell phone?" André asked.

"I do," replied David.

"Could I borrow it?"

"If you pull over to use it," David replied. André was irritated. He was tired and didn't feel like being treated like a teenager. But he also didn't want to offend these guests.

"All right. Thanks," André said as he steered the Honda over to the side of the road. "Jacques, hi. We're on 101 somewhere outside of Falmouth. Any news from tonight? OK, we'll be there by seven. Okay. The search is finished for today. I guess they didn't find any new evidence or anything."

Joe asked, "Could I talk to Jacques for a minute?" Andre passed him the phone. "Hey, have y'all eaten? Okay, can you get to a store? Then I want you to write down this list." Joe proceeded to list several ingredients with which he was going to cook supper. "We gotta eat, and I need something to do."

He clicked the phone shut and handed it back to David as

André got back on the highway. He couldn't see any other cars in either direction.

"Jacques and Michelle are waiting for us at the Cottages. Michelle said she really wanted to see Uncle Joe."

Joe said, "Michelle and Monique are so close, like sisters. How is she handling this?"

"Truthfully Joe, she is convinced Monique is still alive," said André. "She thinks that she'd know if she was . . . you know, if something happened. She fell apart for a day or so, but now she meditates and yesterday she said she saw the Virgin Mary. And one day at the beach she talked to an old man. He disappeared and an old sweater he had on was left on the sand. The police picked it up, and she says it's a sign . . . I guess all this sounds a little crazy, huh!"

"Not too crazy for me," said Joe. "Michelle has always been a little psychic, just like her Grandmère Melanson, and for now I'm going to believe what she believes."

"I believe it, too," mumbled David from the back seat.

"I wish I did," said André. "I find this all pretty spooky."

The three men drove silently for awhile. They reached the exit at Avonport and were soon at Blomidon Cottages. André's friend Bill had arranged for the group to have several adjoining rooms to accommodate the additional people.

Everyone said hellos and Joe got a hug from Michelle. She introduced him to Jean-Paul and Jack the cab driver, who Jacques had invited to join them. Most of them settled into the large living room of the central suite where cold beers were handed out. Joe was already in the kitchen pulling pots and pans out of the cabinet. Andre, curious about what he was doing, had followed, and asked, "Is there anything I can do to help?"

"Sure is. Get the meat and the rest of the groceries out of the fridge there and you can help me start getting everything ready."

"What are you going to cook?"

"Well, I thought a nice pork and sausage jambalaya would be pretty good."

"Sounds great."

André unpacked onions, mushrooms, a large bag of rice, various seasonings, some smoked sausage, pork chops, and pork ribs cut across the rib bones. Joe surveyed the spread, "We're ready now." André had the feeling that he was embarking on an adventure into new territory.

As Joe began the meal, André had a thousand questions. "When do you put the rice in? Do you cook it first? Won't the meat burn?"

"Well, let me see," Joe said, stirring the large pot with all the meat already starting to sizzle. "First, you have to brown the meat until it is almost completely cooked. When it is all getting pretty well browned, you add all the onions, mushrooms, and seasonings and let those cook down before you add the uncooked rice. The important part is what's going on in the bottom of the pot. The meat, onions, mushrooms and seasonings have all helped to make a wonderful browning on the bottom of the pot. These pots don't have the non-stick surface, and that makes it easier to get a nice deep browning. You don't want any of it to burn. This is not blackening, it's browning. Big difference, *cher*. I don't blacken my food, that's for restaurants. But when you add the water and stir up all the browning from the bottom of the pot, all those wonderful flavors cook into the rice.

"I like to take all the big pieces of meat out when I add the water. That way I can get all the good browning from the bottom of the pot cooking in the boiling water. Last you add the rice."

André had listened carefully and asked, "How long does the rice take to cook?"

"It depends. You add enough water to more than cover all the rice. When it's all boiled below the level of the rice, you turn the heat down, cover the pot, and let it steam until the rice is completely cooked. I usually stir it a few times to be sure that the flavors and the seasonings are spread throughout."

"Then you add the meat and stuff back into it?"

"Yep, as soon as the rice is almost finished cooking."

"Joe, the smell from that meat roasting is amazing!"

"Yes, that's the real secret to this dish. You're smelling the meat browning, and the more brown it is, the better. Not hard, but takes some time, close attention, and good timing."

About two hours later, Jean-Paul couldn't stand it any more and walked into the kitchen. "Wow, that smells incredible!" he said, sneaking a peek into the pot. "What is that?"

"It's jambalaya, *cher*," said Joe as he stirred the pot full of rice, meat and seasonings.

"How do you get the rice that color?" asked Jean-Paul.

Joe smiled. "I think André can explain that to you. But if y'all are hungry, this is ready." David was first in line. After almost everyone got seconds and some third helpings by a few, what remained of Joe's huge pot full of jambalaya was just enough for him to offer Jack the Taxi Man a plate to take home to his wife.

Chapter 26

A Gathering of Friends

Late April 1756

"I am so sorry to report that I could not get permission from the parish committee to perform a burial ceremony for François," Reverend Wilson told Father Allain one morning. "They would not consent to the burial of a Roman Catholic in an Episcopalian cemetery."

"Thank-you for risking your own reputation to even ask them," replied Father Allain. "I will continue to wait on God's will for my brother, François."

"Ton frère est mon frère!" exclaimed Reverend Wilson in the French he had been practicing for the past few weeks, gesturing from the missionary to himself.

Father Allain gave him a pat on the back. *"Merci,"* he said.

"I walked around the cemetery and found a spot just outside the fence," said Reverend Wilson. "It is in a quiet little spot at the back, with the forest beyond. No one will ever discover it there. However, we will have to conduct our business in darkness."

"I do not want you to take the chance," said Father Allain at the same time as he struggled to contain his enthusiasm for the idea. When Reverend Wilson said he would gladly take the small risk in such an important matter, Father Allain asked, "May I see where it is?"

"Yes. I dropped two shovels there earlier, in case you decided that this is the proper resting place for Francois' remains."

The two walked out around the cemetery and followed the side of the fence for many yards to the back, pushing away branches and bushes until they reached the back where the woodlands came up nearly to the fence.

"It will be difficult to get to, but I myself will keep the brush cleared so that Louise can visit François," said Reverend Wilson.

"And I will help you. I wonder if you could call me Siméon when it is just the two of us."

"And I would like you to call me Jim." They sealed the agreement with a handshake. The two men crouched down and began to brush away the sticks and stones from the small lot. Father Allain, feeling the grass in his hands, had the feeling that François would like this spot. It was secluded and peaceful, with the shade of large pine trees overhead.

"I am sorry, Siméon." He had caught Siméon's sweater with a twig, putting a small hole near the elbow.

"A second hole," said Father Allain as he showed the first one to Jim. "This one I got in Fitchburg, and I think of Father Cormier when I look at it. Now I have one from you also, a very appropriate memory of a wonderful act of friendship today."

"What was François like?" asked Jim, as he stood up and reached for one shovel. He handed it to Siméon, then reached for the other one. As the two men broke ground together, Siméon reminisced about the Mélanson farm and one special memory he had of helping François to repair a hole in the kitchen wall. He told Jim about the wedding, and how quickly the day had changed into a horrible one.

"I miss François very much. But I am also relieved that he did not have to suffer. God spared him by bringing on an injury that would not allow him to come to the deck and see his beautiful farm brought to the ground in cinders."

"I am so sorry for your people."

"*Oui,* our people. We lived in such a tranquil place, not without problems but so beautiful there. Then we were torn like down from a pillow, and set to the wind to drift north, south, east, west." Father Allain stopped for an instant, panting. "The soil here in Waltham, it seems much rockier, not like the red clay of Acadie." He struggled to lift a very large rock out of its bed of soil, turning the shovel this way and that to wedge further under it. Jim bent down and dug around it with his bare hands, trying to widen the bed for the shovel. Eventually, the two men were able to push and pull it out, and Jim rolled it away from the hole.

"We can use this rock as a marker. Perhaps Louise will want to plant flowers around it. The rich red soil of Acadie produced wonderful crops, from what I have heard."

"*Oui,* we brought in the last of our crops in October, and just like always, they seemed more plentiful than the year before. Then, we were scooped up from our beds like the rock we just dug out. The difference is that this rock will continue to have a place of dignity as a marker for my friend's grave. The Mi'Kmaq believe that all things in creation, even rocks, have spirits. I'm not sure I believe a rock has a spirit, but if it does, then this rock was treated with dignity. We were treated as having no worth. However, God always considers the souls of his children worthy, and He asks us to forgive. In my heart, I know this is my challenge. God did not permit François to be buried in his rightful burial ground at Grand-Pré cemetery, but He did provide for

François' family here in Waltham, by sending you and others to help us. I am indeed grateful to God, and to you."

The two men stood and leaned on their shovels, looking into a hole that was now large enough for a casket. The smell of fresh earth filled the air, and Siméon knelt down. He picked up some of the soil in his hands and blessed it.

"Almighty Father, *sur le terre de* Waltham, Louise, Monique, Cecile, Mariette, and I, as well as our other Acadian family members, have found a place of safety. *Nos amis* have come to our aid. I thank you for this, and ask that you bring peace to the final resting-place of my beloved friend, François. Amen."

"Amen."

After a moment of silence, Siméon stood and brushed his hands off on his trousers. "He would like you," he said, "and he would certainly admire your courage for allowing us to bury him here. François had a wonderful sense of humor, and probably watched us with much amusement from Heaven as we dug out that rock just now."

Later that day, Father Allain presented his news to Louise as they walked toward the stores. He knew that her mind would be filled with thoughts of shopping for wool and would be perhaps more receptive to the idea of François' burial outside the cemetery fence. When he explained that he and Reverend Wilson had dug a grave earlier, she did not respond for several minutes.

"It is undignified, of course, my dear Siméon, to bury such a wonderful man in such a lonely place, so far away from everything he loved. But Reverend Wilson is a good man, and François, I believe, is happy that Monique and I, Cecile and dear little Mariette, and you, his dearest friend, have been given such a wonderful home to live in. I suppose we can ask for God's blessing on all of it, even my beloved husband's burial behind a fence."

The plans were set for an evening graveside ceremony on Wednesday of the following week, and Father Allain spent several hours alone each day, writing and rewriting. He acted distracted and cross, and Monique mentioned to her mother that he did not seem like himself. Even the *poulet fricot* that Cecile and Louise cooked did not seem to ease it. Mariette, Monique, Cecile and Louise sat with Father Allain as Louise offered him his third bowl at supper one night. The two other couples had strolled down to the stores.

"You are trying to fatten me up," Father Allain said. The four women watched him intently as he ate, hoping the third bowl would be the charm. "Mr. Hutchinson kindly did all the arrangements for François' funeral. He is a good man, and offered to pay for a wooden coffin. He said he will deliver it himself tomorrow."

"Mariette, tell Father Allain your wonderful news," said Monique, making an attempt to lighten the subject for the missionary's sake.

"I went to Mr. and Mrs. Smith's house this afternoon," said Mariette. "Mrs. Hoskins came too. Their house is filled with so many books, I do not know if I can ever read all of them. I am to move there next week."

"That is good news," said Father Allain.

"Speaking of books, I have one of yours that I would like to give back, but I have been afraid to tell you that it is quite a mess."

"What book is that?"

"Do you remember you let me borrow the one called *Introduction to the Devout Life*? You were packing up to go to winter camp when I visited you the day of Monique's wedding. You said I could borrow it and I put it in my apron pocket. I read it at Aunt Louise's house when I stayed over to help translate things she wanted to tell that awful Colonel Winslow. I carried the book with me everywhere. When I was in the hold of the ship, I used my apron as a pillow and threw up on the cover during the voyage. I tore off the cover and threw it away, and was scared to show you that I had damaged the book so I never gave it back. Are you mad at me?"

"No, of course not. Please go and get it." His deep brown eyes sparkled with excitement.

While they waited for Mariette, Monique turned to Father Allain. "Last night I had a dream about you."

"I hope it was a good dream, Monique. When the subject of dreams comes up, I remember being at the Mi'Kmaq camps and sitting with my brothers and sisters as the shaman gave interpretations of their dreams. He had learned the ways of Chief Membertou, who understood their spiritual meanings. I myself had no pleasant experiences with dreams, so prefer not to have any. Unless it is pleasant, I must say with apologies that I would hesitate to hear about any."

"This one was very pleasant. Puzzling, but pleasant."

"Please then, describe it to me."

"I was standing under a willow tree. It was lovely there, and the shadows of late day danced on the grass beneath. A cool wind rustled them, and I could hear the sound of seagulls in the distance. You held out your hand to me, Father, like this." Monique extended her hand to within inches of his and smiled at him sweetly. "Then you turned and said, 'Come, Monique, God calls us northward.' Did I say that you were much older in the dream? Your voice was the same, but as I looked into your eyes, your face changed to that of a very old man. Suddenly Michel came through the branches with his fiddle, playing a song he played at my wedding. Someone was following him. He said to the woman behind him, "*Dit bonjour*, Catherine." I looked at the woman and thought she looked familiar, but I was not sure. Then Michel's fiddle turned into the cross that I took from our kitchen in Grand-Pré, the one the soldiers threw in the fire. Michel handed this cross to the woman, and she took it and placed it on the ground beside her. She picked up a box that was there, and lifted a cover to show me what was inside. I could see Angeline's quilt, which was old and discolored. There were pages from a book, and other things, but before I could see them she shut the box. She wanted me to take it, so I reached for it and after politely thanking her, my hand was suddenly in yours and my arm felt so heavy, like I was lifting a horseshoe. Do you remember when we were on the transport ship? I had a strange experience then, when I held your hand, when we saw . . ."

"Yes, I did too," he said.

"Well, Father, it was just like that. It was such a vivid dream, and it has stayed with me all day today. I think I shall never forget it."

"When you mentioned the large willow tree, I thought of the ones in Grand-Pré. Did anyone else?" He glanced around the table, and received a nod of agreement from Louise. "If Chief Membertou was here, I think he would say that north is one of the four directions, indicating death and renewal. Perhaps this relates to François' funeral. And the wind rustling through the willow . . . . What does the wind mean to you, Monique?"

"Hmm. The wind felt refreshing. I felt alive, maybe even chosen for something special. The wind came in from the north, the same direction as we turned and from where Michel and the woman came."

"*Oui*, refreshing."

Mariette was now back at the table holding a well-worn book.

"May I read something I like?" she asked, and receiving nods of consent, she began:

> *When St. Catherine of Genoa became a widow, she gave herself up to work in a hospital. Cassian relates how a certain devout maiden once besought Saint Athanasius to help her in cultivating the grace of patience; and he gave her a poor widow as companion, who was cross, irritable, and altogether intolerable, and whose perpetual fretfulness gave the pious lady abundant opportunity of practicing gentleness and patience. And so some of God's servants devote themselves to nursing the sick, helping the poor, teaching little children in the faith, reclaiming the fallen, building churches, and adorning the altar, making peace among men. Therein they resemble embroidresses who work all manner of silks, gold and silver on various grounds, so producing beautiful flowers. Just so the pious souls who undertake some special devout practice use it as the ground of their spiritual embroidery, and frame all manner of other graces upon it, ordering their actions and affections better by means of their chief thread which runs through all.*

Mariette sat up straighter than Monique had ever seen her. She was turning into a young lady, and Monique knew at that moment that Mariette was going to grow beyond the rest of them, beginning today. Monique's heart both rejoiced and ached to think of it.

"I have read this often," Mariette explained, "and each time I do, the words 'teaching little children in the faith' make me think of you, Father Allain." Mariette paused to smile at him, then continued. "It also makes me think of me, for some reason. Do you think that it is possible I will one day teach children, when I am grown?"

"Yes, Mariette, I do think it is entirely possible. I think it is possible for you to do whatever it is you ask God to help you do. Keep reading and praying, and you will know, my child." He looked at her with the look of a loving father, and then asked if he could borrow her book for a few days.

"I think there is something in it that is my favorite, and I believe it will be fitting to say at the burial of François."

"Actually, did you forget that it is your book?" she asked, getting a laugh from all who sat at the table. "The book smells a little, but if you hold your nose and read, it will be fine." The second comment produced even more laughter.

He thanked her as she handed him the book, then said to her, "I will return it to you after the ceremony. This book's words have had special meaning in my life. I hope they do the same for you. That is why I wanted you to have it. It is yours to keep."

The following evening just before 8 o'clock, Reverend Wilson led the group of Acadians through the thicket of brush on the side of the fence and around to the clearing in the back. Father Allain was dressed in a black robe, as was Reverend Wilson. Father Allain's was adorned with the Mi'Kmaq scarf that he had worn the day of Monique's wedding, and Monique marveled that he had kept it through their journey. Behind the men were Monique, Mariette, Louise, Cecile, Jean and Adele Bourque, and Baptiste LeBlanc. Irabelle LeBlanc had stayed home with a case of the flu. Mariette walked carefully, determined that the lit candle she carried would not go out, no matter what.

The group of mourners crowded together in front of the grave. Father Allain and Reverend Wilson had placed the coffin into the grave earlier and covered it over.

Father Allain offered prayers, and then Reverend Wilson said one of his own. They sang "Ave Maris Stella" and some other familiar Acadian hymns. Father Allain was about to say a short homily when Louise grabbed the sleeve of his robe.

"Father," she said. He stopped speaking to look at her, and saw that she had a finger over her mouth. Her eyes told him that there were intruders, and the mournful call of the whippoorwill split the air. In the darkness, the shadows of three men emerged from the fog, and Father Allain motioned for everyone to remain quiet until they left. Monique felt her heart jump when she realized that they had been spotted, and when Mariette tugged at her sleeve anxiously, she reached down toward her cousin's hand.

"Father Siméon Allain, are you here?" said one of them.

"Father Cormier, is that you?" The three men walked closer, toward the other side of the back fence. Mariette let go of Monique's hand and stepped up next to the fence, shielding the candle to ensure that it would stay lit as they identified themselves.

She lifted it to the man who spoke first. "Hello everyone," said Father Cormier. "We found your house, and Irabelle said that you were here, in the cemetery. She did not say you were behind the cemetery. We do not want to interrupt, so please continue."

"Perhaps you should introduce your companions first," said Father Allain, trying to remain solemn but betraying a tinge of excitement in his voice.

"Yes, forgive me, of course," said Father Cormier. "The young gentleman beside me here—young lady, perhaps you would be so kind as to illuminate his face. He is the nephew of a friend of mine, from the Mi'Kmaq tribe.

Mariette lifted the candle, and emitted a scream of joy, "Eyes of Black Bear?"

"Actually, this young man's Christian name is Stephen Humblewa," said Father Cormier with a chuckle, "but apparently a young lady here knows him better by his Mi'Kmaq name." Mariette reached up with her other hand to steady the candle that had begun to shake.

"Eyes of Black Bear! It is I, Mariette. You have changed, your voice is much deeper. I cannot believe you are here. Eyes of Black Bear . . ."

"You have changed also, Mariette."

"And the other gentleman is Acadian," said Father Cormier. "He has come to reunite with his beloved bride, and I have good news. Mr. Hutchinson has arranged for him to help us in the construction of a new town hall, so he has permission to stay and live with your family, at least for the time being. Perhaps you will place the candle closer to his face, so I can introduce Pierre Doucet." Monique watched, stunned, as the candle slowly moved to the right and illuminated Pierre's face. He smiled at her, straining his eyes to see her better. He had never looked more handsome, his complexion weathered into maturity by the winter elements and the hardships he had endured.

"Monique? Come to the fence my darling."

Monique stepped forward, and he reached to touch her face. "Mariette," he spoke, "please shine the candle on Monique so I can see the face I have missed every day since we parted." Mariette complied, and Pierre reached out and touched Monique's hair, then her cheek.

"You are alive."

"And you are alive." Neither their hands nor their eyes left each others' faces for several moments.

"Well, shall we all get on your side of the fence?" ventured Father Cormier after allowing the young couple their moment. Pierre scaled the fence. Eyes of Black Bear helped Father Cormier over and followed him to join the rest of their friends.

As the other two newcomers were greeted, Pierre guided Monique past the reach of the light and into the darkness beyond. Their lips joined and Pierre whispered, "I have planned this moment for so long . . ."

"My dear Pierre, I was beginning to fear this moment might never come." Monique clasped her hands behind his neck, drawing him close for another kiss. He pulled her body against his, so that she could feel his pent-up passion. "My darling," she sighed, "we must be patient a little longer. But I have some wonderful news that I have not shared with anyone yet. I am carrying our child!"

Pierre's hands went up to cradle her face as he looked into her eyes. When he could again speak, he whispered, "This day I am the luckiest man alive." His hands felt his wife's stomach, soft and just barely showing the first signs of its impending growth.

Their reverie was disturbed by Father Allain's voice. "If our bride and groom will rejoin us, we should continue." As they reemerged into the ring of light, Monique reached for Pierre's hand and felt the sensation of a lightning bolt going up her arm and straight to her heart. A glow seemed to envelop both of them, and where their hands touched it felt as if they had been joined for all time. Her Pierre stood beside her as she bade a last good-bye to her Papa, and it was all such a dream. On the other side was Mama, who sniffed into her hanky and whispered the Lord's Prayer along with Father Allain. Monique looked up into the starry skies above, and felt a peace that rested on their small congregation at that moment. She closed her eyes and listened to every word of Father Allain's dedication to her Papa, her husband squeezing her hand as if to say "I am right here, and I will always be."

"I have found my favorite passage," Father Allain said. "And I would like to share this with all of you gathered here, my dear friends:

> *Truly it is a blessed thing to love on earth as we hope to love in Heaven, and to begin that friendship here which is to endure forever there. I am not now speaking of simple charity, a love due all mankind, but of that spiritual friendship which binds souls together, leading them to share devotions and spiritual interests, so as to have but one mind between them. Such as these may well cry out, "Behold, how good and joyful a thing it is, brethren, to dwell together in unity!" Even so, for*

the precious ointment of devotion trickles continually from one heart to the other, so that truly we may say that to such friendship the Lord promises His Blessing and life forevermore.

Father Allain paused for a few moments, and then asked if Louise would like to say anything.

"Yes," she replied. She stepped forward and knelt down toward the freshly-turned earth that held her husband in its womb. "François, our precious Monique has been reunited with her husband Pierre tonight. It is indeed a miracle that he is here, along with Father Cormier and Eyes of Black Bear, our Mi'Kmaq friend. We thank God for Reverend Wilson and for Mr. Hutchinson, without whose kindness we surely would have not survived. You said it before, François, just before you died. We do belong there, in Acadie, but whether or not we are ever able to return to our cherished land, Acadie will always belong in us, in the ties of love and kinship that knit us together, no matter where we are."

After everyone made the sign of the cross, the group began to walk back around the fence and down the street toward town. Monique suddenly noticed that Father Allain was walking by her side. Taking her hand, he whispered, "Monique, I think it is time for us to go."

She looked up at Pierre, who had moved slightly ahead of her

Cemetery Departure

to say something to Eyes of Black Bear. She allowed the heaviness in Father Allain's grip to lead her, and everything began to swirl in a flash of blinding light.

Chapter 27

Return to Grand Pré

David reached up to place another empty beer bottle among the collection on the counter behind him. He was talking about his pending lawsuit with a land development company that was attempting to take his property from him.

"The owner is a scoundrel," Joe chimed in, "although he never had the decency to introduce himself to me. My daughter went out with his son for two years. There were times when I thought Monique was lost to me forever. Do you know they never asked to meet me in all that time? I know they are prejudiced people."

"I think Monique finally listened to Michelle's advice and dumped him," said Jacques.

"She told me that he didn't respect her family at all," added André.

"Those people don't respect anybody. They take what they want," remarked David, shaking his head. "And they have connections, which worries me. I'm in for a battle, but I'm taking my lawsuit just as far as I can."

"Well good luck to you," said Joe. "You will have Monique and me on your side."

"And us too," Jacques chimed in. "So," he said suddenly, raising his beer bottle, "here's to finding Monique."

"Tell us again Jack how you're related to Acadians," said André.

"I ain't one myself," said Jack excitedly, "but my wife started askin' round and, gee wankers, she found out her mother's last name Comeau could be Acadian! She was reared in Belliveau's Cove down there in Digby County, and her cousin said that the grandparents talked nothin' but French—no English a-tall. My wife, she's feelin' so much better these days. The doctor says the cancer's . . . there's a word, but anyway, she's better. She's been real interested in learnin' more about her own roots since Monique went missin' and we all searched around for her. It's funny how they talked on the news about Acadians more with all this happnin'. I guess it was one good thing in a whole pile of bad. It was good for my wife, anyways." Jack smiled broadly, his eyes sparkling in his thin and weathered face.

Bull Session

"And how are you related to the Acadians, Jean Paul?" asked Jacques. "I know the Cajuns in Louisiana come from Acadians who came down right after the expulsion, but I didn't hear how you're related."

"Actually, the exiled Acadians didn't go to Louisiana right away," explained the professor. "In 1755, around ten thousand were dispersed to nine colonies. Crowded boatloads of them landed at cities down the Atlantic coast, at Boston, New York, Philadelphia, Annapolis. And they were sent away penniless. Some walked north up through New Hampshire and Vermont and into Quebec, some returned to areas of Acadia where they would still be permitted to settle, and some ended up being transported overseas, to be prisoners in England. In France they started a colony at one point, but it didn't last. There were other places they went too, like Santo Domingo, French Guyana, the Falkland Islands. When they were able to colonize Louisiana beginning in the 1765, thousands went there over the next two decades and made it their permanent home."

"It's a wonder anybody lived to raise more children," Joe said. "But the strongest ones who made it must have found happiness and prosperity again in Louisiana."

"Yes, they did indeed," David confirmed.

"Now, you'd think that people don't have to go through terrible things in this day and age," said Joe, "but I saw some awful things when the hurricane hit. People were stuck on their roofs, hoping to get rescued. When I go back, we'll have lots of work to do at the shelter in Lafayette to help the people get taken care of and feel safe again. But anyway, Jean-Paul, Jacques wanted to know how you're related, and I don't think you told us yet."

"I think that's my fault, Joe," said David. "I rambled on about history, my favorite subject." He smiled at Jean-Paul in a silent signal to share his story.

"My family's from Fitchburg, Massachusetts," explained Jean-Paul. "The story goes that my ancestors got off one of the ships in Boston. It was headed for Philadelphia but stopped in Boston and the conditions on board were awful so they were allowed to get off. After that, about sixty of them were sent out to Fitchburg, where they eventually found work and stayed.

"My father and mother got really interested in their genealogy at some point and joined a group who got together at the Fitchburg library. Once they learned how to access information on the Internet, it became much more than a hobby. They go to all the big celebrations and came back from *Congress Mondial* 2004 so thrilled with the reunions and celebrations there!"

"Thank-you for everything you've done this week," said Jacques. "You've been great."

"Well, you're great to work with too, Jacques. I couldn't believe how easy it was for you to fix the sound problem last Saturday. That was impressive."

"Aw, it was nothin'," said Jacques.

"Yeah, right, nothing," said André. "Do you guys know what he did? Halfway through the show, remember when he said they'd be taking a short break because some news was coming in about Monique? Well, actually, some news did come in, but they wouldn't have taken a break if they didn't need to. I don't think the crowd even noticed because Jacques took care of it right away. It was the amp on the left side of the stage that gave them a problem. It got too much load and then it blew. Jacques knew the signal would have to be rerouted to run off a different amp, so he just went down and rewired the load himself. It took about fifteen minutes and was as good as new."

"Those kinds of problems are why I'm hiring André as my sound engineer," said Jacques. "After he finishes his engineering degree, that is."

Michelle finally said her "good-nights" to the men, who didn't show any sign of wrapping up their conversation any time soon. They sat around the large cherrywood table drinking beers until they ran out, then David made some decaf coffee. Jacques sat at the end of the table closest to the hall, and Jack sat to his left. A sheet of paper on the table between them contained a list of tentative dates for an upcoming tour. On the left side of the table sat David and Jack the Taxi Man. At the far end of the table from Jacques was André, and on the other side, Joe sat next to Jean Paul. A hanging lamp directly above provided the only remaining light for the group.

Jacques talked about how he, Michelle, and Jean-Paul had returned to Halifax to finish some business left over from the Festival. Jean-Paul praised him for the great reviews their performance had brought, and the many requests he received for their time and talents.

Jacques said he had tried to thank people for helping in the search. He hoped that there would be a group to show up tomorrow, although they'd run out of places to look. Many people were still calling Michelle and offering prayers for Monique's return.

"Jacques?" called Michelle sleepily from the bedroom.

"Well, guys, I guess I better go," said Jacques.

"Me too," Joe chimed in.

"I need to see Sgt. Williamson back at the Police Station early tomorrow morning," said André. "So I'm turning in too."

Jack thanked Joe for the jambalaya and left with his plate. The men all scattered to their separate sleeping places, and Jacques, as quietly as possible, snuggled in beside his wife. Both were sleeping peacefully as Joe turned the light out in the kitchen.

"Yes, right now!" David exclaimed. "We need to go there now! I just had a dream about the old man . . . he called me Beausoleil, said he was Father Allain. Monique was standing right beside him. I was there, in Grand-Pré. I saw her as clear as I see you both now. Don't say anything, just drive us to the park!"

As David hurried off to awaken Joe and André, Jacques told Michelle, "Stay here. We'll just check this out and be right back. I'm sure it's nothing."

"I don't believe for one minute that it's nothing," said his wife. She was instantly wide-awake and throwing on a sweater. "I felt all day yesterday that something was going to happen."

André stepped on it, and they pulled into the parking lot at the park a few minutes later. David jumped out of the back seat and was gone, running across the parking lot toward the park. André and Jacques sprinted to catch up to him, leaving Michelle to accompany

Joe at his slower pace. David had reached the first willow tree and was standing beside it, looking at something on the ground underneath it.

"Monique?" David asked. "Are you all right?" André came closer, and could see the outline of a body lying on the ground.

Dazed and looking from one man to the other, Monique struggled to sit up. "Papa?" she said to the man now standing with them, and her father fell to the ground, his large hands cupping his daughter's face.

"*Ma cherie*, I can't believe my eyes. It's a miracle, praise God! Where have you been? We've all been worried sick!" The other two men helped Joe and Monique up from the ground. She and her father stood in a tight embrace for a few moments.

The three men and the woman who loved her all had questions.

"Monique, do you know what happened to you?

"Where did you go?

"Do you remember anything?" Her ashen face and blank expression told them nothing. Instead, she waved absently, "Hello, *mes amis*. Pierre, I am so glad to see you."

André didn't care what name she called him. Relieved that she knew him, he grabbed her and gave her a hug. She hugged him back just as joyfully.

"What are you doing here?" she asked David.

"I came to help find you, Monique," he answered. Her response to him was completely in French. The men turned to each other, each trying not to panic the others.

"She is speaking Acadian French," said David. "I understand the dialect, and she is saying she is happy I sent Pierre away from Acadie and back to her."

"Let's get her to the hospital," said Joe.

"I'll go get the car," said André. "I'm going to drive it right up here on the lawn, so don't move."

"Joseph Broussard, *dit* Beausoleil," Monique said sweetly, still looking at David. "It is so nice to make your acquaintance. It is true, you do have a wonderful smile!" She extended her hand to him, and he reached to shake it. His arm suddenly felt as though it weighed a hundred pounds. He tried to move it, but it felt frozen in place at the elbow. Electric fire ran up to his shoulder and into his chest, and he felt so anxious that cold sweat broke out on his forehead and he thought he would have to sit on the ground. Was he having a heart attack? Monique let go, still smiling shyly, and the feeling unleashed its grip on him.

The Honda sped across the lawn toward them, high beams lighting a path. "Oh my God, slow down boy!" yelled Joe, as he stepped aside. André threw the door open, and David took the front passenger seat. Michelle sat on Jacques' lap in the back, with Joe and Monique crowding in beside them.

"Don't speed!" ordered David. "We're not driving safely." André agreed, saying he would be cautious. Monique turned to her father and mumbled something in French.

"Do you know what she said, David?" asked André.

"It's puzzling," said David, "but I do believe she just asked for goat cheese and ale."

André pulled into the front parking area at Valley Regional Hospital in Kentville a few minutes later. The emergency room was almost empty, and the receptionist on duty appeared irritated when David requested service immediately. André borrowed David's cell phone to call the cottage.

"Jean-Paul and Jack are on their way and they'll call and let the police know we found her," he said to Joe. David was over by the reception window, explaining to a doctor that they had brought Monique LeBlanc, the girl who had disappeared last week. Immediately they were ushered through a door labeled "outpatients."

"André," Monique said suddenly. "I tried to call you tonight."

"Sweetheart, that was last Thursday, don't you remember?" replied André. A nod from Joe told him not to press her anymore for now. Joe and Monique left to see the doctor, and the others took seats in the waiting area.

"Do you want something from the vending machine?" asked André. "I'm starving."

"Sure," said David. "Anything, chips, soda, whatever." He handed André a five dollar bill.

They munched on chips and soda, their fatigue and excitement being replaced by numbness. David looked at the clock in the waiting room and commented that it was after two. They turned when the automatic doors opened and Jean-Paul and Jack walked through.

"Jean-Paul called," said Jack excitedly. "an' the wife answered. She says to me, you git over there and see if you can help, so here I am." David filled them in on how they'd found Monique, until the night receptionist came over and firmly told him to "pipe down." Joe returned, accompanied by the doctor on call, a Dr. Thibeault.

"There is no evidence that your daughter was the victim of an assault, as far as we can tell in our initial examination of her," he said. "I would be interested in getting a police report of her disappearance. Have you notified them? She keeps talking about someone called Father Allain. Do you know who he is?"

"No," Joe answered.

"Hmm," said Michelle. David glanced at her quickly, giving a nonverbal message that the name was familiar to him also.

"She also said she came from Acadie," said the doctor.

"That doesn't make much sense," said David. "since Acadie is the historical name for Nova Scotia. Monique is from Louisiana. She said some other strange things on the way here, too."

"She is acting somewhat delusional," said the doctor, "so I am worried about her mental state. However, when I told her I was meeting you out here, she said that she is Monique LeBlanc and that she is here for a visit from Louisiana. She said she lost her way and wandered all over the place for awhile, but when I asked her where, she said somewhere near Boston. We're going to keep her in here for observation and a few tests."

The automatic doors opened for Sgt. Williamson, who immediately came over to André.

"Hello, Dr. Thibeault," he said. "I've been on this case for the past week since Monique disappeared, and I can give you any information you need."

"When can we see her again?" asked Joe.

"Why don't you go in and say good-night to your daughter, Mr. LeBlanc," said Dr. Thibeault, "and Sgt. Williamson, you may come also. I would like the rest of you to wait until visiting hours, and I hope you understand. Rest and sleep could improve her condition."

The doctor ushered Joe and Sgt. Williamson back into the hospital room, and the others stood in silence.

"Well," Michelle said after a moment, "I'm a little ticked off! I really want to see her!"

"Me too, Hon, but we got to do what the doctor says. Uncle Joe will tell us how she's doin' and we'll just have to be happy she's alive. We'll get back in here as soon as visiting hours start. In fact, André, let's go ask when they start."

Chapter 28

Old Problems, New Solutions

Friday, September 2

At Blomidon Cottages, Jacques was serving coffee at 7 am. Jack had said good-bye to everyone when they drove him home from the hospital, and said his wife would love to hear from Joe when he got the chance to call. Joe promised he'd call with an update when they got back to Lousiana. The others gradually straggled out to get some of the caffeine they hoped would help them get going.

"The doctor said we can come in at 8 a.m.," said Joe. "He's making an exception because of the circumstances. He knows we want to get a flight back home as soon as we can."

"I can arrange a ride for all of us to wherever we need to go," said Jean-Paul. "I called for the limo to be up here this morning, and I'll tell him to be here by 8. I don't think he can get here any earlier though. We can also go to the airport together once she gets discharged."

"Thank-you," said Joe, visibly moved by the generous offer.

When they got to the hospital, they all visited Monique for a few minutes, then Michelle asked Uncle Joe if he minded her talking to Monique alone for a moment. He agreed, and Dr. Thibault suggested that they all go outside and bring the limo up front. Michelle tried to prepare Monique for the reception she was about to receive on her discharge. Somehow, the word was out, and when she had checked with the nurse's station about Monique's condition they had told her that the press was waiting outside, among others who were excited about Monique being found.

Both young women were surprised by the hundred or more well-wishers awaiting Monique. Michelle, accompanied by a nurse, wheeled her out the front door to the waiting limo. So many faces Monique didn't know—Bill, Mr. Daigle, Jack the Taxi Guy, Jean-Paul, the custodian at the Chapel, hospital personnel, and many others—who had been taken in by her disappearance and subsequent return.

Knowing how strange the situation must seem to her, they all stood smiling quietly, waiting.

"Did you know that André is making plans to come back to Louisiana, so he can be closer to you?" asked Michelle. "I think he is a man in love. He was looking for you night and day. If you want my opinion, he's a keeper. Monique?"

Monique glanced around to see that the nurse was talking to someone. "Michelle, the doctor told me this morning that I'm four months pregnant!"

"What! How could that be . . . Ted?"

"No, I don't see how." Monique felt a cool sea breeze on her face. "Mmm, smell the salt air."

Michelle could not smell salt air. "Are you sure you're feeling alright today?"

Monique was momentarily lost in memories carrying the smell of dust and iron, and the sound of breaking waves. "Let's get this over with," she said as people seemed to wait for something from her.

Her voice unsteady, she tried her best to thank everyone for every little thing they might have done to help with her return. Muffled applause followed as she finished and she and Michelle took each person's extended hand on the way to their waiting car.

The entire group loaded in for the ride to Halifax Airport. Joe sat next to his daughter, with André on her other side, and Michelle and Jacques beside André. David and Jean-Paul found seats across from them. They all waved at the crowd by the road as the long, black limo pulled onto the 101 toward Halifax. Jean-Paul got cold drinks for everyone as they settled in for the ride.

"I can't believe how much trouble I put everyone through," Monique said as she accepted her cold Sprite, which her father took and opened for her. "And y'all have been so sweet about all this. I'm kinda embarrassed."

"Honey, I told you, there were more people than even I know who helped in more ways than I would have ever imagined," smiled Michelle. "So, don't worry about that. Everyone is just glad you're back and safe. Let's toast to Monique, a member of the Lafayette Trio."

Everyone raised soda cans with a "Hear! Hear!"

Monique replied, blushing slightly, "Thank you. But you are the performers. I could never measure up to you two."

"Darling," said her cousin, "You are part of this group, now and forever. And I keep telling you, your voice is wonderful, and with a little work, we could have some awesome three-part harmonies. Although y'all are goin' to be kind of busy . . . ."

Michelle instantly realized she had said something Monique wasn't ready to talk about. "You'll probably want to go back to grad school," she added quickly.

"Speaking of school, Jacques, I could finish up my courses online and go on the road with you anytime," André said as he put his arm around Monique's shoulders. I'd like to visit Lafayette this fall and we can talk about it some more. I definitely owe Monique a good time, if I can bum a room from someone down there."

Joe LeBlanc jumped in, "André, after all the help you've been to me, especially the last two days, you have a room at my house any time you want it. As far as I'm concerned, you're a part of the family now."

"Thank you, Mr. LeBlanc," André said graciously. "I've been wanting to visit Jacques down in Louisiana for years. So, I'd love to accept your invitation."

"Joe, we might even be able to show him the Atchafalaya Basin, if he has enough time. And if there's much left of it," said David. "But I'm not sure how he'll like the slower pace of life there, as much as he likes speed." Several of the friends chuckled, all knowing André's passion for speed, and his penchant for getting citations for it.

Joe asked, "David, I know you've got a lot on your plate trying to protect your land and with your job at LSU, but if you have any time you're also welcome to join us whenever you want to. We open our house to friends and family during the music festival weekends."

"Thank-you Joe."

Holding Monique's hand, Joe spoke to her gently, "Baby, you should just take it easy for awhile. I met a woman, her name is Dorothy, and she'll be at the shelter for awhile. She could probably help me some, and she likes to cook so maybe she could come over to give you a hand when you need it. I'd like her to meet you."

She squeezed her father's hand and smiled brightly. "Of course, Dad," she replied. "You'll have to tell me all about how you met Dorothy. How old is she?"

"Oh, around my age," he said with a grin. "And I had the feeling she liked me when I rescued her from her roof."

"Way to go, Joe!" said Jacques. "Michelle, since you're psychic, do you see romance in your Uncle Joe's future?"

Joe chuckled. "It's possible. I'm just glad I could be there for her. It was an awful day, seeing people on their roofs. I'll never forget it."

"Yes," Monique chimed in, "I saw some terrible things too. I got so seasick and I was sure we were all going to drown. Finally they let us outside on deck for awhile. And thank God I found Mama and Mariette in Boston. If I hadn't, I don't know how I would have made it."

Stunned, awkward silence filled the limo for seconds that seemed more like minutes.

"Monique, it's okay," reassured the professor, taking the initiative.

"I saw on the news this morning that people down South are getting help from the National Guard. I'm sure they'll recover. And you're safe here with us." He alone among the group suspected she was describing a different horror from that happening in Louisiana, and wanted to deflect attention from her comments.

The limo passengers were still a little shocked and confused by Monique's comments. They tried not to make eye contact, for fear of showing what they were feeling. Monique seemed to sense that something was wrong. She looked at her cousin Michelle with raised eyebrows, as though to ask her if everything was OK. Michelle smiled tentatively.

Finally, Jacques spoke. "I would never have planned it this way, but all we've been through this past week, I think it made Michelle and me realize how special this place is for our people. And I mean all Acadians—from Louisiana and everywhere."

"This is not the vacation to Nova Scotia that I dreamed about taking!" said Joe boisterously as he hugged his daughter closer. "So, we'll have to come back soon. Jacques, you're right, this place has a special pull on me that I didn't expect."

André offered, "Any time you guys want to come back up this way, I would love to take care of you. You should come to Shediac, my hometown in New Brunswick. My mom would love it. She's been calling everyday, and was so happy about Monique." He turned to her and squeezed her hand. "And I also plan to show you a good time up here in the Valley if I ever get the chance. I promise you, it'll be different next time."

Joe moved across to get another round of drinks for everyone from the small fridge, then sat next to David. Monique could hear them talking about the Basin.

But her attention was diverted, as André gently held her hand in his own. She turned to look at him. She could see in his eyes that he truly cared for her, and she placed a hand on his cheek tenderly. He leaned over and kissed her, and she suddenly wished they were all alone in the limo. She had been so disappointed when André hadn't showed up as he had promised, but that was all behind her now. He did love her, and she had loved him ever since . . . that first time she saw him in le Canard, fixing the dykes.

"I do want to return here," she said softly. "Somehow, I think it's important. I don't quite know what happened to me, but I think this place will be part of my future somehow. I've been thinking about graduate school, studying Acadian history. David's class opened my eyes to a whole new world. André, I loved the campus at Acadia University . . . . I have a strong feeling that I have a story to tell. It may take awhile to get it out. I don't know what it's going to be yet, but I'll figure it out."

The couple's quiet talk was interrupted by Jean-Paul, who said he wanted to make an announcement. "I hope to get all you guys up here again," he said. "Monique, your cousins turned lots of heads up here with their performance at the festival. They were incredible. I wanted to save the good news for the right moment, and this seems like it. I've had so many offers over the past few days, people begging me to get you back here to perform, recording guys interested in signing you to their label, more opportunities than I can list right now. I see the Lafayette Duo making it in large venues. I'd like you to think about letting me put together a tour next year. We'd start in Louisiana, and make our way up here to Nova Scotia, up to PEI, over to Quebec, west to British Columbia, and finishing in California, where there is a huge Cajun music following. I've already been in contact with people at twelve different locations in the places I mentioned. If you'd like, I think we can put together a dynamite tour, and you would just explode on the music scene."

Jacques was the first to react, "Wow, I don't know what to say. Man, that all sounds like a dream come true." He looked at Michelle and squeezed her hand. "I know we still have lots of work to do, but I think we need to do some serious talking, Jean-Paul. Man, you have been so awesome! I don't know how I could ever thank you enough . . ."

"That's not even necessary," answered Jean-Paul. "Getting to know you guys and being involved up here has showed me that I've got a part to play in preserving and promoting our culture. It seems we've all had some kind of epiphany up here. All of us have found something special over the last few days. It might sound kinda corny, but I may have found my life path for the next few years, if it works out like I think this can. It sure feels like I'm starting a new chapter in my life, if that makes any sense."

David replied, "*Mon ami*, it makes a lot of sense. I think you've expressed what many of us have been feeling over the last two or three days."

When the limo pulled up to the terminal, David and André helped carry Joe's and Monique's bags through to the ticket counter. By the time they reached the security checkpoint, they could tell their flight would be almost ready to board when they reached their gate. They all took turns saying goodbye and more thank-yous to André and Jean-Paul. Monique approached André last. He had pulled something from his sports bag, which he showed her.

"Monique, I'm not sure what to do with this," he said. "Sgt. Williamson gave it to me after they found it on the beach the day after you disappeared. I think you should have it."

He handed Monique a ragged old, gray sweater. She reached out to take it, stunned. As she brought it up to her face to smell it, she whispered, "Father Allain." Only André and David, standing just beside her, heard what she had said. The professor's jaw dropped in amazement and his face betrayed his shock and some fear. Neither he nor André were quite sure they really heard what they thought they'd heard. Monique reached up to touch André's cheek, and they embraced in a lingering kiss. David quietly drifted back to where the others were.

André's voice was hoarse with emotion. "It's going to kill me to have to let you go right now. There's so much I want to tell you."

"We'll have time. I promise," Monique replied, holding him tightly. "I have some thinking to do, but we do need to talk, so you'd better find a way to get a phone soon," she joked. "I do hope you can come to Lafayette next month like you said."

"Count on it," he promised. "I'll make it happen somehow. You're an incredible girl, and I've only known you a few days. I'll keep bugging Jacques about hiring me on."

After one final tender but short kiss, they said goodbye, their hands the last to lose touch.

David returned and shook André's hand, then gently took Monique's arm to guide her toward where the others waited. She was still clutching Father Siméon Allain's old sweater to her chest as she walked with Joe and David toward the gate to board their flight to Louisiana.

André watched until he couldn't see her anymore. His mind was on overload with emotions for Monique LeBlanc, confusion over what had happened and what it all meant, and sadness over their parting. He asked Jean-Paul if he minded if he sat for awhile before they headed back up to the Valley.

Inside the plane, Monique settled into a window seat, with her cousin next to her and Jacques on the aisle. Joe had taken a seat several rows behind them. All were quiet through take-off. Soon after, Jacques's heavy breathing told them he was asleep when Michelle broke the silence.

"André really cares for you."

"I feel the same way about him, Michelle, even though it's hard to understand. We've only seen each other a few times, so you must wonder how can we have feelings like that already?"

"Honey, with everything that has happened the past few days, nothing can surprise me anymore." She looked over to be sure Jacques was asleep and continued at almost a whisper, "Do you feel okay? About being pregnant, I mean."

"I have to get used to the idea. But I feel good. I don't think I can explain it right now, but I'm sure it's not Ted's. We were only together twice, and the second time hardly counted. Besides, we took precautions."

"Then you and André . . . ?"

"No!"

"Then, how . . . ?"

"That's what I can't explain. This baby . . . I know this sounds crazy, but I think it has something to do with my mom."

"Your mom!" said Michelle, trying to keep her voice down. She looked more closely at her cousin and could tell that the pregnancy was starting to show. "Monique, your body is already changing, you know. Your breasts are getting bigger."

"And my stomach's getting bigger too . . . . Can you tell?"

"Yes, a little. Do you feel anything happening there?"

"Not yet. I feel like my hormones are going wild, and I get hungry a lot."

"Maybe your hormones are making you talk crazy. Let's face it, everybody's gonna think it's Ted's. And it can't be André's—you two just met. Your father . . . what will he think?"

"I don't know. But I'm going to try and explain my feelings to him. You don't think I'm nuts, do you?"

"Don't forget you are talking to your cousin who is psychic, Monique. When you were gone and I was meditating, I saw something. Since you are saying crazy things, it's my turn to tell you something that happened to me while you were gone."

"What?"

"I was meditating one night, and I saw you . . . God this is gonna sound bizarre, but you were in a little barn or something like a barn with a boy, actually the guy was probably our age. He wasn't dressed like us. He looked like he was out of a movie from the 1600s or something, and looked a little like André, actually. I remember there were horseshoes on the floor. It felt like I was floating around. And I . . . I know this will sound nuts, but I drifted around and through your bodies when you were lying down with him on the floor. You were . . . well, making love, and I could feel the most incredible energy . . . like when Jacques and I make love, or when we are on stage and the audience is really with us and everything is so in place that I think the whole universe is flowing with us. It was like just like that! And I came out of the meditation feeling as though, no matter whether you were alive or dead, I had just spent time with you and you were incredibly happy. Maybe your mother knows that too. I guess there are so many things that happen in life that are unexplainable, it's possible she could have something to do with you disappearing and coming back."

"I believe she did. She left me several things, remember? Her journal, some stories she had written, our family history, an old baby's blanket. And now this old sweater that the policeman found on the beach. André gave it to me to keep."

Michelle glanced down to see for the first time what Monique was holding on her lap. Oh My God! she thought.

"Anyway, where did you think I was when you meditated that time?"

"I don't know. An old building with horseshoes on the floor."

"I sort of remember something about that, but it seems like I dreamt it. And before, back at LSU, I started having dreams about a guy named Pierre when I started taking the Historical Fiction class. I even told David when he called on me in class. I felt really stupid that day, I was so embarrassed because I wasn't paying attention. When I talked about the dream . . . it was after that when we became friends. Maybe we can both talk to him about that sometime. He believed something paranormal was happening, and he told me about an experience he had right at Grand-Pré too. I believe that what I experienced was because my mother gave me an incredible opportunity. It scares me to think about what's going to happen from here, but I feel somehow that this baby is another part of that gift from her.

"Sometimes over the last day I've felt her presence so powerfully. I dreamt last night that she was speaking to me, and it has helped me to feel at peace about this baby and to begin to try to make sense of where I went. I keep asking myself, what does all this mean? Why did this happen to me? Maybe my mom wants me to tell the story of what happened to our ancestors, just the way she did when she was alive. She gave me her love of our culture and now she has somehow given me this. I feel this story deep inside me, and now I've also got a new life inside me. This life feels like it's both Acadian and Cajun, and Mama somehow gave this baby to me. Crazy, huh?" Michelle just shook her head as she looked into her cousin's eyes. "You're the only person I would even consider telling all this to, and even you are looking at me like I need help."

Michelle laughed. "I have to confess, even for me this is kind of overwhelming. But everything has a way of coming to light sooner or later." As the aircraft streaked southward away from Nova Scotia, Michelle reached for her pregnant cousin's hand and closed her eyes to meditate again. She felt an incredible tingling through her arm and into her shoulder, as though her hand and Monique's, as well as their spirits, were knitted together in some inexplicable way.

Catherine just smiled.

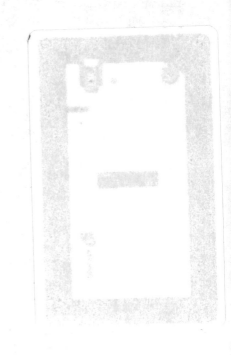